# A SUDDEN VENGEANCE

# A SUDDEN VENGEANCE

## AN EVERETT CARR MYSTERY

## Matthew Booth

First published by Level Best Books/Historia 2026



This novel is entirely a work of fiction. The names, characters, and incidents portrayed in it are the work of the author's imagination. Any resemblance to actual persons, living or dead, events, or localities is entirely coincidental.

Matthew Booth asserts the moral right to be identified as the author of this work.

Author Photo Credit: Personal collection

First edition

ISBN: 979-8-89820-225-5

Cover art by Level Best Designs

This book was professionally typeset on Reedsy.
Find out more at reedsy.com

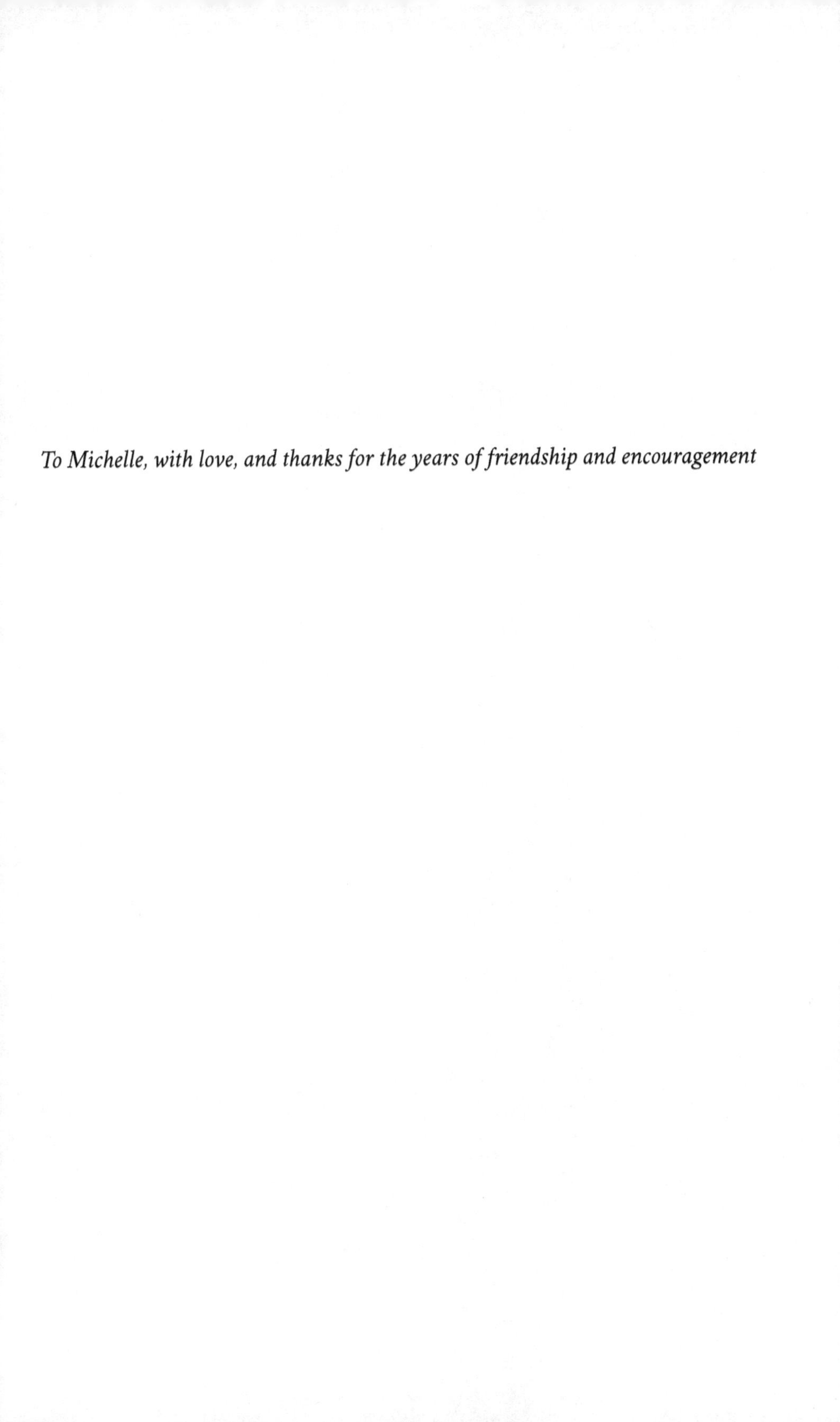

*To Michelle, with love, and thanks for the years of friendship and encouragement*

# Praise for the Everett Carr Mysteries

"Everett Carr makes an excellent detective. He has his own sufferings, which make him compassionate as well as a shrewd judge of human nature, and he's observant of every unexplained detail. …*The Serpent's Fang* is everything you want in a 'Golden Age' mystery: a country house, stolen poison, a missing will, and the denouement in the library where Carr reveals the final shocking twist. I couldn't put it down, and such is the dastardly ingenuity of Matthew Booth that I didn't guess whodunnit."—**Jean Briggs**, author of the Charles Dickens Mysteries

"…an engrossing mystery, with a despised murder victim and a group of suspects, each of whom has a strong motive to kill the victim. The description of each character is finely drawn, the setting atmospheric, and the conclusion to the mystery eminently satisfying. So many secrets. So many suspects. So many twists and turns. *The Serpent's Fang* offers a sting in the tail." **Laraine Stephens,** author of The Reggie da Costa Mysteries

"… a macabre but satisfyingly cosy crime. Booth handles the introduction of his quite significant cast with grace and ease. …the opening scenes flow so beautifully together, and the murder itself does not disappoint."—**Mairi Chong**, author of the Dr Cathy Moreland Mysteries, Amazon

"Everett Carr is…a marvellous protagonist. This is a descriptive, well-paced mystery…a recommended read for mystery lovers."—**Fiona Alison**, The Historical Novel Society

"Booth's work is about as good as it gets. We see the master craftsman at work.His characters not only behave in a believable fashion, but they speak in a believable fashion.  Echoes of Christie and Sayers here, and the plot, characters, and dialogue are all of the best and all fit together perfectly."—**John Hall**, author of *Death of a Collector: A Freddie Darnborough Mystery*

"A classic locked room mystery in the finest tradition which will delight old and new readers alike"—**Dr M Jones**, Amazon

"A classic page-turner and must-read for all fans of Christie, Sayers, James and the country house murder mystery genre"—**Ms M Powell**, Amazon

"An Everett Carr Mystery is not to be missed. The sense of time and place is there on every page, and author Matthew Booth knows how to spin a tangled web of people, murder and blackmail in a fashion reminiscent of the best 'Golden Age' mysteries."—**Helen** (helenfrominyocounty), Goodreads

"Enter the marvellous and enigmatic Everett Carr, who sees beyond the seemingly impossible...a wonderful homage to the Golden Age of crime"—**intheamazone**, Amazon reviewer

# Chapter One

It was Eric Hirst who discovered the latest act of sabotage.

He did not think the word was too grandiose for the various practical jokes and petty vandalism that had been inflicted on the factory and offices of Bayliss Textiles Incorporated over the last few weeks. It was true that no professional secrets, assuming there were any, had been stolen, but Hirst still considered these recent outrages could be classified as sabotage. They were criminal acts that resulted in serious disruption to the firm, both in terms of property and reputation.

This new example was what Hirst believed was commonly called a poison pen letter. The envelope was pinned to the outer door of the mill so that Hirst had seen it as soon as he arrived on that morning. Picking it off the door, he entered the mill and made his way to the iron staircase that led from the factory floor to the gallery overhead, along whose corridor were various offices of different purposes: Bayliss' sanctum, Hirst's own office, one for the two typists employed by the firm, and the remainder used for storage of records, archives, and supplies. If the envelope had simply been posted in the usual fashion or even dropped on the gallery floor, there would have been nothing about it that might have caused it to stand out. By fixing it to the outer door of the mill, the phantom responsible for these pranks had ensured it would be discovered immediately.

The incidents prior to the letter had been less venomous, at least initially. The first, six months earlier, had been the smashing of a headlamp on one of Bayliss' cars, closely followed by the breaking of a window on the ground floor of the mill. Compared to the infringements that followed, these were rather innocuous events. Arthur Bayliss had read nothing into them. In his view, windows got broken, and how they got broken was perhaps something of a moot point. What mattered was that the window was replaced with the minimum of fuss and interruption to the firm's business. Hirst had agreed at the time, but his view had changed when he had discovered the tyres on his bicycle had been slashed only the other evening. A relatively minor inconvenience, as Bayliss had pointed out, but to Hirst, it had seemed personal. It had been a direct attack on his property, rather than a random smashing of a window in a large building. He had voiced these concerns to Bayliss, of course, who had typically dismissed them with a sneer.

Bayliss' attitude had changed when he had entered his office and found the carcass of a rat in his desk drawer. Although he had not witnessed the discovery, Hirst could imagine the horror of Bayliss opening the drawer, perhaps as he spoke on the telephone, and reached into the depths of it, not looking, his attention fixed on his conversation, and his fingers coming to rest on the blood-matted fur. It would have been at once an alien sensation to him, and his inevitable glance into the drawer would have revealed the obscenity of rodent insides, exposed like a vile secret, and the slack open mouth and long teeth fixed in a revoltingly mocking smile. Hirst could recall vividly the sight of Bayliss in the doorway to the office, crimson with anger, the dead animal hanging from an outstretched hand like a loathsome, dripping trophy.

Then, there had been the Carnaby order. It was a lucrative deal, one which would have made the firm (and Bayliss himself) a significant amount of money. It had been a particularly welcome order, which would have greatly increased revenue, after the struggle of the consequences of the stock market crash of the last decade. Bayliss Textiles had weathered the storm, but it had hardly been an easy journey, and the firm had survived only on account of the efforts of the workforce, Bayliss' business acumen, and Hirst's own financial skill. The Carnaby order would have been a significant injection of profit. As it was, the Bayliss Textiles poltergeist had learned about it. Bayliss discovered that the deal had been cancelled when he had telephoned Jeremiah Carnaby himself to advise on the progress of the order. Carnaby, whilst apologetic, had been unable to assist: he had been advised that Bayliss Textiles could no longer fulfil its promises and was on the verge of bankruptcy. Carnaby had pulled the order immediately. When asked to whom Carnaby had spoken, he could not give a name but said only that it had been a woman. It had been a very real disaster. It had not necessarily been about the money, Hirst knew that; it had more to do with Bayliss' reputation, the suggestion that he was nearing bankruptcy, that he was a failure. That would have hurt more than any loss of money.

Now, there was this anonymous letter.

There was no address, only Bayliss' name typed across the centre. Hand-delivered, then, thought Hirst instinctively. The implication of the idea was immediately apparent. An insider, one of the workforce, a serpent in their garden. The suspicion unsettled him more than it should. He was not naïve enough to suppose that Arthur Bayliss had no enemies, either at work or in his family circle, but the suggestion that this poltergeist that haunted the mill might be someone close even to Hirst was unsettling. He did not open the envelope; to do so would be a form of invasion of privacy, and Bayliss would not thank him for reading it. Instead, Hirst placed it in his jacket pocket and walked along the gantry to his own office.

Despite his determination not to read the letter before Bayliss had been given the opportunity to do so, the envelope seemed to call to Hirst, luring his attention towards it like the songs of the Sirens to a doomed sailor. From somewhere in his mind, a memory stirred. Had he not read of an outbreak of such letters causing a sensation in Littlehampton a little over a decade ago? Several hundred miles south of the Bayliss mill, of course, and separated from the present by several years, but the events of the Littlehampton letters at the close of the last decade suddenly seemed to Hirst to be ominously relevant.

He scoffed at himself. These thoughts were pointless. The existence of the letter spoke for itself. It had happened, and not in some distant seaside town but here in Darton Vale, at the heart of the Lancashire hills. Hirst prided himself on being a sensible, practical Northern man, and idle fancies were alien to him. The letter was a fact. What mattered now was what it said and what he and Bayliss were going to do about it. With an assured nod of his head, he secreted the letter away in his desk drawer, the memory of Bayliss' dead rat only vaguely coming into his mind, and pulled an accounts ledger towards him. Opening it, he busied himself with the latest invoices paid and outstanding. Work was the best antidote to any anxiety, as his father would have said.

It was perhaps a quarter of an hour later when Hirst heard some movement from the office next door. He had been so engrossed in his work that the sound of the neighbouring door opening and closing and the scuffle of sounds as someone prepared themselves for the working day ahead startled him. It was Arthur Bayliss himself, of course. Hirst felt a catching of his breath, a small display of nerves because the inevitable could no longer be ignored. He reached into the desk drawer and took out the envelope. It felt like a ton of lead in the palm of his hand.

He walked to Bayliss' office and knocked on the door, obeying the gruff call for entry that came from within.

"Any word on the Denby payment, Eric?" asked Bayliss.

No formal greeting, no cordial words before business began. Hirst was not surprised, but he and Bayliss had been colleagues for so long that he felt he had earned some sort of respect from his employer. In other circumstances, they might even have been friends after working so long together, and Hirst supposed that in some way they were. Hirst was a regular visitor to Bayliss' house for dinner, family parties, and other social engagements. He and Bayliss had played rounds of golf together, shared many glasses of beer and wine, and they had confided in each other on several personal matters over the years. Beyond the use of his first name, however, there was never any sign of comradeship between them in the workplace. There was no room amongst the mules and looms and the noise of the mill for any indication of friendship between them, but over a late-night glass of port, Bayliss would allow a glimmer of it to show.

"Not yet," said Hirst. "They are now a week overdue. I shall get Miss Murchison to send a final notice."

Bayliss snorted and took out a cigar from the top pocket of his waistcoat.

"People think this mill is a charity, Eric."

"We haven't yet paid Del Cartwright for fixing the window after the last incident," Hirst felt obliged to say.

"Get Miss Murchison to write a cheque, and I'll sign it." Bayliss puffed on the cigar. When Hirst did not reply, Bayliss frowned from behind the smoke of his cigar. "What's wrong, Eric?"

"There's been another one."

Hirst handed the envelope across the desk. Bayliss took it in his large hands, so big that they always reminded Hirst of the paws of a bear. The ursine qualities of the man did not end there. His shoulders were broad, and his forearms and thighs were so thick that his boasts of school records for rugby were easy to believe. He was large without being obese, so his heft appeared to be muscle rather than fat. As an athlete, in those days on the rugby field, for example, he would have been strong but not perhaps fast, of more use in a scrum than in racing to the tryline to score points. He was not a conventionally handsome man, but his features were proud and had about them a certain dignity. His eyes were dark and determined, the hair still thick around his temples despite the increasingly apparent tonsure at the crown of his head, and the thick lips were often pursed in an expression of alert resolve. The nose was broken, another remnant of his days on the playing fields, but instead of marring his features, the deformity somehow managed to add a dimension of nobility to them, offset slightly by the few broken veins and the slight glow of crimson in his cheeks that suggested an increasing love of alcoholic beverages.

Bayliss turned the envelope around in his hands. "Where did you find it?"

"Pinned to the outer door."

"Have you told anybody about it?" A pointless question, so Hirst made no comment. Bayliss looked carefully at the seal. "You haven't opened it?"

"Of course not," repeated Hirst. "It wasn't my business."

Bayliss reached across the desk for a letter opener. The paper made almost no sound as it was slit open, and Hirst found himself foolishly admiring such a delicate touch from those massive hands. From the envelope, Bayliss pulled a single sheet of paper, folded twice, which he slowly extended to reveal its contents. If Hirst had expected the traces or outlines of words composed from newspaper letters, he was to be disappointed, since he saw none. Another flight of fancy blown away by the wind.

Bayliss tossed the page over to him. "He's surpassed himself, whoever he is."

Hirst picked up the letter, and he saw now that it consisted only of three lines of typewritten text:

*"You gross, obnoxious pig. You make me sick to look at you. What good is all that wealth if everyone around you hates you and wants you dead? Do everyone a good turn for once—hang yourself. Better still, put a bullet in your head. Or shall I do it for you?"*

"God, what filth," muttered Hirst, throwing the letter back onto the desk. "This is terrible. We must show it to the police."

"Out of the question." Bayliss inhaled deeply on his cigar.

"It's a direct threat against your life, Arthur," said Hirst, leaning forward over the desk.

"Made by somebody who so far has only mustered the guts to break a window and slash the tyres of your bicycle?"

"Whoever it is came close to damaging the reputation of this firm and you personally."

Bayliss had not forgotten it, and nor did he want to be reminded of it. "People intent on murder don't warn their victims first, Eric. This is a hoax."

"So, you're going to do nothing about it?" Hirst put his hands in his pockets and shook his head.

Bayliss' eyes narrowed behind the swirl of cigar smoke, and a crease formed on the bridge of the broken nose as a sneer fell across the bulbous lips. "No, Eric, you misunderstand me. I don't take this piece of muck seriously as a threat to my life, absolutely not, but it doesn't follow that I don't intend to do anything about it. By sending this, whoever it is has gone too far."

"Then go to the police."

One of the huge paws slammed down on the desk. "For the last time, no! I won't bother Tommy Barber with any formal complaint about this bastard,

Eric, but don't think that means I'm not going to do something about it."

"I thought it didn't bother you, Arthur."

Bayliss smiled. "This spineless phantom of ours isn't going to kill me, Eric, which is why his little love letter here doesn't trouble me. But nobody pulls my chain like he's been doing forever, not without me doing the same to him."

"What are you going to do?"

Bayliss leaned forward across the desk himself now so that he and Hirst were in close proximity to each other. Hirst could smell the sickly-sweet cologne that had been applied so liberally that it still overpowered the more recent odour of the cigar. Hirst looked into Bayliss' eyes, and he saw the familiar and predatory malice, almost animalistic in its intensity.

"Nothing," said Bayliss, screwing the letter into a ball. "There's nothing to be done."

Hirst watched as the letter was tossed into the nearby wastepaper basket. Whispering a quiet but resigned "Very well, Arthur," he rose slowly to his feet.

"You know where I'll be if you need me," he said.

Bayliss nodded. "Give me an hour or so, then pop back in. We'll have a look at the Denby account, then go and have a wander around the shop floor. Give some of them a good boot up the arse."

"Very well, Arthur," Hirst said again, with an even greater sense of resignation than before.

He was almost out of the office when Bayliss called him back. "Don't forget dinner on Saturday night. You can still come, can't you?"

"Yes, I can still come."

"Excellent." Bayliss grinned widely, satisfied with himself. The poison pen letter might almost have been forgotten. "I've got rather a special friend coming from London."

"London?" Hirst was furious with himself for repeating it. Ever since Bayliss had made social contacts down in the dirty metropolis, he had taken any available opportunity to indulge himself in talking about it. Hirst had feigned both interest and admiration, but in truth, he had felt and continued to feel neither.

Bayliss was nodding. "From the Icarus Club, no less. I have mentioned that they've allowed me to become a member, haven't I?"

"You may have done," said Hirst, with almost no irony.

"One of the most exclusive clubs in London, Eric, and they've accepted me." Bayliss stubbed out the cigar at last. "Not bad for a nothing lad from Salford, wouldn't you say? Hard work and ambition, Eric, they can't be beaten."

Hirst had heard variations of this theme before, and he had no intention of listening to another one now. "Who is this guest of yours?"

"Chap called Carr, Everett Carr." Bayliss waited for any indication that Hirst knew the name; none came. "A retired judge, as a matter of fact, and from what I can gather, something of a sleuth."

Hirst's nose wrinkled in distaste. "A sleuth?"

"Solved a few murders, so I understand." Bayliss picked up the poison pen letter. "Perhaps we should ask Mr Carr, the detective, if he can work out who sent this bit of grubby nonsense. If he can tell us who it was, maybe we can give our little poltergeist a bloody good whipping."

It was said with a smile, but Eric Hirst knew that there was not a single ounce of humour behind the words.

# Chapter Two

Everett Carr was sitting in one of the private bars of the Icarus Club with an awkward sense of regret hanging over him like an unproven accusation.

His mind wandered back to the evening a few days ago, when the invitation had been made. Somehow, it seemed more like a matter of weeks rather than days since he had found himself accepting Arthur Bayliss' offer of a weekend in the Lancashire hills. Carr supposed that such bad decisions preyed on one's mind more acutely than pleasant thoughts, so that they seemed to plague one for longer than was the case. Certainly, he seemed to have been living with his decision to accept Bayliss' offer of hospitality for more than a couple of days. Not that it had been an offer, Carr reflected; it had been more of a demand, an insistence that Carr visit Bayliss' home, and one that would brook no denial.

Bayliss was only a recent acquaintance. Carr could hardly imagine calling the man a friend, even if they had known each other for several months. If he were to be honest with himself, Carr would confess not only to an instinctive dislike of the man but also to an apprehension that Bayliss was in any way a suitable candidate for membership of the Icarus Club. This was, in part, a personal snobbery, and Carr could not deny it, but nor was he prepared to apologise for it. He had heard another member, an old naval commander by the name of Fleming, expressing his disgust that Bayliss had ordered a half-bottle of claret to accompany his grilled sole and, later in the same evening, that he had insisted on gulping the club's finest single malt and slurping at the Napoleon brandy. Carr had listened to these condescending complaints with amusement, but he was aware that their triviality spoke of a deeper problem with the man. To Carr, it had been best personified when he witnessed Bayliss failing to rise from a dinner table when a lady was introduced to him. It was not simply a matter of a lack of finesse. It spoke more of the man's lack of respect than his boorish manners. One of Carr's closer acquaintances at the Icarus had said that he would not be surprised to learn that Bayliss cheated at cards. There was no proof of it, nor any genuine foundation other than prejudice to suspect it, but once the possibility had been planted in his mind, Carr had found it difficult to disengage it.

"You must come and stay with me for a few days, Mr Carr," Bayliss had said, blowing a cloud of intense cigar smoke in Carr's direction. "I'll give you a tour of the mill, one of the finest in the North West, and if I may say so, one of the most profitable."

"The American stock market crash did not affect your business, Mr Bayliss?" Carr had asked. It was an unnecessary question since Bayliss was fond of boasting about the subject.

"Hard work and business sense, Mr Carr," he had replied. "That's all you needed to shelter from that storm. Mills like mine went under, no doubt about it, but only because those in charge didn't have what we had. Brains and experience, sir, brains and experience."

Carr had sipped his *café noir* with a polite smile. "I am pleased to hear you came out of it unscathed. So many still suffer the consequences, I fear."

Bayliss had leaned back in his chair, taking an obscene mouthful of whisky and wiping his lips with the back of his hand. "An old friend of mine, Conrad Toole, he died a few years back and left his own mill to his son, George. He's a good lad, is George, engaged to be married to my daughter, as a matter of fact. A nice and decent lad, he is, but he's not got what it takes to run a mill. Conrad knew what he was about, but George hasn't got the spark you need in business. Well, he's a case in point, Mr Carr. If it weren't for me, George Toole would have seen his father's legacy burn to the ground."

"You assisted him?" Carr had said. "For the sake of your daughter, perhaps."

"Don't you believe it, sir." Bayliss had seemed genuinely offended by the suggestion. "I don't believe in any of that nonsense. The young learn nothing if you give them a steer all the time. No, no, sir, it was a matter of business."

Carr had felt himself losing his way. He had never been a man of business, and he had always found the intricacies of profits and losses, turnover, revenue, and similar concepts of which he knew nothing to be of little interest.

Bayliss had inhaled deeply on the offensive cigar once more. "I'm in negotiations with George Toole to take over his mill. If I don't, he'll sink, you mark my words. And he knows it too, I might add. It is a good business opportunity and one which I'd be foolish to overlook."

"And how does Mr Toole see the matter?" Carr had asked.

"As I said, he can see the sense in it." Bayliss smiled. "Besides, he knows he hasn't got a choice about it."

This last remark had been curious, and Carr's eyes had narrowed in suspicious interest. Before he could probe the issue further, however, Bayliss had turned back to his original topic. "So, you'll come up to my neck of the woods, Mr Carr? Have a look over the mill, meet the lads and lasses on the shop floor, and see my little empire at work. You'll stay with us at Darton House, of course. We've plenty of room."

"Well, if truth be told..."

Bayliss had ignored him. "Have you ever been to Lancashire, Mr Carr?"

"I have not."

"I never knew a Lancashire man who didn't swear by his county, and I do so myself. You'll never find a more beautiful landscape than the hills and moors of Lancashire. I wonder sometimes if the poet who talked about England's green mountains and pleasant pastures had been to Lancashire, and Darton Vale in particular."

It was a measure of the man, Carr had thought, that Bayliss could quote Blake's poem without appreciating the irony of the fact that it condemned the very mills from which Bayliss profited as satanic. It was difficult to imagine a poem less likely to be appreciated by Bayliss had he properly understood it, but quoting from it was a deliberate act, designed to demonstrate his cultural knowledge and intelligence. Typically, all it had done was to suggest the opposite.

"You make your home county sound idyllic," Carr has said diplomatically.

"So it is," Bayliss had beamed, "as you'll see when you come. There's a train from Euston, but you'll have to change, of course, and I can have a car meet you at Darton Vale station. How about you come down next Thursday?" Bayliss had taken out a diary from his jacket pocket. "That'll be the 16th September. You're free, I presume?"

If Carr had found this presumption of lonely idleness offensive, he had no time to express it. He had confirmed it almost without thinking and, as soon as he had done so, the matter had been settled. That had been on the previous Saturday evening, and in the intervening time, Carr had been unable to think of any suitable or convincing excuse to break the arrangement. He disliked dishonesty in any event, even on a minor scale, and he had allowed himself to become resigned to the fact of the matter. But that did not mean he could not still feel regret about it, and this he emphatically did.

The following few days had passed without incident, and further comment on the trip to Darton Vale. Bayliss had stayed at the club on the Sunday night, Carr had been led to believe, but he did not see him. As far as Carr was aware, Bayliss had travelled back to Darton Vale on Monday, presumably along the same route Carr would travel, and he would now be back in his familiar surroundings, amid the noise and the smells of the mill and the warm domesticity of his family. Assuming, Carr supposed, that there was warmth in the Bayliss family.

Now, breaking his reverie, Carr rose to his feet and made his way down the main stairway of the club. He collected his hat and coat from the cloakroom and stepped out onto St James' Street. It was only a five-minute walk back to his rooms in the Albany, but the air was getting cooler as the autumnal winds began to make their presence known, and the cold would make the short journey seem almost interminable. As he walked, Carr's mood began to darken. He prided himself on his optimism, on his hope for life, on his belief in the goodness of people, so that these bouts of melancholic pessimism were as irritating as they were crippling.

He knew the cause of them, of course, only too well. He had thought that he was coming to terms with the murder of his wife at last when the first wave of guilt hit him. He had known for some time that he would never get over Miranda's death, but he had never hoped to. It would seem to be something of a betrayal of her if he were able to accept what had happened. It seemed imperative to him that he should always remember and mourn her. The fragment of bullet in his shattered knee seemed to him then and now to be a physical reminder of the importance of never letting go of the pain and the sense of loss, and, as far as he was able to have a conscious say in the matter, he had never allowed those emotions to abandon him.

But if Carr strangely wished these negative emotions would stay with him, if he somehow welcomed their effect on his life, this new sensation of guilt, which threatened to overshadow them, was decidedly not welcome. It was an intruder into his private grief, a trespasser on the grounds of his emotional healing, and Carr wanted it gone. But, like all weeds in a garden or plagues in an infected area, the guilt returned continually. In his more practical moments, Carr was able to feel close to understanding it. Miranda had died in a hailstorm of bullets that had been meant for him. It was she who should be living, not him. His logical, analytical mind was able to explain to him that the burden of responsibility for that situation was understandable. But was it normal?

As he walked slowly past Jermyn Street, Everett Carr realised at last why he had been so frightened over the past few months. He had thought it was the guilt itself that terrified him, but he saw now that it was the uncertainty of it that unnerved him. These feelings of culpability over Miranda's fate might be explained as an intellectual response, but were they a human one? Did other people feel them? Did a soldier who returned home alive from war feel the same sense of responsibility over his survival as Carr felt? Did that soldier ever feel an unfairness that he had endured where his closest ally had not? Carr could assume it, and perhaps he did, but he could not know it. None of the medical journals he had ever read had given a name for this feeling of survival culpability. If the best medical brains in the land had no name for it, did it even exist as a condition? Or was it only his own self-absorption and indulgence that allowed Everett Carr to succumb to it? And there was his dilemma: he had survived an assassination that should have killed him, but which had taken Miranda's life, and he felt guilty for it, but he had no assurance that he was entitled to have such a response.

He turned from Piccadilly into the Albany, and for a moment, the sides of the buildings which surrounded him seemed to close in on him. They loomed over him with suggested menace as he stood in the courtyard of the residence. It was an illusion, he knew, brought on by his paranoia and that final, unnecessary glass of whisky. He stood motionless for a few moments, leaning heavily on his silver-handled cane, breathing in the night air with a grateful intensity. The chill of the air in his lungs was invigorating, almost cleansing, and he took a moment to relish in it. He opened his eyes slowly, and his nerves seemed to soften and relax. He began once more to limp towards the door to his rooms. His mind was not perhaps perfectly clear, but he knew with a sudden keenness that he was at that moment so thoroughly sick of London that he could almost convince himself that he wouldn't care if he never saw the wretched city again. It was filled with ghosts, phantoms that plagued him, and emotions that crippled him. In that moment, he wanted rid of them.

Arthur Bayliss' voice, with its talk of pleasant pastures and the green mountains of Lancashire, came back to him. Carr had seldom travelled to the north of England. He had been a frequent visitor to Scotland, both in his youth and in adulthood, and a return to the Highlands had been an unfulfilled promise to himself for many years. But northern England was an unknown territory to him, although it was becoming an increasingly attractive idea to him that he should become familiar with it. Bayliss might be an insufferable bigot, but his offer for Carr to stay with him for the weekend now seemed impossible to resist, if only because it served as an escape from London, and his previous regret at accepting the invitation almost instantaneously evaporated. It was replaced by a calm assurance that a few days in the bracing atmosphere of the unknown north might well clear Carr's mind of his guilts and anxieties, and the certainty that if a stay at Darton House succeeded in doing so, the overbearing personality of Arthur Bayliss was a small price to pay.

Once in his rooms, Carr decided that he felt better about himself and the forthcoming weekend. He would rise early and pack his case, a task that he had delayed in performing solely on account of his reluctance to make the trip at all. Now, however, he was almost eager to do so, and the packing of his case would be closer to a relief than a chore. He picked up his Bradshaw and reminded himself of the times of the trains and connections which would allow him to arrive in Darton Vale a little before teatime. Of these, he made a careful note in his notebook, in his careful and precise handwriting, and with a slightly lighter heart, he took himself off to bed.

# Chapter Three

Rosamund Bayliss realised that she may not love George Toole as much as she should, as they were walking along the moors overlooking Layton Brook.

It was one of those sudden flashes of inspiration that occur without warning, and that seem so obvious once they have made themselves known that it is almost incredulous that their truth had not been obvious from the start. It wasn't that there was anything wrong with the man. He was certainly handsome, well-built, and kind. He was capable of making Rosamund laugh in almost any situation. He was not a natural businessman, as her father had often said, but he was hard-working nevertheless, and he had a healthy dose of integrity, something she often feared was lacking in her father. In many ways, he was the perfect choice for a prospective husband.

And yet, she had known for some time that she was not comfortable with the engagement.

She had put her doubts down to the nervous anxiety she had assumed all girls felt when they had accepted a request to share their life with a man. It was, after all, a daunting prospect, thought Rosamund, for both parties. She had no doubt that George felt similarly anxious about the commitment they were making, although whether this assurance of his reciprocated nervousness was in fact a product of her own desire to feel better about her qualms or a genuine appreciation of his emotional state was difficult to say. He had never voiced any concerns about their future, but then neither had Rosamund. She had been content to dismiss them as passing worries, nothing to concern herself with, and she had told herself that they would disappear as time went by. But they had not; if anything, they had increased slowly, until the present moment when they had silently shrieked their insistence in her mind.

She looked at him, suddenly aware of how momentous the next few minutes would be. He was gazing out over the expanse of green and brown which formed the extensive fields and hills below them. The water of the brook, so clear and fresh, rippled its way beneath them, the sound of its passing seeming to come from the distance, as if entirely independent of the visuals of the brook itself. The trees that latticed the view had begun to lose their leaves, and various birds, from crows to sparrows, could be seen perching on the exposed branches. To the left, there was the notorious curve in the road, sharp and unforgiving, that had been the cause of many a road accident, earning itself the sobriquet of Devil's Corner. George stared out over the whole vista, his blue eyes squinting against the sun but still betraying the almost childlike wonder with which he viewed nature in its glory. Rosamund found herself looking again at the clarity of their colour, and at the patrician angle of his jaw, the classical nobility of his nose, and the gentle curls of hazelnut hair that flickered in the wind beneath the rim of his peaked, tweed cap. She found herself again admiring, as if for the first time, his tall, lean body, the muscular arms, and the long legs that had served him so well on the athletics tracks of his youth. She found herself finding him as attractive in that moment as she had when they had first met at whichever social event it had been, now lost to time. Despite her previous fears and feelings, and in a wave of contradiction, she found herself unable to imagine life without him, and her previous doubts suddenly seemed foolish and destructive. The change of heart was as superficial as it was sudden, and it irritated her. This romantic dithering over another human being was beneath her, and she was at once angry with herself for yielding to it and with George for inspiring it.

"I never tire of this view," he said, waving his arm across it as if he were showing off his own artistic endeavour.

"George, I think we need to talk."

He seemed not to have heard. "Don't you think it's amazing? I'd like to bring an atheist up here and ask him what he makes of it. I don't know how anybody can take in a view like this and not accept the existence of God. Or, at the very least, wonder about it."

"Are you happy, George?"

This time, he turned to face her, and the majesty of the view surrounding them seemed to be lost to him. It was as if the directness of the question, or its implication of her own answer to it, had shaken Toole's assurance of the presence of a divinity in the world. "What sort of question is that?"

"I just want to make sure."

He looked into her dark eyes, more like her father's than she would have cared to admit, and he saw in them a troubled honesty. "Are you not happy?"

The evasion did not trouble her. "Yes, I think so."

She was staring ahead, fighting the urge to look at him, despite his need for her to do so. Her cheeks were softly pale but tinged with crimson by the crisp open air. It was a stark contrast to the darkness of her hair, so intense that its waves resembled the silk of a raven's wing. Her features were angular without being harsh, so that there was a suggestion of the aristocrat about her profile, and her habit of tilting her head back gave the illusion of gentle superiority. This trace of nobility was carried over into her voice, which suggested authority but without any obvious pomposity. She looked at him now with the sun in her face, so that her eyes were narrowed and the nose wrinkled, and he thought at once how childishly vulnerable she looked, and he felt his heart lurch at the sight. Ruefully, he smiled to himself, knowing only too well that she would have hated the comparison.

"I thought I was happy until a few seconds ago," he said. She smiled for a moment, and it turned into a gentle snort of humour. At least, he thought, he could still make her laugh. "Are you having doubts about us?"

Yes, she thought, although she couldn't in the moment find the words to say it. Her indecision frustrated her, and she let out a heavy sigh before she replied. "Not really, no."

"Just nerves, I expect," said Toole, putting his arm around her shoulders. "Perfectly natural. I get them, too."

She looked up into his eyes. "Have you been having doubts?"

"Not doubts, as such," he replied, without elaborating.

Rosamund found that she only half-believed him. She was not sure whether this was because of her own reservations, however, or on account of a genuine concern. "I sometimes feel as if my father wants this marriage more than either of us."

And this, too, was a consideration that had occurred to George Toole. He thought back to the moment when the question of marriage had first arisen. Looking back, it was strange that it had been a discussion between Arthur Bayliss and Toole rather than between Toole and Rosamund.

He recalled that lunchtime meeting in the Midland Hotel in Manchester, all luxury and extravagance, where the chandelier lights flickered on the cut-glass champagne flutes like the sparks of sunlight on an ocean wave, and the elegance of the furniture and upholstery suggested wealth without descending into ostentation. It was typical of Bayliss to hold court in such a place, both because he had made a sufficient fortune to be able to do so and because it pleased him to let people know it.

They were enjoying, assuming Toole could accept the word as appropriate, a cigar and a brandy. Again, it had seemed to Toole that such pleasures were better saved for after dinner rather than in the middle of the afternoon, but Bayliss had insisted. In accepting, Toole avoided offence, but he had not been able to avoid the feeling that he had somehow betrayed part of himself in doing so. The business talk was over. Bayliss had called their venture a joint one, referring to it as a merger that would benefit them both, but Toole was not so naïve that he did not understand what was happening. It was a takeover, friendly rather than hostile, but still not a merger. Toole had wondered whether his father would have agreed to it. The reality was that Toole did not have the same business acumen that his father had possessed, or, for that matter, that Bayliss had. To Toole's mind, the proposition that the Toole mill be taken over by Bayliss Textiles Incorporated was sensible, however unpalatable, and that one thing his father would have hated to see was the firm crash into bankruptcy, which was surely now more of a probability than a mere possibility.

"It's a sensible and potentially profitable decision, my lad," Bayliss had said, blowing a cloud of smoke up into the air. "Your father would have been proud of you for having the guts to make it."

"I hope so, sir," Toole had said. "And the workers will be kept on? You've given me that assurance."

"No question, my boy, no question." He ordered two more glasses of brandy. "We may as well have the one we came for," he had said with a leering smile. Toole had heard the phrase too often now for it to be funny; if anything, it now screeched across his nerves like a badly played violin.

When the unwanted brandy had arrived, Toole had merely sipped at it politely, without any enthusiasm or appreciation of it. "Forgive me, sir, but everything we've discussed this afternoon seems to me to be things we've already gone over. Was there something else you wanted to talk to me about?"

Bayliss had grinned. "Wise lad, indeed. You may not be a businessman, George, but you've got instinct and a head on your shoulders."

The compliment, if it was one, had seemed capable of being ignored. "What did you want to say, Mr Bayliss?"

"Since we're talking about unions, lad, I thought I might suggest another one to you. I've noticed that you've been seeing a fair bit of our Rosamund."

Toole had felt immediately cornered as if he had been caught stealing boiled sweets from a jar. "I enjoy her company."

Bayliss had rolled his cigar along the rim of the ashtray, feigning a little social coyness. "I take it she feels the same?"

"I would like to think so."

"And it is nothing more than that?"

Toole had felt himself flush. "I rather think that we feel more than friendship for each other. Perhaps we're both too hesitant because we've never actually said the words."

"But you do love each other, am I not right?"

Toole had smiled. "I believe so, sir."

And then, Bayliss had leaned forward in a swift movement in his chair. Toole had been reminded of a bloated cobra pouncing on a mouse.

"You see, my boy," Bayliss had said, "I have a son who is a total disappointment to me. Now, I'm expected to leave some or part of my money to that wastrel, and for what? So that he can fritter away my hard work on a dream of being a painter. And not a good one at that."

Toole had not been interested in these personal prejudices. "Surely you can leave your money to whomever you choose."

Bayliss had shaken his head. "Rosamund is a very high-spirited girl, and she knows her own mind, but she's very loyal to her family. Sentimentally so, if you take my meaning. All it'd take would be a tug on the heartstrings from Henry, and she'd give him any amount of money he asked for."

"I think you're underestimating her, if I may say so," Toole had remonstrated.

Bayliss had glared at him. "I know my children, lad. Trust me on that."

"Very well."

And the glare had softened into a smile. "Now, every father wants to walk his girl down the aisle, and I want to be able to say I did it and gave her to a man I respected."

"I see."

"And if she had a husband I could trust, he could give Rosamund an allowance. See? That way, I could ensure that Rosamund got her money, but be equally sure that this bloody painter son of mine got nothing."

The revelation had been momentous, and Toole, for a moment, had thought that he had misheard the words or else misunderstood them. "Are you suggesting…?"

"Think it over, my boy." Bayliss had stubbed out the cigar. "You and Rosamund seem on your way to marriage anyway, and I'd be proud to have a son-in-law like you, and if I could find a way of assuring Rosamund got the benefit of my money without having full control over it, Henry wouldn't be able to take advantage of her. I win on both counts, you see."

"Yes," Toole had said quietly.

Bayliss had drained his brandy. "You think it over, my boy. Now, shall we get a taxi back to the railway station?"

And that had been the end of it. Bayliss had mentioned it several times since, of course, since Toole had not put the plan into immediate action. It hadn't seemed right, feeling as it did part of a business arrangement rather than anything to do with love. Toole would have preferred to ask Rosamund to marry him on his own terms, and he would have liked the proposal of marriage, when it was made, not to be a cynical one, made with the stench of Arthur Bayliss soiling it. Toole had wanted it to be sincere, to matter, rather than being somehow engineered by Bayliss, his money, or his hatred of his son.

But there was the reality of Toole's life to consider. There were the sleepless nights, the anxiety, the constant threat of violence against him. And here was a possible solution to all of it, a chance to put right what he had so seriously allowed to go wrong. Once resolved, Toole would never permit this horror in which he found himself to repeat itself. Marriage to Rosamund Bayliss might save Toole's skin, but it would also give him a cause to fight for, a reason to change that skin forever. All it would take would be to swallow his pride and make the proposal on Arthur Bayliss' terms rather than his own. After all, love was one thing, but self-preservation was quite another. And so, it had happened. And Rosamund had accepted. For George Toole, that had been the end of it. Safety was only a few months away. Once married, his turmoil and fear would be confined to history.

Except now, standing over Layton Brook, his mind raced back to the present, where that sense of stability and sanctuary against the violence he dreaded was in danger of capsizing. When Rosamund expressed doubts about their engagement, Toole felt his world stumble and quake. The tide had to be turned.

"I do love you, Rosamund," he said, making no apology for it.

She looked up at him and smiled. "I know you do."

He waited desperately for her to reciprocate the words, but they did not come. He wondered whether he should tell her the truth about himself, throw himself on her mercy and beg for her forgiveness. Perhaps honesty, he thought, could save him anyway, without recourse to Bayliss' scheme. Of that, Toole could say nothing, of course. Rosamund would see him as a collaborator in the plan and herself a pawn in it, neither of which she would appreciate. But would she appreciate the truth about Toole any better?

Not for the first time, Toole wondered when his life had become such a mess. But he knew. Of course, he knew.

"I love you so much," he said. This time, the words were an urgent rush of intensity.

She continued to stare into his eyes until at last he pushed himself towards her and kissed her forcefully, the hairs of his moustache bristling against her lips. With a sigh of frustrated and confused emotion, she had embraced him.

"Just nerves," Toole whispered into her ear. "We're getting jumpy about it all. There's nothing more to it than that."

"I know," she said, "I know."

They stayed there for a long moment, their arms locked around each other, the birds circling in the cool blue skies above them, and the rustle of water over rocks from the brook beneath them. It was so idyllic, so curiously romantic, that neither of them realised for some time that the wind had risen and brought with it a more bitter cold.

"Come on, darling," said George Toole, "let's get back and have a stiff drink. Calm those nerves a little bit."

Rosamund pulled away from him slightly so that she could look into his dark eyes once more. She kissed him, gently this time, and told him that she loved him.

"Just nerves, as you say," she whispered in his ear.

It must have sounded convincing, because she almost believed it herself.

# Chapter Four

The contents of the anonymous letter lingered in Eric Hirst's mind for the majority of the day, so that only the more intricate accounting duties and administrative tasks of the working day distracted him from it. His profitability and professionalism were not unduly affected, but he was aware that his mind was not always concentrated on his work and that the mystery and the threat behind the letter were causing his attention to drift. It was not surprising, perhaps. Anonymous death threats, Hirst supposed, could hardly be said to be a matter of routine for any business, so they presumably would always be a cause for distraction and concern.

It was not the letter itself that troubled Hirst, not in isolation. It was the escalation of the seriousness of these outrages perpetrated by this prankster that had begun to taunt them. To call him a prankster seemed foolishly trite. It implied a practical joker, someone who put sugar in the salt cellars in the canteen or removed lightbulbs from the staff lavatories; someone who disrupted matters without causing any real harm or distress. But this was not the case with the phantom that haunted Bayliss Textiles. Some of the earliest acts of sabotage might well have seemed trivial. The broken windows, for example, might have been put down to a group of naughty schoolboys searching for cheap thrills on their walk home from a day of tedious education. But the cancelled order, Hirst's slashed tyres, and the dead rat without question had not been the work of mischievous adolescence. They had been acts of malice rather than mischief. And now, they had elevated to a direct threat against a human being. A dead rat was one thing, but a dead man, even by threat alone, was something quite different.

And yet Bayliss had remained defiant throughout the day. There was no question of alerting the police, despite Hirst's repeated and increasingly anxious pleas to the contrary, and Bayliss seemed content either to ignore the letter completely or, at best, to ask this man Carr to consider the position. It all seemed, in turn, reckless and ridiculous not to inform the police and to confide only in a man Bayliss knew from an elitist club in London, even if this Everett Carr person claimed to have solved serious crimes in the past. The notion of an amateur sleuth seemed more ludicrous each time it crossed Hirst's mind, but there was nothing he could say to Bayliss that would change the man's mind. In the end, Hirst had been told in no uncertain terms that the topic was closed.

"I'm not repeating myself, Eric," Bayliss had snapped. "The damned thing was addressed to me, and it's mine to deal with, as I see fit. Leave it be. If you must think about it, do it on your own time and not mine."

There had been so many things Hirst could have said in return, so many replies he could have given, but he had said nothing. He had walked back to his office, sullen and morose. Damn Bayliss, Hirst thought. If the letter writer made good on his threat against him, good luck to him. Nobody could say afterwards that Hirst hadn't tried to do something to help prevent it.

He pulled on his overcoat, scarf, and hat, turned off his office light, and carefully locked the door. He walked along the iron gantry, down the spiral staircase, and across the mill floor. A few of the lads were still working, and he called out a friendly warning not to stay too late and to have a good evening. A few, but not all, thanked him and reciprocated. Michael Arden, Hirst noticed, only stared at him with contempt. Hirst felt nothing about that. He did not even return the glare. Arden meant nothing to him, not before Emma's death and certainly not now after it.

Outside, it was as dark as twilight, although it was only a little after six o'clock in the evening. The moon was bright, and the stars glistened around it, and Hirst took a moment to gaze at the majesty of them and to wonder what lay beyond them. Broken windows, rats in drawers, death threats, or even Michael Arden meant nothing when compared to those divine lights in the sky that had endured longer than any of mankind's troubles and would no doubt exist long after those troubles had come to their end. It was both a sobering and an inspiring thought, one that startled as well as soothed Hirst. He had not been to church as regularly as he had done before Emma's death, but looking at the moon and its surrounding freckles of light made him wonder whether he should make a return to the house of the God that had created them. He was surprised at how strongly this minor religious resurgence swelled within him, and it was almost impossible not to take it as a sign to attend the service on Sunday morning and make his peace with God. The decision made, Eric Hirst began the familiar walk of a couple of solitary miles from the factory to his home.

He contemplated half a glass of beer in *The Black Bull*, but there was beer at home, and the whisky decanter if he desired anything stronger, so there seemed little point in walking through the door of the public house. Besides, he reminded himself, Michael Arden was a frequent—perhaps *too* frequent—customer of the place, and there was every possibility that he would call in for a drink or two after his shift at the mill. Quite how Arden could contemplate the social gathering of a public house, or even the noise of the working environment, so soon after his mother's death was beyond Hirst. There was something to be said for distracting oneself from grief, of course, but Hirst could not reconcile his experiences of it with the bustling murmur and laughter of a public house. For him, after the death of both his wife and daughter, solitude had been his closest ally against the trials of mourning.

He dismissed the thoughts, sour and unwelcome, from his mind and continued the walk home. As he turned into Church Lane and the looming stone edifice of the bell tower of St Andrew's came into view, he tried to recall the last time he had heard those bells ring. The last clear memory of their peal had been Emma's funeral, six months ago. It was a memory spurred by his emotions rather than his logic because he knew that he would have heard the bells ringing every day on the quarter hour and at length on every Sunday. But those memories, undeniably real, were meaningless. He may have heard them, he thought, but he had not registered them. The last time the bells had consumed him, the last time they had held any meaning for him, was when he buried his daughter in the grounds of this noble, Anglo-Saxon church. Their sounds thereafter were hollow silence to him.

His thoughts might have darkened further if he had not seen the figure coming towards him from the opposite end of Church Lane. Even though she was silhouetted by the overhanging trees of the lane, Hirst could recognise the elegant sway of movement that was peculiar only to Lydia Stansfield. She was dressed, as she often was, in dark blue or black; it was impossible to tell in the darkness of the evening, and her narrow-brimmed fedora hat was pulled down over one eye, at an angle that might have been deemed jaunty, but that struck Hirst as deliberately careless. The darkness of both the evening skies and the glare of the street lamps made the vivid blonde of her hair seem almost unnaturally bright, like some sort of impossible halo of sunlight in an otherwise impenetrable dark.

She suddenly became aware of him, and she gave a smile of recognition, the rose lips parting smoothly and the cobalt eyes squinted at him from under the brim of the hat. He lifted his own hat in greeting and gave a short, foolishly old-fashioned bow.

"Finished for the day, Eric?" she asked.

"Yes, just on my way home. I had thought about a quick drink in *The Black Bull* but decided against it. Although perhaps now we could go together?"

Lydia smiled warmly. "A wonderful idea, Eric, and I'd love to, but I can't. I'm heading into town to meet a friend."

"I see." Hirst's manner changed instantly. His eyes had darkened, and he lowered his gaze to his feet. "I suppose I can guess who that friend is."

He regretted the words as soon as they were spoken. They betrayed his pettiness, his envy, and his disapproval. Lydia's smile faded. She had hardly expected his petulance to come out so quickly and so vehemently.

"Please, Eric, let's not fight about it."

"I'm sorry," he said, meaning it. "The thought of you being with him makes me so..."

"I can't help how I feel," Lydia said. "About either of you."

She had not meant it to be cruel, but it had hurt him nevertheless, this reminder that she could not reciprocate whatever feelings he had for her and that romance could never develop from their friendship. He could not complain, however. She had never pretended otherwise, and it was foolish and childish to expect her to do so. He could not inspire love in her any more than he could spin straw into gold, even if what he felt for her was love. And was it? He thought so, but there were times when he could not be sure of it. Thinking one was in love was not the same thing as being in love. And if he had doubts, how could he say he loved her? Lydia, of course, had no such doubts. To her, the situation was entirely plain.

"I've no wish to force you into anything," he said.

"I should hope not." Her voice was momentarily hostile, and he knew he deserved it. His remark had been fatuous. But her smile soon returned. "Eric, we've been friends for so long, why can't that be enough?"

"Perhaps it's not so much that you don't want me but rather who it is you do want."

This was an old, tired argument, and she was not about to have it again. "As I said, I can't help how I feel about either of you."

He nodded. Looking into her eyes, his expression was apology enough, he hoped, but he supported it with words. "I'm sorry. I didn't mean to say any of this. It's been a long day."

She took his hand in hers. "Would it be made any better if I told you that the friend I'm meeting isn't who you think he is?"

He laughed. "It might."

"Perhaps we can have that drink in *The Black Bull* some other time?"

"Most certainly," he said. "Whenever is best for you."

Lydia detected in his manner a sense of distraction. "Eric, are you all right?"

Hirst shook his head. "There was an anonymous letter at the mill."

"My God…" She frowned heavily. "This prankster again?"

Hirst shrugged his shoulders. "We have to assume so, I suppose. It was filthy. Worse, I think it was dangerous."

"Dangerous?"

"Despite how I feel about you and Arthur, I'm worried."

"Arthur?" She watched him affirm it with a flicker of his eyes. "What did this letter say?"

"It threatened his life."

For a moment, she seemed not to have heard him. She stared blankly, making no response at all. Then, as if her ears had caught up with the words, she frowned heavily, her brow furrowing, and her blue eyes questioning. "I'm sorry?"

Hirst knew that he did not need to repeat himself. "He refuses to take it seriously. I've told him to go to the police about it, but he insists it means nothing. He wants to show it to some crony of his from London, but that's all he's prepared to do about it."

"Then why are you taking it so seriously?"

He glared at her. "It's a death threat, Lydia."

She nodded vaguely, still reeling from the shock of his revelation. "Perhaps I can talk some sense into him. Is he at the mill?"

"No, he left early today."

"Damn. I can't very well telephone the house either. I need to speak to him as soon as I can."

"To try to get some sense into him?"

She looked at him as if he had said something that had been designed to hurt. "To make sure he's all right, Eric."

He felt suddenly foolish. "Of course, I'm sorry. I didn't think. But I've told you," he added, as if in his defence. "He doesn't think it's anything to worry about. If you say anything close to what I said, you'll get the same reaction."

"I've still got to try. Take care, Eric, and thank you." She leaned into him and kissed his cheek. He tried to retain control of his knees. "Let's have that drink."

And with that, she walked away from him, down the slope of Church Lane and into the town. Hirst watched her disappear from view, the ghostly traces of her lips still lingering on his cheek and the scent of her perfume still haunting the air around him. As he turned on his heel and began walking again, he regretted almost immediately having said anything about the threatening letter. Surely it could only make Lydia feel sorry for Bayliss, encourage her sympathy towards him, and drive her closer into his arms. Hirst cursed himself for the worst type of fool, the sort of man who must delight in misfortune and who cannot be happy unless he is tormented by misery. And worse, the type of man who wallows in his own self-pity. He cursed himself again, this time with a cruel vehemence, and he quickened his pace. Forget the beer at home, he thought grimly; as soon as he was inside, he would attack the decanter of whisky and damn its effects in the morning to Hell.

# Chapter Five

The cottage in which Michael Arden had been born and raised was at one end of a narrow row of identical cottages dating back to the early part of the previous century. They were modest, simple, and functional, but to Arden, they were his childhood, his adulthood, and more than likely his retirement. They had moved with the times insofar as utilities were concerned, but these modern additions to them were equally perfunctory, so that the overall impression of the narrow domiciles was no different now than it had been over a hundred years previously. When Arden had sat with his mother on either side of the fireplace, waiting for the iron kettle to whistle its purpose, it would occur to him that they were no different from their Victorian ancestors. Their living arrangements may have been updated with electricity and gas, but the opportunities and the hardships of the inhabitants had not shifted in the slightest. A hundred years of industrial and economic progress had done nothing to alter the fortunes and the prospects of people like Michael and Beatrice Arden.

It was almost seven o'clock when he returned to the cottage. Contrary to Eric Hirst's predictions, Arden had not gone into *The Black Bull* after finishing up at the mill, although he did plan on nipping in for an hour or so before last orders. He would once have acted exactly as Hirst had imagined, and it had suited Arden to do so. A couple of drinks after work, just to unwind, and then back to the cottage for some food with his mother and a couple of hours together in front of the fire. Since Beatrice Arden's death, however, Arden had come to realise that the nocturnal peace by the fire could be as lonely as it could be soothing. As a result, he had taken to coming straight home after the mill, having a wash and perhaps a change of clothes, a quick meal of bread and cheese, and only heading out to *The Black Bull* for the last hour or so of trading if he felt like it.

And if he did feel like it, once there, he would indulge in two or three pints of beer, perhaps a slice of a pork pie that was always a day or two past its best, and a couple of games of darts. He would pass perhaps an hour and a half in this way before deciding that he had best get home for one last beer or, more sensibly, a cup of hot tea, a couple of smokes, and bed, before the whole cycle of living in Darton Vale repeated itself on the following day. Arden had heard some people call it a simple life, but those people were usually the ones with money. To him, there was nothing simple about it. It was hard graft for low wages and even less respect. Yes, he had money for food, beer, and smokes—and why shouldn't he have some pleasures in his life?—but there was very little left behind for anything else. No dinner parties, no social balls, and no prospects of getting on the next Honours list like Arthur Bayliss, if the rumours were to be believed. Not that Arden would want any of it, but it would be nice to be in a position at least to refuse it.

He pushed open the door of the cottage, its hinges reminding him yet again that they needed oil. And, to judge by the temperature of the sitting room, the fire required fuel. The air outside was cold, but the interior of the cottage was unforgiving. It amazed him how so small a room could be so cold. The stone floors would not help, of course, and the small rug, knitted by his mother, that was placed in front of the cast iron fireplace was hardly big enough to compensate for the harsh cold of the floor. There were two armchairs on either side of the fireplace, threadbare but purposeful, with cheap rugs thrown over the back of each, and a small table between them. A wooden sideboard was set against the back wall, inside which were plates, dishes, and glasses, with a wooden board on top for slicing cold meat and bread. A pair of candlesticks was at either end, and a lace-trimmed cloth spread across the centre, its white now faded a faint yellow and the edges slightly frayed. Through an archway to the left of the room, there was a small kitchen and a wooden table with four chairs set at it, although only two of them had ever been used with any regularity. The bedrooms were accessible by a wooden staircase that led up from the corner of the sitting room. Outside, through the back door, there was a small flagged yard with little more than a small toolshed, a coal shed, and an outside convenience. The whole place, Arden would think to himself, inside and out, could have fitted into Arthur Bayliss' dining room, and it seemed to Arden both cramped and depressing, little more than a reminder of how little he was expected to achieve and how futile any attempts to better himself would be. Beatrice Arden had a saying, one that would both irritate and embarrass Arden: "Be it ever so humble, there's no place like home." To Arden, the word *humble* was inappropriate. It suggested quaintness, cosiness, and charm when the reality was cold, restrictive, and despondent.

It took a few moments to get the fire going, and once it had caught, Arden went through the archway into the kitchen and filled the iron kettle with water. He lit the ring on the stove and placed the kettle on it. It was a mechanical act, one which he performed without thinking, and one that he did whether he went to the pub later in the evening or not. Beatrice had always enjoyed a hot cup of tea before supper, and Michael had always made it when he came in from work. Now, though, she was gone, but not putting the kettle on when he returned home seemed almost to be a betrayal of her memory, as if not hearing the kettle whistle would be some sort of indication that he had forgotten her. The kettle would boil now, and he knew that he would take it off the stove, make a cup of tea for his mother, take it through to the sitting room, and place it on the wooden table between the armchairs. He would get himself a bottle of beer from the pantry, and he would sit in the other chair and remember her. The beer would be drunk, the tea would go cold and be poured down the sink, and he would go up to bed. If it was a habit, it was one he could not break; if it was maudlin sentimentality, he made no apology for it; if it was grief, he made no effort to understand it. It was just something he had done in the two weeks since she had died.

He sat now with the bottle of beer poured out into a glass and the steaming tea set at the other side of the table between the chairs for nobody to drink.

He missed his mother; there was no doubt about it. In the weeks leading to her death, her conversation had become repetitive and increasingly trivial, but Arden had never complained. Beatrice had been a strong and independent woman, as he had always known, and she had been a considerate and effective mother. She had chastised him when he had deserved it, even if in the childish moment he had not understood that he had deserved punishment, and she had taken his side when he had been maligned or blamed by other children for their misdemeanours. She had been unafraid to speak her mind if it had been necessary, but she had never been anything but fair. Looking back, with mournful and adult eyes, Michael Arden could recognise that she had been a strong and supportive mother to him, and he had found himself more than once wishing that he had told her as much. He had loved her, without question, but he had also both admired and respected her. Now that she was no longer there, it seemed less difficult to admit than it had been when she was alive. Perhaps, he thought, all people feel like that, so that with grief comes inevitable regret.

Beatrice had brought him up alone. He had never known his father, and he had never been subjected to a paternal influence. He had always been led to believe that his father had died soon before he was born, the victim of a railway disaster somewhere between Manchester and Leeds. He had been out on some business or other, Arden had been told, and a collision had occurred in the midst of the Pennines. Only later had school ground rumours begun to surface that his father had not died but had deserted, that he had not even been married to his mother, that she was nothing less than whatever word they chose to call her. Arden had won and lost several brawls, had his eyes blackened and his knuckles bloodied, defending his mother against the charge of being a liar and much worse. The taunts and the fights had continued into his working life, so that by the time he had turned fifteen, Arden had no longer been able to suppress his desire for the truth. If he were to continue fighting for his mother's honour, he had thought, he might as well understand why he was doing it. And so, one evening, a little over ten years ago, and sitting by this same fire, his lip swollen and his face bruised, he had dared to ask her for the truth.

"Did my Dad die in a railway accident?" he had said, without warning.

Beatrice had been stoking the fire, and she had risen to her feet swiftly, holding the poker out towards him like a vengeful sword. "What makes you ask that?"

He had shrugged, suddenly regretting his decision to speak. Beatrice had turned her back on him slowly and replaced the poker in its stand. "This is what all these fights are for, is it?"

He had nodded, having previously refused to explain what the blood and bruising had been for. "They say you're a liar. And worse."

"Who says?"

"Kids at school."

"Repeating what their parents say, of course." She had looked down on him, her face shrouded in shadows caused by the orange flicker of the fire's flames. "Don't you listen to them, Mikey. They're just wicked lies."

"From all of them, Mum?" he had asked. "One or two, maybe, but not all of them."

Beatrice had sat down in the armchair beside him and rubbed her hands together. She had brushed a wayward strand of dark hair from his face and looked at him with her slate-grey eyes. Her expression had not been fierce, but it had held purpose, and the fifteen-year-old Michael Arden had known that it was a moment to listen rather than to speak.

"Very well, Mikey," she had said. "If you're old enough to get into fights to defend me, you're old enough to know what it is you're defending. Your father didn't die in a railway accident, and I should never have told you he did."

"So why did you?"

"Because, Mikey, I thought it would mean that you'd never ask no more questions about him. I thought it was better for you to think he died honourably than know the truth of it. But you've asked me outright for the truth now, so I'll give it to you. I suppose you're old enough to understand it." She had looked sadly into his eyes. "But I'll give you the full truth, nothing held back. And just remember, you asked for it."

He shuffled in his chair now, as if the memory of her confession caused him physical discomfort. He gulped at the beer as he saw the ghost of his mother sitting in the chair next to him, her elbows on her knees and her hands clasped in front of her, as if in some silent prayer not only for the strength to talk but also for her child's forgiveness. He seemed to hear her voice coming from beside him rather than from the cellars of his mind. He felt as if he was the same fifteen-year-old boy, hearing the truth about his lineage for the first time, rather than an adult who had long ago come to terms with the reality of his parents and who had forgiven his mother over a decade previously, so that it had hardly mattered anymore, until her death had brought it back to the forefront of his conscience.

"The truth is, Mikey," his mother had said, "I know very little about your father. I know his name was Frank, that he lived in London, and that he was a travelling salesman up in Darton Vale on business. I know he was full of charm and cheek, and I know he could have had any girl in Lancashire if he'd wanted. I know all that, but I don't know him as a person; I never did. I can imagine a lot of things about him, though. I can imagine he was married, and I can imagine that when he left here, he found another Beatrice Arden in some other town somewhere. I can imagine that when he got back to London, he kissed his wife and children, sat down to a family dinner, and made love to his wife, and kissed his kiddies goodnight, and forgot all about the Beatrice Ardens across the country, who sat waiting for him to come back like he promised he would. I can imagine that, Mikey, only too easily."

She had begun to weep, he recalled, her cheeks glistening in the firelight. He had wanted to hold her, but somehow even his juvenile instinct had told him that it would have been an unwelcome gesture.

"He bought me some drinks in *The Black Bull*," Beatrice had continued, "and he charmed me. He had something none of the lads in the town had. You won't understand, my lad, you're too young. But he had style, swagger, and stories about London, which made it seem like some fairy tale world far from here. And he had promises, Mikey, promises that meant the world to girls like me but nothing to him. They were just ways of getting girls like me to fall for him, to make fools of ourselves for him, to give ourselves to him. It never mattered where: his hotel, the woods, the back of his car, alleyways, anywhere he got the urge, and always with a new promise of love and a new flattering compliment. Until one day, he was gone, and you were here."

The tears had flowed freely during the speech, and Arden, just about old enough to understand the words she said but too young to appreciate the complexity of emotions she felt, had been unable to resist his instincts any longer. He had got to his feet and gone to her, flinging his arms around her and holding onto her as if she would vanish into the air if he dared to let go. She had kissed his head, his cheeks, and he had felt himself succumb to tears as she did so. Whatever he had imagined the truth about his father might be, and he had never doubted the story about his death until the schoolyard malice had forced him to question it, not once would he have envisaged anything like this. In that moment of revelation, he had forged an instant hatred for this man he had not known, and, simultaneously, his profound love and admiration for his mother had intensified. Suddenly, it had not mattered whether his father was alive or dead. He did not care whether the kids in the schoolyard mocked and teased him for having no father. In his youthful mind, all that mattered to Michael Arden was his mother and her love for him. If this man, Frank, was what fathers were, young Michael Arden wanted none of it.

"I love you," he had whispered into his mother's ear, "and I am so sorry, Mummy."

"You've no need to be sorry," she had replied. "If anyone should be apologising, it's him and me. Him for never coming back like he promised, and me for lying to you all these years."

Her son had held onto her even more tightly. "I never want him to come back, and I never want you to go."

"I'm not going anywhere, Mikey," she had said. "I'm never going nowhere, you watch."

Except now, she had gone, and it would be forever.

Arden felt an itch on his cheek, and he was surprised to find that he was weeping. He had not realised it, and now that he did, he was embarrassed by it. He drained the beer and got to his feet. He picked up his mother's cup and poured the cold tea down the sink, and left both her cup and his glass in the small sink. He washed his hands and threw some of the ice-cold water from the tap onto his face, rubbing away any trace of those stray tears. He stood for a moment, his hands on the edges of the sink and his head bent forward so that droplets of the water dripped from his nose and chin into the ceramic bowl. He was breathing heavily and erratically, he thought, until he realised that it wasn't breathing which was causing his lungs to lurch and his shoulders to tremble, but sobbing. At last, with another dose of water to his face, he stepped away from the sink and walked back through the arch to the stairs.

His intention was to go into his room and strip, have a proper wash, and put on clean clothes suitable for a visit to the public house. As it was, he only carried out that intention almost half an hour later. First, without really knowing why, he went into his mother's room. It was the first time he had come in it since she had died, and he could only imagine that the reason for coming in it now was the moment of reflection and recollection that he had experienced downstairs. He had a sudden desire to see his mother's face, not simply in a memory but as close to reality as he could. There were photographs, he knew, albums that she kept hidden away in drawers in her dressing table and wardrobe. She would sit and look through them with him sometimes, telling stories about her grandparents and her aunties, often laughing at some memories and sometimes crying at others. He had thought of those sepia images as frozen moments of time from another world, one far away from his own reality, a life experienced by a woman whom he had only ever seen as a mother and a parent, but who these photographs showed had lived a life. And now, with that life over, Michael Arden was suddenly desperate to see evidence of it again.

He found the albums in the drawers of the dressing table and boxes in the wardrobe, as he had expected to, and he had carried them over to her bed. Sitting on the edge of the mattress, he had pulled one of them towards him. Several minutes passed as he delved once more into the past, some of the images being familiar and some so lost to time that he might have been seeing them for the first time. Pictures of Beatrice as an infant, his own childhood features being so obviously recognisable in her face; pictures of her in her pubescent years, slightly more identifiable as the woman he had known; pictures of her around the time that she had met a lying travelling salesman who had taken advantage of her, but no pictures of him with her. There were other items in these personal memorabilia, none of which meant anything in particular to him, but all of which would have meant something to her: pebbles and shells from some distant beach, a thimble, several bookmarks made (by Beatrice, perhaps) with pressed flowers, a paper napkin from somewhere called *Sinclair's*, handkerchiefs with initials which meant nothing to him, a matchbox filled with his baby teeth for each one of which she had left a penny under his pillow, Christmas cards he had made for her.

And then, eventually, he had found the envelope. It was addressed, in her neat but somehow childish handwriting, to "My Mikey". He felt a sudden nausea come over him as he picked it up and turned it over in his hands. How long it had been in these boxes, he could not say, but something told him that she had written it only recently and that she had known that, sooner or later, he would feel the urge to look at the photograph albums. It meant, he supposed, that she had not been able to give the envelope and its contents to him while she was alive. In turn, it seemed to him that it must follow that whatever was inside was something momentous, perhaps even monstrous.

He tore it open and pulled out the letter. He read the words to himself, but it was her voice that he heard reciting them in his head. He could hear every inflexion of tone, every breaking sob in her voice, and he could almost feel her arms around him, holding him close. How many times he read it over, he could not say, but however many times it was, the words still seemed to make no sense to him. At last, having read it for the final time, Michael Arden, nauseous and angry, marched out of her room, slamming the door behind him, and running downstairs and out of the cottage.

He made his way down the narrow street to the main road and up the hill to the town square. He needed beer, not only to comfort him but to wash away the taste of blood that had seemed to coat his tongue and the roof of his mouth. He wondered if he had bitten his lip or something, but it did not seem to be the case. Only as he passed the gates of St Andrew's did Michael Arden realise that the bitter taste in his mouth was not actual blood, but was instead the blended taste of deceit, vengeance, and murder.

# Chapter Six

Rosamund helped herself to a second glass of sherry, ignoring the disapproving look that she had no doubt was being cast in her direction by her mother. She made no apology for it. The afternoon walk with George Toole still preyed on her mind, for one thing, and, for another, she had always faced family dinners with a stifled disgust.

It was her father's fault, of course. It always seemed to be her father's fault. There had been a time when she hadn't hated him, but she had to force those childhood images from deep within her memory. They didn't come easily to her. She could remember her father reading bedtime stories to her, dutifully rather than enthusiastically, perhaps, but she could recall still hanging on each word, staring up into his florid face until slumber eventually overcame her. And she could remember the sensation of towering over the town of Darton Vale, like a giant making its way through the fairytale kingdom, her head brushing the branches of trees as she passed, on those occasions when he would carry her on his massive shoulders. She could even bring to mind performing songs for him before dinner, complete with childish dancing and his rigorous applause both during and at the conclusion of the performances. She could remember all those things when she tried.

At least, she thought she could. Now, all those years later, there was the gnawing doubt, the incessant fear that these memories were not real, that they were only fabrications of a mind that so strongly wished them to be true.

It was these fears that made her remember other aspects of childhood, this time certainly genuine memories. Of sitting alone in her bedroom, the door locked and the key taken away by her father, a punishment of isolation for some minor misdemeanour. A lie told, an order disobeyed, a house rule transgressed. And sometimes, it wasn't her bedroom. It was the cellar, cold and dank, among the spiders and the mould, the lightbulbs removed by him, so that she could have no distractions whilst she thought about her behaviour. Those had been his words, the last ones she would hear for hours before he closed the cellar door and bolted it. Sometimes, perhaps worst of all, it had been the cupboard under the stairs. No spiders there, but the same darkness, and somehow, to the infant Rosamund, the cramped, claustrophobic space that forced her into unnatural and uncomfortable contortions simply to be able to sit down was more terrifying than the cold, arachnid-infested cellar.

There was never any physical reprimand. That was always saved for her brother, Henry, but she would feel compelled to watch it, to listen to it, sometimes in the room and sometimes in the corridor outside. In her childish selfishness, Rosamund had wondered whether her ordeal was not worse than the beatings her brother endured. Bruises, welts, and cuts could be treated. There were creams, ointments, and sticking plasters. Bruises faded, broken flesh healed. Her wounds would come back to her in her sleep, night after night, haunted even her waking hours, and infiltrated her mind when she was trying to concentrate in the classroom. Her adult self had understood the situation better, however. It had been the same for Henry, of course. How could she have thought otherwise? Perhaps it had been a means of coping with the horror.

Strangely, neither she nor Henry had ever dared ask the other about their suffering. The pair of them, she thought, had grown up in suffering silence, not daring to confide, each perhaps thinking the other got off lightly, always hoping it would end, knowing it never would. She assumed, then and now, that Henry had felt as powerless against the abuse as she did, that he had equally felt unable to fight back. By the same token, she deeply suspected that Henry, as she had herself, had always dreamed of exacting on her father some terrible but so very satisfying revenge.

These thoughts had swarmed into Rosamund's mind during dinner, as she watched her father gorge himself on the roast beef like a cannibal at a sacrifice. Her hatred towards him, her disgust at his pride and his greed, had intensified over the years. As a child, she had feared him. As an adult, she despised him, and this loathing seemed even more acute when he was indulging himself in gluttony, as if he was capable of making the most basic human need seem unnatural and horrifying. This evening, her revulsion towards her father seemed more ferocious than ever.

Rosamund had been conscious recently of a new manifestation of unease circling her. It was not only her growing suspicion about the motives of her father, the roots of which were firmly planted in the question of her engagement to George Toole, but also in the increased and ever more tangible dislike that had been forged between her father and her brother. It had always existed, of course, but over the past few weeks, it had seemed to Rosamund as if it had mutated into something altogether more dangerous.

Henry, to give him credit, would try to underplay the tension if either Rosamund or their mother was in the room, but Arthur Bayliss made no such concessions. It had begun to make any occasion when the two of them were in the same room almost unbearable, but to Rosamund, it was dinner, with its expectations of polite conversation and appropriate manners, that was the most awkward example of it. Sitting around the table had ceased to be a pleasure and had become a trial as if they were sitting on a keg of gunpowder and either father or son, and possibly both, held a lit match in his hand. Rosamund had never spoken of these concerns, but she felt certain that she was not alone in having them. Surely, she thought, the disquiet was too obvious not to be noticed.

As it was, however, Marjorie Bayliss was entirely aware of the fractious relationship between her husband and son, and she not only shared her daughter's certainty that it was felt by the whole family but also the same reluctance to talk about it. If Marjorie thought that Rosamund's second glass of sherry was inappropriate, she did not say so. She looked carefully at Rosamund and tried to find something of herself at that age in her daughter's expression. There was a resemblance, without question, but Marjorie wondered how defined it was. Superficially, it was easy to see. Rosamund shared Marjorie's luxuriously black hair, although she did not have the streaks of grey that swept back from Marjorie's temples and which she considered distinguished rather than intrusive. Rosamund's eyes were as dark as her mother's, too, and the angular nobility of the features was present in both women, although they were perhaps slightly softer in Marjorie. In temperament, however, the differences between them were more distinct. It was perhaps a generational thing, but Marjorie had always felt that she was less outspoken than her daughter, who was capable of saying things without always appreciating the effect her words might have. To Marjorie, this tendency to express any opinion, wanted or otherwise, was both reckless and disagreeable.

"Do you know anything about this man who is coming to stay for the weekend?" Rosamund asked.

"Mr Carr?" Marjorie shook her head. "No, dear, I don't know very much about him at all. He's somebody your father met at this London club he has been accepted into, but I don't know any more than that."

"I hope he isn't a bore." Rosamund sipped at her second sherry. "Do you want anything, by the way?"

"No, thank you, dear." She adjusted the scarab brooch on her evening dress. "How is George?"

Rosamund shrugged. "He seems to be working late a lot these days."

"I expect it's this merging of businesses with your father. It's bound to keep George busy."

Her daughter nodded vaguely. "Possibly, but for someone who claims to have no head for business, George seems very involved in it all. I didn't see him at all last night. I went to the mill, but neither he nor Daddy was there. Why can't he just let Daddy do everything? They'd both prefer that, I'm sure."

It was a sensible question, but Marjorie Bayliss had no answer to it. "Have you decided on your wedding dress, dear?"

"Not yet." Rosamund sat down in one of the drawing room armchairs. "I feel as if I should just flip a coin and be done with it."

"I hardly think that would be satisfactory, Rosamund. I prefer the more traditional one you tried on, but I suppose that is a question of age. No doubt you are more inclined to the white lace with the pleats, which made you look rather like a flapper, I'm afraid."

"The other made me look like something out of Wilkie Collins," argued Rosamund. "Did you have this trouble when you got married?"

Marjorie smiled. "No, dear. But then I had rather less say in the whole matter than you have."

Rosamund laughed. "And that's an age thing too, I expect."

"Very much so."

The conversation, without warning, was interrupted by the door being opened and the subsequent appearance of Henry Bayliss. Both Marjorie and Rosamund had expected it to be Arthur Bayliss, and they each noticed in the other their own expression of relief reflected back at them. If Henry was aware of it, he made no comment, although he returned their smiles of greeting and, had he been able to sense it, he would have shared their gratitude at the absence of his father. The three of them knew that it was only a delay of the inevitable, but they were all grateful for any respite from the guaranteed and awkward unpleasantness of the coming dinner.

Henry helped himself to a sherry, his long, thin fingers treating the crystal with respect and delicacy as if the glass and decanter were two of his instruments of artistic endeavour. He had dressed for dinner, but it was obvious that he found the formality of the evening suit both oppressive and uncomfortable. He was more accustomed to open-necked shirts, loose flannel trousers, and the occasional smock when the fancy took him, so that the stiffness of the collar and tie and the restrictive cut of the dinner jacket seemed to him to be the equivalent of a noose around his neck or a straitjacket around his shoulders. Had he voiced the opinion, any single member of the family would have accused him of melodrama, putting his exaggeration down to his artistic imagination rather than any foundation of fact. His father, in particular, would have called him a vile name, no doubt, a slur against his sexuality that would have been both offensive and inaccurate. Similarly disgusting words had been used by his father in those frequent disagreements about Henry's general appearance: about the length of his curling fair hair, about his lack of hair elsewhere on his body, about his preference for painting and poetry over machines and engines, and about his incapability to kick a football or his inability to wield a cricket bat with any measure of success. To his father, Henry's tall frame and broad shoulders were wasted standing in front of an easel instead of being put to use in one sporting arena or another, or, for that matter, in general hard work.

"Painting is fine as a hobby, lad," Arthur Bayliss would say, "but it's no job for a man. A man should be out grafting, not playing around with paints."

"I do graft, just not in a way you understand, but that doesn't make it any less honest as work."

"Painting pictures is not hard work. Look at you, boy. Hair too long, no callouses on your hands, no blood in your veins. Some bloody son you are. We should have called you Henrietta." The remark was childish, and even as a taunt, it was close to worthless, but the motivation behind it and the actual insult glossed over by it were both ignorant and dangerous.

"Is Father not in for dinner?" Henry asked now, kissing his mother on the cheek.

"He is expected, darling," said Marjorie.

Henry winked at Rosamund. "I thought it was too good to be true."

"Don't let him hear you talk like that," cautioned Rosamund with a smile. "He'll take away your paints and brushes."

Any further reply from Henry was prohibited by the arrival of Bayliss himself. Behind him, smiling amiably, was George Toole. When she saw him, Rosamund felt her insides contract, as if a serpent had coiled itself around them, and she felt the cold tingle of nervous anxiety prickle her skin. George looked at her, retaining his smile, although now it was rather sadder than it had been a moment before.

Bayliss had thrown open the door with a malignant flourish, and he now closed it with more force than was necessary. Marjorie, on an instinct that disgusted Rosamund with its submissiveness, rose to her feet. For a moment, Bayliss looked at his family, as if wondering what he had done to be cursed with them, then smiled and crossed the room to the drinks table.

He poured Toole and himself a large whisky each, blithely looking over his shoulder as he did so.

"Anyone else want one?" he said. "Marjorie, my dear? No? Very well. Rosamund, you have a sherry, I see. And so have you, Henry." Now, he turned to face them, and the smile had spoiled itself into a sneer. "Sherry, lad? How appropriate."

Henry bristled, but Rosamund's hand on his forearm relinquished any idea of a response from him. It went unnoticed by all but Toole, who crossed the room now and kissed her on the cheek. Rosamund could not help but think that the whole process was perfunctory.

"Hello, George," she said.

"How are you, darling?"

Rosamund feigned good humour. "Oh, you know. Same as always. Are you staying for dinner?"

Toole's eyebrows raised, and he inhaled air into his lungs as if to brace himself for an ordeal. "I'm afraid not, my darling. I have to work."

Bayliss was standing behind them and, hearing the exchange, he intruded into the conversation. "Not on my account, you haven't. What're you doing that's so important?"

Toole managed to smile with an affable innocence, but he felt sick at how close the lie had come to being exposed. He was aware of Rosamund's gaze on him, but he dared not return it. She would have read deception in his eyes as easily as he could taste it in his mouth.

"Just some figures to be gone over, sir," he said. "Nothing important, and something I can easily undertake myself."

Rosamund was still glaring at Toole. "Is it more important than having dinner with me?"

"Of course not." How he hated lying to her. Almost as much as he hated now what once had been a thrill for him. He took her hand in his and kissed her knuckles. "I'm afraid it can't wait."

Rosamund pulled her hand away. "No, I don't suppose it can."

Toole cursed his predicament. Even if he felt able to tell her the truth, he could hardly do it here, in front of the Bayliss family, whose eyes he seemed to feel burning into his soul. He looked at Rosamund once more, and the look of disdainful mistrust on her face scared him more than the danger that was closer now than ever to consuming him. For the first time, Toole wondered whether telling her the truth might alleviate the burden rather than increase it, but still his cowardice prevented him.

"I'm sorry," he said, the words as futile as they were meaningless.

Rosamund walked away from him and sipped her drink in silent loathing. For his part, George did likewise, but Arthur Bayliss was already filling his glass for the second time.

"Shame you're not staying, Toole, my lad," he barked with a foul laugh. "I was looking forward to having some strong male conversation at dinner."

This time, Henry gave in to his instincts. "For God's sake, listen to yourself. Do you realise how childish you sound?"

Bayliss laughed. "It was only a joke, lad. You artistic types, you don't have much of a sense of humour, do you? Take offence at any little remark. Altogether too fragile, if you ask me. No more robust than a flake of snow, the lot of you."

"Anybody would take offence if they had the misfortune to get into a conversation with you," snapped Henry, suddenly caring nothing for any potential consequences of the argument.

Bayliss was still smiling, however. "How you'd cope with something really serious, I wouldn't like to think. Have a breakdown, no doubt, rather than looking it square in the face."

"Serious like what?" asked Marjorie, hoping in some way to deflect the discussion elsewhere.

"A death threat."

Bayliss said the words as if they meant nothing, but their importance could hardly fail to impress itself on the three people standing in front of him. Marjorie Bayliss glared at her husband, her eyes blurred with shock and disbelief. Rosamund's fingers tightened around the stem of her glass. Nobody spoke, however, and the silence drifted on, deepening in ominous intensity with each second, until one of the ice cubes in Bayliss' whisky cracked under the temperature of the spirit. The silence in the room was so profound that the noise from the glass sounded like a gunshot.

"A death threat?" stammered Marjorie.

Bayliss turned to face her. "The mill poltergeist is at it again, that's all."

"Have you called the police?" asked Toole.

"You sound like Eric Hirst, lad," Bayliss replied. "And that is exactly what I'm talking about. People not having the guts to stand up to difficult situations. People like Henry, here, who are offended if someone calls them a dirty name. How do you think you'd cope, lad, if someone threatened your life?"

"Nobody would. I'm not hated by almost everyone in Lancashire like you are."

Bayliss prodded his chest in self-aggrandisement. "You have to inspire hatred, boy. You have to mean something to people for them to have strong feelings, one way or the other, about you. Who do you inspire? Nobody. That's why you never sell any of your paintings. People don't care enough about you."

Marjorie walked across the room and stood between the two of them. "Must we do this in front of George?"

Bayliss laughed. "He's not afraid of a bit of unpleasantness, are you, lad?"

Toole was looking at Rosamund. "I think perhaps I should go."

She glared back at him. "Yes, you don't want to be late for whatever it is you have to do."

Toole tried to ignore the scorn. "I'll telephone tomorrow."

"I'll try to remember to be at home," said Rosamund.

He drained his glass and walked towards the door. As he passed Bayliss, the older man grabbed him by the arm. "You be careful, lad. Some folk don't play fair."

Toole glared at him, suddenly fearful that Bayliss knew the truth about him. He couldn't know, Toole told himself, but when Bayliss smiled back at him, Toole was reminded of a cobra, with its predatory grin and its dead, impassive eyes.

Once Toole had left the room, Bayliss laughed grimly. "He's a good lad, that George Toole. I wish I'd had a son like him."

Henry's face was scarlet with outrage and anger. "Why don't you go to Hell?"

Rosamund stepped forward and glared at her father, shielding her brother from him. "Why have you always hated us so much?"

"I don't hate you," said Bayliss, the smile still on your lips. "As I said, you have to inspire hatred. All you do is inspire disappointment."

Rosamund's eyes blazed with fury. "I could kill you, so help me God!"

Bayliss glared at her, his eyes drifting over her entire person. "At least you've got some fire in your belly, lass. Comes from having the nerve to brave the cellar, eh? You should thank me for it."

"That's a monstrous thing to say!" roared Henry.

For her part, Rosamund had felt as if a fist had struck her in the stomach. The horror of the words, of the memories they invoked, almost caused her to double over. She felt nausea and fear battle for dominance inside her, neither one winning, but both causing equal damage to her feelings.

"How could you?" she whispered, barely able to breathe.

Marjorie went to her daughter's side, but her attention was fixed on Bayliss. "Get out! Get out and leave her alone!"

Bayliss scoffed. "You didn't complain when I put her in there all those times. What's changed? Found a voice, have we?"

Marjorie's cheeks flushed with horror. "How dare you? I never wanted you to treat them like you did."

"You didn't stop me, did you, woman?" Bayliss leered. "And you didn't let her out either, did you?"

"She was too scared, that's why?" screamed Rosamund. "I never understood why she let it happen at the time, but I do now!"

"Scared of what?" mocked Bayliss.

"You!" Rosamund wailed.

"Because you're a bloody monster!" hissed Henry, lunging towards his father.

"You look as if you might be a man after all, lad." Bayliss stopped Henry's lunge with a hard hand against his chest. "You caused this scene, boy. I don't say these things because I don't care. I say them because I want you to be worth something, to count, to matter. To have some fight in you!"

Henry shook his head. "You say them because you want me to be like you, but I'm not. I won't ever be like you."

Bayliss nodded slowly. "And that, my boy, is your tragedy."

"It's not a tragedy to me." Henry drained his sherry. "I'm not the one getting death threats, after all."

Bayliss shook his head, an arrogant and mocking smile on his lips. "Whoever wrote that is a coward. Like you, boy. Whoever it is hasn't got the guts to carry out the threat."

"How can you know that?" asked Rosamund. She wiped away what remained of her tears and was fighting to regain her composure.

"Because if they had, they'd do it. They wouldn't waste time writing about it."

"So why mention it at all, if it doesn't bother you?"

"To make a point to your brother. To try to explain to him that serious and bad things happen, and he can't always be offended by them. Sometimes, he has to do something about them."

"Nothing bad has happened to me," said Henry. "All you're doing is insulting me for no reason."

"Eventually, something will happen, son, and you need to be ready for it." Bayliss spoke through clenched lips as if he were talking to a child whose stupidity was frustrating and impossible to understand.

"Why do we have to have the same argument all the time?" asked Henry.

And now, Bayliss roared. "Because you don't bloody listen, lad!"

Henry flinched at the violence of the reply and at the fleck of whisky and spittle that peppered his face on account of it. He slowly shook his head.

"I'm sorry, I'm not the man you wanted me to be," he said. "If it's any consolation, you're not the father I wanted you to be either."

As a response, he was proud of it; as a statement of fact, he was saddened by it. Whichever way he viewed it, Henry Bayliss knew that there were no words that could possibly follow it. He replaced the sherry glass on the drinks cabinet and slowly walked out of the room.

Bayliss watched him leave. Then, he drained his whisky and slammed the glass back down on the silver salver of the drinks' table. He had reached for the decanter once more when Rosamund spoke again. When she did, it was a vicious hiss of venom spat down his ear as he poured that second glass of whisky.

"I hope you choke on it, you old snake."

She marched out, shaking her head at her mother as she passed, and hoping to find Henry in the hallway. But he had gone. She could make a dozen guesses where he would have escaped to, but she acted on none of them. Perhaps Henry wouldn't want her company, even if it was in a show of solidarity. There were times, as she knew only too well, when a person wanted only to be left alone, and she had an instinct that this was such a time for her brother. She turned on her heel and walked slowly up the main staircase to her room.

Back in the drawing room, Bayliss was standing at the window, staring out over the driveway that stretched across the lawn and down towards the road. He watched Henry walking down it, his fists clenched and his head sunk on his breast. Where he was going, Bayliss could not say; perhaps he did not care. By the time Marjorie had joined him at the window, their son had disappeared from view.

"Why must you provoke him in that way?" she asked gently.

"If he had anything about him, he wouldn't get so easily provoked." Bayliss looked at her with mild contempt. "Can't you see that's my whole point? Too soft. Or worse."

"Comments like that don't help. He's sensitive, always has been, but that doesn't mean what you insist on thinking it does."

"Not married, though, is he? No sign of any girl in his life."

"He hasn't met the right one, that's all."

His contempt for her seemed to rise, and he turned away from her before it consumed him. "You're so bloody certain of everything, aren't you, Marjorie?"

"I know my son." She sat down on the settee. "I wish you did, too."

"I do know him. I just don't like what I know."

"If you know him, you don't understand him." She leaned forward. "Why don't you look at some of his paintings? You might find you like them."

Now, his darker feelings for her swelled further. "You stupid cow. I don't want to like them. I don't want to look at them. I hate the bloody things. Sometimes, Marjorie, I hate *everything* about this family."

It felt as if a knife had sliced into her heart. Slowly, she got to her feet. Her expression was hostile, but a force of her will demanded that it retain its dignity. When she spoke, her voice was laced with poison.

"How nice of you to say so," she said. "Don't for a moment think, Arthur, that everything in this house doesn't sometimes hate you back."

She left the room, and the slow closing of the door and the gentle click of the latch seemed far more ominous than if she had slammed it shut with all the bitter ferocity she felt inside her.

# Chapter Seven

It was Neville Pym's custom to pop into *The Black Bull* for half a pint of beer, possibly two if the mood was upon him. The ritual had become automatic now, of course, but Pym could not recall precisely how it had first come into effect. He supposed that it must have begun as an impulse, one of those sudden decisions that come from nowhere and shock even the person who made it with how uncharacteristic it was, for Mr Pym was not a man who had ever felt the need to frequent public houses. It had nothing to do with temperance or any religious beliefs, but rather more to do with the fact that he found pubs both too noisy and too crowded to enjoy any sort of libation properly. He preferred a couple of glasses of sherry in the comfort of his own home, as a rule, so what had prompted him to enter the local pub several weeks earlier was unknown to him but once he had done so, he had discovered that he rather enjoyed it and, human nature being what it is, he had swiftly become consumed by the habit and now it had become a tradition that he could not break. Nor, he thought as he sipped the beer, did he want to particularly. On some days, the couple of half pints were a reward for a productive day; on others, they were a consolation for a tedious one. That day, however, he could not say had been either. It had been something altogether more sinister.

He had paid some bills in the town, then taken the train into Manchester and had lunch with an old friend, whom he had not seen for several months and who had told him not only of the birth of his nephew but also of a rather unpleasant skirmish with a couple of servicemen outside a public house in the city centre. The pub in question was one that Mr Pym knew only by reputation, having never dared step into it himself, and his friend's experience only showed how right Mr Pym had been to avoid the place. It was lamentable that only certain places accepted certain gentlemen, but it was a cruel fact of life, and, however much he wished for it, Mr Pym could see no change in attitudes coming any time soon. But the fear of being prey to a physical attack like the one his lunch companion had suffered was sufficient to keep Mr Pym safe from such reprisals for his particular caprice of nature.

"It isn't so much the intolerance," Mr Pym had said to his friend, "although that is hideous enough, but it is the hypocrisy. After all, what were the servicemen themselves doing in that pub?"

"Looking for people like me," his friend had replied.

"That's my point."

"Don't be naïve, Neville. I mean that some people go out looking for us to do us harm."

The notion had astounded Mr Pym. "Are there such people? That is pure wickedness."

"It's a wicked world, Neville, and the less you see of it, the better."

It had been a much more despondent Mr Pym who had travelled back to Darton Vale that afternoon. He had returned home and scrubbed his hands violently as if to wash away not only the grime of the city but also the horror of what he had learned. By the end of it, Mr Pym's hands smarted and stung as if he had plunged them into a bed of nettles.

He had spent an hour or so reading and listening to music, both of which had helped to raise his spirits, even if the spectre of his friend's tale had not vanished completely. Fresh air, he had thought, might help to eradicate it and finish the job that the music and the novel had begun, and so Mr Pym had put on his hat and coat, wrapped his scarf around his neck, and set out for an early evening walk. The air had been cool without being freezing, and the early evening skies had glowed with an orange-red intensity that was almost impossible to resist. The elements, the brisk freshness of the evening, and the vigour with which Mr Pym walked amongst them had a stirring effect on him. By the time he was walking down Church Lane,

Mr Pym had been able to say to himself that perhaps there was wickedness in the world, but there was also beauty in it, and that a man like himself should not permit one to extinguish the other. The conclusion reached, he had determined that it should be celebrated with a trip to *The Black Bull*.

As he had walked down Church Lane, he had seen Eric Hirst talking with Lydia Stansfield. Instinctively, he moved into the shadows cast by the overhanging trees of the churchyard. He had felt at once that his presence, although coincidental, was embarrassing, for Hirst and Lydia as much as for himself. Mr Pym was well aware of Hirst's feelings for the girl, and even if they had not been close friends, he would have been able to guess them. And had Mr Pym not done all he could to persuade Eric Hirst to abandon those feelings? He had, not out of malice, of course, but out of honest friendship. Furthermore, if they had seen him, they would surely have drawn the obvious conclusion. Mr Pym was aware of how people thought about him in the village, and he had no wish to be accused yet again of gossiping. And so, he had stayed lurking in the shadows, watching them closely, trying hard to hear what was being said, without once considering the irony of his actions.

At last, he had watched Lydia walk away. Hirst had continued walking, and Mr Pym had waited as long as possible before stepping out into the light and continuing down the lane, hoping that he had managed to convey some impression of coincidence.

"Good evening, Eric," Mr Pym had said, tipping his hat.

Hirst had smiled in greeting, but it had been evident that he remained distracted. "Hello, Neville. Forgive me, I was miles away."

"I was just nipping into *The Black Bull* for a quick drink if you would care to join me."

Hirst had smiled. "Funnily enough, I had the same idea."

Mr Pym had smiled warmly. "Splendid. Truth be told, I've had rather an unpleasant afternoon. Perhaps we can talk about it."

But Hirst had shaken his head. "I'm sorry, Neville, I'd rather get home. Splitting headache," he had added, touching his temple.

Mr Pym could not have failed to detect the lie, but if he was offended by it, he had not said so. "Another time perhaps."

"We could have a game of chess at the weekend if you like."

"I should very much like to do that, yes." Mr Pym had tipped his hat once more, not only in gratitude for the invitation to chess but also in acknowledgement of the fact that not all men were like those servicemen outside a grim Manchester pub. As Hirst had walked on, Mr Pym had called after him. "Is everything all right, Eric?"

Hirst had turned to face him. Even in the growing dark, Mr Pym had seen the glimmer of a smile on his lips. "Same as ever, Neville."

Mr Pym had detected the fatigue in his friend's voice. "I do wish you'd be careful when it comes to Miss Stansfield."

"Not this again, Neville, please."

"I just don't want you to get hurt."

Hirst had nodded his understanding. "Because of her and Arthur Bayliss?"

"Bayliss has had a string of lovers," Mr Pym had said. "I've seen him with them, you know. Some of them half his age, and some of them you wouldn't imagine could behave in such a way."

"Indeed?"

"It is Mrs Bayliss I feel sorry for, of course."

Hirst had conceded the point. "I can share that sympathy, certainly. I feel it for Rosamund and Henry, too."

Mr Pym had sneered. "And what about all the other children he may have fathered? After all," he had added in response to a look from Hirst, "he can't have affairs with all these ladies and not run the risk of...consequences."

Hirst had frowned. "I suppose not."

"And now, there is Miss Stansfield."

"Lydia won't allow herself to get into any trouble, I'm sure."

"Very possibly. She may at least think she is in control. But with a man like Bayliss, there is only ever one person in command."

"It won't happen," Hirst had insisted.

Mr Pym had now detected a trace of hostility in the voice. "If Bayliss throws her over, what will she do? Come running to you, and then you'll fall for it, but she won't feel the same as you, not really."

"I didn't know you were such an expert in relationships." The barb had been insensitive and almost cruel.

If Mr Pym had thought it unfair and beneath Eric Hirst, he had not said it, but perhaps his expression had spoken the words for him. "I'm simply giving a friendly word of warning, Eric. Nothing more."

And Hirst had bowed his head. "I'm sorry, Neville. I'm just a little riled, that's all. I have no doubt you're right, but I can't pretend that I won't fall into the very trap you're afraid of."

Mr Pym had smiled. "If you do, you know where I am if you need me."

Hirst had nodded. "Enjoy your drink."

And now, Mr Pym sat in *The Black Bull*, with his half pint of beer and his solitary thoughts. His current drink was his second, and this would normally be sufficient. However, no sooner had he taken his first sip of it than something happened that made him wonder whether he ought to stay for a third.

The appearance of Henry Bayliss was surprising, not because he was an unfamiliar face in the pub, but because he was in full evening dress. Such formality was not common in the smoky, bustling interior of *The Black Bull*, and when Henry walked to the bar, eyes followed him with a mixture of admiration, fascination, and suspicion. Henry ignored it all, ordered his drink without fuss, and paid for it with no complaint. It was not difficult to discern in his appearance some degree of concern and anxiety, and Mr Pym's long nose quivered at the possibility of some interesting story to be told behind the young man's brooding silence.

He watched several people walk past Henry, some scowling and some nodding a polite if cautious greeting to him. A few of them evening, gave a verbal word of acknowledgement of his presence and welcome. Those, Mr Pym could understand; the scowlers, he could not. He assumed it was some sort of inverted snobbery, an inherent belief that people like the Bayliss family should stay out of good, honest pubs as if such places were the exclusive domain of working men. If this were the prejudice behind the hostility, Mr Pym wondered for the first time whether it extended to him. He was not wealthy, by any means, but nor was he a labourer. How far, he wondered sadly, did prejudice in all its forms discriminate? He rose from his chair at his usual corner table and walked gently towards the bar. A third drink was now a certainty, although Mr Pym undertook the desire with more than a little trepidation.

As soon as Henry saw Pym walking towards him, he felt an irritation take hold of his mind. He knew Pym well enough to know that any cordiality that he was about to offer would be a mechanism for discovering some sliver of gossip over which Pym could chew. Henry hated gossips. They made him wonder whether people had anything in their lives at all, if the lives of others were so much more interesting. Why could they not mind their own business? Henry, for his part, was never happier than when he was in his studio, locked away from the world, existing only in the world of his paintings. He suddenly began to wonder why he'd come to the wretched pub at all.

Pym was upon him now, and Henry was reminded of the man's smoothness of skin and the faint aroma of cologne that exuded both flora and expense. He was a small, fussy man, with a pencil moustache that was trimmed so neatly and thinly that Henry wondered why he bothered wearing it at all. His hair was swept back from his forehead and so carefully styled that it seemed as if no force of wind could affect it. His suit was plain but fashionable, the shoes highly polished, and the handkerchief that peered out from the jacket pocket was so crisp that it could never be anything other than decorative. His appearance and manner suggested something that Henry's grandma would have called prim, what his mother termed dapper, but what his father and others derided as unnatural.

"How very nice to see you here, Mr Bayliss," said Mr Pym. "Perhaps I could get you a drink."

"No, thank you," said Henry, his politeness sounding less forced than it felt. "I'm not staying for long."

"I would have thought you'd be at dinner at Darton House now, sir."

"I wasn't hungry."

The lie was suitably evasive, but Henry knew that it was a mistake. Instead of deflecting the issue, to a man like Neville Pym, it was bait. "All is well up at the house, I hope."

"Everything is fine, Mr Pym, thank you."

Pym was not one to force a conversation. "How's the painting? Have you managed to sell one of your works as yet?"

"I have some interested parties, yes." This time, the lie tasted bitter in Henry's mouth, and he hated his vanity for forcing him to tell it.

"What wonderful news," Mr Pym was saying. "Of course, it is so difficult to get started in the arts. I once knew a young man who almost put himself into an early grave trying to make a name for himself as a poet. The last I heard, he was sailing to America to try his luck there. I never heard from him again."

Curiously, Henry was struck by the story, not so much by its trite reminiscence but by the sudden realisation it invoked in him of how far away America was from Darton Vale. It seemed a solar system away from Henry's life in a Lancashire mill town. What hopes did he have of having his name known even in London, let alone New York? Even Manchester, a mere train journey away, seemed an impossible star to catch. Suddenly, his father's derision screamed loudly in his ears, and Henry felt depressed and hopeless.

"Do you know, Mr Pym," he said, feigning a smile, "I think I will have that drink if you don't mind."

Mr Pym, taken aback by the sudden change of heart and its impact on his pocket, stammered for a moment, wondering whether he could protest on the grounds that it had only been a polite but perfunctory offer in the first place. As it was, however, he simply smiled and nodded, and requested a large whisky from the barman, handing over the coins with an external smile and an internal moan.

The time now was a little after half past seven, and Mr Pym was adamant that he was going home. He had drunk one more glass of beer than he should have, and the pub itself was now becoming oppressive. Henry Bayliss ordered yet another drink, and Mr Pym was mildly disgusted by this sudden apparent need for drunkenness. He assumed it was all part of the artistic temperament. His friend, who had sailed to America, he recalled, had been far too fond of a drop of gin, and it tended to make the man rather rougher than Mr Pym might have wished. The memory, coming back quickly and unpleasantly, convinced Mr Pym that three half pints of beer were bad for him and a fourth might well lead him into a dark state of mind, so he bade a swift but civil farewell to Henry Bayliss, collected his sleek leather gloves, and put on his hat and scarf. He had taken only a few steps from the bar when it happened, and, not for the first time in his life, Mr Pym cursed the devils of coincidence that forced men like him, who are so interested in people and the world, to stay in a place or situation from which they had determined to walk away. But when Michael Arden walked into the pub, Mr Pym found himself unable to go home, fourth glass of beer be damned.

Arden was a large man, heavily built, and it seemed to Mr Pym that he had seldom looked content with life, even before the death of his mother. His eyes were dark and brooding, his hair a mop of nocturnal curls, and his chin was square and prominent, like those images of the Greek Gods and mythical heroes over which Mr Pym had fawned in his youth. His hands were rough and, now clenched into fists, they seemed almost unnaturally large and powerful.

He walked up to the bar and ordered a pint of beer. He stood next to Henry Bayliss, on purpose as it seemed to Mr Pym, who now felt within him a concerning sense of foreboding. One part of his soul was desperate to leave before any unpleasantness occurred; the majority of it compelled him to stay, both eager and fascinated to watch whatever malevolence was surely about to unfold. Looking back on it, Mr Pym could have convinced himself that Michael Arden had entered the pub with the intention of causing a scene.

"Don't often see you in here," Arden said.

It seemed to take Henry a moment to realise that the comment was meant for him. He was not sure how to respond, so he simply said, "No."

"Come to see how real people live, have you?"

"I beg your pardon?"

"This place is for working folk," said Arden. "For them who have worked up a thirst."

The barman, experienced enough to see signs of a disturbance even in their infancy, strove to intervene, but Henry waved aside his polite warnings. "I thought it was a public house. Meant for members of the public, that is to say."

Arden, who had been leaning forward on the bar, straightened himself to his full height and turned to face Henry. "You're not welcome here."

"Does that apply to everyone here?" asked Henry, looking around. "Or just you, Arden?"

"Take it how you want."

"Just you then," smiled Henry. "In that case, I won't take it at all."

He turned his back on Arden, intending to speak to Mr Pym once more, but Arden grabbed his shoulder and spun him around. His dark eyes flared with rage.

"You think you're so much better than us, don't you?" he snarled. "You don't know nothing about what life is really like."

"For God's sake, what's this all about, Arden? What have I ever done to offend you?" Henry looked around the crowded pub for some support. "I hardly know you."

"But we all know you, *Mr* Bayliss." The emphasis was sarcastic, designed to be an insult rather than a mark of respect. "Had it easy all your life."

Henry was fighting to keep control of his temper. "I don't know what this is all about, but I'm asking you to let me finish my drink in peace."

Mr Pym nodded in agreement. "Let's go back to my table, Henry, and we can chat there."

Arden laughed. "You two are a fit for each other."

Mr Pym stammered a response, but it was Henry's voice that was heard. "Don't be so bloody offensive! Apologise—*now!*"

Arden shook his head. "I'm not apologising to a bastard like you, Bayliss, who's had his whole life handed to him, who's never had to go hungry, or never had to shiver in his bed."

Henry's mind snapped back to the argument with his father. "You don't know the first thing about me, Arden."

"I know you're only able to piss your life away as an artist because your Dad keeps you."

"You know nothing about it."

"Tell me I'm wrong."

"You're wrong."

"A liar, as well as a waster."

Henry was now in Arden's face, his spittle now freckling Arden's cheeks. "Leave me alone."

It was then that Arden called Henry a name that Mr Pym had heard only a few times before and one that he had hoped never to hear again. And its effect was devastating.

Henry, instinctively, pushed Arden away from him with as much force as their proximity to each other would allow. Arden had not anticipated the move or perhaps had not thought Henry capable of it, for he stumbled backwards, knocking himself into a bar stool over which he stumbled again. Regaining his balance, Arden tossed the offending barstool to one side and charged forward. Mr Pym, sensibly, stepped out of the way as Arden barrelled into Henry at speed, knocking the wind out of him. If Mr Pym had not acted as he did, they would have crashed into him, and a trio of men would have fallen in a heap on the stone floor of the pub.

As it was, only Henry and Arden landed there, beside the fireplace, their breaths snorting from their nostrils and between gritted teeth as they grappled with each other. Arden pulled Henry to his feet, but he gained no advantage. With a fierce lunge forward, Henry brought his forehead into accidental collision with Arden's nose. He then arced his fist upwards, striking Arden on the jaw. It was a momentary victory only, however, because Henry was not the fighter Arden was. The labourer's massive hands were again clenched, and he used them to inflict a massive blow to Henry's stomach, forcing him to buckle forward and make his face an open target. Arden took advantage and delivered a terrifying punch to Henry's face. Blood flew upwards, spotting the stone floor, and Henry collapsed, barely conscious, and reeling with painful nausea.

Arden moved towards him, but the barman and some of the regular drinkers held him back. He roared profanities at them, insisting they let go of him, but they held him fast. Mr Pym, sensing the only opportunity for him to act with any meaning, raced to Henry's side and lifted him slowly from the floor. Henry coughed violently, spitting out more blood, and took a moment to steady himself.

The barman took control of his own establishment. "Out you go, Arden. I don't stand for unprovoked brawling in here. Out!"

Arden protested. "He pushed me first."

It was a childish comment, and the barman ignored it. He barked an order to the two regulars holding Arden. "Get him out of here."

"All right," roared Arden. "I don't need to be thrown out. I'm going. I don't like the stink of this place anymore anyway," he added, spitting nastily in Henry's direction.

Henry was given a brandy to steady himself, and he drank it at Mr Pym's corner table, dabbing at the blood with his handkerchief. The barman loomed over him, and Henry shook his head.

"Don't worry, I'll leave of my own accord," he said, "once my legs get working. I'm sorry for the whole scene. Quite unnecessary and most undignified."

"But young Arden's fault, sir," said the landlord. "I'll not hear otherwise."

"I did push him first," said Henry.

"At his provocation, my lad." The barman smiled. "Now, you finish that brandy and get off home."

Henry complied and got slowly to his feet. He looked at Mr Pym. "What caused him to say all that? He must hate me."

"He has just lost his mother," said Mr Pym. "No excuse, of course, but perhaps he isn't himself."

Henry nodded. "Yes, of course. I'd forgotten. But why take it out on me?"

For that particular question, however, Mr Pym had no answer to give.

# Chapter Eight

On the following morning, Everett Carr travelled north to Darton Vale.

It was not a particularly arduous journey, although there were moments during it when Carr wished that he had been able to decline Arthur Bayliss' invitation, thereby avoiding the occasional periods of tedium that occur during any long period of travel. The change of trains had been irritating but not onerous, and the branch line was serviceable if not overly comfortable. Arthur Bayliss had been as good as his word, however, and a motor car was waiting for Carr at the small, quaint railway station of Darton Vale. It proved to be only a short drive to Darton House, and the chauffeur was mercifully silent during it. The air was cold but not unpleasant, although Carr had wrapped his scarf luxuriously around his neck and jaw so that only the tips of the white moustache peered over the edges of it. At last, the car drove through some gates and up a long driveway, and the splendour of Darton House finally appeared before him.

The house was a three-storey edifice in the Georgian style, built from washed roughcast brick on a stone plinth. The roof was slate, and set into it were four brick chimneys, from which Carr could see wisps of smoke billowing in the air. Each end of the house had semi-circular turrets that formed the east and west wings, and into each of which were set a bay window on the ground floor and four-paned sash windows on the upper floors, peering out from the intentionally sparse growth of ivy that descended each turret. The entrance to the house was formed of a protruding porch supported by fluted columns and topped with a steepled glass roof. The house was surrounded by trees, so that it had the appearance of an oasis in a desert of green, as if man had opted to make his presence known in a space otherwise intended purely for nature. It was an impressive property, opulent without being extravagant, but it was a far cry from the smaller brick terraces that the car had passed on its way through the town. Those had been remarkable for their simplicity, their honesty, and their functionality. The manor house might possess an extravagance that the workers' cottages lacked, but Carr wondered, possibly, and to his shame, for the first time, whether those more frugal dwellings were not more homely than the high-ceilinged rooms and expansive hallways of the gentry. In London, the distance between the rich and poor seemed greater, separated by the expanse of the Thames, but in Darton Vale, it was much closer, more immediate, and as a result, it was far more chillingly obvious.

The chauffeur led him to the front door, carrying his luggage with ease, and he pulled the chain of the doorbell. It took only a moment for a maid to answer, with a courteous bow of greeting to Carr, and the chauffeur placed the luggage in the hallway. With a tip of his cap, he walked back to the car, no doubt to drive it around to a garage and provide it either with a service or a cleaning. The maid ushered Carr into the hallway and closed the door behind him. He was standing in a rectangular hall with curved corners, a slate floor covered with an immense Turkish rug, and a staircase leading up to the upper floors. A series of panelled, mahogany doors led off from the entrance hall into what Carr presumed would be a drawing room, a study, a library, and similar rooms frequently found in houses such as this. He found himself surprised at the grace of the interior of the house. There was none of the vulgar ostentation that he might have associated with Arthur Bayliss, no trace of a man who failed to rise from his chair when a lady entered or left a room or who drank claret with fish. Carr felt certain that there would have been some evidence of Bayliss in the décor of the house, even in the entrance hall, had he possessed a monopoly on the appearance of the place. Accordingly, Carr could not help but infer the involvement of a person with some degree of taste, most likely the feminine instinct of a wife. Bayliss was married, after all, Carr seemed to recall, and he had no doubt that this lady was responsible for the understated elegance of the family home.

The maid took his hat, scarf, and coat, and hung them on one of the hooks of a highly varnished coat stand whose base was a carved but rather ugly representation of an elephant's foot. Perhaps this, thought Carr, was Bayliss' only contribution to the furnishings. The maid, now perhaps a little over-helpful, asked if she could take his walking stick, but he held firmly onto its silver handle and said gently that he would keep it. The girl, if it were possible, had not seemed to notice his limp.

He was shown into a drawing room that looked out onto the driveway across which the car had come. There were two occupants of the room, both female, and the dark hair and similarly angular features of both suggested that they were mother and daughter. Almost immediately, Carr had the notion that he was intruding. There was evidence of anxiety in the expression of the elder woman, and Carr was certain that he could discern some semblance of tears in her eyes. The younger woman displayed no such distress, but there was a hardness about her glare that suggested that a recent argument or disagreement between the two had come to an end. Again, Carr felt sure that he had been the cause of the termination, and he felt an irrational but impulsive need to apologise and excuse himself. As it was, the elder woman got to her feet, thanked the maid, and requested that tea be brought in. The maid gave a brief curtsey and closed the door behind her.

"You must be in need of refreshment after such a long journey, Mr Carr," the elder woman said.

"You are very kind, dear lady," said Carr, with a bow.

It was clear that neither Marjorie nor Rosamund Bayliss had expected this unknown associate of Arthur Bayliss to be as polite and softly spoken as he was. Perhaps not unreasonably, they had expected someone as brash and uncouth as the husband and father, so that the sight of the dapper man with the limp and the elaborate moustache was an understandable shock. Whatever conflict had existed between them seemed momentarily to dissipate as they glanced at each other briefly. Marjorie, quick to recover her composure, introduced herself and Rosamund and invited Carr to take a seat on the settee.

He held up a finger. "Perhaps you would not mind if I stood for a little while longer, Mrs Bayliss. I have been sitting in railway station waiting rooms, on two trains, and then in your very comfortable motor car, and I think it will do me good to stand for a while. It helps with my leg, you see," he added with a coy and almost unconscious gesture towards the shattered knee.

"Of course, Mr Carr," said Marjorie. "As long as you are comfortable. Whenever you're ready, please do sit down. No need to wait for an invitation."

She gave a small laugh, as nervous as it was hospitable, and Carr returned it with a smile. Before she turned away from him, he caught again a trace of those shadows of disquiet behind her eyes. Whatever else he might have expected to find at Darton Vale, fear in a woman's eyes had not been foremost in his mind.

"You are very kind, thank you," he said gently. He walked to the mantelpiece, taking a moment to admire the marble casting with its golden laurels. "Your husband is at the mill, I presume."

"Yes, I'm afraid so."

"He's always at the mill." Rosamund had lit a cigarette. "Apart, of course, when you need to speak to him, and he isn't there, like I did the night before last."

"Where was he then?" asked Carr politely.

"Haven't a clue," said Rosamund. "All I'm saying is that if you know him well enough, Mr Carr, you won't be surprised that he isn't here to greet you. Manners aren't exactly his *forte*."

"Don't be rude about your father, Rosamund," said Marjorie.

The girl was not swayed by the rebuke. "Why isn't he here to greet his guest, then?"

Marjorie looked at Carr. "It is unfortunate that Arthur isn't here to welcome you, I admit. I can only apologise for him."

And here, perhaps, thought Carr, was the cause of the anxiety. Was it possible that he had interrupted an argument about Arthur Bayliss himself? Carr felt the stirrings of intrigue in the back of his mind and the cold fingers of instinct along his spine.

Further comment was avoided by the arrival of tea. Marjorie poured and handed a cup to Carr and Rosamund. For ease, Carr placed his on the mantelpiece. There was a plate of sandwiches and one of what appeared to be seed cake, but neither of them appealed to Carr. Afternoon tea was not a meal he particularly enjoyed. Marjorie Bayliss did not eat any of the food either, although Rosamund helped herself to a sandwich of ham and mustard and a slice of the cake. Her eyes remained hardened, and if they were not fixed on some point in the distance, they were staring at Everett Carr. He kept his focus on her mother.

"Have you known Arthur for long, Mr Carr?" asked Marjorie.

Carr shook his head. "Only for a month or two, dear lady. He has recently been accepted as a member of a club to which I belong, back in London."

Rosamund inhaled on a cigarette. "I hope you're not easily embarrassed, Mr Carr. There is bound to be something about this weekend that will be regrettable."

"I'm afraid I don't follow you, my child."

Marjorie was on her feet now. "Take no notice, Mr Carr. Rosamund is teasing you, and she really shouldn't."

Rosamund stood up. "Very well, mother, you win. But it doesn't change anything," she added in a whisper as she passed her mother. She smiled at Carr, taking his hand and shaking it warmly. "My apologies if I did offend you, Mr Carr; you must take no notice. I'm delighted to meet you."

"I shall see you at dinner, perhaps," Carr said with a smile.

But Rosamund shook her head. "I'm dining with my fiancé tonight, I'm afraid. You had remembered, Mummy?"

Marjorie indicated that she had done so. Rosamund, smiling slightly, nodded a farewell and crossed the room to the door. Everett Carr watched her leave, his brows creased, and a disconcerting sensation of ice crawling up his spine. Marjorie now lit a cigarette herself and sat down once more on the settee.

"Take no notice of her, Mr Carr," she said. "Rosamund likes to shock, and it isn't an attractive quality. She's perhaps more like her father than she cares to admit."

Carr made no immediate reply. Instead, he gently stroked the Imperial beard. "Forgive me, but I thought that I was shown into this room at an inconvenient moment."

Marjorie shook her head and stammered a remonstrance, but it was too clearly a performance. "Of course not, no. Everything is fine."

Carr looked down at her. "I sense some unease, dear lady, that is all."

She shook her head, giving him another smile of pretence. "Rosamund and Arthur are just having one of their little spats, that's all. She made the mistake of sticking up for her brother last night. Henry and Arthur aren't getting along at the moment. Dear me," she added with a humourless laugh, "I make it sound as if Arthur is at odds with everybody."

A moment passed before Carr spoke once more. "I should hate to intrude into any personal problems."

Marjorie looked up at him and seemed to see him properly for the first time. She took note now of the black suit, the white hair, and the elaborate moustache, and she somehow felt alarmed by the lurid necktie and pocket handkerchief, but it was the darkness of the eyes that captivated her. They were almost black, she thought, but there was a compassion in them, an almost intoxicating benevolence, that was strangely at odds with their profound colour.

She took a long breath. Tears were not far away. "What must you think of us? This can hardly be the welcome you had expected, and it certainly isn't the one you deserve."

Without waiting for an invitation or permission, Carr sat down slowly beside her. "All is not well, dear lady, I can see that."

Slowly, and without any melodramatic hysteria, the tears began to fall. Somehow, their silence and unobtrusive arrival seemed to make them all the more tragic. "I can't deny, Mr Carr, that you have been invited here at a rather difficult time for us."

"I am sorry to hear it."

"Not that we could have known some of it, of course," she said as if by way of some apology. "My son, Henry, had something of a quarrel in the local public house last night with one of the young men from the mill."

"Was he hurt?" Carr's voice was filled with sympathetic concern.

"A black eye and a bloodied nose, but nothing more serious. And he seemed to give as good as he got, by his account."

"There must have been some reason behind the altercation."

"Henry insists there wasn't. He says it was just Michael Arden being aggressive. Michael lost his mother recently, so he is naturally angry and grieving."

Carr nodded his understanding. "And your son?"

Marjorie took a handkerchief from her sleeve and dabbed gently at her eyes. "Henry won't have been in a good mood when he left here to go to the pub last night. And he hadn't eaten."

"Because of whatever happened last night?"

"Henry argued with Arthur before dinner. As I told you, it isn't anything new."

Carr shifted gently in his seat. "May I ask what it was about? Confiding in an impartial stranger can often be helpful, I find," he added with a smile, in response to the look she had given him.

Looking back, Marjorie Bayliss would wonder why she had found it so easy to talk to this stranger about such intimate matters, but at that moment, there had been no question in her mind that it was the right thing to do. Perhaps it was the gentleness of his voice, his politeness of manner, or the kindness of his expression that prompted her to take him into his confidence. Or perhaps, she had thought later, it was nothing to do with him at all, but everything to do with her. How long, after all, had these fears and apprehensions been eating away at her unchallenged? When was the last time somebody in the house had thought to ask her how she was feeling, how she was coping, and whether she had anything preying on her mind? And yet now, there was this dapper and ingratiating stranger offering her not only comfort but possibly reassurance.

And so, she told him about last night, and he listened. Once the tale was told, she felt better but not entirely at ease. For his part, once she had finished speaking, Everett Carr had remained silent for a moment, his eyes fixed on the ashes in the grate.

"Forgive me, dear lady, but is there something else?" he asked now. "Something that troubles you more than family quarrels and scuffles in public houses?"

Marjorie stared at him once more, but he did not return her look and nor did he speak further. He simply waited for a response, and it seemed to Marjorie that he would have waited an eternity for it. Slowly, she turned away from him and rose silently to her feet.

"Something wicked is going on at the mill," she said, at last.

Carr's eyes closed softly. "I see."

"It started as small acts of vandalism. Broken windows, a smashed headlamp on one of Arthur's cars. Eric's bicycle tyres being slashed."

"Eric?"

"Eric Hirst, the mill's accountant." Marjorie was shaking her head. "He told me of other acts of sabotage. A major client of Arthur's, Jeremiah Carnaby, said that a woman had called from the mill to cancel a major order. It was a hoax, but Arthur nearly lost an important customer in Mr Carnaby and a significant contact worth a lot of money."

"I see," murmured Carr.

"Arthur has dismissed it all as trivial. Windows can be replaced, he said; Eric has repaired his tyres, he said; orders can be reinstated, he said. None of it matters to him."

"You do not agree?"

Marjorie shrugged, as if she were unsure of how to reply. "It does all seem petty, of course, but at the same time, it is so spiteful. So malicious."

"And it strikes you as dangerous?"

"I'm afraid it does."

"And, tell me, dear lady, have these incidents perhaps become more serious?" Now, Carr did look at her, and she was strangely transfixed by those dark eyes.

She nodded, lighting another cigarette. "Arthur found a dead rat in his desk drawer."

"How long has all this been going on for?" asked Carr.

"About six months, spasmodically."

"When was the last incident?"

"Only yesterday." She paused, but not for effect, only to summon the will to say more. "And it was the worst of the lot."

Carr rose to his feet and limped slowly towards her. The tea that he had left on the mantelpiece was now cold, like the ice of instinct that continued to freeze around his spine. "In what way, dear lady?"

"An anonymous letter." Marjorie wondered whether Carr could hear the horror in her voice or see the trembling fear that had seized her body. "Addressed to Arthur personally."

Carr nodded slowly, and a gentle, almost imperceptible smile of assurance crept briefly across his lips. "What did it say, this letter?"

Again, she felt somehow convinced that he knew already. "It was a death threat."

When spoken aloud, the words seemed more terrible than when they were in her head only. There followed an ominous silence as if the presence of this warning of death had robbed them both of the power to speak. At last, it was Everett Carr who interrupted the gloomy quiet.

"Tell me, dear lady," he said. "Is it possible that your husband knows who is behind these outrages?"

She glared at him, a sudden and confused fear leaping into her eyes. "Why would you say that?"

Carr gave a simple shrug of his shoulders. "I'm trying to understand his reluctance to inform the police of a threat against his life."

Marjorie shook her head. "My husband is a stubborn man, Mr Carr. Telling the police would be like confessing to a weakness."

The attitude was a foolish one, but Carr found that he had no difficulty in ascribing it to Arthur Bayliss. "Do *you* have any idea who might be behind these acts of sabotage?"

She stared at him with an expression of outrage. "Certainly not."

"But you are frightened, aren't you, dear lady?"

The single word of reply came in a choking sob. "Yes…"

Carr watched her wipe away the tears. "Because you think that someone close to you wishes harm to your husband?"

She inhaled deeply, fighting for the breath to say the words. "After that letter, I can't stop thinking about it."

Carr removed his hand from her arm, lowering it to his side. There seemed to be something almost portentous in the movement. "You imagine that someone, a member of the family, perhaps, or somebody close to it, or even someone from outside of it…"

Marjorie was already nodding, her eyes wide with frantic horror. "…wants my husband dead."

# Chapter Nine

News of the fight between Henry Bayliss and Michael Arden had spread so rapidly in a short space of time that even before Arden arrived for work, his conduct was common knowledge. When he appeared at work with his eye blackened and his knuckles raw, there were cheers at his appearance from some workers and cries of derision from others. For his part, Arden offered no response to either faction, simply taking off his coat and cap, pulling on his overalls, and starting work. Today, he had no time for conversation with anyone. He wanted only to be left alone to work and to think. But, unlike in the fairy tales his mother used to read, Michael Arden knew that wishes very seldom came true.

His eye still throbbed with a dull ache, and the knuckles of his hands still smarted from the cold water and carbolic soap with which he had washed this morning. Worse, his head felt as if it were clamped in a vice, and he regretted now the alcohol that he had consumed after getting home from *The Black Bull*. Despite his drunkenness, he had slept badly, and his muscles groaned in protest at everything he asked of them. He had considered not turning in for work and spending the day in bed, but he knew that it would only be taken as a measure of weakness and embarrassment on his part, and he could not bear to have people think about him in those terms. For that reason alone, he thought, staying away from the mill and sleeping off his stupors and pain could never be an option. Besides, he thought with a grim smile, his mother would never have allowed it. Thoughts of his mother reminded him that it was impossible not to feel some shame at the events of the previous night, but Arden refused to apologise for it. His shame was not borne from regret but from the knowledge that his mother would have been horrified at his actions.

"What will people think now, Mikey?" she would have said. He could hear her voice, strident and accusatory, ringing in his ears as it would have rung around the stone walls of the cottage and the cast-iron grate. "Dignity, lad, that's what we need, because we've precious little else."

What was dignity, Arden thought. Was it bowing to people who were only considered better than oneself because they had money and power? They still had to eat and sleep, same as he and his mother did. Nature still had to take its course with them, just as it did with him. They weren't any different, not where it mattered, and only a bank balance said otherwise. No dignity in any of that. But there was dignity in standing up for oneself, in showing people you weren't afraid of anything, any more than you were ashamed of anything.

And Emma would have understood, he thought. She would have told him how much he mattered, that his bank balance meant nothing to her, that what was important was honesty, decency, and love. He had believed her when she had said it, and he had clung to the words. By doing so, the anger he had felt since childhood had been suppressed, if not silenced altogether. When Emma's car had gone off Devil's Corner near Layton Brook, it had returned, this rage at the unfairness of life and the injustice of its caprices that made some people suffer and others only prosper. And then, in its wake, there came the death of his mother, and history had seemed to repeat itself with greater cruelty.

He realised that he had stopped working, his mind distracted by thoughts of the past and this increasing tendency to self-pity that he was growing to despise about himself. On impulse, Arden looked up at the management offices, and he saw Eric Hirst staring down at him from the gantry above. It seemed a cue for Arden to return to his work.

For his part, Eric Hirst had watched Michael Arden attempt to bury himself in his work but slowly become disengaged from his duties by some internal machinations of thought. He had seen the bruises to the young man's face and the scraped knuckles, and he had heard the rumours that it was Henry Bayliss with whom Arden had been fighting. The reason for the brawl still appeared to remain a mystery, and Hirst was not about to speculate on it. It hardly mattered. Arden was a thug, and starting fights was in his nature. The identity of his opponent was seldom of importance to him. Not for the first time, Hirst thought about his daughter and her relationship with Arden that had ended as tragically as possible, leaving behind nothing but bitterness and reproach. On Arden's side, those emotions were directed towards the world. It was too much to hope that he would bear any responsibility for the life he had ruined. For Hirst, the resentment and blame were much more personal. To him, only two men were responsible for what happened to Emma: Arden and himself. On the one hand, Arden had destroyed her; on the other, as her father, Hirst had failed to protect her.

Arden was staring up at him now, and it seemed as if he were preparing himself for a confrontation. He was glaring up at the gantry, and, despite the distance, Hirst felt strangely intimidated by the motionless figure below, with its clenched fists and square shoulders. Hirst felt his fingers tighten around the metal gantry as he watched Arden pick up a hand iron from his workbench. Hirst tried to shout a command to desist, but the words froze in his throat. Time seemed to stand still. To Hirst, it was as if the workers below him had been turned to stone, with the sole exception of Michael Arden, whose legs now bent to give him momentum and whose arm arced back with devastating power. Hirst watched in horror as the iron was projected on a terrible journey upwards. Hirst thought he heard a cruel, almost inhuman roar of anger and hatred come from below him, and he seemed to see Arden's features contort into a feral caricature of their normal state. At last, there came the terrifying clang as cast iron collided with metal, and the second unsettling clang as the iron clattered against various surfaces on its sudden descent. Simultaneously, Hirst let out a hoarse curse as he dropped to his knees on the gantry, hoping that the metal frame would protect him from harm.

Hirst was suddenly aware of being hoisted to his feet. He was grateful for it, because he doubted his knees would have supported him if he had been compelled to stand on his own accord. He still had hold of the gantry as he stared after Arden, who, by now, had turned his back on the scene and walked away, reaching for his cigarettes and matches. Fellow workers watched him as he strode past them, not one of them attempting to engage with him as he passed. Even those who had supported his actions in the pub on the previous evening now remained quiet.

On the gantry, Hirst looked into the eyes of Arthur Bayliss. "Did you see that?"

"Aye."

"He tried to kill me."

Bayliss raised an eyebrow. "Let's not get carried away with ourselves, Eric. The lad could never have hit you at this range."

This unsympathetic confidence in mathematical physics didn't reassure Hirst. "I want him fired."

"The lad's grieving, Eric," warned Bayliss.

"He's a thug, and I want him gone." He broke free of Bayliss' grip. "Did you see him staring up? I did nothing to provoke him. Or perhaps you think I did."

"I saw it all, Eric. I came out here to see what the bloody hell you were doing with yourself. I thought you were thinking of jumping." He laughed, coarsely and offensively.

Hirst was not amused. "Are you going to fire Arden?"

"No."

"Arthur, I'm warning –"

But Bayliss's glare silenced him. "I don't think you're warning me about anything, Eric. I'll put your little outburst down to high emotions, and I won't fire you for it."

"Fire me?" Hirst's face was crimson with outrage.

Bayliss put his arm around the accountant's shoulder. "I'm jesting, you silly bastard. I can't manage without you, Eric, you know that. Now, come into my office, and we'll have a little pick-me-up."

"No, thank you."

"I want one, and you need one," said Bayliss. "Do as you're told."

And so, Eric Hirst obeyed.

The smell and taste of the whisky at a little after half past nine in the morning was sickening, but Bayliss seemed unaware of it. Nevertheless, Hirst found that his natural repugnance at this early consumption of alcohol was assuaged by the soothing and warming effect it had upon him. His breathing became more regular, and his anger seemed to subside. Bayliss watched him keenly, a smile stretched across his lips, and a mocking glint in his heavy-lidded eyes.

"Feeling better?"

"Not much." He drained the last few droplets of whisky from the glass. "Although that helped, surprisingly."

"Good. Now, let's get back to work, Eric. Put this little bit of nastiness behind us and move on with the day."

The condescending tone of voice was irritating, but Hirst did his best to ignore it. "I'd have thought you'd want to see the back of Michael Arden as much as I do. After all, he gave Henry a bad time last night, by all accounts."

Bayliss laughed. "I should promote him, then. Henry no doubt deserved what Arden gave him."

Hirst stared coldly at his friend. "You can't possibly be serious."

"Deadly." Bayliss seemed to savour the word whilst simultaneously making it seem like the final word to be said on the subject. "One other thing, Eric," he added, after a pause, "I spoke to Lydia last night."

At her name, Hirst seemed to feel himself tremble. Bayliss was looking at him dangerously, his eyes heavy with menace and his lips pursed with intent. Hirst knew that he was expected to respond, but he could find no words to say.

"Anything you want to tell me, Eric?"

"I don't think so."

Bayliss glared at him for a long moment. "Nothing about an item of post we had yesterday?"

Any more efforts to avoid the inevitable were clearly fruitless. "I see."

"I don't like my private business being discussed behind my back, Eric."

"I thought she should know, given your relationship." The final word was almost impossible for Hirst to say.

"I told you that letter meant nothing. All you've done is worry Lydia."

"And I told you I don't agree. Besides…"

Bayliss waited for something more, but nothing came. He walked over to Hirst and put his hand on his shoulder. He smiled coldly. "Don't think you can use my private business to worm your way into Lydia's bed. She doesn't want you, Eric, so don't you go trying your luck at a bit of poaching. We clear?"

The shoulder was almost numb with pain now. "We're clear."

There was a sudden relief as Bayliss uncurled his fingers and released his grip. "Good lad. Now, let's make some money, eh?"

Hirst was rubbing his shoulder, trying to bring some feeling back into it. "Just so we are clear, Arthur, I wasn't trying to get into Lydia's bed. I genuinely am concerned about you, whether you can believe it or not."

Bayliss grunted out the semblance of a laugh. "As long as I'm alive, Eric, you'll never have her."

And this final assurance, Hirst realised, really was the end of the conversation. With a snarl of contempt, he closed the door gently behind him and went back to his own office.

# Chapter Ten

Despite his best efforts, Everett Carr had not managed to persuade Marjorie Bayliss to confide in him very much further than expressing her fears about her husband's life. For his part, Carr could believe in her anxiety. Bayliss was surely a man who it could be imagined would make enemies far more easily than he would make friends, and although Carr felt rather sordid in having the thought, it was a notion that it seemed impossible to refute. The question that was settling in Carr's mind as Marjorie spoke, however, was whether she had any definite suspicions, either about the identity of the poltergeist at the mill or about who might be keenest to bring physical harm to her husband. A secondary, rather obvious thought, of course, was whether these two as yet unknown persons were one and the same or whether Bayliss had multiple enemies. As to that, Carr felt inclined to keep an open mind. There was nothing to suggest that the two matters were connected, but, likewise, the possibility of them being cause and effect could not be discounted.

But Marjorie clearly felt that she had divulged too much to this stranger who now sat with her on the drawing room settee. Indeed, now that she had said the words aloud, she wondered why she had felt so compelled to confide in Everett Carr at all. She would not usually give away her confidences so freely, but it had somehow seemed the most natural thing in the world to do so to him. It was, she supposed, something to do with his calm, gentle manner and his politeness. Most of all, she thought, it was the compassion behind those dark eyes that she had found so intoxicating that she had been unable to resist it. She now felt foolish for this weakness, of course, but the matter was done, and time could not be reversed. Her sense of stupidity was increased by the idea that she had not realised how keenly she felt about the possibility of harm being done to Arthur until she had said the words out loud. And now they were said, they seemed impossible to ignore, as if they had been released from a private cage after too long in captivity and had now come out roaring.

Carr had tried to compel her to say more, but she had resisted. "I have no doubt I'm imagining it," she had said.

"Are you so sure, dear lady?" he had replied, and the tone of voice indicated that he either knew the answer for sure or certainly strongly suspected it.

"I don't know why I even said it."

"You had a reason, dear lady," Carr had insisted. "Please, I wish only to help you and your husband."

She had looked at him keenly, and she had seen an assurance of his pledge in his expression and the warmth of his hands around hers. He had looked at her expectantly, almost hopefully, and she had felt the urge to smile at him in gratitude, but the curve of the mouth would not come. Instead, she had nodded vaguely and removed her hand from his grasp.

"You must forgive my foolishness," she had said. "Arthur usually knows best about these things, and he sees nothing to be concerned about in this business at the mill, nor in the anonymous letter. So, I am sure I am worrying about nothing."

Everett Carr did not share her casual attitude, nor did he believe in her dismissal of her fears or her pretence of it, and Marjorie had been aware of the fact. His expression had made it clear, and she had turned away from him so that she could no longer see it.

And it was then, as an uneasy silence descended on them, that she saw Mr Neville Pym walking up to the house. A foolishly giddy sense of relief surged within her. She had quite forgotten that she had invited the man round for afternoon tea several days previously, and she recalled now that she had regretted the invitation almost as soon as it had been made, Mr Pym being an inveterate gossip, but now she was so overwhelmed with gratitude at his arrival that her previous reluctance was entirely forgotten.

Carr had greeted Mr Pym with customary politeness, and it had been received with an almost childish enthusiasm. Mr Pym's cheeks were flushed with the exertion of his walk and the brisk afternoon air, and he was slightly out of breath.

"I do apologise for being a little late, Mrs Bayliss," he said. "I'm afraid I rather rushed here to make up for it, and now I'm suffering for it. A touch of asthma, you know," he added, looking across at Carr. His voice was ingratiating but low, as if in a perpetual whisper, and there was a trace of gentle conspiracy about it, as if he were constantly letting his partner in conversation into some secret or other.

"Not at all, Mr Pym," said Marjorie, now with no trace of her previous concern, Carr noticed, but instead with an almost exaggerated display of hospitality. Her relief at Mr Pym's arrival was almost palpable, and Carr allowed himself a little smile.

"I see you've already eaten," Mr Pym said. "Please don't order more on my account."

"It is no trouble." Marjorie looked across at Carr. "More tea, Mr Carr?"

He did not want any more tea, but his politeness prohibited any rejection, and he bowed his head in compliant gratitude.

If he was afraid that the conversation might be awkward, he need not have worried. It became apparent almost immediately that Mr Pym could find words for any occasion, about any subject, and for a seemingly indefinite time. And yet, unlike some garrulous people Carr knew, Mr Pym never seemed to dominate the conversation. He could listen as well as talk, so that his presence never seemed to drift into annoyance, and Carr suspected that Mr Pym was a man who knew when it was time to leave and who would never outstay his welcome. Again, Carr allowed himself a little smile. Being a gossip, he thought, was almost like being a finely tuned instrument, and there was no doubt in Carr's mind that Mr Pym might be considered a star of the orchestra.

"Of course, even without your kind invitation, Mrs Bayliss," he was saying now, "I should have taken the liberty of calling here anyway."

"Really, Mr Pym?"

"Oh, indeed. To see how young Henry is, naturally." The silence that followed, brief but significant, told him that further explanation was required. "I was in *The Black Bull* last night," he added. "I saw everything that happened between Henry and the Arden chap. I helped to break it up, actually," he added, nodding affirmation at Carr. The exaggeration of Mr Pym's role in the events of the previous night was seemingly taken for granted, although Carr had his doubts.

Marjorie was slowly chewing a square of cake. "Henry is feeling rather sorry for himself, and quite rightly."

"It was entirely unprovoked," said Mr Pym. "I suppose Arden was drunk. He usually is."

Carr wondered whether this charge carried any foundation. "Who is this man, Arden?"

It was Marjorie Bayliss who replied. "A young man who works at my husband's mill."

If Carr had wanted further information, Mr Pym was to deny him the opportunity. "Not for much longer, surely, after last night."

"That will be a matter for my husband," said Marjorie.

"I suppose Mr Bayliss might be lenient," said Mr Pym, sipping the tea.

"On what basis?" asked Carr innocently.

"Mr Arden is having a rather difficult time, at present," explained Marjorie.

Mr Pym nodded his agreement. "A lot of people around the town are excusing his antics from last night on the grounds of his mother's death, but I simply cannot go along with it."

"Why not, Mr Pym?" asked Carr, sipping his tea with polite enquiry, although if Mr Pym had looked across to Carr, he would have seen those dark eyes glaring at him with an intense fascination.

"Well, after all," declared Mr Pym, "we all lose people close to us, but we don't all go around hitting people in public houses, do we?"

"Henry is hardly innocent in the business," said Marjorie Bayliss. "He should have walked away the moment he sensed trouble."

Everett Carr cleared his throat softly. "Is there a history of animosity between your son and Mr Arden, dear lady?"

"I don't remember there being any," Marjorie said. "Not until last night, at least."

Mr Pym was less reserved. "Michael Arden has always had a temper and something of a chip on his shoulder about wealth and privilege."

"Everything my husband has, he has worked for," Marjorie felt obliged to say.

Mr Pym, it seemed, had no interest in the origin of the Bayliss wealth. "Brawling in public houses is certainly not the behaviour of gentlemen. Would you not agree, Mr Carr?"

Everett Carr sipped his tea and replied that he certainly agreed with Mr Pym on that point. It was impossible to see how any sensible person could disagree, although Carr saw no reason to point out the obvious. He said nothing more.

Mr Pym continued. "Michael Arden has always been a bit of a tearaway, I'm afraid. Comes of having no father, I suppose."

Marjorie was anxious to direct the conversation elsewhere. "Can I offer you more tea, Mr Carr?"

"Not at the moment, dear lady, thank you." He turned to Mr Pym. "This man, Arden, seems to have had his share of misfortune."

"And more again," agreed Mr Pym. "Two deaths he's had to weather in a matter of weeks. Such a terrible shame."

"Another death, as well as his mother's?"

Mr Pym nodded. "Only a couple of weeks ago, that was, although she'd been ill for a while, of course. It was a relief in the end, I shouldn't wonder. But before dear old Beatrice went, there was Emma Hirst."

Something stirred in Carr's memory. "The wife of Mr Bayliss' accountant?"

"His daughter," corrected Mr Pym. "Eric and I are very good friends, Mr Carr. After Emma's tragedy, he would come round to my cottage on occasion. For the company, you understand, and a sympathetic ear. Over time, we started to play chess, to take his mind off things, so to speak."

"I'm very fond of chess myself," said Carr, smiling politely.

Mr Pym seemed excited by the admission. "Really? Oh, then you must come to my cottage and have a game." He took out a small notebook and pencil and scribbled an address on a leaf of it, handing it over to Carr. "That's where you'll find me, just along Church Lane. Come for coffee and a battle of wits, whenever you like," he added with a purring amiability.

"I shall do so, thank you," said Carr, folding the paper and placing it in his waistcoat pocket. "I suppose Mr Hirst was grateful for your distractions, Mr Pym."

"Very much so, yes."

Marjorie placed her cup on the table between them. "It was all such a tragedy for him."

Carr looked from one to the other of them. "May I enquire what happened?"

"A motorcar accident," Marjorie said, her eyes distant with sadness at the memory. "Emma was such a good girl. Kind-hearted and very mature for her age. She looked after Eric very well after the death of his wife, even though she was only a girl at the time. She grew up to be a fine young woman."

Mr Pym shook his head sadly. "She was driving across Layton Brook, you see, Mr Carr, and there is a notorious bend in the road there that we call Devil's Corner. Everybody knows how treacherous it is."

"Which is why the inquest said it was a stranger to the area," said Marjorie.

"Who drove away from the scene," added Mr Pym.

"How terrible," said Carr. "When was this?"

"Not quite six months ago," said Marjorie.

"It put poor Eric off motor cars for life," said Mr Pym. "He hasn't driven since."

"And I presume, from what you have said, that Mr Arden and Miss Hirst were in love," Carr said.

"Michael was in love with Emma, certainly," said Marjorie.

Mr Pym's eyes glittered. "The rumour was that there was a baby on the way."

Carr looked across to him. "But no marriage planned?"

"No." Mr Pym sipped his coffee. "There was a post-mortem, of course, that confirmed it. You can imagine the scandal."

"Indeed," said Everett Carr. "Such a tragedy."

"But still not an excuse to start brawling in public houses," said Mr Pym with a forced air of dignified superiority.

Carr had risen to his feet to exercise his leg. "Did Mr Arden have any excuse for starting this fight?"

"None whatsoever," said Mr Pym.

"And they have never had any disagreements before," said Carr gently, and to himself.

"Not that I have ever witnessed," said Mr Pym.

Marjorie confirmed it. "Michael has something of a dislike for the upper classes, but he had never acted on it before."

"Then why should he do so now?" asked Carr, stroking his moustache gently. Then, an idea occurred to him. "Forgive me, but did young Mr Bayliss have feelings for Miss Hirst, perhaps?"

Marjorie laughed, a response driven by shock rather than humour. "If he did, he never mentioned it to us, and he certainly never acted on it. I don't think there is any suggestion that they were romantically involved with each other."

Eager to please, Mr Pym shared the laughter. "And even if that were the case, why would they brawl about it now, so long after her death?"

Carr smiled and gave a little shrug of his shoulders, as if to dismiss his own stupidity. But something much darker was lurking in the back of his mind. Something had prompted Michael Arden to attack Henry Bayliss, and Carr was inclined to blame a rivalry between the two young men for the love and affections of a young woman. And yet, Mr Pym had made a valid point when he asked why, after six months, it only seemed to matter enough to Arden that he acted now and not in the immediate aftermath. Carr turned away from them and stared out of the window, as if he believed that the solution to the problem lay somewhere across the impressive lawns of Darton House.

# Chapter Eleven

Rosamund Bayliss leaned against the door frame of the old outhouse that Henry had converted into a studio for himself. A cigarette hung loosely from her fingers, her legs were crossed casually at the ankles, and her head was tilted to one side as she stared with a confused eye over what appeared to her to be no more than coloured swirls and blotches on the canvas of her brother's easel. Art had never meant very much to her, unless it was a painting of something she could either recognise or appreciate. She could accept the skill of any painting that showed the beauty of a country landscape, or the dignity of a 17th or 18th-century nobleman, or even the adorable innocence of a puppy or kitten. But the monstrosities that Henry produced seemed to her to be the products either of a nightmare or a total lack of talent.

She watched him now, his left hand holding a palette that seemed to her to have seen better days, and in his right was a brush of similar condition that he would flick towards the canvas at irregular intervals with what she supposed was an artistic flourish of inspiration but which seemed to her to be more like a blindfolded fencer trying to score a point. On occasion, he would step back from the easel, occasionally murmuring with satisfaction and just as often snarling with frustration. Rosamund was unsure quite how he could have any emotional response to the painting he was creating, other than baffled annoyance. If she had to guess, she would say that it was a pig. There was certainly the suggestion of a huge pink bulk, but there was no snout and no trace of the characteristic tail of the animal. Instead, she could make out what seemed to be a bowler hat, a winged collar around the neck, and a necktie represented by what she thought was a snake. There were swirls of colour around this indeterminate subject. In the centre of the figure was a large red blemish, out of which seemed to flow yellow circles and repugnant-looking insects or something similar. The backdrop was a distorted vision of what appeared to be a rugby playing field, overshadowed by portentous, dark skies of purple and blue paint. The only item that could be clearly recognised was hovering above the whole image, and it was a smoking pistol.

"I'm sure it's very good, Henry," Rosamund said, "but what is it?"

He did not turn to face her, but his tone of voice betrayed the expression on his face well enough. "It's Father."

Rosamund stared blankly at the ugliness in front of her. It was now, she supposed, easier to understand as an image of her father characterised as a pig, which he most assuredly was, the bowler hat being their father's status as a businessman, and the background a reference to his sporting days. And yet, she was certain that she was missing the point.

"Why hasn't he got a face?" she asked, not unreasonably.

"Because I don't know who he is anymore."

"He's the same old sadist he always was." Her voice was cold, detached, somehow lethal.

Henry looked at her but did not reply. Rosamund seemed not to have expected any response in any event. She was still scrutinising the painting.

"What about the yellow circles?" she asked.

"Money." Henry turned to face her. The blackened eye had turned a dull purple now, its edges framed in a hazy yellow, and the strangely attractive colours of violence seemed to blend perfectly with the accidental smears of paint that blemished the cheeks and chin. "He lives for money. It's his lifeblood."

"I see." Rosamund remained unconvinced. "And the snake around his neck?"

"Evil," said Henry without emotion. "The Garden of Eden, and all that. Choking the humanity out of him."

"He never had any to begin with." Again, she did not expect a reply. "And the smoking gun?"

To this, however, Henry made no reply. Instead, he put down the palette and brush and wiped his hands on a rag so discoloured that Rosamund could hardly expect it to make his paint-coated hands any cleaner.

"What do you want, Rosa?"

Rosa. He was the only person to call her by any shortened version of her name. It had once struck her as incongruous, simply because she had never heard of it before, but she had grown accustomed to it over the years, and now, if he had called her by her full name, it seemed inappropriate.

"I just thought I'd come to see you working," she said. "You're always so passionate about painting, but none of us ever gets to see you doing it. We don't even get to see the finished results." She had stubbed out her cigarette now and had walked over to the easel. "Perhaps now I can see why."

Henry took a long drink from a glass of clear liquid. It was probably water, Rosamund thought, but she wouldn't have been surprised if it had turned out to be gin. There was also a plate with some bread and cheese on it, a slice of each he now cut to make a rudimentary sandwich, of which he took a brutal bite. "You didn't come here just for that."

She paused, wondering how long she could pursue the lie, but her brother's expression was too severe for it to be worth her time. "All right, I came to see how you are."

"I'm fine."

"Boxing in *The Black Bull*? Quite a different side to your character than paints and brushes."

"Don't patronise me."

She threw her head back. "I'm not, honestly. I'm trying to be nice to my big brother. If he'll let me."

"I'm fine," Henry said sullenly. "Embarrassed by it all, more than anything else."

Rosamund smiled. "I understand Mummy gave you Hell about it."

Henry shrugged as if what Marjorie had said to him had not affected him. His eyes, however, told quite a different story. "Where is she now?"

"Having tea with Mr Pym and our guest."

"Have you seen him?"

"Mr Carr? Yes, I have. Nothing like what you'd expect a friend of Daddy's to be like." Her eyes danced with impish excitement. "Very polite and extremely posh. A cripple, too."

"Really?"

"Well, he limps." There didn't seem to be a great deal to be said about Everett Carr after that. "Listen, don't worry about Mummy. She just worries about us."

"I know." Henry drank some more of the water. "I hate how he treats her."

Rosamund walked over to him and rested her head on his shoulder. He smelt of old paint and Turpentine, and vaguely of sweat. "How he treats all of us, you mean."

"I heard her the other day, talking on the telephone. I don't know who to. Mrs Bridges, I suppose."

"It usually is," said Rosamund. Then, she looked up at her brother. "What did she say?"

His voice lowered as if burdened with the importance of what he was about to say. "She said, 'Arthur can't go on like this, and I won't stand for it. Something needs to be done about him.' It almost didn't sound like her."

"I wonder what she meant," said Rosamund. "Divorce, do you suppose?"

"On what grounds?"

"Dozens," said Rosamund, daring to smile. But then the terrible thought came to her without warning or premonition. "You don't think she meant… ?"

Henry glared at her. "Don't be ridiculous."

Rosamund pointed to the painting. Suddenly, its meaning and its intent were painfully obvious: the red blemish in that pink body, the blood money spilling out of it, the smoking gun. "Mummy wouldn't be the only one having those sorts of thoughts, would she?"

Henry, sullen, shook his head. "It's just a painting."

"It might become proof of something."

"You're being melodramatic."

"Am I?" She tapped her finger incessantly on the depiction of the smoking gun, smearing the paint and soiling her finger. Neither of them seemed to care.

"It's just a painting," Henry repeated, his words barely audible.

Rosamund stared at him, willing him to say something more, but he kept his eyes on the floor. She sighed quietly to herself and walked towards him. "I've had similar thoughts myself, you know. More than once, over the years."

The unspoken act seemed to hang in the air between them, and their inability to say its name seemed to make it all the more terrible, both as a concept and in its oppressive effect on them. Henry shook his head, forbidding her to say any more, as if even thinking of doing it was a hanging offence. He stood with his head bowed, his attention fixed on the floor of the studio, and his hands clenched in front of him, like a schoolboy about to receive a beating for a minor transgression of rules he didn't understand.

Rosamund perched on the edge of the workbench, shifting some old jam jars filled with filthy, discoloured water to do so, and looked over at him with an expression of shared sadness. A moment passed.

"I was furious with George last night," Rosamund said at last.

"For leaving?" Henry shrugged. "It would have been worse if he'd stayed and witnessed the full scene."

"I suppose so," said Rosamund. "One thing's for sure. He wouldn't have stuck up for me as you did."

"Of course he would. He loves you."

She looked at him significantly. "I'm beginning to wonder."

Henry moved over to her and took her hand in his. He was surprised to see tears in her eyes.

"Rosa, what's happened?" he asked.

And she wondered how to reply. The words were easy to conjure, but almost impossible to say. She wiped away a tear with the palm of her hand. "I'm having doubts."

"About the marriage?"

"About everything."

"Why?"

Rosamund knew that her reply would make her sound petty and selfish, but she could hardly stop the conversation now. "He's working all the time. I hardly see him."

"He's busy with the merger with our place."

"That's what Mummy said."

"But you don't believe it?" He watched her shake her head as the tears began to fall in earnest. He held her close to him, making himself her protector now as if in return for all those years of childhood. "Why, what's happened?"

And now she said it. "George is lying to me."

"About what?"

She pulled away from his embrace and pulled out a tissue from under her sleeve. "I don't know. Something, everything, *anything*." She gave a humourless, coarse laugh. Henry's expression remained painfully serious, however, and she gave a hearty but disgusting sniff and sighed heavily. "He says he's working late and, like you and Mummy, he blames the merger with Daddy. But I know George, and something doesn't feel right."

"An instinct?"

She nodded. "One I couldn't shake off. So, last night, I did something about it."

"What?"

"He was supposed to be working at his office, so I telephoned him."

"He wasn't there?"

"Nobody had seen him since the late afternoon."

Henry perched on the workbench next to her. "What did you do?"

"I called him just now, and I asked him where he had been last night." She gave her brother a sly, malignant smile. "He said he'd been working in the office."

"A double lie."

Rosamund lowered her head. "I won't marry a liar, Henry."

Henry nodded his understanding of the defiance. "Have you told him you've caught him out?"

"Not yet. I'm supposed to be having dinner with him tonight, but I won't be going."

"I think you should."

The idea appalled her. "Don't be ridiculous!"

But Henry, more forceful and angrier than she had ever known, was adamant. "Damn it, Rosa, he has a right to defend himself. He might have a perfectly good reason for not telling the truth about last night. A lie doesn't automatically mean something sinister."

"What else can it mean?"

"He might be planning a surprise for you."

She scoffed. "Don't be naïve, Henry. Let's be realistic, for God's sake."

Henry was persistent. "He still has a right to the opportunity to defend himself."

"And what about my right to my own feelings?"

Rosamund walked over to him and sank her head on his shoulder. "It's all a bit of a pickle, isn't it?"

He could not help but smile. "What are you going to do?"

Rosamund gave a small shrug of her shoulders. "Go to dinner with George tonight and tackle him about what he's been up to, I suppose."

"You don't think George is in love with someone else, do you?"

Rosamund shook her head. "I doubt it. One thing does terrify me more than anything."

Henry turned to face her. He knew what she meant, not least because the thought had occurred to him too, and he shared her fears of it. "Father?"

"What's he going to say when he finds out I won't marry George?"

"I dread to think." Henry smiled, but there was no humour behind it.

Rosamund sighed heavily. "It is hard enough to deal with. Daddy just makes it twice as hard."

Henry found that he had snapped a paintbrush in half, and he now held the two broken pieces in either hand, as if they were two pistols in the hands of a sharpshooter from the Wild West stories of his youth.

"It would be so much better if he weren't here, wouldn't it?" He felt her eyes burning into him. "How much happier we would all be."

She turned his face to confront hers. "But he is here, Henry. And there's nothing we can do about it."

Henry Bayliss shook his head. "No, there isn't, is there? Nothing we can do at all."

That unspoken word from earlier now descended between them once more, but this time they felt it more keenly, and its horror seemed far more acute. And then, in harmony, brother and sister both turned their collective gaze to the painting of the huge pink pig with the livid red gunshot wound in its side, the blood money pouring out of it, and the smoking gun hanging ominously in the darkly painted sky.

# Chapter Twelve

rthur Bayliss was finished for the evening. He filed away the various papers in the appropriate cabinets, locking them afterwards, placed his notebook and fountain pen into the upper drawers of his desk (no more dead rats, he thought grimly), and replaced the paper on his blotter. This latter action was a daily ritual, arising from the original idea of a new blotter representing a new day. It was a habit he wished he could break, since blotting paper was not inexpensive, but it had become so regular that it was almost comforting, even if the economical impracticality of it was impossible to ignore. The business done, he rose from his desk, put on his jacket, coat, and hat, and walked to the door of the office. He pulled the door closed as he stepped onto the gantry, smiled at the memory of Eric Hirst's fear earlier in the day, and locked the door behind him.

As a working day, it had been otherwise uneventful. There had been the usual orders, which were always a welcome sight, and he and Hirst had gone through the books in some detail. Finances were healthy. Bayliss had spoken to George Toole about some issues surrounding the merger, and it had struck him that the lad had sounded tired. Well, he knew the likely reason for that, after all, he thought with a malicious grin. Not for the first time, he wondered whether Rosamund knew how George Toole liked to spend his evenings. He doubted it. If she did, she certainly wouldn't like it and, perhaps, as her father, Bayliss might have been expected to do something about it. As it happened, however, what Toole did suited him very well, and what Rosamund didn't know certainly couldn't hurt her. Silence on the matter, thought Bayliss as he stomped down the iron staircase, was by far the best policy, and honesty be damned.

The day had not been entirely satisfactory, however, as there had been the difficult lunch with Lydia Stansfield. Bayliss felt no regret at its outcome, nor did he feel any remorse at the tears it had caused for Lydia. What was said had to be said, and that was the end of it. Still, he thought, looking back on the meeting, it had been annoyingly fraught, not to say socially embarrassing, but he blamed the girl for it entirely.

"You can't do this to me," she had hissed. "I won't let you do it to me."

"Don't be so ridiculous, my girl," he had said. "You must see that things have come to their natural end. Besides, I'm old enough to be your father. Much better that you find someone of your own age. Much better for you," he had repeated, patting her hand with his and smiling warmly at her.

But Lydia had seen no warmth in the smile, only patronising arrogance. "Don't you dare presume to tell me what is best for myself. You won't be leaving me, Arthur, and that is final."

His eyes had hooded dangerously. "I don't think you understand the position, lass. I'm very possibly going to be mentioned in the next Honours list. It won't happen if I have a mistress."

She had seen an opening for leverage, and her eyes had sparkled with success. "Then you'd better make sure you keep me happy, Arthur. Otherwise, I could make life rather difficult, wouldn't you say? And the first thing you can do to make me happy," she had added triumphantly, "is to leave your wife."

His hand had still been resting on hers, but now, with the speed of a cobra, his fingers had closed tightly around her wrist, and a numbing pain shot up her forearm. She had winced, and that feeling of victory had dissipated as swiftly as it had arrived.

"I don't think you quite understand my meaning, girl," he had said. "You need to look at this matter from your own point of view. I'm a well-respected businessman, a pillar of the community, and a prospective member of the peerage. You work in a hat shop in a side street of a small Northern town. You see my point?"

"Yes." The word had been a gasp of agony.

But he had clarified it for her, nevertheless, as if to prolong her discomfort. "Who's going to believe you if you say anything about me? They'll see you as a money-grabbing little whore, desperate to escape her insignificant employment, a slut minx who wanted status and wealth."

"That's not true," she had whimpered.

"They won't care if it's true or not, my girl. That's what you'll be. Believe me, I know the way people's minds work. They won't think I looked at you with anything but contempt, and they'd be right about it. And even if they did believe there was anything going on between us, you'd be the harlot of the piece. I'd be a flattered old man. Do you think Mrs Roper would want you in her shop after that?"

"I hate you," she had said, but the words were barely audible under the pain and the tears.

"Slung out on your ear, that's what you'd be. No money for rent, so no roof over your head. No job, no prospects. Only yourself to sell. You know the old saying, don't you, lass? Know your place." He had emphasised the words with a hideous cruelty, only then releasing his grip on her wrist.

Lydia had yanked back her arm, the fingers slowly beginning to tingle with feeling as she rubbed her hand vigorously. She stared at him with eyes of murder, wondering how he could have changed so much from the man who had first flattered her with words and seduced her with gifts and promises. And then, in a fierce moment of realisation, she wondered whether he had changed at all and whether all those acts of kindness were in fact means to an end, to this mortifying and humiliating final confrontation between them.

"I hate you," she had repeated.

He had smiled. "You'll find someone else, lass. No need to pine for an old bugger like me. Find a good stallion to ride over the plains."

"I love you," she had said, knowing its truth was the biggest shame of all.

"Nothing lasts forever, girl." He had risen from the table and grinned salaciously at her. "Except, just maybe, *me*."

He smiled now at the parting words. In a way, they were true. Not in an immortal fashion, obviously, but in his legacy, his mill, and his lineage. They would all outlast his own body and soul, but he would live on in his achievements. Like Christ surviving in all the churches built in His name. In a smaller but arguably no less impressive way, Bayliss thought he would be remembered and admired long after his death. And the feeling made him feel warm inside, despite the coldness of the night air.

He saw nobody on the walk back to Darton House, other than Jock McGregor, the mechanic, who was walking home from his day's work. Bayliss both liked and respected McGregor, but whether the mechanic reciprocated the admiration was impossible to know. The gruff Scot was not known for any display of emotion, other than a passing pride at seeing a broken vehicle healed and back in motion. The two men spoke amiably enough for a few moments before shaking hands and moving on towards their respective destinations.

It was as Bayliss reached home that he saw it. Later, he would wonder whether the chance meeting with McGregor had been an omen of the disaster that followed. Now, walking up the gravel driveway, he saw a figure lurking around the garage that stood to the side of Darton House. It had been a subtle movement of black that had alerted Bayliss to the presence of an intruder, one of those barely discernible shifts of focus that are noticeable only because they are so unexpected. Whoever it was, Bayliss took note as he squinted into the shadows, was tall, wearing a peaked cap of some description, and possibly a scarf around the lower part of the face.

"Hey!" Bayliss called out. "Who's there?"

The figure spun round and seemed to hesitate. Bayliss did not do likewise. Despite his age and the effects of his gluttony, something of the old speed of the rugby playing fields came back to him as he hurtled towards the intruder. The figure seemed to brace itself for a confrontation, and Bayliss had the idea that his adversary seemed almost to relish the thought of a ruckus with the old brawler coming towards him. As it was, however, the prowler took to his heels and raced around the back of the house. Bayliss followed, his chest heaving and his heart protesting against the strain. His throat seemed to have contracted, and the harsh taste of bile and vomit began to coat the back of his mouth. He ran on, though, coughing up phlegm and spitting it to the ground as he moved.

There was a high garden wall that surrounded the property of Darton House, and Bayliss knew that he would not be able to scale it. Inevitably, he thought as he watched the intruder racing towards the impassive stone, the race was over. He watched in curious admiration as the figure in black leapt up into the branches of an overhanging tree, using them as leverage with which to swing himself onto the top of the stone wall. From there, it was a simple matter to drag himself over its edge and leap down onto the side road beyond, and to safety, leaving Bayliss wheezing and snorting like a stuck pig in a suit, his hands resting on his knees and his whole body screaming in agony.

He lurched back to the garage. He turned on the electric lights, expecting to see some signs of burglary, tools missing perhaps, or evidence of the contents of the garage being ransacked. He saw neither, and a later inventory of the garage itself showed that nothing had been taken. And yet, a serious and unforgivable crime had taken place in the darkness of the garage, and when Arthur Bayliss saw it, he was consumed by fury and repulsion, but also, to his surprise, a sudden desire to weep.

As he turned on the lights in the garage, they illuminated the sleek bonnet of his Bentley motor car, the shining trims of the headlamps and chassis, and the elegant burgundy curves of its design. It was an impressive design, a testament to the ingenuity and skill of mankind, and Bayliss had dreamed of owning such a vehicle since he had first seen motorcars on the streets of Manchester in his youth. The car was one of many in the garage, but the Bentley was the pinnacle of his collection.

And now, after this nocturnal malice, the beauty of this particular motor car was scarred and cracked. The paintwork had split, exposing the bare metal beneath. There were ugly blisters across the bonnet, its violation spilling down over the chrome of the headlamps and grill. The whole effect was to make it look as if the car had somehow melted, like the faces of victims of vitriol throwing, and it was this thought, immediate and startling, that suggested the use of acid to Bayliss' mind. It had to be so: this molten vandalisation could not have been achieved with any tool. It was the work of some form of acid, poured liberally over the front of the car. Bayliss walked around the side of the car, but he found that the attacker had confined his malicious attention only to the front. The sides and back remained undisturbed and immaculate, which served only to exaggerate the effect of the violence inflicted elsewhere.

He fought to bring his feelings and his breathing under control, walked out of the garage, and slammed shut its door. He took in the fact that the lock had been broken, so that he could not even have the pleasure of firing the chauffeur for carelessness. He waited a moment, debating whether to wake the staff to secure the garage door, but he decided against it. The intruder would not return now. His lust for hatred and destruction had been satiated for one night.

# Chapter Thirteen

Everett Carr woke early on the following morning, Friday 17 September, and he realised at once that his journey on the previous day must have been more arduous than he had thought, since he had no recollection of any of the dreams that so often plagued his sleep, and he had only a vague memory of settling down in bed at all. The journey north had tired him more than he had felt upon his arrival in Darton Vale, obviously, but now he awoke refreshed and ready to face the day.

He came downstairs to find that breakfast had been set, but nobody was yet present. It was not a meal that ever truly appealed to Carr, and he left the covered salvers of fried bacon and scrambled eggs alone, instead pouring himself a cup of strong, black coffee and setting himself down at the table. He was about to sample it when a commotion outside disturbed his tranquillity.

From the window opposite him, Carr could see Arthur Bayliss and what he took to be Bayliss' chauffeur engaged in as violent a quarrel as can exist between master and servant. Bayliss was roaring in the other man's face, pointing and gesticulating violently, his face a livid shade of crimson. The other man, as far as Carr could tell, was refuting whatever it was Bayliss was saying, but was doing so with sufficient reticence as to ensure future employment. It was, Carr felt, a definite but polite defence to whatever accusations were being made to him, and Carr had the idea that the chauffeur's calmness would be serving only to enrage Bayliss even more than the incident at the heart of the quarrel.

Carr got slowly to his feet and made his way outside.

The chauffeur was walking away as Carr approached, but Bayliss remained standing where he was, lighting a cigarette with an expression of disgust.

Carr approached gently. "What is the matter, my friend?"

Bayliss was glaring after the chauffeur. "Not his fault, I suppose. The lock had been broken, after all, so he must have locked the garage last night."

The words, spoken to himself rather than to Carr, seemed to be reconciliatory, almost apologetic, but the tone in which they were spoken suggested a frustration that the concession had to be made at all.

"But what has happened, my dear fellow?" asked Carr.

And now, Bayliss seemed to see him for the first time. He stared at the smaller man, initially with an expression of confusion, as if Carr's presence was something it was impossible to understand. Finally, Bayliss smiled and offered his hand, squeezing Carr's fingers together with a monstrous but not malicious grip.

"My dear Mr Carr, do forgive me," said Bayliss. "Damned rude of me not to be here when you arrived yesterday. Work, I'm afraid. Do forgive me."

Carr gave a dismissive shake of his head. "Mrs Bayliss looked after me with due diligence and kindness."

"Did she? Well, she's good at all that. Has to be good at something, right?" He laughed at this, but Carr was not sure whether it had been intended entirely as a joke.

Almost tiring of asking the question, Carr posed it again. "And what has happened to so upset you?"

"I'll show you." The voice now was as dark as the expression.

Bayliss led his guest to the garage, the doors now flung open, so that the savage defacing of the car was visible. It had struck Bayliss that in the dawning light of a new day, the horrors of the previous night seemed even more appalling. The effects of the acid, the cracked and blistered paint, and the smeared and melted chrome now seemed more vivid and repellent than they had done in the deep twilight of the previous evening.

Carr, who was not a man with any knowledge or admiration for motor vehicles, stared grimly at the vandalism before him. "Good Lord."

Bayliss grunted in agreement. "My pride and joy, that car. Look at the state of it now."

Carr took a step forward and peered at the exposed metal and shattered glass. "Forgive me, but could this be linked to the acts of sabotage at the mill?"

Bayliss stared blankly at him. He wondered for a moment how Carr could know about the poltergeist, but a second's thought gave him the answer.

"My wife had no business telling you anything about that, Mr Carr."

"She is naturally worried about it."

Bayliss closed the garage doors and turned to Carr. "I've told her she has nothing to worry about."

Carr was staring at those same garage doors. Softly, he said, "I should say there is a great deal to worry about, my friend."

"But it's for me to do the worrying, not Marjorie." Bayliss walked towards him, wiping his hands on his handkerchief.

"If this is the work of the poltergeist, he has attacked your cars twice now, I understand. First, the smashed headlamps, and now this."

Bayliss glared at Carr with a terrifying ferocity. "That's neither here nor there."

"Your expression suggests that you consider otherwise," said Carr gently. "If I may say so."

Bayliss inhaled on his cigarette. "I haven't taken a single one of these practical jokes seriously, and I don't intend to start doing so now."

"I should hardly call them practical jokes," said Carr.

Bayliss ignored him. "But when I find out who did this to my Bentley, I'll murder him."

Carr stared at him for a long moment. "You should be careful what you say to people, my friend."

Bayliss seemed not to have heard him. "I'll have to get the car to McGregor's garage for repairs. Bloody vandals," he added with a snort. Then, a moment later, the savagery of his expression had melted, like the paint on his car, into hospitable amiability. "Now, shall we get some breakfast, Mr Carr? Don't know about you, but I could eat a horse."

Carr followed slowly behind Bayliss, who marched back to the house without giving any thought to Carr's slower pace or the chilled pain that had seized his shattered knee. At the door to the house, Carr stopped and looked back towards the garage. There was a familiar uncertainty coiled around his instincts, the strong impression that something was not right, a detail that had been overlooked, an untuned note in the symphony. For once, however, it was not beyond Carr's reach, and the conclusion he had drawn about the identity of the prowler last night, as compared to the mill poltergeist, seemed impossible to ignore. As he stepped inside the house once more, Carr felt more keenly than ever that he was correct to suppose that the instigator of the acts of malice at the mill was not the same person who had poured acid over Arthur Bayliss' car. And that, of course, was a thought that troubled Everett Carr beyond measure, simply because it meant that there was more than one dangerous enemy in the midst of the mill owner's life.

Breakfast passed pleasantly enough, but Carr's disturbed thoughts continued to plague him. He had been formally introduced to Henry Bayliss and had made a reacquaintance with both Marjorie and Rosamund.

"Did you enjoy your dinner with your fiancé and his family last night, Miss Bayliss?" he asked as she took the seat next to him.

"As much as I ever do," she said.

There was something about her tone that unsettled him. He looked across at her and saw that the natural paleness of her skin now seemed almost spectral, an impression emphasised by the darkness under her eyes and the obvious traces of recent tears.

"Are you all right, my child?" he asked.

She smiled at him. "I'm fine. I just didn't sleep very well, I'm afraid."

Carr nodded in sympathy. Her plate, Carr noticed, was filled with bacon and eggs, with a slice of toast fighting for survival beneath them. He wondered how she would ever manage to empty the plate, and the thought of the quantity of food she had set herself to eat at this hour of the morning turned his stomach.

"It has not affected your appetite," he said.

Rosamund looked at him curiously for a moment, as if she had not understood his words. Then, following his amused gaze towards her plate, she laughed suddenly.

"Force of habit, I'm afraid," she said. "Normally, I eat a ton at breakfast. In my defence, I rarely have lunch and very little at tea time." She was babbling, she knew it, and she brought herself to a halt before she made a fool of herself. Carr was watching her closely. "As it happens," she added, looking back at the food, "I don't think I can face anything at all."

Carr smiled politely. "My mother would always tell me that breakfast was the most important meal of the day."

She looked at his single cup of black coffee. "Did you not listen to your mother about many things, Mr Carr?"

He laughed softly, she reciprocated briefly, and the moment passed. Despite her words, she began to eat, chewing slowly and mechanically, and it was only as she lifted her fork to her mouth that Carr registered the fact that the engagement ring she normally wore was curiously absent from her finger.

The news about the attack on Bayliss' car was broken to the family, and they received it with varying degrees of concern. Marjorie expressed a loyal outrage at the vandalism, Henry remained moodily silent, and Rosamund asked the natural question.

"Do you know who did it?"

"Not yet," said Bayliss. "I saw the bastard running off and scrambling over the wall."

Henry sat upright. "Who was it?"

Bayliss scowled and shook his head. "I couldn't see who it was, you idiot. He was dressed in black, his face covered. But I'll tell you this. Whoever poured bloody acid on my Bentley is whoever put a rat in my desk and sent that letter."

"Not necessarily," said Rosamund.

"I thought you didn't take all that seriously," said Henry, almost simultaneously.

Bayliss glared at him. "Well, maybe I do now. Is that all right with you, boy?"

Henry rose from his chair. "Whatever you want, Dad. I can see that to a man like you, acid on a car means more than a threat to your life."

"You bloody filthy—"

But Henry was out of the room before the obscenity, whatever it might have been, could be spoken. The remainder of the meal was eaten in awkward silence.

After returning to his room momentarily, partly to escape the atmosphere of the breakfast room and partly to appraise himself of his appearance, Everett Carr announced that he would like to take a walk in the town, to find his bearings. Bayliss had already said that he had work to do at the mill, and Carr had no wish to obstruct what he called a busy man carrying out his duties. Bayliss had expressed his thanks and promised, to Carr's dismay, a tour of the mill later that afternoon or perhaps on the Saturday morning. Marjorie volunteered to accompany Carr on his walk, but he declined the invitation.

"A solitary walk, dear lady, is good for my knee and my spirits, if you would allow it," he said.

"Of course. Lunch will be at noon."

Carr had bowed, and after donning his hat, coat, and scarf, he made his way into the town of Darton Vale. In truth, his curiosity had been piqued about various matters, and he had conjured up the notion that a visit to Neville Pym might prove instructive. This minor act of social subterfuge did not detract from the truth of his words to Marjorie Bayliss, nor from his very real desire to flee from the house and its tensions and lose himself in the bracing and clean open air. It had been fortunate, he thought, that Mr Pym had given his address, and Carr checked the details from the folded notepaper in his waistcoat pocket only once before setting out.

He enjoyed the walk into the town of Darton Vale. The air was cold but not unbearable, and Carr was grateful for his scarf. The rolling hills of the northern moors loomed high above him in the distance, and he noticed for the first time how beautiful they were. The words of Blake's poem came back to him, and he let his eyes drift over the green and pleasant land of which the poet had spoken and fought valiantly to protect from industrialisation. The hills undulated across the horizon, like the green and brown waves of an agricultural sea, interspersed here and there by clumps of dense evergreens, which gave Carr the unavoidable impression of nocturnal rituals being carried out by witches amongst the shadows cast by the dense leaves and branches. His mind continued along similar, if less superstitious, lines, and he found himself wondering about the dark deeds that might have been enacted across the centuries on those peaks and troughs of the northern landscapes that now rolled across his view. Beautiful they may be, he thought, but they possessed an alluring mystery of their own, one that was enhanced by the mists that swirled across the tops of the hills and the leafless branches of the trees that surrounded them, whose spindly fingers, like the witches' of Carr's imagination, gave the impression that he was looking at the landscape through a broken pane of glass. Here, he thought, was nature at its wildest, seemingly stretching to infinity, whilst the relatively minor advancements of mankind functioned beneath its majesty. The houses of the town, the smoke from the passing engines over the viaduct, and even the mills that Blake had decried, all seemed minuscule in scale of achievement compared to the vastness of the wild countryside that surrounded them.

He did not have to ask for directions to Church Lane, but he twice had to ask for assistance in finding Mr Pym's cottage. Eventually, he found it nestled in a small space of its own between the back of the church and what seemed to be an allotment beyond it. Carr wondered whether the cottage might once have belonged to the church, given its proximity to it, and he found himself idly theorising about Mr Pym being granted domesticity through religious charity and wondering on what grounds that might have come to be. Similarly, and conversely, he thought, the church might have sold the cottage to Mr Pym for a favourable price, one that benefited the buyer and assisted the seller in some sort of restoration or other. Or, Carr conceded, it might simply be that the cottage had been built close to the church as much on account of coincidence as purpose.

The cottage itself was unremarkable. It was built from white stone with four simple windows cut into it, the upper two latticed and the lower two plain glass, with an arched doorway cut into the centre. There was ivy stretching across the front of the edifice, and the windows all displayed various ornaments and trinkets, including potted plants, china figures whose details were not clear from a distance, and, in the upper windows, small rows of books, what appeared to be a skull carved from wood, and various candelabra. A vase of flowers stood in the centre of the left lower window, and Carr assumed this would look into the sitting room. A small gate was set into a low garden wall, and this Carr pushed open, grimacing slightly at the creak of protest from the hinges. The garden was small but well-tended, and Carr felt certain that the vase of flowers in the window had come from it. A trellis had been erected along one side of the garden path, and growing on it was a mass of green with purple flowers scattered around it. If Carr's grandfather, a devoted horticulturist, had been with him, he would have been able to identify the plant as clematis, but to Carr, it was no more than an impressive display of natural beauty.

It was when he reached the front door that he sensed a serpent in the Edenesque surroundings.

The door appeared to be closed, but on approach, Carr noticed that it was not. In fact, it was merely pulled to, so that it swayed slightly in the breeze, although it was too sheltered by the stone archway and the surrounding flora to be affected too much by the morning wind. Carr leaned towards the opening and listened hard, but he could hear nothing. He called Mr Pym by name, but there was no reply. Gently, he raised the silver handle of his cane and pushed the door. Unlike the gate, the hinges offered no complaint.

Carr stepped into the small hallway from which the stairs led to the upper floor ahead of him. To his right, there was an open door that he could see led to a kitchen. To his left, there were two more doors, both closed. The first was immediately facing him, and the other was further along the passageway. It was this first one that seized his attention, and Carr knew from his earlier deduction that it would be the sitting room. He knocked twice, gently but firmly, and on both occasions his only reply was silence.

Turning the handle, he opened the door slowly and stepped into the room.

As he had thought, it was a sitting room, neatly furnished with a symmetrical and almost feline finesse. The room was perfectly balanced, with two armchairs facing each other on either side of the room and a settee between them along the inner wall. The outer wall, opposite, was dominated by a large cast-iron fireplace surrounded in bare brick, whose frank appearance seemed to give it a strangely opulent effect. The mantel was decorated with another wooden carved skull and two candlesticks at either end. It must have produced an atmospheric, if ghoulish, effect if the candles cast the shadow of the skull onto the wall behind, particularly if the flames of any fire in the grate did likewise from below. Next to the skull, there was a framed photograph of a young man, whose almost feminine beauty was impossible to deny, but whose eyes displayed the arrogance of a man who is handsome but only too aware of the fact. There was nothing to identify the man as a relative, a friend, or a lover, but the prominence of place and the frame around his image were enough to suggest that he was a man of some importance to Neville Pym. Carr would never discover the boy's identity or his relationship with Mr Pym, but he had an immediate impression of an abandoned and forbidden love, and that first instinct never left Carr's conscience. The wall opposite the fireplace was decorated with a large print of Tuke's *August Blue*, whose open inclusion in the room intrigued rather than offended Carr. On a table in front of the hearth, there was a chessboard, the pieces carved representations of the court of Henry VIII, which were placed in positions that suggested a half-played game in which, as far as Carr could tell, white was in serious danger of losing. A book, concerning FD Yates' best chess games, lay open, face down, on the edge of the board.

All of this, Carr noticed afterwards, as he waited for the police. Upon entering the sitting room, his attention was held by the armchair with its back to the window. Slumped in it, the arms dropped loosely into the lap, and the legs outstretched, was the body of Neville Pym. He was dressed in the same grey suit he had worn when Carr had met him on the previous day, although he wore a velvet smoking jacket in place of the suit's own, and the feet, pointed inwards, were not encased the shined shoes of yesterday, but elegant black carpet slippers, whose toes were adorned with a golden stitched *fleur-de-lis*. His head rested against the back of the chair, his mouth hanging open as if singing a silent note. As he looked down at the body, Carr could almost have believed that the man was sleeping. There was no wound that Carr could see, and there was no obvious sign of any means by which poison might have been administered. The hands in the lap, the quaintly, faintly ridiculous twist of the feet, and the open mouth and reclining head gave the innocent impression that a sudden weariness had overcome the man. But the unnaturally blank stare of the eyes told Everett Carr the truth of the matter, because only they showed that Neville Pym was dead, and that this sleep, the deepest of all, would last forever.

# Chapter Fourteen

The inspector's name was Tommy Barber.

He appeared in the doorway of Mr Pym's cottage without any verbal announcement, as if the dark act of murder had conjured him from an abyss. He was silhouetted against the light behind him, shrouding his features in black, which intensified this impression of ethereal menace. Carr was aware only of the outline of broad, rounded shoulders and a build of stocky authority. Only when he stepped into the cottage could Carr see the heavy brows, the slightly widened blue eyes, and the naturally pursed lips that gave his features a permanent suggestion of mistrust. His hands were in his coat pockets, but Carr could not dismiss the notion that they were clenched into fists. Everything about the man seemed to suggest confrontation. His hat and coat were crumpled, as if he had only just ceased brawling on the ground with some miscreant, the hems of his trousers were slightly frayed, and his tie was crooked. Carr could not be sure, because he could not see closely enough, but he had the impression that the top button of the inspector's shirt was unfastened. If it wasn't, his appearance was disordered enough to suggest it; if it was, it hardly came as any surprise.

A few preliminary questions, asked in a gruff and perfunctorily polite Lancashire accent, ascertained Carr's identity and his purpose for being in Mr Pym's cottage. Inspector Barber listened to Carr's answers without paying him much personal attention. Instead, his eyes were scanning the room, and only the occasional nod of understanding showed that he was listening to Carr at all.

"There was no sign of any burglary that you saw, sir?" he asked.

"None, Inspector. In fact," Carr added, "the door was only pulled to."

"You think someone was in here?" Barber watched Carr give a slight shrug of his shoulders. "No sign of any weapon or wound, is there?"

"No," Carr conceded.

"I mean, sir, it looks, doesn't it, as if he's died in his sleep?"

"Possibly, Inspector," said Carr, "although I do wonder about that cushion."

He pointed to a crimson velveteen cushion that was one of a pair resting on the settee. They were both embroidered with gold stitching in the shape of tulips, a single one on each cushion. It was to the one nearest the door that Carr was pointing.

"It's upside down," said Barber.

"Precisely." Carr looked around him. "You must have noted the symmetry in this room, Inspector. Mr Pym was obviously a very particular man. Does it seem likely to you that he would have placed one of those cushions upside down?"

"You're suggesting that someone has moved the cushion?"

Carr's eyes were fixed on the lifeless body of Neville Pym. "A dead man, no wound or weapon evident, and a cushion out of place."

"You think someone stuck that cushion across his face and killed him?" Barber fought hard to keep the insolence and the disbelief out of his voice. Again, Carr offered only a shrug of his shoulders, and Barber did not press the point. "We'll have to wait for the quack to have his say, no matter what."

"Of course," said Everett Carr.

Barber walked back to the body in the chair. "You say you're a visitor to Darton Vale, Mr Carr?

Carr nodded. "I am staying with Mr Bayliss at Darton House."

"A friend of his, are you?"

"An acquaintance," corrected Carr.

"Would you mind telling me, sir, where you were last night?"

Carr was not offended by the question. "I was at dinner with Mrs Bayliss and her son."

"Where was Miss Bayliss?"

"Dining with her fiancé."

"And Bayliss himself?"

Carr shook his head. "I presume he was at the mill. He was late for dinner. He arrived back at Darton House a little after eight o'clock."

Barber contemplated the information for a moment, casting a further glance over the motionless horror of what had once been a living man. "You didn't know Mr Pym very well, I take it?"

"I met him for the first time yesterday."

Barber stroked his chin gently. "And you just called here this morning by chance?"

"He invited me for coffee sometime, and I took the opportunity this morning."

"Why?"

"Pure whim, Inspector." A silence followed, during which Carr mentally dared the inspector to contradict or question his motives. "If I may make a suggestion, Inspector, you may wish to send someone for Mr Eric Hirst. I understand he and Mr Pym were good friends."

Shortly before Eric Hirst's appearance on the scene, the police doctor had arrived and conducted a brief preliminary examination. The time of death could only be estimated at this stage, he had declared, but he wouldn't be surprised if it were not around seven or eight o'clock on the previous evening. For Barber, it was an infuriatingly vague guess, but he knew that there could be no improvement on it until the post-mortem had been undertaken.

"What about the cause of death?" he had asked.

This time, the doctor had been certain. "Asphyxiation. He was smothered to death. Probably with that cushion. It seems out of place, doesn't it?" He had pointed to it.

And Inspector Barber had looked across at Carr with a degree of malice. Carr had offered only a smile in response.

The body had been removed, and the doctor had left by the time Eric Hirst arrived at the cottage. Carr saw at once that Hirst had not finished dressing, since he wore neither tie nor jacket. His shirt sleeves were rolled up, his forearms and his braces were twisted. There was a slight trace of shaving soap at the angle of the jaw, near the ear, showing that he had just finished shaving but had not properly cleaned himself afterwards. This carelessness of appearance suggested urgency to Carr, and that on hearing the news, Hirst had acted promptly.

"Is it true?" he asked. He looked at the chair, and it seemed to pass through his mind that the absence of a body meant that the news was false and the whole business of murder nothing more than a perverted hoax.

As if reading the idea clearly from Hirst's mind, Carr rose to his feet. "It is true."

Hirst stared back at the empty chair. "I can't believe it. I only saw him the other night."

The comment, perfectly natural but almost always irrelevant, hung in the air but received no further reply that could dispel it. Barber walked over to Hirst and took out his official notebook. "You knew Mr Pym well, I believe."

"Yes, we were friends."

"Would it surprise you if I told you that the door to this cottage was not properly closed?"

"It would, yes."

"Would you expect it to be closed and locked?"

"Neville never locked his door until he retired to bed."

"What time would that be as a rule, sir?"

"Half past ten, eleven."

"So, anyone could have got into this cottage last night until somewhere around those times, sir?"

Hirst glared at the inspector. "Why are you asking these questions? Are you suggesting that Neville was killed?"

Barber seemed to loom over Hirst. "I'm not *suggesting* it, sir."

The implication of the inspector's reply was absolute, but Hirst still struggled to believe it. He ran a hand through his hair and shook his head slowly.

"Why would anybody want to kill Neville?"

"Can you think of no reason, sir?"

"None."

Carr cleared his throat gently. "Forgive me, but I understand Mr Pym was very…talkative."

Hirst glared at him. "You mean he was a gossip?"

"I did not wish to use the word," smiled Carr.

Hirst began to pace the room, his hands in his trouser pockets. As he passed the chessboard, he stopped for a moment and gazed down at the position of the game. He saw the Yates book and smiled softly to himself. Then, picking up the black bishop, he moved it towards the white king. He looked across to Carr and Hirst and said simply, "Mate in three moves," before walking on. He looked at the paintings on the walls, the skulls on the mantel, and the flowers in the window. Carr had the sense of a man who had been aware of these representations of taste and life but who now felt as if he were seeing them for the first time. At last, having completed almost a full circuit of the room, he stopped and looked up at the Tuke print. For a long moment, he lingered on the painting, on its depiction of naked young men in a small boat, and he reflected on how much Neville Pym had admired it. He remembered one night when Pym had confessed that he coveted the boys in the artwork, not in a perversely sexual way, but in the purest way possible. To Pym, they had represented freedom from prejudice, protection from loneliness, innocence, companionship, and love. And who, Hirst wondered now, could blame his friend for coveting such things? A tear fell down his cheek, and he allowed it. To wipe it away seemed to him to be too much like a betrayal.

"Neville was a gossip," he said softly. "It's useless to deny it. But I can't for a moment believe it got him killed." He turned to face them. "It was harmless tittle-tattle, nothing more."

Carr had opened his mouth to ask something more, but Inspector Barber strode forward and spoke first. "Would you mind telling me where you were last night, Mr Hirst?"

"I was at home."

"Doing what?"

"Listening to music. Mahler, if it matters."

But it didn't seem to matter to the inspector. "Alone?"

"Yes." The word was clipped with resentment. "Am I a suspect, Inspector?"

Barber smiled grimly. "A little early to be talking about suspects, sir. Just ascertaining facts at the moment."

"Well, the fact is that I was at home, listening to music."

"Very good, sir, thank you." Barber looked intently at him. "And you're sure you can think of no reason why anyone would want to kill Mr Pym?"

Hirst, for reasons he did not understand, looked at Everett Carr. "As I say, the man was a gossip, but he never said anything malicious. Not really."

"What do you mean by that, sir?" asked Barber.

Hirst shuffled his feet. "People don't like to be talked about, do they?"

Barber now leaned closely into Hirst's face. "Are you trying to tell me something, sir?"

Hirst shook his head. "I don't know what I'm saying. I'm just trying to be honest."

"If you have any suspicions, sir, I suggest you tell me them."

"I don't have any suspicions, Inspector. All I'm saying is that Neville liked to talk, and some people don't like it. You asked me for a reason to kill him, and that's my attempt to answer you."

Barber did not reply immediately, but when he did, his voice was heavy with intimidation. "Then thank you, sir. That'll be all for now."

After a moment's deliberation, Hirst nodded and walked slowly to the door. Barber watched him closely, then shifted his gaze to Everett Carr. There was no doubt about his wishes, and Carr was more than willing to oblige. He bowed politely, assured the inspector that he would gladly assist in the investigation, and without waiting for a response, followed Eric Hirst out of the cottage.

# Chapter Fifteen

Outside, Carr found Hirst leaning against the front gate of Mr Pym's cottage, his head sunk on his breast and his face buried in his hands. Carr approached him slowly, not wishing to disturb him without warning, and having no intention of intruding into the man's obvious grief. At the gate, Carr stopped and held his breath in a moment of dignified respect. At last, however, Hirst must have sensed his presence, for he lifted his head from his hands and looked over his shoulder before moving to one side with an apology. Bowing gently in acknowledgement, Carr lifted the latch of the gate and stepped onto the pavement.

"My condolences on the loss of your friend, Mr Hirst," he said.

"Thank you." Hirst now looked keenly at Carr, as if the importance of what he had said had finally struck him. "You know my name?"

"Forgive me, yes, I do. I am staying at Darton House."

Hirst smiled gently. "You're Arthur Bayliss' friend from London."

"Everett Carr." He held out his hand, and Hirst shook it politely. "I hope you didn't mind my suggesting to the inspector that he send for you."

"Not at all." Hirst looked back at Pym's cottage, and for a moment, the sight of the horror inside returned to his mental vision. "It was rather a shock, though. Poor Neville."

"I had no wish to be rude when I mentioned that he was fond of talking."

Hirst smiled. "It's only the truth. He was a gossip."

"Indeed."

"You were about to say something, I think, when the inspector interrupted you," said Hirst.

Carr seemed not to have remembered, although, had Hirst known him better, he would have recognised the deliberate obfuscation. "Oh, yes, of course. I was only wondering, you see, whether Mr Pym's tendency to gossip might have meant he discovered something dangerous without him knowing it."

"Dangerous?"

Carr murmured assent. "I'm trying to account for his death, you see."

Hirst's expression seemed to darken. "To be honest, Mr Carr, if anyone in this town was going to be murdered, I should say that Neville Pym would be far down the list of possible victims."

"And who would be first?"

"I wouldn't like to say, but you could draw your own conclusions, no doubt."

"My host, perhaps?"

"Has he told you about the incidents at the mill?"

"Yes, including the threatening letter." For a long moment, Carr was lost in silent thought, his eyes drifting back and forth from the cottage door. "Mr Pym is altogether the wrong victim."

Hirst thought for a moment. "Unless…?"

The word, so simple and common, seemed to Carr to be suddenly momentous. He waited for Hirst to continue, but nothing came, and it was not until Carr repeated the word that Hirst brought his thoughts back into focus.

"Unless Bayliss murdered Pym himself," he said.

Carr frowned. "But what motive could he have?"

"Pym's fondness for gossip, as you said." Hirst now lowered his voice. "Pym knew something about Arthur Bayliss. Something Arthur wouldn't want getting out."

"Indeed?"

Hirst began to walk slowly down the lane, Carr following painfully behind. "There's a young lady who lives close to here, Mr Carr, called Lydia Stansfield. She's a very beautiful girl, kind, generous. The sort of girl that makes you remember why you keep getting up in the morning."

"I see." There was an inflexion to Carr's voice that showed that an inference had been made.

Hirst smiled. "I'm afraid she may not feel that way about me. We're friends, but I don't think it would be anything more than that. She loves someone else."

And Carr drew another inference. "Mr Bayliss?"

"You see now what I'm driving at about Neville?"

Carr nodded. "A wealthy businessman, married, and a younger lover?"

"And only a lowly shop assistant at that."

"And Mr Pym knew about Mr Bayliss and this lady?"

Hirst gave a muted acknowledgement. "Arthur was in line for the next Honours list. I doubt such an affair would do him much good if it became known. Does that constitute a motive for murder?"

"It may well do," conceded Carr. "You should tell Inspector Barber."

But Hirst shook his head. "No, Mr Carr. For Lydia's sake, I won't do that. It isn't my secret to divulge."

Carr could admire the morality of the sentiment, even if he was forced to question the wisdom of it. "Is it possible that Mr Pym was the mill saboteur?"

The question brought Hirst to a standstill. "Whatever makes you think that?"

"Last night, someone threw acid onto Mr Bayliss' motor car. He said that he would murder the person responsible if he ever got hold of him."

"Acid on the pride and joy?" Hirst was more amused than shocked. "Yes, that would cause Arthur a great deal of outrage."

Carr continued with his thoughts. "The mill poltergeist had already smashed the headlamps of Mr Bayliss' motor car, I understand, so I wondered whether the same person was responsible for the acid attack. And now, Mr Pym lies dead, and as you say…"

"Bayliss might have killed him." Hirst thought for a moment, then shook his head. "I can't imagine Neville putting a dead rat in a drawer, Mr Carr. He wouldn't have had the courage to pick one up, for one thing. And acid? He'd be too frightened of spilling it on his suit." Hirst smiled fondly for a moment.

"Besides, Neville wasn't that sort of person. He wasn't confrontational in the slightest."

"Nor was it he who received a threatening letter," said Carr. "And so, we must ask ourselves again why he was killed."

"And that brings us back to Lydia. Or one of the others," Hirst added softly.

"Others?"

"According to Neville, Arthur Bayliss has had numerous affairs."

"Dear me," was all Carr said, but he felt so much more. He was not sure if it was disappointment or disgust; it might conceivably have been a combination of the two.

Hirst had also fallen silent, his brows furrowed and his mind racing with thoughts and memories of Neville Pym. "You know, there's something else he said about Bayliss' affairs. He wondered about the consequences of them."

"Consequences?" Carr felt he knew what Hirst meant by the word, but, likewise, he felt that clarification was perhaps sensible.

Hirst stared coldly into Carr's eyes. "He said Bayliss couldn't expect to have these affairs and not run the risk of what he called the consequences. He meant children," he added needlessly.

"There is perhaps another motive," said Carr. "If Mr Pym knew of such a child, Mr Bayliss may have wanted to ensure he was kept silent about it."

"But it was only an idea of Neville's," Hirst said. "A casual remark. There was no proof he was right."

Carr smiled. "Quite so."

He was about to speak again when he saw that Hirst seemed to be captivated by something in the distance. Following his gaze, Carr saw the figure of a young woman crossing the main street of the town ahead of them. She was too far away for Carr to distinguish any features, but he had an impression of grace and style emanating from the way she walked and the poise with which she carried herself.

"There's Lydia," said Hirst, pointing in the woman's direction. "I'll go and break the news to her. It'll be best coming from me, I'm sure. Would you excuse me?"

Carr limped slowly back down Church Lane, his mind drifting back over the events of the morning. In particular, he found himself fascinated by the personality of Mr Pym. The question of motive gnawed at Carr's mind like a plague. The man had been murdered, that was certain, and murder had not in Carr's experience ever been committed without reason. The closest thing to a motive Carr could consider was Mr Pym's nature and his fondness for gossip. It was not a stretch of the imagination that such people might unwittingly uncover secrets that certain other people would wish to keep buried. And therein, as Carr well knew, could lie a motive for murder.

And yet, it was Arthur Bayliss whose children seemed to hate him. It was Arthur Bayliss who was unfaithful to his wife. It was Arthur Bayliss who was the subject of persecution and threatening letters. It was Arthur Bayliss who was a much more likely victim of murder than Neville Pym. But still, it was Arthur Bayliss who was alive, and Neville Pym who was dead. The wrong way round, as Eric Hirst had put it.

Carr was now at the church. He walked up the small pathway to the door and entered. He did not expect to find any religious salvation or sanctuary, but he suddenly craved the special sense of peace that comes only from the house of God. It was a silence like no other, a divine quiet perhaps, and it was one that Carr now needed in order to allow his thoughts to develop and his understanding to grow. And perhaps, if his conscience and abandoned faith could allow him to do it, to offer a silent prayer for the soul of Neville Pym, a man whose life, for whatever reason, had been stolen from him.

Sitting in the calm silence of the church, these thoughts raging in his mind, Everett Carr repeated over and over to himself that Neville Pym had been murdered. And with each repetition of the thought, Carr became increasingly certain that he wanted, very badly indeed, to understand why.

# Chapter Sixteen

It did not take long for the news to break. Darton Vale had witnessed many things over the centuries of its existence. It had been a party to civil war, to revolution, both economic and industrial, to manufacture, to famine, and to the horrors of global conflict. Some said it would soon be witness to a second if Germany could not be assuaged, and some said the opposite. Some had seen enterprises like the Bayliss and Toole mills be opened and closed, victims of bankruptcy and financial disasters. The town had seen and experienced much, but never had it been home to murder. Rumours that the most dreadful crime of all had been committed circulated almost immediately and, with a speed that amazed even Everett Carr, those rumours became matters of undeniable fact.

That Carr had discovered the body was a detail that was less widely known. In various parts of the town, the identity of the person who had discovered the crime was reduced to being, in turn, a friend of Mr Bayliss, a stranger, a passer-by, a visitor, or a guest of them up at the house. A distinct identity, or even a name, was not applied, save at Darton House itself and those people who had been directly concerned with Neville Pym.

Carr had spent perhaps an hour in the church, being disturbed by the vicar only once, with a polite and gentle enquiry as to Carr's well-being. Carr had assured the vicar of his health and had expressed a hope that he was not intruding. The vicar had given suitable assurances on the matter, and Carr had been left in subsequent peace. But the spiritual silence that he so enjoyed had done nothing to calm his mind or to provide answers to those questions that beat in his brain like an orchestra of hammers. At last, he had left the church and returned to Darton House, frustrated and confused, and seemingly as far from any grasp of the situation as he had been before.

His arrival back at the house had been heard, it seemed, because Marjorie Bayliss emerged from the drawing room and invited him to join her. Carr was grateful for the diversion, and he hung up his hat and coat with care before limping towards her with a smile.

"We have heard the news, of course, Mr Carr," she said. "We wondered what had happened to you. Are you all right?"

He bowed. "I am perfectly well, dear lady, thank you."

"Such a terrible business," she said breathlessly.

"Everything is fine, I assure you," he felt obliged to say. "Although I should very much like a cup of coffee."

"Of course, of course. At once." She escorted him to the drawing room and rang for refreshment.

As he entered, Carr saw Arthur Bayliss sitting in an armchair, a newspaper held in front of his face, and a glass of what might have been sherry on a small table to his side. Carr was strangely surprised to see him, and it must have shown in his expression, because when Bayliss lowered the newspaper, he stared at Carr and smiled broadly.

"Not at the mill for once," he said. "That's what you're thinking, isn't it, Mr Carr?"

"Not at all," lied Carr.

Bayliss got to his feet, slamming the newspaper back into the chair. He walked to Carr and gripped his hand, shaking it warmly. "I've been a rotten host, sir, and I hope you can forgive me. I invite you up here and then neglect you, leave you to your own devices, and then find you've discovered a murder. Damned rotten, it is."

Carr waved aside the apology. "You have much on your mind."

"Shame about Pym," said Bayliss. "Harmless enough, I suppose."

"Did you know him well?" asked Carr.

"Didn't know him at all, really. Knew what he was, of course, but that was obvious to anybody."

"A gossip, you mean?" asked Carr tauntingly.

"Partly," sniffed Bayliss. "Bloody unnatural. No wonder Henry was drinking with him the other night, is it?"

"For God's sake," hissed Marjorie. Her eyes burned with malice, and when she spoke next, her voice struggled to contain its anger. "Must you be so disgusting?"

"It's men like Pym and Henry who are disgusting," barked Bayliss.

Marjorie almost screamed in outrage. "The man is dead! Have some respect!"

She stared at her husband for a long moment, and then, as if she had forgotten his presence, her eyes flickered to Everett Carr. She muttered an apology and said something about having letters to write, after which she left the room. Carr had detected the lie about her correspondence, but he did not express as much. Instead, he looked sadly at the door she had closed behind her and tried to extinguish the embarrassment he had felt at the outburst. At last, accepting defeat in the attempt, he turned back to Arthur Bayliss, who was now helping himself to more sherry.

"Marjorie has always been a little highly strung," he said. "Trying times all round, of course, so she's bound to be upset."

Carr did not reply. There was nothing to say in response, but even if there had been, he doubted he would have been able to utter the words without displaying some degree of revulsion at the attitude of his host. There was an awkward silence that neither of them knew how to break, and Carr suspected that Bayliss was a relieved as he was when the maid came in with the coffee.

Finally, as he sat back in his armchair, it was Bayliss who broke the stalemate. "It was murder, then? Pym, I mean."

"I'm afraid so."

"Can't imagine why anybody would want to kill him."

"Can you not?" asked Carr, softly.

There was something about his tone of voice that seized Bayliss' attention. "Are you suggesting I should have an idea about it?"

Carr shrugged. "I wondered about it."

"You might have to explain that, Mr Carr." Bayliss' voice was now openly antagonistic.

Carr looked across at him, his dark eyes alive with purpose. "Tell me about Lydia Stansfield."

Bayliss had the grace to look surprised, but it lasted only for a moment before a grin broke out across his face. "People have been talking, have they?"

"Tell me about her," Carr repeated.

"Nothing to tell. She works in a hat shop in the town, lives in a small house off the high street, and gave an old man a wild good time for a couple of months."

Carr's disgust threatened to overwhelm him. "You had an affair with her?"

"She'd call it that, yes. I call it something quite different."

"It is over now, I take it?"

"I ended it yesterday."

"May I ask why?"

Bayliss lit a cigar. "I'm likely to be mentioned in the next Honours list, Mr Carr. A kiss and a grope with a shop lass wouldn't do much to help those chances."

"Perhaps you should have thought about that before you betrayed your wife," said Carr.

Bayliss blew a smoke ring. "I thought you were a man of the world."

"Not, perhaps, of your world," said Carr gently. "Mr Pym knew of this affair?"

"He told you that, did he?"

"No."

"Then how do you know?"

"He told someone about it."

Bayliss nodded slowly. "Eric, I suppose. It's something Pym would do. They were friends, and it would have given him a sick pleasure to tell Eric of all people. He thinks he's in love with Lydia himself. But she's not interested in him. Too besotted with me."

The arrogance was appalling, and Carr felt the best thing to do with it was to ignore it. "But now you've ended it…"

"That won't matter. She still won't give Eric what he wants." He inhaled deeply on the cigar. Then, slowly, he got to his feet. He picked up the sherry glass and sipped at the drink thoughtfully. "So, Pym knew about me and Lydia, did he? Didn't have the guts to speak to me about it, true to bloody form."

"How might he have found out?"

Bayliss glared down at Carr with an undisguised malevolence. "Because he was a bloody spy. He thinks I didn't see him all those times he was snooping on me with his binoculars."

"With Lydia Stansfield?"

"And others." Later, Carr would wonder whether Bayliss secretly chastised himself for this indiscreet admission. "I've seen him all over the place. Up near Devil's Corner, lurking along Church Lane, sitting across from me in tea shops, in pubs, always watching, always spying."

"Did he ever talk to you about seeing you?"

"Blackmail, you mean? Never. He'd know how I'd react to that."

Carr felt he knew it too, but he was also considering the very real possibility that Bayliss' story was fuelled by paranoid guilt and coincidence rather than any active snooping on Mr Pym's part. Was it not possible that Mr Pym just happened to be in the same places as Bayliss and his illicit lovers?

"Could Mr Pym have been the poltergeist?" Carr asked.

"Unlikely, I'd have said. Why do you ask?"

Carr rose slowly to his feet and limped over to stand in front of Bayliss. His dark eyes were coldly authoritative. "I'm trying to understand some motive for Mr Pym's death."

"Am I being accused of something, Carr?" Bayliss' eyes hooded with suppressed anger.

"Not at all," said Carr. "But the question of why Mr Pym was killed has to be asked, and as far as I can ascertain, nobody can understand the motive for the murder. It must be found and explained."

"You're saying that Lydia is a motive for me to kill Pym?"

"I'm suggesting that it is not something you would wish to become known."

"Same thing," said Bayliss. He inhaled deeply on the cigar. "The affair was over. There was nothing to tell."

Carr shrugged. "You must see how it might look to the police. They need a motive for the crime, and you have one in Miss Stansfield. You may have two, if we include the possibility that Mr Pym was the saboteur. Where were you last night, before you arrived home?"

"What business is it of yours?"

"None." And yet, his stare and the honesty of his response seemed to make any refusal to answer seem simultaneously squalid and petty.

"I was walking home from the mill," said Bayliss.

"Alone?"

"Of course. Nobody was around, the place was as quiet as the grave."

"You saw nobody at all?"

Bayliss thought for a moment, and a memory stirred. "Actually, I saw old Jock McGregor, the mechanic, on his way home."

"Did you speak to him?"

"We had a natter, aye."

"I see." Carr thought for a moment. "Might I ask how Miss Stansfield responded when you ended your relationship with her?"

Bayliss gave a dismissive snort. "Like they all do. She refused to believe it and then tried to blackmail me into continuing it. None of them has any self-respect, don't you find?"

"No," said Carr seriously. "No, I don't find that at all."

It was a rebuke, and Bayliss could hardly have failed to recognise it as such, but he made no comment or remonstrance against it. He simply smiled to himself, keeping his eyes fixed on Carr, and smoked his cigar. The sherry was drained completely, the glass placed on the mantelpiece, not to be refilled just yet.

"I realise that you're offended by my behaviour," said Bayliss. "Adultery is reprehensible, of course it is, but I cannot change my nature. I wish I could.

Some pleasures, I cannot resist."

Carr shook his head. "You are not entirely consistent."

"I beg your pardon?"

"You say that you broke off the affair with Miss Stansfield because of the risk of scandal affecting your potential peerage. Now, you say you cannot escape your natural urges. If that is true, there will be future Lydia Stansfields, and your peerage is endangered in any event. You cannot have it both ways."

Bayliss nodded slowly. "A fair assessment. Perhaps the reason I gave Lydia was a little...manufactured. The truth is," he added, lowering his voice, "I'd grown tired of the girl. She wanted me to leave my wife for her."

"Is that so unreasonable a request in the circumstances?" asked Carr.

"I love my wife, Mr Carr. I don't expect you to believe that or even to understand it, but it's true. Marjorie has been with me for years, by my side through the very worst times in my life. She means everything to me. The others mean nothing. They're distractions, diversions, and they have nothing to do with love."

"You are right," said Carr, sadly. "I neither understand nor believe you, but I have no right to an opinion on it," he added. "And I certainly have no right to judge you for it. But I caution you."

"Against what?"

"Revenge. A life lived the way you live yours will never be free from danger. And we know you have at least one enemy."

Bayliss laughed grimly. "I've always been aware that I have enemies, Mr Carr, but not one of them has defeated me. On the contrary, I've got rid of all of them. Believe that if you don't believe anything else about me."

Carr was contemplating him closely, a vision of Neville Pym's dead face flickering across his memory. "Yes, that I can believe."

Bayliss leaned closely into Carr's face. "If anybody comes after me looking for blood, they'd better be prepared to shed some of their own for the privilege."

It was not meant as a threat against Carr personally, but it was almost impossible not to be taken as one. Carr took a step back from it, swallowing hard, and for the first time, he seemed keenly aware of the malevolence in Arthur Bayliss. For once, he did not see the brash vulgarity, the obnoxious attitude, nor the uncouth tastes. All he seemed able to see was the malicious violence of the man, and what he saw was a capacity for violence that alarmed him. He felt as if he should speak, but no words seemed to matter, and nothing he might have said seemed relevant. All he could offer was silence.

"Now, Mr Carr," Bayliss purred, his voice ingratiating and all trace of his internal malice gone, "I think I have been a bad host for long enough. Perhaps you would like to have some lunch with me. We can go down to *The Black Bull*. How does that grab you?"

In truth, Carr could think of nothing he would have disliked more, but he did not have the heart, or perhaps the courage, to refuse. And it occurred to him, as he donned his hat and coat, that Arthur Bayliss would not have expected or accepted any such refusal. The invitation had not been a request, but a command in disguise, and Everett Carr had felt as if he had no option other than to obey it.

# Chapter Seventeen

Everett Carr was not a man who frequented public houses with any regularity. They had never held much of an appeal for him, his preferences having always been for restaurants and, latterly, the confines of the Icarus Club, as well as the sanctity of his own rooms in the Albany. Public houses, by comparison, had always seemed to him to be cramped, crowded, and unduly noisy places, where excessive drinking was more prevalent than polite conversation, and where the possibility of unwanted unpleasantness and raucous argument could not be ignored.

Nevertheless, as he entered *The Black Bull* in Darton Vale, he could not deny its aura of simple hospitality. It had turned cold outside, and the first thing inside the pub that attracted Carr's attention was the blazing fire in an impressive grate in the far wall where, if he only knew it, Henry Bayliss and Michael Arden had scuffled together, only a couple of days before. Beside it now, sitting across from each other, were two aged drinkers, engrossed in a game of dominoes, at whose feet lay two supine dogs, who were seemingly as old as their respective masters. Scattered around the pub were similar types, some engaged in gentle conversation, some reading newspapers, some playing cards, and some sitting in silent, private thought.

Bayliss led him to the bar and ordered two pints of local ale. Carr at once held up a hand in protest.

"Forgive me, but I do not tend to drink beer," he said. "Perhaps a glass of wine, if I may. Or a small whisky."

The landlord bowed, but Bayliss slammed his hand down on the bar with a grin. "Nonsense. Best brew this side of the Pennines, Mr Carr, and once drunk, you'll never go back. We're proud of our Darton beer, aren't we, Jack?"

The landlord bowed again. "Aye, sir, we are."

Bayliss looked at Carr. "Old Charlie Beech runs the Darton Vale Brewery, Mr Carr. What Charlie doesn't know about hops and mash isn't worth knowing, you take my word for it."

Carr was willing to do so, and he smiled politely as the landlord began to draw a pint of the stuff. It drained into the glass like bathwater down a drain, a deep brown and foaming liquid rising up the side of the glass. Carr watched with barely disguised distaste in his eyes, although the smile remained fixed on his lips.

"Perhaps half a pint for now," he forced himself to say.

The landlord obliged, and Carr took a suspicious sip of the foaming drink. It was everything he had expected, but he smiled a forced appreciation of it. Bayliss was not fooled, however, and he gave a guttural laugh as he turned away from the bar and took a mouthful of his pint of Charlie Beech's product. As he did so, and as Carr followed suit, they both saw Eric Hirst and Lydia Stansfield staring at them from a table in the far corner. Bayliss nodded a greeting, raising his glass in a facetious toast, and he directed Carr to a table on the opposite side of the pub. Carr glanced only briefly once more at Hirst and Lydia, and then joined his host.

"Do you want to leave?" Eric Hirst asked as he watched Bayliss and Carr take their seats.

"No," said Lydia with determination. "I'll be damned if I'll let him force me into hiding."

"If you're sure." Hirst drank some of his own beer. "I could kill him for what he's done. To you, I mean," he added, as though it needed clarifying.

"Don't talk like that." She sipped at her gin. "You must never talk like that."

"Even if it's true?"

"Especially then," she said with a forced smile. "Let's just ignore him. Who's that little man with him? With the moustache and beard?"

Hirst was aware of Carr's eyes on them, and he wondered for a moment what Bayliss was saying. The only thing that stopped Hirst from thinking that they were talking about him and Lydia was the distracted expression in Carr's eyes. Whatever Bayliss was saying, Hirst thought, Carr's attention was not reserved for it, exclusively or otherwise. He was more interested in them, it seemed, and that meant surely that Bayliss was talking about something else entirely.

"His name is Everett Carr," Hirst said in reply. "Some friend of Arthur's. It was he who found Neville's body."

"Good God," said Lydia under her breath. "He looks far too nice to be a friend of Arthur's, though."

It was true, and Hirst himself had felt something similar when he had spoken to Carr earlier that day. But he wondered whether Lydia felt it only because of the negative feelings she currently held for Bayliss. Would she have said anything like it before their affair had ended? Somehow, Hirst doubted it.

"I suppose he'll be there tomorrow night," said Hirst.

"Tomorrow night?"

And now, he regretted saying anything. "I'm dining at Darton House."

"With Arthur?"

His voice lowered. "Yes."

"I see."

"I can cancel the appointment."

She shook her head, smiling at him. "You don't have to do that, and nor will you. I can't expect you or anyone else to avoid him on my account. I'm jealous, that's all," she added with a subtle breaking of her voice. "Foolish, of course, to be jealous of a dinner invitation."

"You have no reason to be jealous."

"Perhaps not," she said, wiping away a tear. "But would you do something for me?"

"Of course."

She looked at him with a dark seriousness. "Let me have my jealousy."

In that moment, as she turned her head to look back over to Bayliss, Hirst felt something of his heart break irreparably.

"What will you do now? After Arthur, I mean."

The question surprised her, and she was taken aback by its abruptness. The truth was that she had given it no thought. There had not seemed time to her to contemplate the future, only to deal with the present, however dreadful and bitter it was.

"I hadn't thought," she said. "I'm too busy trying to understand my here and now, Eric, to worry about my future."

He felt an immediate stupidity. "Of course, I'm sorry. I just…"

*Don't want you to leave.* Those were the words he managed to prevent from coming out of his mouth. If he said them, he knew, there would be no turning back. Not for her, and not for him. It would be a declaration of some sort, a revealing of private thoughts that he was not perhaps ready to share and which he felt sure she was not ready to hear.

"I just don't want you to do anything rash," he said instead. "That's all."

She smiled at him. "Such as what, Eric? Shoot him down like a dog?"

"No," said Hirst, frankly.

"It's you who talked about wanting to kill him, not me."

Hirst closed his eyes in frustration. This was going so badly. "I didn't for a moment think you'd want to kill him."

Lydia drank more gin and looked into his eyes. "Perhaps it isn't such a bad idea after all. It couldn't make me feel worse than I already do."

Eric looked over to her. "I think we had both better stop talking about murder."

Lydia took his unspoken point immediately. "You're right, I'm sorry. Murder is very real, isn't it? We shouldn't joke about it, not after Mr Pym."

Hirst drank some beer and glanced unwittingly over to Bayliss. "Neville knew about you and Arthur, you know." It was clear from her expression that she did not know it. "I'm afraid it's true," Hirst continued. "It rather gives Arthur a motive, wouldn't you say?"

Her reply was emphatic. "No, I wouldn't say, Eric."

He looked over to her sharply. Initially, he had taken her decisive response as being in defence of her former lover and, as such, he had felt anger swell within him. When he looked into her eyes, however, he saw the other interpretation of it clearly defined, although he was quick to dismiss the idea.

"You wouldn't have killed Neville because he knew of the affair," Hirst argued. "You didn't want it kept secret, only Arthur did, because of his bloody reputation and this business about the Honours list."

"I love him, Eric," said Lydia, her voice low but without emotion. "Women have been known to kill to protect the men they love."

The words, so difficult for him to hear, were nevertheless impossible to deny. "You didn't kill Neville Pym."

Lydia shuffled in her seat. "Can we stop talking about murder, please, like you said just now? It gives me the jitters."

Hirst drained his glass. "You're right. Let's have another and talk about something else. Another drink?" he added with a smile.

"No, thank you. I have to get back to the shop soon. But you stay and have one."

"I suppose I can, since my boss is doing it," Hirst smiled. "Although perhaps I'd better not, thinking about it." An idea occurred to him. "Look, why don't you come to my house tomorrow night for a drink?"

"You're dining at Darton House, if you recall."

"Before that. How about it?"

Lydia thought for a moment, her instincts telling her to refuse, but the eager anticipation on Hirst's face suggesting strongly that it would be churlish to do so. "I wouldn't want to intrude."

"You wouldn't be doing. One drink, that's all."

At last, she nodded. "One drink, Eric. And no talk about…" But she left the word unsaid, and it had not needed to be spoken at all. He understood only too well.

Even if Eric Hirst had needed an explanation, however, he would not have received it, as matters beyond his control were about to overtake him. Without warning, and with an almost violent attack on its hinges, the door to the pub opened, and Michael Arden entered.

# Chapter Eighteen

s Arden disappeared inside *The Black* Bull, Rosamund Bayliss was walking down Church Lane, her mind ablaze with conflicting thoughts and emotions.

On the previous evening, she had followed Henry's advice. She had gone to dinner with George Toole and his family, and she had eaten the food and drunk the wine with polite appreciation of both, but at the back of her mind had been her purpose for the evening. Henry had said that George had a right to defend himself against the lies she had uncovered, and on reflection, Rosamund had come to agree. And so, she had told herself, before the men retired for brandy and cigars, she would give George that opportunity. If she had any premonition or prejudice about whether he would pass the test or not, she did not voice them, nor did she consider them.

It had been as they filed out of the dining room that she had pulled him to one side. He had been surprised by the action, and he had stared at her for a long moment, his confusion soon becoming replaced by disagreement.

"What do you think you're doing?" he had asked.

"I want to ask you a question, George, and I want the truth."

"All right." He had pulled himself free of her grip and had stood in front of her, his poise balanced, almost belligerent, as if he was prepared for anything that she might say, although she could not believe that he was.

"Last night, you said you were working late at the office. This morning, I asked you again where you were last night, and you said it again."

"Because I was."

She had resisted the temptation to shout, and she had felt herself fighting the urge to cry in frustration. "I telephoned you at the office last night. Nobody had seen you since the late afternoon."

"And?" The word had been said with an attempt at confrontational defiance, and for the most part, it had been successful, but Rosamund had seen the faint glimmer of embarrassed fear in his eyes, and the swift movement of his fingers to scratch the side of his nose betrayed the untruth.

"Where were you really?"

"At the office." He had shaken his head in what she had assumed was perceived outrage at her paranoia. "Just because people didn't see me there doesn't mean I wasn't. It only means nobody saw me. Nobody came to the office, so nobody would see me."

"Why didn't you answer the telephone?" she had asked, refusing to be deflected.

"I must have been away from my desk." He had shrugged dismissively.

"So, you were wandering around your mill, which meant you didn't hear the phone, but still nobody saw you?"

It sounded incredible, and Toole had known it. He had replied, "Yes," but the word had held almost no meaning.

Rosamund had glared at him. "You're a liar, George. *A liar.*"

For a moment, she had thought he was going to strike her. His eyes had burned with disgust, and his lips had hardened into a grim sneer of suppressed violence. Rosamund had prepared herself for a blow, refusing to cower from it or show any weakness in the wake of what she knew had been the truth, but nothing in fact had come, and yet it had seemed to her that they were standing in the silent aftermath of something momentous.

"Why are we getting married, George?" she had asked.

He had not known how to reply. Memories of that fateful lunch in the Midland Hotel in Manchester had come back to Toole's memory, but he had denied them any voice. Instead, humiliated and impotent, he had said nothing.

"Neither of us knows, do we?" Rosamund had answered for them both.

And still, Toole had found no words, feeling himself strangled into silence by his own cowardice and folly.

Slowly, Rosamund had removed the ring from her finger, taken one of his hands in hers, and placed it in his palm. "I think you'd better have this back."

"Please, don't…" His voice had found itself, but the words had been nothing more than faint whispers of useless protest.

"I'm doing it so we can both be happy," she had said, walking away from him, and longing for an excuse to go home.

"We can be happy, Rosamund," he had said. "Please, don't do this. I just need to sort a few things out with some people, that's all. I just need a little time."

"To sort what out? What people?"

She had waited for him to reply, but he had only rolled his eyes and sighed in what she had taken to be exasperation. Later, thinking about it again, it had seemed more like frustration, possibly even desperation.

"You can't be honest with me, can you?" She had said, when he had offered no reply. "Is there someone else? Is that it?"

"No!" He had seemed genuinely horrified by the idea. "It's nothing like that. Look…"

But the words had not come. They had been stifled by an exhalation of meaningless, futile air.

Now, stroking the empty space where the engagement ring had once been, Rosamund began to feel again those spasms of regret that had plagued her at breakfast. Her finger seemed somehow unnatural without the ring, the pale skin strangely and almost indecently exposed. Everett Carr had noticed its absence at breakfast; she was sure of it, and she was grateful then and now that his politeness, good manners, discretion, or all three had prevented him from mentioning it.

She put her hands in her trouser pockets, as if to hide her naked finger from herself, and continued to walk towards the town. She tried not to think about George Toole, but it was perhaps inevitable that her mind would not permit it. But when she thought of him now, it was not with any degree of regret, but with a determination. He was lying to her, certainly, but she did not think that it was a pathological necessity for him. There was a definite reason for his deceit, and Rosamund needed to know what it was. Her instinct was another woman, but she dismissed the idea.

Which meant it was something else he wanted to keep secret…

"Rosamund?"

His voice, clear and commanding, startled her. It brought her out of her internal conflicts so abruptly that, for a moment, she seemed not to recall where she was. The high street, the church, and the surrounding hills all seemed alien and unfamiliar to her in that brief moment of surprise.

"George…" she stammered.

Toole was standing ahead of her, his hands behind his back, and an expression of determination on his face. "I want to talk about last night."

She rolled her eyes. "Oh, George, what's left to say?"

"I think there's plenty to say." He stepped towards her. "I should apologise to you, at least."

"For lying to me?"

"Amongst other things."

She seemed to lurch physically at the words. "Is lying to me not enough?"

Toole held her gaze for a long moment. "I will tell you the truth, Rosamund, about where I've been and why I've lied. You deserve the truth, although in light of what happened last night, I don't suppose it can matter now. All too late," he added with a deflated laugh.

"Far too late," she said. Then, after a moment, she asked: "Are you in trouble, George?"

"Nothing I can't get out of, I don't think," he replied.

It was not enough, she thought, but Rosamund had to admit that it was honest if nothing else. "What sort of trouble?"

"Look, that is my problem, and I can deal with it. What I wanted to talk to you about concerns us both."

"What is it?"

Toole inhaled deeply. "You asked me last night why we were getting married. I couldn't answer you then, but I will now."

"What *is* it?"

"It's your father, Rosamund. It's all to do with your father."

"What are you *saying*, George?"

She felt as if she could scream the question into his face, and she cursed the limp, pathetic manner in which the words came out of her mouth. She glared into his eyes, her mouth hanging open uselessly, and her brain seemed to collapse under confusion. If there were not such an earnest and apologetic urgency in Toole's expression, she would have slapped his face and pushed him aside. As it was, she stood staring blankly at him.

"Let's go somewhere," Toole pleaded. "We have to talk. I have to explain."

Rosamund was about to respond, without knowing quite what she would say, but her words were interrupted by the sound of shouting. She glanced over Toole's shoulder and saw her father and Michael Arden standing outside *The Black Bull*. She watched as Arden marched away from the pub and her father gesticulated behind him. She could hear her father's raised voice, but she was too far away to distinguish actual words, so that the sounds were merely angry grunts. Her father then turned on his heel and disappeared back inside the pub.

"What's going on?" asked Rosamund.

Toole shook his head. "It doesn't matter. What matters is your father and us, Rosamund!"

"Just give me a moment, George."

She ran down Church Lane, so swiftly that on occasion she feared she might lose her footing. She did not, but by the time she caught up with Arden, her lungs were ablaze with effort, and her brow beaded with sweat. She overtook him slightly, so that she stood in his way, and he was forced to stop walking.

"Michael, what's the matter?" she asked.

"Leave me alone, Miss Bayliss." His eyes were livid with anger.

She seemed hurt by the formality. "Rosamund, please."

Toole had raced after Rosamund and was now pulling at her elbow. "Come on, darling, let him be."

She pulled herself free of his grasp. "I saw you with my father, Michael. What's he said to you?"

Arden stared at her as if seeing her for the first time, and his expression changed slowly from hatred to something approaching confusion. The angry hatred returned to his face. Under his breath, Arden growled words that sounded to her like "Your fucking family," before spitting at her feet and pushing her aside. As farewells went, it was as ignoble as it was offensive. Toole made a comment of disgusted protestation, but to Arden it meant as much as the barking of a stray dog.

Rosamund, shaken and disturbed, looked towards the pub, and an image of her father came into her mind. In that moment, she could think of nothing but how wonderful it would be to be free of him. Not only for her, but for others. How many lives had he blighted? How many people had he damaged? It was not the first time such a thought had entered her head, but something about that morning made it seem altogether more enticing. And what would it require, this taking of his life? Only a moment's nerve, a second's worth of courage on her part. Suddenly, to herself alone, Rosamund smiled.

Just that one second of wickedness, and then no more torment.

# Chapter Nineteen

oments earlier, as he had entered the pub, Arden had seen Arthur Bayliss immediately.

He was sitting with a stranger, a gentleman who appeared old but whose dark eyes suggested a vitality that belied the white hair of the head and the ornate moustache. Arden took very little notice of him. He paid no attention to Bayliss either, apart from the initial recoil at seeing the man. Arden had no wish to speak to him. He had come for a quick lunchtime pint of ale, and nothing more. He wanted no trouble. He wanted no conversation. He wanted nothing from anybody, least of all from Arthur Bayliss.

He ordered his drink and stood at the bar, his elbows resting on the edge of it, and his head slumped forward. He wondered whether it would have been better to turn on his heel and walk straight back out of the pub the moment he had seen Bayliss, but it was too late now. The decision had been made, and Arden did not regret it. Nothing he had learned about Bayliss would drive Arden from his local. He wouldn't give the bastard the satisfaction. But how he hated the man. It was impossible to deny it, just as it was impossible to deny how good it would feel to have his hands around Bayliss' throat, choking the life from his obscene carcass, or seeing his blood flow from a gunshot wound to his chest, to see those nasty eyes widen in horror at the advent of death.

And Hirst was in the pub too, Arden had noticed. He could feel those eyes on his back, too, throwing invisible knives between his shoulder blades. Arden didn't mind that Hirst hated him, but it angered him that the cause for Hirst's animosity was unfounded. What had happened to Emma had not been Arden's fault, whatever Hirst believed. Arden had tried to convince him of it too often in the past, each time being ignored and disbelieved, so that now he had stopped trying to justify himself. He no longer cared what Hirst believed, and he cared even less about what Hirst thought about him. Let him hate; it was his own time he was wasting. But Bayliss was something entirely different. In his case, the hatred was mutual.

Arden was halfway down his pint of beer when he sensed a movement at his elbow. He didn't need to look up to know that Bayliss was standing beside him. Arden kept his focus on the foam head of his drink, and he tried not to listen to Bayliss' voice when it ordered another pint for himself and a glass of wine, this time, for Everett Carr.

"Get you one, lad?" he asked.

The word, at once patronising and loathsome, rankled. Arden shook his head, willing himself not to speak. It was as if engaging in any form of conversation with Bayliss would mean some sort of bond between them. He fought hard against the memory of a couple of nights ago, when he had gone through his mother's papers, and when the first thoughts of murder had come into his head.

"Just having the one and then going back to the mill, eh?" said Bayliss. "Very wise."

Arden did not know what to make of the comment. Was it a rebuke for drinking in working hours? Surely not. Arden made no secret of how he spent his lunchtimes. If it were a problem, either Bayliss or Hirst would have taken pleasure in telling him so, but neither ever had. So, why say anything at all?

"I wanted to have a word with you, as it happens, Arden," Bayliss said. It did not require a response, not really, and Arden was not about to provide one. "I wanted to thank you."

Arden frowned and, this time, his resolve failed. He didn't speak, but he moved his head to look up at Bayliss. The man was smiling, but something about his eyes seemed blank, almost dead. Like looking at a snake, Arden thought.

"Thank me?" Arden hated himself for speaking.

"For giving my boy a good hiding the other night."

Arden turned away now. "Leave me alone." And then, with only a perfunctory show of respect, "Sir."

"I mean it, lad." Bayliss clapped him on the shoulder, but Arden recoiled from the touch. "It's about time someone showed my son what a man should be like."

"I don't hold anything against your son," said Arden.

Bayliss laughed unpleasantly. "You always beat up blokes you like, is that it?"

"It was a mistake."

"Didn't sound like it to me, lad." Bayliss leaned on the bar, his face now disconcertingly close to Arden's. The younger man tensed at the proximity of the encounter. "I'm not angry about it, lad. Henry's a grand disappointment to me. No backbone, no guts, no fight in him. He's all easels and Turps. Away with the fairies, you see, lad, which is pretty much where he belongs." Bayliss laughed again, even more unpleasantly. "Not like you, is he?"

Arden was breathing erratically, fighting to keep his temper under control. "Look, sir, just leave me alone, all right? I've nothing to say to you."

Bayliss ignored him. "I wish my Henry were half the man you are, Arden. Breaks my heart, you know, to think that I've got a son I despise, and you had no real father to be proud of you. Not fair, is it? The wrong way round, like."

"Shut up," hissed Arden. He wanted to take a slug of his drink, but he feared he might choke on it. "Don't mention my father."

"I'm trying to be nice to you, son. Can't you see that?" Bayliss was grinning. "I mean what I say. I don't blame you for what you did to our Henry. If you were my son, I'd be proud of you, as I'm sure your dear old mum was. That's all I'm saying."

Arden slammed his fist on the bar. "Well, stop saying it!"

The words were a roar of anger and rage, forcing the murmured conversation of the other patrons to come to an immediate halt. From his table in the corner, Carr felt his nerves tighten, and he frowned ominously at the two men ahead of him. Eric Hirst did likewise, his hand instinctively reaching for Lydia's arm in a gesture of protection. Only Bayliss seemed undisturbed by the outburst, although it was clear from his expression that he had failed to understand it.

"Easy, lad, we don't want any trouble."

Arden was close to Bayliss' face. "Don't you mention my mother again. You're not fit to talk about her, see? Hate your son if you like, but don't use me against him, or next time, it won't be him I clout in the face, right?"

Now, Bayliss' eyes hardened. "You're forgetting who you're talking to, my boy."

"Don't call me your boy," snarled Arden.

Bayliss towered over him. "You reckon you can go a few rounds with me, sonny, then you go for it. I might be older, but I'd whip your arse before you'd even broken a sweat."

Arden was unperturbed. He had not noticed that his hands had curled into fists. "God help me, I could kill you."

Whatever reaction Arden had hoped for or expected, the low and guttural laugh of contempt that rumbled in Bayliss' throat was not it.

"You wouldn't have the brains or the guts, boy." The last syllable was a derision, spat out as if it were a rancid bit of meat.

Arden, as hard as he could, slammed his fist into Bayliss' cheek. Afterwards, sitting alone and distraught in his mother's cottage, he would tell himself that the punch had been nowhere near as satisfying as it should have been. Far from being proud of it, he would feel devastatingly ashamed of it and himself. For now, however, there was a collective gasp of shock from the drinkers in the pub, and both Everett Carr and Eric Hirst rose to their feet.

Bayliss spat out a small globule of blood and spit, and dabbed his lip with his handkerchief. His eyes aged with mortification. "Big mistake, son. Big mistake."

Arden, feeling tears of anger welling behind his eyes and refusing to allow them to fall publicly, turned on his heel and marched towards the door. Bayliss followed, his embarrassment turning swiftly to anger and resentment.

"Come here and finish the job, Arden, you little bastard!" he was shouting. "No? Not man enough for it! Prefer writing letters, do we, sonny? Did you happen to write one to me at the mill, Arden? Did you, you dirty little coward?"

Everett Carr watched his host pull open the door of the pub and follow Arden into the street. He heard no more from Arden, but he could hear the raised voice of Bayliss still, as it shouted after the younger man.

"Don't go back to the mill, boy! You're fired, you bastard! You hear me? Fired! And I hope you rot away in the cottage that slut brought you up in!"

It was an undignified end, and Bayliss was not proud of it. But it had happened, and he would have no regrets about any of it. He marched back inside, so consumed by his own anger that he failed to see Rosamund run down from Church Lane and speak with Michael Arden.

Sitting quietly at the corner table in the aftermath of the storm, Everett Carr peered down at the surface of the wooden table and frowned heavily, lost in deep but dark thought.

# Chapter Twenty

Rosamund banged on the door of Michael Arden's cottage. She seemed to have been doing so for hours now, but it could only have been a few moments. It was the lack of response that made the time bend, the cold and silent ignoring of her hammering on the door and her calls of his name. She felt isolated, frustrated, and more than incensed.

Earlier that evening, she had left the dinner table at Darton House in a storm of fury and insolence. Her father had forbidden her to make the journey to Arden's cottage, but she had defied him without a single thought as to the consequences. There might be some hell to pay in the morning, even later this evening if he sat up and waited for her, fuelling his outrage with brandy, but Rosamund found it close to impossible to care.

She had spent the earlier part of the late afternoon and early evening wondering whether she should confront her father about the argument she had witnessed between him and Arden. She knew it was both inappropriate and unwise, but something inside her told her it was vital that she knew. There was a devil of inquisitiveness on her shoulder, whispering in her ear, and yet Rosamund knew that it was not simple curiosity that was prompting her to ask the question; it was also, she told herself, a genuine concern for Arden's welfare.

"By the way, father," she had said, as the soup course was cleared away. Rosamund had barely touched hers. "I saw you and Michael Arden arguing outside *The Black Bull* this afternoon. What was that all about?"

"Mind your own business, girl." Bayliss had dabbed his lip with his napkin, more to conceal the physical evidence of the quarrel than to remove traces of stray food. "We had a spat, he lashed out, and I fired him. That's all you need to know."

He had said it so casually that it seemed to Rosamund, already horrified, that the news was made all the more dreadful on account of his tone of voice. "You fired him?"

"Of course." Bayliss had displayed an almost cherubic innocence on his face. "What else could I do? He attacked me in public."

"And entirely unprovoked, no doubt," Henry Bayliss had said.

His father had glared at him. "Speak only when you're spoken to."

Marjorie had placed a hand on her son's arm. "Do as he says, dear, please."

Rosamund had seemed to hear nothing of the exchange. "Do you realise what you've done, Father? Michael won't get another job here. What's he going to do?"

"No concern of mine."

"How can you be so heartless?" Rosamund's disbelief had choked her so much that it had left her breathless.

Bayliss had stared at her, and when he spoke, his finger had jabbed maliciously in her direction. "And what's your interest in Michael Arden, all of a sudden? You're an engaged woman, girl, and I expect you to behave like one."

"I'm not engaged anymore," Rosamund had said, instantly regretting it.

Bayliss' glare had intensified. "Say that again."

Marjorie, her own cheeks pale with shock, had turned her attention to her daughter. "Rosamund, what has happened?"

"I've ended it with George." She had spoken dismissively. "But we're not talking about that right now."

Bayliss had slammed his fist on the table. The cutlery had rattled in shock. "We bloody well are talking about it. The marriage goes ahead!"

"What are you so adamant that it should?"

"He's a good match for you."

"He's a liar, Daddy, and I know he is!"

Bayliss had sneered. "Every man's a liar at some time in his life, girl. Toole is a good match for you, because I say he is. Right?"

Rosamund had got to her feet. "I'm going to see if Michael is all right."

Bayliss had stood over the table like a spectre. "You're going nowhere, lass. I forbid you to go to see Arden, you hear me? Forbid it!"

"I don't care," Rosamund had challenged.

"I want to know what's happened with George Toole. Tell me now, or be sorry."

"Don't threaten me, Father." She had spoken the words with confidence, but it seemed to have no effect on him.

Bayliss' eyes had narrowed. "Well, my girl, whatever it is, you put it right. You hear me? You're marrying Toole, or you're done with. I can change that will in a heartbeat!"

"I don't want your damned money, you pig!"

She had screamed it, the words bursting forth in a mixture of hatred and frustration. Marjorie had tried to make the peace, and Henry had stood up in a futile attempt to support his sister, but nothing came of it. He had stood meaninglessly at his place at the table. Only Everett Carr had remained seated, his brows furrowed, and his lips pursed in quiet contemplation.

Rosamund, for her part, had run from the room, although she had heard her father calling after her. "You'll think differently soon, lass! It's a tough life when you're penniless on the bloody streets!"

But Rosamund had not replied. She had run, taking no shawl or coat with her, out of the house and into the town of Darton Vale. She had not felt the cold then, but now, standing at Arden's cottage, the night air bit into her skin like the lash of a whip, and the tears which had started to fall felt like slivers of ice on her cheeks.

She banged on the door one more time, calling his name, but still there was nothing but the cold silence of the unopened door.

Suddenly, without warning, it was broken by the kind, gentle voice behind her. "Perhaps, my child, you should have this."

Startled, Rosamund turned to find herself staring into the dark eyes of Everett Carr. He was holding one of her long raincoats out to her, and she grabbed it quickly and gratefully, stuttering a word of thanks as she shuffled herself into it. The warmth of the coat was immediately obvious and, more importantly, it was instantly gratifying.

"Thank you, Mr Carr," she said. "I'm afraid I've made rather a fool of myself."

"Not at all." Carr's smile was both reassuring and, she felt, entirely genuine. "Being concerned about someone is never foolish."

She smiled briefly at his response, but anxiety soon reclaimed its hold over her. "Father won't like that you've come after me, Mr Carr."

"Perhaps not," he replied, "but that is a matter for him. It doesn't concern me."

She looked into his eyes and, for the first time, she was able to see the kindness behind their darkness, and it impressed on her the truth of his presence there. He would have had to excuse himself from the dinner table, collect his own hat and coat, take hers from the hook in the hallway, and make his way to the town as quickly as his limp would allow. She wondered whether her father had tried to stop Carr and, if so, what Carr had said in retaliation that now meant he was standing in the street with her. A new respect for him dawned within her because she had to believe that her father would have said something to prevent Carr from leaving the house, and yet he stood there now with her, which could only mean that whatever Carr's reply had been, it had silenced Arthur Bayliss. And now, like a benevolent saviour, Everett Carr stood in front of her, bringing her warmth and seemingly offering her friendship, all without any fear of her father's reaction.

"You're very kind," she said, uselessly.

He bowed his head gently. "It is very cold, dear lady, and you have had a trying evening. Might I suggest a brandy in the public house?"

She had started to weep, but she tried clumsily now to laugh. "I should like that very much, Mr Carr."

He offered his arm for support, a gesture that seemed to her foolishly gallant given his own disability. "Come, then, dear lady, and let us warm our bones and clear our minds."

As they walked away from Arden's cottage, neither of them took the trouble to look back one last time. If they had, and if their eyes had wandered to the upstairs windows, they would have seen Michael Arden staring down at them. But still, he would have been too shrouded in darkness for them to have been able to see the twisted malice in his expression and the dark intent in his eyes.

# Chapter Twenty-One

The pub was busy, but not intolerably so, and Carr and Rosamund had no difficulty in finding a table that would allow both the warmth from the fire, blazing merrily in the grate, and a satisfactory degree of privacy. Carr left Rosamund alone for the brief moment it took to order a glass of brandy for her and a whisky for himself. It might have been a short space of time only that he was away, but the curious stares and the surprisingly judgmental glances in her direction, and the suddenly hushed conversations made it seem to her like a lifetime. She wondered what sins and shame they were applying to her, the mistress of the manor, hair dishevelled by the nocturnal winds and eyes crimsoned with tears, sitting in a public house with a man, a stranger, old enough to be her father. Or was she being paranoid? Was this fear of disapprobation from the working people of the town merely a product of her confused emotions, her personal fears, and her internal anxiety? Rosamund couldn't say for certain, but she felt that neither explanation would necessarily come as a surprise to her.

Carr returned holding her glass of brandy, and a barmaid carried his whisky. Rosamund felt a sudden embarrassment that she had not offered to help him with the drinks. It had never occurred to her that he would be unable to carry two glasses and make the necessary use of his cane, and she felt a sudden, selfish disgrace threaten to overwhelm her. She stammered something of a useless apology, but Carr, with a warm smile, waved it aside, saying it was of no moment and that she should trouble herself about it no longer. She had smiled, both at his exaggerated eloquence of speech but also, perhaps primarily, at his natural kindness. She felt as if she could tell him everything about her life, every secret and every blemish, and that it would be received with neither prejudice nor judgment. She watched him over the rim of her glass, and he sipped the whisky like a connoisseur, savouring its taste before he swallowed, then gently dabbing the luxuriously waxed moustache clean from any droplets with a pristine handkerchief.

He looked across to her and smiled. "Are you getting warm now, my child?"

"Very much so, thank you, Mr Carr. You're so very kind. I'm sorry for making a show of myself this evening."

"Not at all."

She saw his eyes flicker to the fingers of her left hand. "I don't think my announcement came as a shock to you, did it?" About George and me, that is."

"Perhaps not."

"I was sure you'd seen at breakfast that I wasn't wearing my engagement ring anymore."

He did not confirm or deny it. The smile had faded, and his eyes had dimmed with a serious concern. "Will you treat me as a friend, Miss Bayliss?"

"Of course."

"I have no wish to pry, and I ask this question only out of concern." He shuffled delicately in his seat. "What is it that troubles you?"

For a moment, Rosamund did not know how to reply. She felt sure that Carr would recognise and reject any form of deception from her, and she dismissed the idea of lying to him immediately. And yet, knowing that the truth was her only response, she could not find the words to say it. The directness of the question somehow made any of her replies seem foolish and inadequate. She took a gulp of the brandy and allowed it to soothe her bones and mind before looking across at him. He was waiting patiently for her to speak, his face impassive, as if he were willing to wait an eternity for his answer but making it clear that he expected one and would receive it.

"There are so many things," Rosamund said at last. Her voice sounded defeated, exhausted, although no tears fell. Perhaps, she thought, she was too tired even for weeping.

Carr now smiled softly. "Then, let us take them one at a time."

Rosamund drained the brandy. Carr asked whether she would like a second, but the girl shook her head. He bowed his head slightly in assent and leaned back in his chair. He waited.

"If you'd come to visit Daddy last month," Rosamund said, "we wouldn't be sitting here now. Until a few days ago, I was fine. Everything about my future was decided. I was in love with George Toole, who was going to go into business with my father and who was going to marry me. We would get a house, raise a family, and grow old together. Everything was settled."

"And what happened to change things?" Carr sipped his whisky.

"I can't explain it," she said. "One day, I met George, and we went for a walk along Layton Brook. He was talking about something or other, and I had a sudden vision of what my life would be with him. He was talking about—whatever it was, I forget now—and I remember feeling utterly bored by him. In that moment, the idea of a family with him turned into shackles around my wrists and feet, and growing old together seemed like purgatory. I could imagine it all: making his supper, washing clothes constantly, a peck on the cheek goodnight, Church on Sundays, and up again the next day to repeat it. I felt stifled before it had even happened. And I asked myself why I was marrying George at all."

"Did you talk to him about it?"

"I tried to. He just said he loved me. But it sounded as exciting as if he'd read me a shopping list."

Carr could not help but smile. "Does he feel the same?"

Rosamund's eyes darkened. "I don't know, honestly, I don't. I sometimes wonder if he thinks saying the words is the same as meaning them. But it's not, is it, Mr Carr?"

"No," said Carr gently, and a little sadly.

She ran a hand through her hair and shook her head. She laughed, but it was one of despair rather than humour. "I've always been so sure of myself, but recently... I don't recognise myself anymore. I feel as if I've lost all control of my life. Isn't that ridiculous?"

"It may not be as ridiculous as you imagine," murmured Carr. "Mr Toole must have loved you in order to propose," said Carr.

But Rosamund offered no corroboration. "I wonder, Mr Carr. This is something else that has been worrying me. You see, I think my father had something to do with it," she added, seeing the confusion in his eyes.

"How?"

She shuffled in her chair, suddenly wishing she had said nothing about it. "I saw George earlier today. He said our engagement was something to do with Father."

Carr tried not to display his fascination. "In what respect?"

She shook her head. "He was interrupted before he could say anything more. By the argument outside the pub between father and Michael. Besides," she added, "I don't believe a word George says at the moment."

Carr was surprised. "Why so?"

"People think George is lovely, a decent chap." Her voice was filled with scorn. "I know he's a liar."

"Indeed?"

"Definitely," she said. And she proceeded to give Carr the full details of Toole's deception.

Having heard it, Carr shook his head sadly. "It would appear that Mr Toole has much to explain."

"He can explain it to someone else," said Rosamund with determination. "I'm not interested."

"Apart from this suggestion about your father and your marriage," Carr felt it important to say.

Rosamund nodded, frowning. "Apart from that, yes."

Carr leaned back in his chair. "Would you allow me to give you some advice, my child? Go to Mr Toole," he added, without waiting for a reply. "Ask him what it was he wanted to tell you."

"Perhaps I don't want to know."

"Very possibly," Carr conceded with a nod of his head, "but it is always better to have the truth, my child, however unpalatable. And it may help to explain his conduct and dispel some of your own confusion."

"Do you think so?"

Carr smiled gently at her. Then, after a moment's reflection, he picked up his glass and sipped the last of the whisky. "Does it not strike you as interesting that Michael Arden had two physical altercations with members of your family?"

It was evident that she had not considered the point. "I see what you mean. I know he hates my father, and always has done."

"Yet he works for him?"

"No longer," said Rosamund sadly. "But he did, yes. He needed a job, of course, and there isn't much employment around here, Mr Carr, if you discount the mills. I know I've been privileged because of Daddy's money, but I've always been aware that there is a fine line for people less fortunate than me between survival and starvation. Darton Vale isn't alone in that, either."

Carr had no taste for a political discussion. "Mr Arden's behaviour cannot simply be a matter of class."

"Perhaps not. Now I think about it, I cannot see any reason for him to attack Henry in the way he did. It is strange."

"Almost as strange as Mr Pym's death," said Carr slowly.

Rosamund suddenly glared at him, and he watched what might have been fear dancing in her eyes amid the glow of the fire's flames. He said nothing more, but twisted instead in his chair, and gestured to the landlord for a second drink for the pair of them. As he turned back to face her, Rosamund's expression was one of nervous anxiety.

"I was very shocked to hear about it," she said. "So unexpected."

"It was murder, my child. You will have heard as much, I expect." He watched her closely as she nodded and mumbled a verbal assurance. "There seems to be no motive for it, however," Carr added. "Can you think of any reason why someone should wish to kill Mr Pym?"

"He was a terrible gossip."

The second round of drinks arrived, and Carr nodded his thanks to the barmaid who had delivered them. He took a sip of his whisky and leaned forward in his chair, his eyes fixed on Rosamund. "Gossip generally doesn't lead to murder, my child."

"He might have said something he didn't know was dangerous to somebody."

Carr smiled. "Now, my child, what makes you think that?"

Rosamund shrugged. "I don't know really."

Carr's smile widened. "Do you consider Mr Pym to be a likely victim of murder?"

"No, I don't." She looked at him with a dangerous glint in her eyes. "But I know what you're thinking, Mr Carr. Why was Mr Pym killed and not my father?"

Carr doubted it would be fair of him to divulge to her what Eric Hirst had told him about her father's relationship with Lydia Stansfield and Pym's knowledge of it, for that matter. It would be unfeeling, not to say cruel, to do so. Nevertheless, in Mr Pym's knowledge of the affair lay a possible motive for murder. Bayliss had admitted to his infidelity with Lydia Stansfield, but had said he ended it on the day Mr Pym was killed. But as vindication, it was useless, as Carr himself had pointed out to Bayliss. Not only would there be other possible mistresses, the scandal of any affair, past or present, might be harmful to Bayliss and his place in the Honours list, and Neville Pym's discretion could not be taken for granted, quite the opposite.

And yet, if Bayliss had a motive to kill Mr Pym, he did not have the opportunity. He had been walking home from the mill and had spoken to McGregor, the mechanic. He might have a motive for Neville Pym's murder, but he likewise had an alibi for it. It was all so confusing and contradictory, and none of it went any great measure towards answering Rosamund Bayliss' question.

Carr looked across at her and saw that her eyes were closing and her head was beginning to drop forward. He wondered whether it was the heat of the fire, the effects of the brandy, or the toll of her emotional stress that was the cause of her obvious exhaustion. Perhaps it was a combination of all three. Whatever the reason, however, it was unforgivable for him to keep her out any longer.

Rising slowly to his feet, he put on his hat and coat and gently walked around to her. With a light touch on her shoulder, he roused her from her shallow slumber, helped her to her feet, and wrapped her overcoat around her. Then, he offered his arm once more, and they walked together slowly out of the public house. Nothing was said between them on the stroll back to Darton House, but in Carr's mind, there was a screeching chorus of questions and problems for which he could find no meaningful explanations.

# Chapter Twenty-Two

The following morning threatened rain, but as it turned out, the rain never came. Nevertheless, the skies were dull and grey, seemingly heavy with portent, and a strong wind shook the trees into a rhythmic but sullen dance. From the windows of his room, Everett Carr looked out over the rolling hills of the northern landscape, and it seemed to him that they somehow appeared even more beautiful in this bleak weather than they had in sunlight, as if the grimness of the weather was better suited to the natural panorama of this part of the country. In London, he thought, such weather would seem bleak and miserable, but here, in the brisk, clean air of the north, it enhanced rather than detracted from the surrounding scenery.

Carr had slept badly and had woken from a turbulent sleep with a feeling of irritation and frustration. He had been unable to sleep, not because of any discomfort of his bed or his room, both of which were more than satisfactory, but even the most comfortable of beds could do nothing against an unsettled mind, and in Carr's case, his mind had refused to allow him to rest. The questions that had plagued him as he walked home with Rosamund on the previous evening had lingered in his brain, but try as he had, their solutions continued to elude him. Lying awake in the silent darkness, their persistent chanting in his head seemed louder than ever, and sleep was impossible, beyond a few unsettled bouts of slumber. He had fallen asleep at some point, he knew that, but he had been awake for more prolonged periods than he had slept.

Now dressed, he made his way downstairs, craving strong black coffee, and even contemplating a plate of eggs and bacon, an occurrence that was not unheard of but so seldom that it could hardly be considered a regular habit. In the dining room, he found Marjorie Bayliss, Rosamund, and Henry, but there was no sign of Bayliss himself. Carr bowed in polite greeting to them all, and from Rosamund, there came a private glance of gratitude which he returned with a smile. Helping himself to coffee, he found his place at the table and sat down.

"Has Mr Bayliss already breakfasted?" he asked.

It was Marjorie who replied. "He has forced down a slice of toast and gone to the mill."

"On a Saturday?" Carr's surprise was obvious, but whether it was entirely genuine was a matter for debate.

"It's better than spending time with us," said Henry, prodding at a clump of scrambled egg with his fork.

"Don't be churlish, darling," said his mother. "It's far too early for it. Arthur has much to do, Mr Carr," she added, looking across at him, "but I'm afraid you'll think he's a terrible host."

Carr smiled. "Not at all."

Marjorie watched him closely, but he kept his attention on the dark surface of his coffee. She would be wondering, he knew, what had passed between him and her daughter on the previous evening, but she would hear nothing of it from him. It was not for Carr to break any confidences. If Marjorie wanted any insight into the evening's events after dinner, she must ask Rosamund about it.

As if she had read his thoughts, Marjorie said, "I'm sorry about the scene at dinner last night, Mr Carr. Quite unforgivable." She stared at Rosamund, but there was no return glance from the girl. "You must think us very rude."

Carr shook his head. "Think nothing of it, dear lady."

"And I must offer my thanks to you for bringing Rosamund home safely." Marjorie's eyes were still on her. "I can't think where she thought she was going."

Rosamund shook her head. "Please, Mother, just leave it alone."

"I don't know how you can expect me to do that, my dear, after the mess you've caused."

Henry tossed his fork onto his plate. "Honestly, Mother, just leave her be. You apologise to Mr Carr for us being rude and then persist in embarrassing him like this. I apologise, Mr Carr," he added, looking across to the guest, "*again!*"

Marjorie nodded slowly. "Perhaps a change of subject would be in order."

Henry played with some egg on his plate. "Any news on Mr Pym's murder? I don't understand why anybody would want to kill him at all."

Rosamund let out an exaggerated sigh. "Must we talk about murder? Can't we talk about something pleasant for a change?"

Henry had the grace to look embarrassed. "Sorry. As a change of subject, Mr Pym was hardly appropriate."

"No," said Marjorie. In an effort to do a more skilful job, she looked across to Carr. "We have another guest for dinner tonight, Mr Carr, but I think you have met him already. Eric Hirst, my husband's accountant."

Carr smiled warmly. "I have met Mr Hirst."

"Such a nice man," said Rosamund.

Carr's smile broadened. "I saw him yesterday in the public house with Miss Stansfield."

Without warning, there was the clatter of cutlery, so unexpected that it seemed almost deafening. Carr noticed Rosamund jump at the sudden noise, and Henry recoiled as if he had heard a gunshot. Marjorie, still holding the slice of toast, was staring at Carr with an expression on her face that suggested he had uttered a sudden and obscene blasphemy in the house of God. For a long moment, she seemed unaware of the disturbance she had caused, but at last, her eyes flickered, and her lips, which had been quivering with unspoken outrage, formed themselves into an apologetic smile.

"Forgive me," she said. "I don't know what came over me."

A sip of her coffee, a smile, and a gentle laugh of embarrassment, and she picked up the dropped knife and continued to butter her toast. Rosamund drank her own coffee, and Henry resumed the eating of his scrambled eggs. Breakfast continued, and the mind of Everett Carr raced.

The meal over, Henry and Rosamund left the table, but neither Carr nor Marjorie stirred from their seats, as if both had understood, in silent agreement, that there was more to be said.

"I suppose some explanation is required," Marjorie said.

Carr shook his head. "Not on my account, dear lady."

"You think it is a private matter, and that it is inappropriate for me to confide in a stranger."

He looked over to her and smiled. "You do not need to explain, because I already know. About your husband and Miss Stansfield. And now, of course, I know that you do, too."

She glared at him, her eyes flickering with tears and confusion. "You mentioned her on purpose. It was a trick."

Carr offered no confirmation or denial of the accusation. "How did you find out?"

"Perhaps I should ask you the same question."

His smile faded, and Marjorie was surprised to see that a seemingly genuine sadness crept over his face. "Your husband told me."

"I see," she managed to say, but it was clear that she did not.

"I presume he did not confess it to you, also."

She shook her head. "Over the years, Mr Carr, being married to a man like Arthur, you learn to recognise the signs. It is not a question of *if*, but rather one of *who*. Who this time? And I have seen Lydia Stansfield and how she looks at him. Funny, isn't it," she added with a coarse, pained laugh, "how easily these young girls fall for him, because he isn't conventionally handsome, is he? It is the power, I suppose. His status."

"Are you aware that he has ended the relationship?" asked Carr.

"No, I was not," she said, shaking her head. Whether she believed it or not, Carr was unable to say for certain.

Carr stroked his moustache thoughtfully. "Might I ask a rather impertinent question, dear lady?"

"If you wish."

"How can you stand by and allow these affairs to happen? The law no longer requires you to suffer such outrages in silence."

For a moment, it appeared that she was going to succumb to a bout of violent sobbing, but no tears came. Perhaps, Carr thought, too many had been shed already.

"I have no doubt people would say I was a foolish old woman," Marjorie said, "but you and I are from a different generation, Mr Carr. We were brought up to respect the sanctity of marriage."

"Your husband is of our generation," Carr was compelled to say. "He does not share our views, it seems."

Marjorie smiled. It was evidently a point that she had debated with herself many times in the past. "Don't they say that two wrongs don't make a right?"

"Indeed, they do," said Carr quietly, and with a smile of understanding.

"Besides, I don't happen to believe in divorce. I made a vow to God, and I personally don't believe that I can break it. Under any circumstances."

"Are you very religious?"

"Once upon a time," she said with a coy smile.

Carr leaned back in his chair, nodding slowly. He found that he felt a keen sense of admiration for the subtle blend of pride and conviction that Marjorie Bayliss displayed. There had been the initial panic in the wake of her shock, of course, but that had passed quickly and, whilst understandable, it seemed to say less about her frame of mind and core beliefs than the stoicism that she now presented to him. And yet, the central question beneath all this politeness of conversation remained in his mind.

"And yet, surely, dear lady, there are times when you find it difficult, if not impossible, to bear?" he asked.

And Marjorie Bayliss nodded, looking across at him without any measure of regret or deception; only, Carr thought, a genuine sadness. "God forgive me, Mr Carr, but there are times when I feel I could kill him without a second thought and be done with him."

If she had expected Carr to be shocked by the words, she was to be disappointed. He merely held her gaze for a long moment, his expression betraying none of the fascination for her response that swelled within him, and his enigmatic smile, somehow both compassionate and playful, remained fixed on his lips.

Marjorie dabbed the corners of her mouth with her napkin, as if her confession had left some bitter taste on her lips. "I suppose that shocks you."

Carr shook his head. "I'm sorry to say, dear lady, that I would have been more shocked if you had said quite the opposite. And yet it is Mr Pym who has been killed," he added softly, lowering his gaze.

Marjorie needed no further explanation. "You think it should have been Arthur?"

"Do you not think so?"

She needed to give the matter only the slightest thought. "It seems so despicable even to talk about such things, Mr Carr. How can we sit here and discuss murder so easily? What have we come to that means it is so easily done?"

It was a question Carr had asked himself many times, but it was also one that he had never satisfactorily answered. There seemed to him, on occasion at least, to be in society a ghoulish obsession with murder. Perhaps it was the lingering aftermath of the war; for that matter, he thought, perhaps it was the increasing possibility of a second war. Or perhaps it was a simple degeneration of society as a whole, little more than a sociological corrosion of the fibres of a collective morality.

"I suppose you're right, Mr Carr," Marjorie was saying. "It does seem more natural for Arthur to have an enemy than Neville Pym."

"It has been suggested by other people." He watched her consider the point with care. "He received that threatening letter, after all."

"I cannot deny that there are people who hate my husband," she said.

"Michael Arden, for instance," said Carr. "And Miss Stansfield, if we are to believe your husband has terminated their affair. Eric Hirst, who has feelings for the girl himself, I believe, and who was jealous of her relationship with Mr Bayliss."

"And me?" Her expression dared him to contradict her, but he did not. "I see what you're driving at, Mr Carr, of course I do. It would be foolish indeed to try to deny it."

"Yet we must explain why Mr Pym has died instead."

"You don't think he was somehow mistaken for my husband?"

The idea was as unlikely as it was ridiculous. "Mr Pym was murdered in his own home. How could anyone mistake him for your husband in those circumstances?"

Marjorie offered no explanation. "Then what do you suppose?"

Carr's eyebrows raised, and he gave a frustrated sigh. "I cannot explain it. There must be a reason, but I cannot find it."

"And I'm afraid I cannot help you, Mr Carr," said Marjorie, rising to her feet. "Now, if you would excuse me, I have some letters to write."

Carr rose as she left the room, but sat back in his chair slowly once she had closed the door behind her. He sat alone for several quiet moments more, wondering whether the trace of satisfaction and suppressed humour at Marjorie Bayliss' confessed inability to explain the puzzle of Pym's murder had been genuine or a mere figment of his own confused and frustrated imagination.

# Chapter Twenty-Three

The remainder of the day passed without incident.

Carr spent it alone and away from Darton House, opting instead for a solitary walk through the town of Darton Vale. He spent a peaceful hour in the church, enjoying as he so often did the architecture and the particular brand of almost divine quiet that emanates from such places, and he exchanged a few amiable words with the vicar. He learned nothing of any great interest from the holy man, however, apart from a further assurance that nobody in the world could have wanted to harm Neville Pym and directions to Layton Brook. He enjoyed a wholesome but frugal lunch at a small tea shop in the town, but he came across nobody he knew or recognised there, and finally he made his way to the brook and the notorious Devil's Corner.

He saw at once how accidents could occur there. The road itself was well preserved, but there was a dangerous blind spot at the point where it curved around the natural landscape of the cliff face that overhung it. No amount of human endeavour could have avoided it, and all mankind could do was take care when approaching it. Beneath, there was a long and vertiginous drop that cascaded down into the rippling stream of Layton Brook, interspersed with visible humps of rock submerged in the water. The branches of trees latticed the entire spectacle, as if it were being held in the thin, bony hands of those old, malignant crones from the dark fairy tales of his childhood. It was an impressive example of natural beauty, but with such loveliness, there must also be ugliness, and in this particular spot, it could not be found anywhere else than in the lurking danger of

Devil's Corner. Carr found himself wondering how many other victims of it there had been, other than Emma Hirst, who surely could not have been its only casualty. It seemed perverse to have such a sombre thought in the majesty of the surroundings, but Carr spent some moments reflecting on it. At last, however, the chill of the wind, the dying of the light of day, and the increasing sense of isolation about the place began to unnerve him. It was as if the area took on another persona in the gathering gloom, and its dangerous ugliness overtook its diurnal attractiveness. Suddenly, Carr had no wish to be there as the light faded, and he made his way as quickly as possible back to the sanctuary of the town.

He returned to Darton House cold but invigorated, and the prospect of a warm bath before an eagerly anticipated dinner was irresistible. The hallway was empty, and the house as silent as the grave as he hung up his hat and coat. Out of little more than blind curiosity, he looked in the library and the drawing room, but he found no trace of anybody in either. He presumed Henry would be in his artist's studio at the far end of the garden, and he knew that Bayliss himself was at the mill. But Marjorie and Rosamund were conspicuous by their absence. Carr shook his head. He accused himself of finding ghosts where there were none, of assuming sinister deeds in innocent situations, and for it, he blamed both his inquisitive nature, the chill on his bones, and the dull, persistent ache in his shattered knee. Slowly, painfully, he mounted the stairs to his room.

It was a couple of hours later that he descended those same stairs for the usual pre-prandial cocktails. Earlier, he had swapped his jacket and waistcoat for his dressing gown, his shoes for his patent leather slippers, and he had sat in a chair by his bedroom window, looking back towards the impressive scenery that he had experienced. He had fallen asleep, he would later realise, but it could only have been for half an hour or so, no more, but as he often noticed with unexpected naps, he had awoken feeling more tired than before. He had rung for some tea, and it had been delivered by one of the maids. A cup or two of it revitalised him, and he had then bathed, a long and soothing soak, shaved, preened his moustache and beard, and dressed for dinner.

The eerie silence of the hall in the afternoon was gone, replaced now with the sounds of dinner preparations in the dining room and the faint sound of music from the drawing room. Entering, he found Marjorie Bayliss sitting alone on the settee, a glass of sherry in her hands, and an expression of distant anxiety on her face. The music, Carr noted, came from a small gramophone playing almost to itself in the corner of the room. The music was not familiar to Carr, and, being altogether too pacy in its rhythm and too insistent in its brass, he supposed it was something modern. Certainly, he thought with mild disdain, it was not Mahler.

Marjorie did not notice him at once. It was only when he approached her that her reverie broke. She laughed politely and rose to her feet.

"I'm so sorry, Mr Carr," she said, "I was miles away. I shall turn off the music. Please do help yourself to a drink. I'm afraid I'm no good at mixing cocktails, so you will have to prepare your own."

Carr, never a great lover of cocktails, declined with a bow of his head. "Perhaps a sherry, if I may, dear lady."

"Of course, help yourself." As he did so, Marjorie silenced the gramophone. "Rosamund will be down in a moment, and Henry is across the hall in the library. He'll be in soon, too." She checked a slim watch on her pale wrist. "And Eric will be here at any moment, I think."

Carr nodded slowly, sipping his sherry. He almost dared not ask the question. "And Mr Bayliss?"

He was not unduly surprised to see a look of concern pass over her face. Perhaps, he thought later, she had some premonition of what was to come, but in the moment, he thought no further than the idea that she was anxious that her husband had gone to the mill on a Saturday and had not yet returned.

"I don't know where he is," she said. "He said he was going to the office for a couple of hours this morning, but he came back for lunch, while you were on your walk. He was sorry to have missed you," she added needlessly and perhaps, Carr thought, falsely. "Then, he said he had to go back later on, but would be back for dinner." She consulted her watch for the second time. "I've not heard from him since."

"He may have been delayed," Carr said. "Perhaps there was more work for him to do than he had appreciated."

"He would have telephoned, I'm sure."

At which point, Henry walked into the drawing room, dressed suitably, and although he was smiling, Carr could not help but think that he had detected a distant glimmer of malice in the young man's eyes.

"Father's not here, I see," he said, preparing himself a cocktail. "I suppose I shall have to be host. Would you care for a White Lady, Mr Carr?"

"Thank you, no," said Carr, indicating his barely touched sherry.

Henry looked at the clock on the wall. "Nearly a quarter to eight, mother. Aren't people supposed to be here by now?"

Again, a nervous reaction only, Marjorie looked at her watch. "They really should be arriving any moment. Where is Rosamund, for Heaven's sake?"

"Preening herself, no doubt," said Henry rather ungallantly.

"Don't be so unkind, Henry," snapped Marjorie. "It doesn't suit you."

Henry, having finished stirring his cocktail, poured it out with a flourish and took a sip. His nod of appreciation and his short gasp at the potency of the alcohol suggested that it was not only acceptable but that he had somehow surpassed himself. Carr allowed himself a small smile under the luxuriant moustache.

Marjorie was about to speak when two bells rang almost simultaneously. The first, deep and sombre, was the peal of the front doorbell; the second, shrill and insistent, was the trill of the telephone. On impulse, Henry marched to the door, pulled it open, and stepped into the hallway. Under the influence of a similar instinct, Carr followed him, although he placed his glass of sherry on the glass-topped coffee table before he did so. In the hallway, there was a commotion of activity. Rosamund Bayliss, resplendent in a satin dress of duck-egg blue with a string of pearls around her slim neck, was coming down the main staircase into the hall. Grayson, the butler, moving slowly but with a solemn elegance, like a spectre through a cemetery, picked up the telephone receiver. Carr heard Rosamund ask him who it was on the other end of the line, but the servant made no immediate reply. One of the maids had appeared in order to answer the door, Grayson clearly being unable to do both, but Henry Bayliss reached it before her and dismissed her with a kind assurance that all was well. Pulling open the front door of the house, Carr saw over Henry's shoulder the friendly face of Eric Hirst. Henry welcomed him, and the accountant stepped over the threshold and into the hallway, offering a smile of greeting to the assembled throng. On impulse, Carr pulled out his watch from his waistcoat pocket and glanced at the time. It was only a fraction after a quarter to eight.

Rosamund was now standing beside the butler. "Who was on the telephone, Grayson?"

"I don't know, miss," came the reply. "She did not say. She simply asked if Mr Bayliss was at home."

Carr had joined them. "What were her exact words, Mr Grayson?"

The butler, slightly perturbed by the polite use of his title, looked down at the guest of the house. "She said, 'Is Arthur Bayliss there? I need to speak to him.' I told the lady that he was not, and she ended the call."

"Did you recognise her voice?"

Grayson did not need to give the matter any thought. "No, sir."

"Did Mr Bayliss indicate to you, Mr Grayson, that he would be home for dinner?" asked Carr.

"Indeed so, sir. He summoned me, told me he was returning to the office, but that he would be back at the house before dinner was served. I was instructed to have his dress clothes ready for him."

"He did not indicate a specific time?"

"No, sir, but from what he had said, I would have expected him to be back by around half past seven."

The assumption was not unreasonable. Returning to the house by then would surely have given Bayliss just enough time to wash, dress, and be back down for a drink before Eric Hirst's arrival at the arranged time of a quarter to eight, albeit with only a few moments to spare. And yet, there was no sign of the man. For the first time, Carr began to feel a real, almost tangible sense of foreboding.

Marjorie, having dismissed Grayson, walked over to Hirst. "Eric, have you seen Arthur today?"

Hirst had shuffled off his coat and removed his hat, and he was standing now in the hallway, rubbing his hands together against the remnants of the cold night air.

"I haven't, no," he answered. "I had no reason to go to the mill today."

"Then where is he?" asked Marjorie, fighting to resist the temptation to shriek the question.

Henry's face was grave. "I don't know why everyone is so surprised. This is typical of him, isn't it?"

It was Everett Carr who replied. "Perhaps, but he had given Mr Grayson the impression that he would be here at half past seven."

"So what?" sneered Henry.

"Mr Bayliss did not need to lie to Mr Grayson." Carr began to pace slowly, his head sunk on his breast, and his voice pensive. "If he had no intention of coming home for dinner, why the directions to Mr Grayson to have his dress suit ready?" To his mind, that one instruction seemed to hint at disaster.

Rosamund seemed anxious to convey a lack of concern. "Henry's right. Either Daddy has decided to avoid dinner with us, yet again, or else he has been sidetracked somehow."

"If he has been sidetracked," said Marjorie, "I can think of only one place he would be."

Hirst, recognising the implication, shook his head. "He's not with Lydia. At least, she had no plans to meet him." In response to the querying glances fixing on him, he added, "She and I had arranged to meet this evening. Just for a drink, you understand."

Carr stood beside him. "Did Miss Stansfield say anything about meeting Mr Bayliss tonight?"

"No, that's just it," said Hirst. "She had no intention of seeing him. She said she was going to go home, have a long soak in the bath, and a couple of hours with a book before bed."

Carr glanced at the telephone. "Might she have changed her mind?"

Hirst shrugged, but he understood Carr's unspoken question. "She didn't seem to have done so when I telephoned her just before I came here."

"And why did you do that?" asked Carr with an ingratiating smile.

"As I was leaving the house just now, I noticed her gloves on the table by the door. She'd forgotten them, so I rang to tell her. It took her a few moments to answer, because she was running her bath, she said."

"And this was only a few moments ago?"

"Yes, my cottage is only around the corner."

"Can you be precise as to the time of your telephone call to Miss Stansfield?"

Hirst checked his watch. "Twenty to eight, perhaps. I put the phone down and came straight here."

Carr's mind was racing now. Would Lydia Stansfield have changed her mind about moving on from Arthur Bayliss, after his rejection of her, in so short a time as Hirst now suggested? It seemed unlikely. And yet, in the darkest corners of his mind, Carr was certain that it was Lydia who had telephoned the house just now. But if what Hirst said was true, why would she need to be in contact with Bayliss at all? Once again, the almost physical weight of anxiety descended on him.

Henry marched forward, the cocktail glass, now empty, hanging loosely from his fingers. "I don't see what any of this is achieving. Father isn't here, that's all we need to know. Asking Grayson to put out his dinner suit only shows an intention to come home for dinner, which he hasn't done. Who cares why?"

"He's just changed his mind, that's all," said Rosamund.

"Don't be naïve, sister," taunted Henry. "The truth is he doesn't care enough about us to be here, so we shouldn't care that he isn't. Simple."

Marjorie had been standing aside from the rest of the company, only half listening to the questions and theories about where her husband might be. If it had struck her as offensive that they should be discussing her husband's whereabouts and his relationship with Lydia Stansfield, she did not show it. It seemed to her now as if she had been separated from her body, as if somehow, she had walked out of herself and was watching proceedings from a dispassionate distance, so that none of the personal hurt and private shame could harm her. But now, with Henry's almost leering disgust of his father, Marjorie seemed to be thrust back into reality with a shuddering violence. She knew and understood her children's feelings towards their father, and she even empathised with it, but it seemed in this moment to be strangely horrifying. Like Carr, she would wonder later if she had some sort of premonition about the future events, but in the present, she felt only outrage and disgust at Henry's words.

"For God's sake, will you shut up!" she roared. "Just shut up, shut up, shut up! You hate your father, we know. You make it so plain that it's impossible not to know. But can't you see, you stupid boy, that something is wrong? Arthur said he would be here, and he isn't. Something has happened, I'm sure of it. Have you all forgotten about the anonymous letter he received, telling him to hang himself? What if he has, and all you can do is gloat about how much you hate him? What if you never get the chance to retract it? What if he's…?" But the word, so obvious that it was almost unnecessary to say it, failed to come, strangled to death in her throat by a choking sob.

Henry stared at his mother, dazed by the shock of her outburst, whilst Rosamund ran towards her, putting her arms protectively around her mother's shoulders. Carr, his attention fixed on Marjorie's pale features, spasmed with horror and fear, pointed towards the drawing room door.

"Take her in there, Miss Bayliss, if you please," he said. The strength of his voice, now so authoritative and commanding, surprised her. "Brandy would be in order, I think. No, Mr Bayliss," he called over to Henry, who had made a move to follow, "your place is with us, I think."

The young man, blanched by the shock of the moment, now seemed little more than a disgraced child, and he paced slowly over to Carr. "I didn't mean to…"

But Carr placed his hand on the boy's shoulder and patted it comfortingly. "We must decide what is to be done."

It was Eric Hirst who spoke. "It seems to me, Mr Carr, that if Bayliss isn't with Lydia, and given that he isn't here, there's really only one place he's likely to be."

"And that is the very place he said he would be all along." Carr nodded. "Quite so. I wonder, Mr Hirst, if you might telephone his office and ascertain the fact?"

"Yes, he has a direct line." Hirst picked up the receiver and made the call. Henry was staring hopelessly into the middle distance, but Carr's attention was riveted on Hirst's face. Finally, the accountant shook his head and replaced the receiver. "No, there's no answer."

Carr thought he had detected a note of anxiety in the man's voice, but he made no mention of it. Instead, he turned to Henry. "Do you know the telephone number for Mr George Toole?"

Henry nodded. "Yes, sir."

"Then, please telephone him and ask him to come here at once. Your sister needs him, however fractious their relationship has become. Then, you and I, along with Mr Hirst, shall go to the mill and see what we can discover."

As Carr and Hirst put on their hats and coats, Henry did as he was told. He tried first the Toole residence, but he was told that George was working late in the office. Upon trying there, however, Henry received a similar response to Eric Hirst. Replacing the receiver, he turned to the two men standing behind him.

"George isn't at home," he said, "and there's no reply from his office."

Carr glanced at Hirst, then nodded slowly. "Very well, it cannot be helped. Now, let us go."

Carr said no more, and further words were unnecessary in any event. Hirst pulled open the front door, allowed both Carr and Henry to leave the house in front of him, and then stepped out into the cold air himself, pulling the door closed behind him.

They made their way to the garage and found the chauffeur inside, his head under the bonnet of one of the vehicles. Henry alerted him to their presence and indicated a Daimler.

"I'm taking this out, Denton. I shan't be long."

"Very good, sir."

Henry opened the door and climbed into the vehicle. Carr was about to do likewise, but he paused and walked as swiftly as he could to the chauffeur. For a few seconds, he spoke with the servant before smiling and nodding his thanks. Then, he walked back to the car and opened the passenger door. Hirst grabbed his forearm.

"I'll run down and meet you there," he said.

Carr, recalling his phobia of motor cars, patted his arm and gave a word of understanding. "As quickly as you can."

During the drive, Henry did not speak, his eyes wide with frantic concern and his bottom lip trapped between his teeth. Everett Carr, too, sat in silence, his mind engaged in deep thought, but his heart consumed with a dark sensation of menace. From somewhere in the distance, he heard a squawk of a bird. In his imagination, diseased by his morbid thoughts of anticipated death, it might have been the cry of a raven, the prophet of evil, either bird or demon, and as he walked, the sinister old poem came into his head, unbidden and unwelcome, yet so insistent that Carr seemed to hear that ominous rapping and tapping at the chamber door of his troubled mind.

# Chapter Twenty-Four

There was something eerie about the mill in the silent darkness. Without the noises of the looms, mules, and other equipment, the cavernous building seemed larger than it was, but it equally felt entirely without life. When the machines were not running, the place had no purpose. Those machines, covered in shadow save for thin slivers of moonlight from the ceiling windows, loomed over the three men as they entered the mill, as if they were sentries on duty, guarding its safety and infrastructure. The quiet, made all the more ominous by the dark, was so intense that the sound of their shoes on the floor sounded like pistol shots in the night. There was a fierce smell of industrial labour and stale human activity. The stench of what Everett Carr assumed was raw cotton or other fibres blended with the coarse reek of dust and grit, and the lingering odour of lubricating oils from the machinery. Additionally, had Carr been able to identify it, there was the faint but comparatively sweet scent of the dyes used to colour the fabric.

Carr had seldom, if ever, been inside a mill, and he was struck at once by the magnitude of the enterprise. He realised now how little thought he had given to the manufacture of textiles. Those sheets of cloth from which his tailored suits were made, the starched aprons of the waitresses who served him in his favourite restaurants, the flag which he honoured every Remembrance Day, all the other examples that did not occur to him in the moment and which he had forever taken for granted in his privileged life began their lives in a place like this. Not once had Carr considered the men and women who toiled at these imposing shadows of industry that surrounded him now so that he could wear expensive suits and gaudy neckties. And never before had he felt so humbled or so aware of his status and good fortune in life as opposed to others less blessed than him. He thought now, only briefly, that of all the notions that might have occurred to him in coming to this place, these were the ones that he would never have predicted.

They were compelled to wait around fifteen minutes for Eric Hirst's arrival, but once there, Hirst took control. He led the party through the mill towards the iron staircase that loomed up into the darkness above them. Carr struggled with its steps, rather too steep for his damaged leg, and he had a sense of dizziness as he looked down from the gantry and out across the maze of the mill. He inhaled deeply, feeling the initial sense of vertiginous delirium wane, and in order to dispel it completely, he focused his mind on what was in front of him. He saw the narrow length of the gantry, taking in the closed doors of the offices leading off from it. Except that not all of them were closed. One, the closest to him, was open.

"That open door..." he said, pointing with his cane.

It was Hirst who replied. "Bayliss' office."

Carr stepped forward, his mind now clearing of its fog of distractions. Behind him, and below him, there was no mill, no iron staircase, no dizzying heights; there was only that open door and what lay beyond it. Slowly, he approached it, conscious at once of his two comrades behind him. As the door came closer, Carr became aware of a key in the lock, on the inside, but no sign of any damage to the door. No forced entry. There was the dull glare of a desk lamp, but no other source of light in the office, and the light offered by the single bulb seemed almost comically inadequate in this overbearing darkness. At last, Carr turned into the office itself, Hirst and Bayliss following him, peering cautiously over his shoulders.

At once, Carr turned around to face them. "Stay away. You mustn't come any further. Mr Bayliss, you go for the police. Immediately."

Henry stammered. "What is it? Is it Father?"

"I'm afraid so, but there is nothing you can do now except go for the police."

"I want to know what's happened," wailed Henry.

Carr placed his hand against the boy's chest. His dark eyes seemed to Henry to have changed. There was now no trace of the amiable politeness behind them, nor was the voice that gentle, almost melodic sound that Henry had come to know. They had both been replaced by a stern authority, a hard briskness that was both compelling and strangely disconcerting.

"I'm afraid he is dead," said Carr. "And it is a matter for the police. Now, go, my boy, and fetch them!"

This last command was almost barked, but it managed to retain something of Carr's natural dignity. And yet, Henry found it impossible to defy, and he ran from the scene, his feet clattering on the iron staircase, and the faint sounds of sobbing drifting back along his path.

And now, Carr turned to Eric Hirst. "You must stay out here, my friend. The less disturbance, the better."

Hirst nodded and took a step backwards. Carr gave him a small smile and turned his attention back to the office.

The second look at the body of Arthur Bayliss was no less terrible than the first. He was sitting at the desk, leaning back in the chair, his arms hanging loosely over the sides. His head was resting against the back of the chair in such a way that he appeared to be staring straight at Carr. The sightless eyes were widened in death, but they had lost none of their malice, so that it seemed as if he was glaring accusingly at this unwanted intruder. The mouth was open, giving the dead face a suggestion of inquisitive surprise, as if Bayliss were about to ask what they were doing here at this time of night. He was dressed in his shirt sleeves, which were rolled up his massive forearms, and the suit jacket was tossed casually over the back of the chair. The tie was pulled loose from his throat, and the top of the shirt was open. His waistcoat was unbuttoned, revealing the bulk of his chest, and, just where his heart would be, there was a small, terrifying hole of destruction. The red of Bayliss' blood was so livid against the white of the shirt that it seemed so fresh that Carr could almost believe he could still smell the gunpowder of the gun that had fired the bullet that had made that single, devastating wound. But he could not. It was a fanciful idea, but there was nothing imaginary about the scene in front of him. There was only the cold, brutal fact of murder.

From behind him, Carr heard Eric Hirst say: "This is the murder we all thought should have happened. And now it has."

Carr nodded slowly, but he did not turn round. He muttered only a single, solemn word, "Yes," and lowered his gaze to the floor. After a moment's silence, he lifted his head and began to look around the room.

"Does anything look amiss to you in this room, Mr Hirst?" he asked quietly.

Hirst leaned into the office and gave a brief glance around. "Not that I can see."

"Nothing is disarranged or out of place?"

"Nothing."

Carr nodded. He had hardly expected there to be any disturbance, but it was as well to ascertain the fact. He pointed to the door handle. "There is a key in the lock. Would Mr Bayliss have locked himself in here for any reason?"

"Sometimes, if he was taking a private or important call, and did not wish to be disturbed."

"But as a matter of course…?"

Hirst shook his head. "No, his office wouldn't usually be locked."

"So, anybody could have walked in here at any time?"

"Assuming the outside doors to the mill were open, yes."

"Which they would have been tonight, because Mr Bayliss was in here himself," said Carr. "So, anybody who knew he would be here, or could guess it, could have killed him."

"Yes, I would say so." Hirst had turned away from the sight of the body. "This is terrible. I didn't like the man very much, but nobody would wish this."

Everett Carr looked across to him, the glow of the desk lamp casting shadows across his face, strangely distorting his features. "Somebody did wish it, my friend."

The statement, whilst true, still seemed shocking. Hirst said nothing more, lowering his head and leaning against the gantry. As Carr turned away from him, his eyes caught sight of something on the floor, a square of white by the side of his foot. Bending down slowly, Carr picked it up with his gloved fingers.

"Shouldn't you leave that for the police to find?" asked Hirst.

"The police will not need to find it," said Carr with a serious, hushed tone. "I shall give it to them."

"What is it, exactly?"

It appeared to be a piece of paper, possibly a leaf from a notebook, but when Carr had bent down to retrieve it from the floor, he had seen at once that it was a paper napkin. On one side, there was a logo in the shape of a fluted wine glass framed by small *fleur-de-lis*, under which was the name *Sinclair's*. Carr held it out for Hirst to see.

"It is a restaurant in Manchester," Hirst said in reply to the unanswered question. "It is—*was*—one of Arthur's favourites."

Carr nodded, but his attention was primarily focused on the other side of the napkin, the side facing him as he held it out to Hirst. With a dextrous flick of his fingers, Carr rotated the napkin so that the words on the other side were visible to Hirst.

"Do you recognise that handwriting?" he asked.

"No, I'm afraid not," said Hirst, shaking his head. But then, the meaning of the words seemed to hit him, and he recoiled from the napkin in shock. His eyes blinked rapidly as he glared from the message on the paper to Carr's dark, impassive stare. "So, *he* did this?"

"That remains to be seen." Carr lowered the napkin. "Do you know anybody else with those initials?"

Hirst thought frantically for a moment. "No, I don't."

"Would he be likely to frequent this restaurant of his own accord?"

"Hardly, but he might if Arthur had invited him there."

"Why should he do that?"

"I can't imagine."

Nor could Carr, and yet the words on the napkin had to be explained somehow. Frowning, Carr read them once more:

*I won't let you get away with it again—MA*

And, like Eric Hirst, Carr could think of nobody else whom he had met in this business with those initials, other than Michael Arden.

# Chapter Twenty-Five

Inspector Tommy Barber leaned against one of the filing cabinets in Bayliss' office, rubbing his eyes with the tips of his forefinger and thumb, and wishing he were anywhere else but here. In the back of his mind, there were images of sandy beaches and lapping waves, of donkeys carrying children, of fish and chips wrapped in newspaper, all flickering together like old newsreels into a collage of hope and escape. He could not remember the last time he and Margaret had taken a decent break from the routine. A year, perhaps? Six months at a push? No less, that was for sure. It just hadn't been possible, a combination of work and finances conspiring against them to keep them locked in Darton Vale. As the rest of the world experienced a wider, more varied existence, Margaret and Tommy Barber scrimped and saved to buy more essential things than ice cream and fish and chips. Things like meat, bread, and warmth. And now, with a little one on the way, he was struggling to see how there could be any escape from the treadmill of a working life. A friend of his, good old Stanley Tideswell, had recently taken a trip to Europe, something he'd always wanted to do, and something that now he never stopped talking about. Barber had lost track of the number of times he'd had to listen to how amazed Tideswell had been at his first sight of Notre Dame Cathedral. Barber had found it amusing at first, given that Tideswell was neither a religious man nor a man particularly interested in Gothic architecture, but he had soon grown to despise the repetition of the tale and others like it. Most of all, he had grown to loathe Tideswell's sudden snobbery. The trip, paid for by a wealthy relative of Tideswell's, had changed the man, and Barber did not like the result. But he knew that there was an element of jealousy in his hatred of Tideswell's boasts, and Barber was honest enough to admit to it. Tideswell had seen something of the world, and Barber envied him for it. Tideswell had seen places that seemed too remote from Darton Vale that they seemed almost mystical, places with names like Vienna and Florence, rather than Salford or Blackburn, places that Tommy Barber would never get to see, and would probably never be able to appreciate even if he did. He had no wealthy relatives. He had a pregnant wife and debts. He would never see fresco paintings, or whatever Stanley Tideswell called them, and he would never see French vineyards or Italian lakes. All Tommy Barber ever seemed to see were dead ends and dead bodies. And now, he was looking at another, the second in as many days.

Somehow, Barber had not been surprised to see Everett Carr, now hovering casually in the doorway, at the scene of this second murder. Idly, his mind had wondered whether it was a coincidence or not, but Carr could hardly be considered a serious suspect. No witness in the land, Barber thought with a trace of malice, would fail to recognise that moustache and Imperial beard, and even if they were disguised, the limp couldn't be. No, Barber did not consider Carr to be involved in either death, but his presence at both was something the inspector felt he could not ignore. He made a mental note, soon to be forgotten, to ask one of the constables to make some enquiries into this man, Everett Carr.

Barber had listened carefully to Carr, Eric Hirst, and Henry Bayliss as they told and corroborated the story of their arrival at the mill and the purpose of their visit. It had seemed natural enough to the inspector, and he saw no reason to pursue that particular line of questioning. He had told them to wait for him on the gantry, and they had complied. His examination of the body had been brief, but without the police doctor, there was little he could ascertain for sure, beyond the fact of the gunshot wound itself.

Now, he approached Carr and leaned against the doorframe. "You say you arrived here at around half past eight?"

Carr nodded. "Just so, Inspector."

Barber looked back at the body. "I'm no doctor, but I'd say he's been dead for at least an hour, making it eight o'clock tonight at the earliest."

"I would concur," said Carr, softly.

"We can't tell the calibre of gun, of course, not until the doctor has had a look, but I'm guessing it was a small handgun."

Carr inclined his head. "I would not like to say."

Barber seemed to take no notice. "I'd say the killer stood pretty much where you're standing now, Mr Carr, square in the doorway, possibly a little bit inside, and took aim. Was the door open when you got here?"

"Yes." Carr leaned towards the inspector. "I took the liberty of asking Mr Hirst whether anything looked amiss in the office. He said not."

If Barber was annoyed by this minor investigative instinct, he did not express it. "You're staying with the Bayliss family, I seem to remember."

"Indeed."

"Did you like him?"

"I did not know him particularly well," said Carr, with diplomacy.

"You accepted his invitation to stay for the weekend," Barber felt obliged to say.

Carr smiled. "I am a man alone in the world, Inspector. Sometimes, one craves company."

Barber did not seem keen to probe the point any further. "When was the last time you saw him alive?"

"Yesterday lunchtime. He took me to the local public house."

*The Black Bull?* Barber could not imagine this dapper little man being at home in a pub. "Did you enjoy it?"

Carr gave a slight shrug. "There was an altercation, I'm afraid, between one of the mill workers and Mr Bayliss."

"Which worker?"

"His name is Michael Arden."

Barber nodded. "I know him."

"He and Bayliss quarrelled, and it ended with Bayliss dismissing the boy."

"Firing him?"

"Indeed."

"How did Arden deal with that?"

"He had marched out of the public house before it happened. Mr Bayliss shouted after him."

Barber was thinking. "This quarrel…"

But Carr had anticipated him. "It was about nothing very significant. Certainly nothing that might be considered a motive for murder."

Barber folded his arms. "Very well."

"However, on the floor there, I found this." He reached into his pocket and produced the paper napkin.

Barber glared at him. "This is evidence, Mr Carr! You can't go around disturbing it as you please!"

Carr clicked his tongue with impatience. "Come now, Inspector, it hardly matters. You would have picked it up yourself, and it would have been disturbed in any case, so what does it matter? Besides, I am wearing gloves, as you see," Carr added, with a sententious smile.

It was hardly the point, but Barber could see from Carr's expression that labouring it would be a waste of time. Shaking his head, in an effort to register some official disgust, he looked down at the napkin. *Sinclair's* was a place he knew, but not one he had frequented. In that regard, it was as unattainable for him and Margaret as Stanley Tideswell's Italian lakes. He turned it over and read the words on the back. Almost immediately, a shiver of excitement danced along his spine.

"This is a threat," he declared. "And the initials…"

Carr nodded. "Michael Arden."

"The man who quarrelled with our victim."

"Our second victim," murmured Carr pedantically. "And this is not the only act of malice against Mr Bayliss. Tell me, Inspector, do you know anything about the mill's poltergeist?"

"About its what, sir?"

Carr smiled. He looked over his shoulder and called Eric Hirst. "Would you please tell Inspector Barber about the poltergeist, Mr Hirst?"

Hirst did so, as succinctly as he could manage: about the broken windows, the dead rat, and the anonymous letter.

"Anonymous letter?"

"It was vile," said Hirst. "Pure bile and malice, and it ended by telling him he should hang himself."

"And last night," added Carr, "someone poured acid all over his favourite motor car."

Barber took a moment to consider it all. At last, he dismissed Hirst and turned his attention to Everett Carr. He held up the napkin. "A second death threat."

"So it would seem."

"Someone wanted to get at Bayliss very badly, and now that someone has succeeded."

Carr held up a warning finger. "We must not allow ourselves to be carried off in the wrong direction. Bayliss himself made a very good point, that people who want to murder a man don't normally give him advanced warning in the form of a threatening letter."

"You don't think these notes are connected with the murder?" Barber asked, astonished.

Carr nodded slowly. "I don't say that, Inspector. What I do say is that we must not allow ourselves to be distracted by them."

"I don't understand, Mr Carr."

"I simply mean, Inspector, that whoever wrote these threatening messages may not be the same person who shot Mr Bayliss this evening."

"It seems to me like cause and effect," said Barber with some obstinacy.

"Then why did this person not put Neville Pym on the same notice of his death as Arthur Bayliss?"

Barber looked at him. "You think it is the same killer?"

Carr nodded. "And so do you, I think."

Barber bowed his head, raising his eyebrows in silent surrender. "Yes, Mr Carr, God help me, I do."

Carr smiled and placed his hand on the inspector's arm. "Then perhaps we should set our minds very seriously to finding out who this killer is."

# Chapter Twenty-Six

It was not long afterwards that the police surgeon arrived. His business was concluded swiftly, efficiently, and without any fuss. It was a professional at work, and Carr found himself admiring the thorough approach of this burly, barrel-chested man with sombre eyes, ruddy cheeks, and large hands and fingers that belied the obvious delicacy of their skill. Inspector Barber obviously knew the man in a personal as well as a professional capacity, since he talked to him in lowered tones about sport results, the doctor's grandchildren (only recently born, Carr deduced from the exchanges), and domestic pressures that the inspector was feeling. At last, the doctor got to his feet and began making notes in a battered, dog-eared notebook.

"Only a guess for now, Tommy, as you know," he said, his voice thick with the local accent, "but he's been dead for no more than a couple of hours."

"He was found at around half past eight," said Barber, looking at Carr. "I thought he'd been dead for at least an hour when I got here, at nine, give or take a couple of minutes."

The doctor nodded. "Not a bad guess. So, let's say between seven o'clock and when he was found. I probably won't be able to be more definite than that even after cutting him open."

"Cause of death?"

Without any trace of irony, the doctor replied. "He was shot, Tommy."

Barber nodded. How ridiculous it was, he thought, that he had to have it said for the official report when it was so obvious. "A small handgun, I thought."

The doctor nodded. "I'd go along with that .22 calibre, if you want my best guess, but I won't say it again without a formal report to back me up."

And that was the medical examination over. Not for the first time in such matters, it had struck Carr how brief these initial examinations were, particularly for something so vital to a murder investigation. There would be more to come after a detailed examination, of course, but Carr's experience was that these basic pieces of information, time and cause of death, were seldom changed from this first estimate, so often carried out with this degree of cold and professional competence.

Barber gave a few instructions to his officers, and the process of removing what remained of Arthur Bayliss to the mortuary was undertaken. Given the hour, the official procedure would have to wait until the morning, the doctor said.

"Not ideal working on a Sunday, Tommy," he added, "and it'll be after church, you know that. I'll say a prayer for the man. Report sometime on Monday, Tuesday latest."

"Just as soon as you can," Barber replied.

Without the corpse in the chair, the office seemed ghoulishly empty, as if even in death, Bayliss was supposed to be in the place. Carr looked across to Eric Hirst and thought he must have been having similar thoughts, as his eyes were wide with an emotion Carr found difficult to define. For his part, Henry Bayliss had sunk to his haunches, leaning against the steel of the gantry, his eyes staring into space. He saw nothing. The momentary shock, which would soon turn to anger, no doubt, before its final transformation into grief, had blinded him to everything but the single point in the middle distance of nowhere on which he was now focused. He was biting his thumbnail, but it looked to all the world as if he was sucking his thumb, and in the instant, he seemed to revert to the fair-haired, innocent child he must once have been.

Once the office was cleared of all people, alive and dead, Barber took the key from the lock, closed the door, and used the key to secure the scene of the crime. He put the key in his pocket. Nobody would gain access to that office now without the inspector's permission being granted, and Carr felt curiously grateful for the assurance.

"Now, gentlemen," Barber said with a professionally courteous, but somehow inappropriate, smile, "I think it's best we all go back to Darton House together."

It was almost impossible not to take it as an official command, and they obeyed it accordingly.

During the journey back to the house, Carr found himself uneasy in his mind. He could not define precisely what disturbed him. It was not simply the fact of murder, terrible enough in itself, nor was it the always distasteful and painful task of breaking the news of sudden death to a family. It was something in addition to those very natural concerns. Something he had heard that had not rung true in his mind at the time, but which now, as typical as it was frustrating, could not make itself known to him. It was a common failing of his, one that he had never grown accustomed to, and he knew that the answer was always to force his brain not to try to retrieve the nugget of information but instead to compel himself to think of other matters entirely. In time, he knew, he would remember it, if only he could bring himself to stop thinking about it.

The solemn party of men went into the drawing room, where Rosamund and Marjorie were sitting close together on the settee. There were glasses of sherry on the table in front of them and a pot of coffee, with cups and saucers, set to one side. It seemed to Carr that the coffee was strangely perfunctory, since he felt sure that the circumstances demanded something calming rather than any significant stimulant. In unison, the ladies got to their feet as the men entered the room, and for the briefest of moments, they remained fixed in an awkward and macabre tableau, which subsequently was broken by Marjorie Bayliss, stepping forward and addressing the group of men as a whole.

"Where's my husband?" The question was so simple that it seemed almost devastating.

Inspector Barber stepped forward, turning his hat around between the tips of his fingers. How he hated such confrontations, one of the few things in life that experience could not make easier. Barber's old governor, a gruff

Manchester man from the Salford docks, had once told him the only way to deliver the news of a loved one's death to the family. "Be honest, be respectful, but don't offer sympathy, lad," he had said. "They don't want it. They want you to get the man who did it. Nothing else."

Barber had listened, and now, as on many other occasions, he implemented the advice. "Mrs Bayliss, I'm afraid I have some bad news. Your husband is dead."

There was a collective gasp from both wife and daughter. Marjorie sank back onto the settee, as if fearful that her knees would no longer support her, but Rosamund remained standing, her eyes alive with confusion and an apparent resolution to disbelieve the fact. She looked over to Henry, whose head was bowed, and she glared at him for what seemed to Carr like a long moment. At last, Henry raised his head, as if in some silent gesture of obedience, and nodded at his sister. Still, Rosamund remained standing, and the look in her eyes dimmed only slightly.

"An accident?" she asked.

Barber shook his head. "I'm afraid not."

"Suicide?" It was clear Rosamund did not believe it.

"Murder," said the inspector. "He was shot. In his office, at the mill."

Rosamund's control was beginning to dwindle, but she fought heroically to maintain it. Her gaze flickered to Everett Carr. "Two bodies in two days, Mr Carr. You have a talent for murder, it seems."

It was an unfair gibe, and Carr felt certain that Rosamund knew it, which is why he offered no retort to it. It was borne out of shock rather than malice, he knew, and it was unfair to punish the girl for speaking offensively when her mind was distorted by suppressed grief. She looked away from him at last and placed a hand on her mother's shoulder. Leaning towards her, she whispered something to Marjorie, so softly that Carr could not be sure of the words. Later, pondering the moment, he became increasingly sure of what she had said.

"He can't hurt us anymore, not now."

Carr said nothing in the moment, and even if he had wanted to, he would have been prevented from it by the voice of Henry Bayliss.

"I can't get the sight of him out of my head," he said. "There was so much blood. His eyes, staring and…" He shook his head, as if trying to dislodge the memory. "I can't believe he's dead."

Rosamund gave a guttural snarl of contempt. "Don't be a bloody hypocrite, Henry. You hated him as much as we did."

Henry glared at her. "I didn't want him dead!"

"Didn't you?" cried Rosamund.

"He was my father!"

"He was mine, too! But that doesn't change anything about how we felt about him, or what's happened." Rosamund's voice was raised, twisted with bitterness, but she cut her words short, as if she had regretted immediately the words that came from her lips.

Henry, however, was appalled by her. "Be careful, Rosa, you might just incriminate yourself."

Eric Hirst glanced at Everett Carr, and they both shared a mutual realisation that their presence in the room was an embarrassing one. It was not without some internal gratitude that Inspector Barber took control of the situation. With interest, Carr noticed that the inspector did not enquire into the cause of the scene that had just played out in front of him. No doubt, Carr thought, he was waiting for tempers to have subsided, so that he could probe the matter in the cold light of day. If that were the tactic, Carr had much admiration for it.

"I suggest everybody takes a moment to calm down," Barber said. "We have much to establish, and you will all have your opportunity to tell me what you need to. For now, though, I will need to ask some practical questions, I'm afraid."

"Can't it wait, Inspector?" asked Marjorie.

"No, Mrs Bayliss, but I won't keep you too long, I promise, although I will have to return in the morning."

"What sort of questions?" asked Rosamund.

Barber shrugged. "All very routine, miss. Where everyone was, for example."

Rosamund looked around the room. "We were all here."

Barber began to pace the room slowly. "The time of death was likely to be somewhere between seven o'clock this evening and half past eight, when these gentlemen"—he indicated Carr and Hirst—"and your brother found your father's body. Where was everyone between those times?"

Marjorie spoke first. "Must we do this now?"

"The sooner I have the information, the sooner I can leave you for the evening, Mrs Bayliss." Barber spoke without emotion. It was simply a statement of fact.

She shook her head. "I was in here. I'd had some letters to write in the afternoon, and I had a long bath, before dressing for dinner, and coming downstairs. I was in here until Mr Carr came in."

Seeing Carr's nod of agreement, Barber asked, "What time was that?"

"Half past seven, perhaps," said Carr.

Barber looked at Marjorie. "But nobody saw you in here before that?"

"No. I helped myself to a drink, so I did not ring for assistance. Henry came in soon after Mr Carr."

Henry confirmed it. "Then we heard the doorbell, and it was Eric."

"What time was that, sir?" Barber asked Hirst.

"A quarter to eight, perhaps," was the reply.

Barber looked back at Henry. "Where were you before you came in here?"

"Across the hall in the library." And then, pre-empting Barber's question, he added, "Alone."

Barber made a careful note. "Mr Hirst, where were you before you arrived here?"

"At my cottage. I left there around twenty to eight."

"You live nearby?" If Barber thought the question was unnecessary, as Carr did, it did not prevent him from asking it.

"Yes," came the inevitable reply. "Before that, I had a drink with Miss Stansfield."

Carr's mind went back immediately to the telephone call the butler had taken. He remained convinced that it had been Lydia Stansfield who had made it, and now that the discovery of Bayliss' body had been made, Carr wondered whether there was any sinister connotation to the call itself. Had

Hirst been wrong all along, and had Lydia wanted revenge on Bayliss for ending their relationship? If so, the telephone call was easily explained, and she would know that Bayliss would most likely be in one of two places: at home or his office. The call might simply have been a process of elimination. Carr remained silent on the point, but it rested uneasily at the back of his mind.

Barber had shifted his attention to Rosamund. "And you, miss?"

"I was in my room. I hope I don't have to say specifically that I was alone." The sarcasm was inappropriate, but Rosamund made no apology for it. "I came downstairs at a quarter to eight, just as Mr Hirst was arriving, and then the telephone rang."

Barber's brows raised in curiosity. "The telephone?"

"A woman, according to Grayson," said Rosamund.

"Did he recognise the voice?" asked Barber.

"He said not."

Barber thought in silence for a moment and scribbled something in his official notebook.

"There will be more questions tomorrow, as I've made clear," he said, "but one I need to ask now is whether anyone in this house owns a gun."

There was a collective shake of heads.

Barber scribbled once more in his notebook. It was impossible to say whether or not he had believed the response to his last question. "For now, I think that is all. I must ask none of you to leave Darton Vale for the foreseeable future. Mr Carr, I hope that is not an inconvenience for you."

"Not at all," said Carr, with a bow.

"I didn't think it would be," said Barber, with only a trace of irony in his voice. "I shall be back here early tomorrow with my officers. I suggest you all try to sleep."

With an official bow of farewell, Barber left the house. Carr watched from the drawing room window as the police car drove the inspector away into the night. His gaze lingered for a few moments but eventually he turned away from the natural twilight outside to face the altogether more unsettling darkness which had begun to rise within Darton House.

# Chapter Twenty-Seven

As he walked into breakfast the following morning, Everett Carr might have expected to detect grief and a sense of loss, but unnatural death produced its own effects, and they were seldom, in his experience, in accordance with the normal feelings that were pricked by any death from natural causes. As a unique crime, murder had unique effects on those confronted by it, and there was no reason why the Bayliss family should be any different. Carr found the three of them sitting in silence at the table, the plates of food before them barely touched, with a cloud of mistrust and recrimination hanging over them. Only Marjorie Bayliss seemed to betray any sense of genuine loss and human grief. Her eyes were ringed with red, and her cheeks were pale and drawn, and Carr could read in them both the evidence of a fitful if not sleepless night. In the children's expressions, however, there were no traces of such sentiment. Rosamund's eyes were restless, glancing at her brother, then at her mother, and then finally back at her plate. Carr found the silent tableau fascinating, and he wondered what it was that Rosamund so obviously wished to say, and why she seemed to lack the courage to say it.

Marjorie stirred from her silence only when Carr sat next to her. Across the table, both Rosamund and Henry did likewise, acknowledging him with cautious smiles and nods of their heads, which Carr returned with an almost noble courtesy.

"I thought I might go to church this morning," Marjorie said to nobody in particular. "To say a prayer for him."

Rosamund was unable to prevent the small snort of derision from escaping her lips. "Is this how we're going to deal with it?"

"Be quiet, Rosa," snarled Henry.

She slammed her hands on the table. "No, Henry, I won't. We can't pretend to be sorry about what's happened. We just can't. Not after everything we've all said before."

Marjorie fought to retain her dignity. "He was your father, Rosamund. And he's dead."

"But what sort of a father was he? What sort of a husband, for that matter? Lydia wasn't the only one, I daresay."

Henry got to his feet, swiftly and violently, knocking his chair over in the process. "We understand, Rosa! He was cruel to us all in one way or another, and he cared more about money, the mill, and his damned car than he did for us. We know it. But, for God's sake, can't you show some compassion? For Mother's sake, if not your own."

"I just hate how we can be such hypocrites so easily," said Rosamund, sullenly.

"Is that any better than sounding as if you're glad he's dead?" said Henry. "You're talking as if you think that whoever killed him did us a favour and we should be grateful to him. It's obscene." A further thought seemed to occur to him. "And you might need to be careful, Rosa, because if Inspector Barber sees it the same way, you might find yourself in serious trouble."

"That's a beastly thing to say," snapped Rosamund.

"Not as beastly as anything you've said," replied Henry, his voice calmer now. He picked up the chair and sat down on it. He looked at Marjorie. "I'm sorry, Mother. If you want to go to church, I will come with you, of course."

Marjorie had said nothing during the quarrel between her children, but Carr could see that it had pained her. Her eyes were tightly closed, and the knuckles of her clasped hands were so white that it seemed as if her nodules of bone of her skeletal knuckles were showing through the thin parchment of skin. Now, she slowly opened her eyes, and Carr saw a single tear roll down one of the pale cheeks.

"I am going to church to say a prayer for my husband," she said. The voice was quiet, barely audible, and weighed down with regret, but no less powerful because of it. "And I would prefer to go on my own."

She rose from the table slowly, Carr doing likewise as a matter of course, and she walked towards the door. It seemed to Carr that she glided as she crossed the room, like a spectral apparition, and when she had left, the sense of unease that he had experienced on entering seemed now to increase. Henry wiped his lips with his napkin and excused himself, saying he would be in his studio should he be needed by the police, and only Rosamund and Everett Carr remained seated.

"I do care," she said. "That he's dead, I mean. It does matter to me."

"I know that, my child."

"But I find it so disgusting that we can feel sad about his death when we all hated him when he was alive."

Carr sipped some of his coffee. "It is not a question of hypocrisy."

"Isn't it?"

He dabbed at his moustache with his handkerchief. "Whatever you thought of him, he was still your father. He had his faults, as we all have, but he wasn't a monster."

"He was to me." Her mind went back to the darkness of the cellar and the cupboard under the stairs.

"That is because you have no perspective, my child. How would you describe your father?"

Rosamund, it seemed, did not need time to consider her answer. "Difficult, arrogant, selfish, proud, vain, opinionated, cruel, deceitful."

Carr leaned forward in his chair. "But not wicked, evil, sadistic, perverted?"

"No." She was not sure why she told the lie. Perhaps, in the wake of his death, it was easier than speaking the truth.

"I have known men like that," said Carr sadly. "Men who kill for pleasure, men who abuse women for sport, men who harm children in ways you could not imagine. These men are monsters, and they should die without being mourned. But your father was not one of them. He was simply a man with traits you did not like. That does not mean he is undeserving of your grief."

Rosamund considered the point in silence, picking uselessly at a slice of toast but eating none of it. "I understand what you're saying, Mr Carr."

Carr smiled at her. "There is only one reason for you to consider yourself a hypocrite in these circumstances, my child."

"And that is?"

His next words were spoken in a colder, darker version of his voice than she had expected. "If you mourn his death when, in fact, it was you who killed him."

Rosamund stared at him in disbelief. She visibly recoiled in her chair and gripped the edge of the table to prevent herself from falling out of her seat. She looked at Carr, motionless and placid, his dark eyes contemplating her with solemn interest, and it occurred to her that somehow, he had changed. The avuncular politeness and the amiable shyness that she had noted on her first introduction to him now seemed to have darkened into something altogether more dangerous.

"How can you say that?" she whispered. "Why would I kill him?"

He smiled benignly. "If you had no reason to kill him, why all this talk of hypocrisy? And last night, you all but confessed to hating him. Why was that, I wonder?"

If he had intended for it to be an invitation to explain, Rosamund was not about to accept it. "I was here, in the house, when Father was killed."

Carr held up a finger. "You were alone in your room, my child. You appeared at a quarter to eight, yes, but before that, there is nobody to say where you were or what you were doing."

"The same applies to Mummy and Henry," she said.

Carr bowed his head. "Quite so."

"You think one of us murdered Daddy?"

"I say only that you have no alibis. And I say it not to scare you, my child, but to prepare you. Inspector Barber will have taken note of it last night, and when he comes here today, he will press you on it. You must be ready for him."

Rosamund shook her head, as if refusing to accept the truth of any of his words. "It's disgusting, all of it. It's horrible."

"It is murder, my child," said Carr gravely, but to himself, because Rosamund had fled the room and his company.

# Chapter Twenty-Eight

The rain that had threatened to make an appearance the previous day now began to fall at last, and it came down in thin shafts like stiletto knife blades. Carr had known heavy rain, of course, but seldom had he experienced it so fiercely as this. The shards of water were almost invisible, but they drenched the town of Darton Vale so heavily that it seemed like a Biblical flood. As he walked down the main street, wrapped in his black overcoat, with the lower part of his face hidden by a large scarf, Carr wondered why the weather up here was so much more ferocious. He was not of a particularly scientific mind, but he assumed it must be something to do with altitude, although it was impossible to reject the notion that these barren and expansive hills that surrounded him were not in some way responsible for the bleakness of the weather. Whatever the cause, and it did not occupy his mind extensively, Carr found himself wishing that he was in the relative calm of London weather, which, although no stranger to cold and wet, was never as harsh as this. As he looked at the shining cobbles of the street and up at the bleak expanse of the moors around him, Carr felt a sudden isolation overcome him, and never had he felt so alone and insignificant in the wake of a shower of rain. He supposed that there was a philosophical, even theological, debate to be had about the sensation, but he was too cold and wet to engage his mind with it.

A brief and subtle enquiry with Mr Grayson had given him the address of the cottage where Michael Arden lived, once with his mother, now alone. Carr had little trouble finding it, but the rain and wind had made the walk a long and uncomfortable one, so that by the time he knocked on the small door, which hardly seemed to be any defence against these raging elements, Carr was cold, soaked, and exhausted. The door opened, and Carr found himself confronted by Arden, who stood in gruff silence, waiting for an explanation for the interruption of his Sunday morning.

"I wonder, sir, if I might come in for a moment," Carr said, his voice muffled by the scarf. "I am drenched, as you will see, cold, and my leg is causing me a great deal of pain."

Arden looked down at the stiffened limb and saw the silver-handled cane that supported it. He saw the reddened cheeks above the scarf, the plea for sanctuary in the curiously dark eyes, and the sodden shine of the black coat and hat. Behind him, Arden could feel the relative warmth of the fire, the heat emanating onto his palm from the mug of tea he had brewed, and he could hear the voice of his mother welcoming this stranger into the parlour with grace and kindness.

He pulled open the door and stepped aside. "Come in."

Carr muttered several words of thanks and gratefully obeyed. "I shall not intrude on your time too long, I assure you. Just a few moments to warm myself and rest this damned leg."

Arden was distracted by an elusive memory of having seen this man before. "An accident?"

"A bullet wound."

"The war?"

"No, a criminal gang."

The words had been spoken with such calm frankness that they shocked Arden. He took a moment to look at this man, who now lowered himself painfully into one of the chairs by the fire. The waxed, extravagant moustache, the Imperial beard, the deep emerald green of the bow tie and handkerchief, at odds with the sombre black of the suit, and the overt, even exaggerated politeness hardly suggested any connection with violent criminals. But the response to Arden's question had come so easily and so candidly that he found he was unable to dismiss it, but nor did it seem like a point he could or should pursue any further. Instead, he hung the man's coat over the back of a chair and placed it by the side of the fire.

"It will soon dry, I'm sure," he said.

Carr nodded his gratitude and accepted the cup of tea that Arden offered. It was strong, rather too strong for Carr's taste, but it was so hot and warming that he felt no ground for complaint. He took a moment to assess Arden, taking in the curling black hair, the determined chin, and the brooding menace in the dark eyes. He thought about the impression he had gained over the past few days of this young man as lonely, grieving, and angry, and he could discern all of those qualities in him, but nothing had prepared him for the kindness that he had shown to a stranger. Carr had expected a door slammed in his face, even a curt word of dismissal, but neither had come, and he found himself considering what Michael Arden might be like once the darkness of his life had been lifted. Once someone treated him with dignity and compassion, perhaps, instead of brawling with him in public houses.

"I'm very grateful to you, my boy," Carr had said. "You can't understand how much of a relief for me it is to sit down."

"Have you walked far?"

"Only from Darton House," Carr replied, "but the cold affects my leg very badly and," he added with a small laugh, "I have seldom known cold as you have up here."

And now Arden remembered. "You were with Bayliss in the pub the other day. You're this friend of his from London."

Carr sipped the tea. "Indeed. My name is Everett Carr."

Arden took the hand that was offered to him. "It was you who found Neville Pym dead."

"I'm afraid it was."

Arden looked into the fire. "I was sorry to hear about that. He was harmless, Mr Pym was, whatever else he might have been."

Carr understood the implication. "You don't think, perhaps, that someone might have killed him because of his nature?"

"Maybe we're not as backward around here as people in London might think." It was a defensive, if not antagonistic, response, and Carr thought it best to ignore it.

"The police don't seem able to find a motive for Mr Pym's death," he said. "I wondered if he might be the person responsible for the pranks at the mill."

Now, Arden did react, but only with genuine surprise. "Why would he be?"

Carr shrugged. "His death must be explained somehow, no matter how ridiculous an idea might sound."

"I can't see any reason for Pym to hate Bayliss. On that, he was alone," Arden added under his breath.

But Carr had heard him, and he nodded slowly. "Yes, there does seem to be a suspicion that the wrong man was killed."

"I'd say so," replied Arden.

"It could hardly be a case of mistaken identity," Carr continued. "Mr Pym was killed at home, after all."

Arden swigged from his mug of tea and continued to glare into the flames of the fire. For a long moment, Carr did likewise. He could feel the heat of the fire soothing his leg, and the crackling of the logs in the grate seemed to reverberate with the tingling of his nerve ends as they prickled into life once more. In this simple cottage, devoid of any extravagance, with its stone walls barely decorated save for a few scattered photographs and prints, and its cold floor furnished only with a simple but threadbare rug, Carr began to feel a glow of honest if plain living. He was oddly content in the place, and he told himself that he was just as comfortable here as he ever was in the Albany or the Icarus, but he was aware that the effect might have been artificial, caused more by the soothing and much-needed warmth of the fire than any genuine emotional response to his surroundings.

"Are you close friends with Bayliss?" asked Arden suddenly.

Carr shook his head. "We are acquaintances only."

One side of Arden's mouth raised in a crooked grin. "You don't seem to be the sort of person who would be friends with him."

Carr took it as a compliment and bowed his head. "I was sorry to hear about your mother."

Arden bristled, but if he had felt the need to respond with violence, verbal or otherwise, he seemed to resist the temptation. "She'd been ill for a while."

"Is it lonely here, without her?"

There was a vague shrug of the shoulders. "I try to keep busy. Right now, I'm looking for another job. Thanks to your friend," he added.

"Yes, I was sorry about that. I think he overreacted."

"He can stick his job," Arden said. "There'll be others."

Carr admired the optimism, however misplaced he considered it to be. "I hope so. Did you enjoy working at the mill?"

Arden gave a grim smirk and lit a cigarette. "Not much else for a man like me to do. What's your profession, Mr Carr?"

"I'm retired. I was a criminal barrister, then a judge," he added after a moment.

"That explains the leg, maybe?"

"It does," said Carr, unable to hide the smile on his lips.

Arden, however, did not share it. "There's a world of difference between you and me, Mr Carr. People like you have options. People like me haven't. That's how simple it is."

"Your view of the world is so bleak?"

The young man did not reply. Instead, he slurped at the mug of tea and stared back into the fire. Carr, momentarily embarrassed by the silence and fearful that he might have offended the lad, did likewise. At last, he became conscious of movement beside him, and he looked up to find that Arden had risen to his feet and was now leaning against the wall into which the small iron fire grate was set.

"I don't think it's fair that some people have everything and others have nothing," Arden said.

"You mean money?"

"Partly." Arden drained his tea and wished that it had been something much stronger. "We're all the same when it comes down to it, Mr Carr. Money divides people. Or am I wrong?"

Carr shook his head. "Perhaps not. I do not see any forcible argument against helping those who are less fortunate than oneself."

"That's one way of putting it."

Carr felt that he had caused some offence. "Perhaps if you told me what you meant, my boy, I could be of more help."

Arden put his cup down on the floor and stretched out his bare hands to Carr. The skin was rough, like old leather, and mottled with calluses and blisters. There was ingrained dirt beneath the fingernails, and among the traces of old cuts and lacerations, there were visible and permanent scars. Carr, subtly and carefully, so that Arden did not perceive it, looked down at his own hands, the smooth skin now tellingly clear of any abrasions or old wounds, and the well-manicured nails.

Arden was turning his hands over. "That's graft, Mr Carr. Hard work, and for barely enough wages to keep this cottage heated. If you came here for dinner, Mr Carr, you'd get bread and cheese, a slice of ham if you were lucky. Not the roast beef you're getting up at the house." The bitterness in his voice was palpable, and Carr felt strangely ashamed by it, but he said nothing. "And some people, Mr Carr," Arden continued, "they get everything for nothing. You don't get old man's hands at my age by painting pictures, do you?"

And here was the truth of it, thought Carr. "Is this the cause of your fight with Henry Bayliss?"

"We're about the same age, did you know that?"

"No."

Arden shook his head. "People don't think it, but we are. I look ten years older."

Carr knew what Arden wanted him to say: that his life had been harder, tougher, that it had aged him, whereas Henry Bayliss had retained his youthful complexion and handsome looks because his life had been the opposite, pampered and privileged. But Carr did not have the words.

"If you wish to have a political response from me, my boy, I have none to give you," he said. "I am not a political animal. But what I think I do have," he added, "is a sense of character. I have seen many men and women come before me when I was on the Bench. Do you know what those years of service to justice taught me?"

"Well?"

"That kindness and wickedness—good and evil, if you prefer, my boy—do not know or care about class, background, or sex. A man may have no money, but it is because he has donated it all to help others. Another man may be rich beyond compare, but treat others with contempt and disdain. A woman may kill, but it is to save another's life. Another woman may poison her husband for money. You see my point? The wealth or privilege of people like Henry Bayliss should matter less than the type of person he is. Do you know what sort of man he is?"

Arden lowered his head. "Spoilt, naïve, worthless."

Carr smiled. The response was belligerent and unworthy of Arden, but its sullenness showed Carr that some of the meaning of his words had penetrated the toughened frame of the young man. "He is a kind, loving, and supportive son and brother. You decry his painting as worthless, Mr Arden, but it is an ambition of his. He does not want the privilege of his life; he wants only to paint. How much money do you think he will make doing it? And yet, he still wishes to pursue it. Does that not say more about him than his father's money?"

Arden sat down once more, clasping his hands together and leaning forward towards the fire, with his elbows on his knees. "Maybe it's his father I hate more than him."

Carr shuffled in his chair. "Did you hate Arthur Bayliss?"

"Didn't everybody?" sneered Arden.

"Somebody most certainly did," said Carr, his voice low and ominous. "Arthur Bayliss was murdered last night. He was shot in his office at the mill."

For a moment, it seemed as if Arden had not understood the words. He was looking at Carr, but there was a distance in his eyes, as if he were looking through his visitor into the recollection of a long-forgotten memory. His lips seemed to attempt to speak, as if he felt that he should make some verbal response to the news, but was unable to find appropriate words to do so, until at last, they closed firmly shut and pursed into a grim defiance. Now, his eyes flickered back to the present, and they burned with malice as their journey came to an end.

"I won't say I'm sorry," he said, more to himself than to Carr. "I'm damned if I will."

Despite himself, Carr admired the honesty. "The police will want to know where you were, my boy."

"Why?"

The question was as foolish as it was naïve, and Carr suspected that it was little more than an instinctive reaction, one that Carr found quite natural.

"You knew a victim of murder. It is purely a matter of routine," he said.

"Let them ask what they like."

"And what will you say in reply?"

Arden shrugged. "That I was here."

"Alone?"

"Until I decided I'd go along to *The Black Bull*. Plenty of people saw me in there who know me. And I spoke to most of them."

"I see," smiled Carr. "What time did you get there?"

"Half-past seven, a quarter to eight, maybe."

Carr smiled gently and sipped some tea. The timings spoke their own tale, and they meant that Arden would have had time to get from the cottage to the mill and back to the public house with time to kill Bayliss. The precise times would need to be established, but Inspector Barber would do that, and Carr doubted that his investigation into those times would alter the fact that Arden had the opportunity to kill.

"Tell me, Mr Arden," Carr said after a moment's pause, "were you also here at the cottage when Mr Pym was killed?"

Arden got to his feet, the callused hands balled into fists. "What are you saying, Mr Carr?"

"I am merely asking a question, my boy," said Carr, not looking at him.

"I was, as a matter of fact," Arden said, "but I don't see what business it is of yours."

"None," conceded Carr. "But there must be a connection between the two deaths, and the police will certainly ask you—"

"I'd like you to leave now."

Carr struggled to his feet. "We must be realistic, Mr Arden. You had a very public argument with Mr Bayliss yesterday, and hours after it, the man is dead."

Arden scoffed. "Hardly evidence."

"No," said Carr gently, "but the threatening message, perhaps, is."

Slowly, he raised his dark eyes to look into Arden's and, for the second time, he saw something approaching fear flicker across the man's face. "Message?"

Carr nodded. "There was a threatening message found near the body."

"Saying what?"

Carr did not need to concentrate to recall the words. *"I won't let you get away with it again."*

"What's that got to do with me?"

"You deny writing it."

"Of course, I bloody do," hissed Arden.

Carr nodded, rather sadly. "It was signed with your initials, my boy."

Arden was shaking his head, and he pointed his finger accusingly at Carr. "That's a bloody *lie!*"

Carr shrugged. "The police will bear me out, Mr Arden. And the note must be explained."

"It's nothing to do with me!" Arden shouted, turning his back on Carr. "I think you'd better leave, Mr Carr. I'm sure your coat is warmed through now."

Carr knew when discretion was required. He bowed slightly in deference to Arden's demand and made it his business to put on his hat and coat. At the door, he paused and looked over his shoulder to the young man who stood seething still in the far corner of the room.

"Thank you for your hospitality and kindness," Carr said. "I am truly sorry if I have caused you distress or offence."

"Forget about it," came the dismissive reply.

Carr maintained his position. "If I might ask one more question…"

Arden turned round, his shoulders square and his hands still balled into those huge fists. "Leave my house, Mr Carr."

But the older man persisted. "Have you ever been to a restaurant in

Manchester called *Sinclair's?*"

Arden's eyes glared with that same blend of fear and rage that Carr had already noticed in them. His breathing intensified, and his head began to shake in protest. "Get out," he began to whisper dangerously, repeating the phrase with increasing volume. Carr, paralysed by this startling reaction, remained fixed to his spot by the door.

"Get out of here," Arden said again, now with a dark menace in his voice. "Get out now, before I damage that other leg."

Carr remained motionless. "If this note means something to you, Mr Arden, I can perhaps help you."

"Whatever you think you know about me," snarled Arden, "you're wrong. Now, go. I'm not warning you again."

Carr bowed stiffly. "Very well. But I warn you also, Mr Arden. Sooner or later, mark my words, you will need a friend, and I think you would be wise to consider that friend to be me."

The words said, the door was opened and closed, and Carr was outside in the cold once more. He leaned back to the door, however, pressing his ear against it. From within, he could hear first the small explosion of what he assumed was one of the mugs of tea being thrown against the wall, then the sound of a chair being hurled across the room, and finally, and perhaps most worrying of all, Carr heard the sound of muffled and stifled sobbing.

# Chapter Twenty-Nine

The rain had eased but not stopped completely when Carr found himself back in the centre of Darton Vale. It was now a drizzle only, but the grey skies above him showed no sign of impending blue, and the sun had never seemed so far away from him in his life. What glimpses of it he had seen had been so brief as to be irrelevant. He began to wonder whether these northern landscapes ever saw extensive sunlight or whether, this far from London, it was never anything other than a seasonal cycle of autumn and winter.

The reverberations of his confrontation with Michael Arden echoed in his mind. And it had been a confrontation, rather than an interview. Carr had known that it was always likely to have been a difficult conversation, but he had not prepared himself for the definite sense of threat and harm that threatened to overcome him in those final moments. It had been, on reflection, a fascinating, perhaps even illuminating, glimpse into Arden's psychology and his obvious capacity for violence. Had Carr felt intimidated by it? Despite his stance against it, he knew that he had felt fear, and he was not ashamed to admit it to himself. But now, with the danger passed, he was considering the matter in more analytical terms, and he was now wondering how much it would take for Arden to take the additional step from threatening violence to committing it. And Carr's own laboured steps as he walked seemed small enough to give him the answer. And yet, there had been the tears that he had overheard. If Arden had committed murder, had those been tears of guilt, of remorse, of regret? Or had they been tears over something else entirely, something much more personal to the young man, something even that had prompted him to murder in the first instance? The old poem came into the mind of Everett Carr, but with a slightly different refrain: *questions, questions everywhere...*

But, as yet, he had no answers to give.

As if to mirror his mental despondency, his shattered knee buckled, and with a grunt of pain and frustration, he sank against the perimeter wall of the church. The pain, caused by the cold and exertion of the morning, seared through his whole leg like a lance of fire, and Carr was unable to prevent another pitiful groan of distress howling from his mouth. The road seemed to rise towards him, and for a moment, he assumed that he was falling to the ground, but he realised almost immediately that it was only the overwhelming desire to fall that was manipulating his perception. He had lived with the persistent pain in his knee for so long now that he had begun to believe that he was accustomed to it, but this sudden and tremendous bout of agony reminded him that he had not done so, and possibly never would. The church bells behind him began to peal, loudly and incessantly, sounding for all the world like a death knell calling him to his final moment of judgment. A vision of Miranda, the wife who had died in his place, swirled in front of his eyes, and in between the harsh gasps of crippling discomfort, he whispered her name, once, possibly twice.

"Mr Carr, are you all right?"

He did not register the voice immediately. First, he felt the strong hands supporting him under the arms, and then the strangely giddying motion of being pulled upright. Helplessly, he looked into the eyes of his saviour, and he saw Henry Bayliss looking down on him with wide-eyed concern.

"I...I..." stammered Carr uselessly. "Can't walk...can't..." The words, barely intelligible, were little more than gasps of air.

Henry pulled Carr's arm around his shoulders and took his weight. "I can't carry you back to the house. It's too far. Can you wait here, Mr Carr? Lean against the wall."

He helped in the manoeuvre, and Carr, breathless, held onto the stone wall of the church, like a penitent man at the feet of Christ. He was vaguely aware of Henry running away and, sensing desertion, Carr tried to call after him, but the pain and embarrassment had robbed his lungs of the air required. Momentarily, although to Carr it had seemed like hours, Henry returned with assistance. Carr allowed himself to be carried away from the wall, helping as much as he could, but only too aware that he was little more than a collection of lead bars in a tailored suit.

Later, he wasn't sure whether he had passed out for a moment or whether his memory had simply played tricks on him, but when he replayed the incident in his mind, the next thing he remembered was sitting in a comfortable armchair, his leg outstretched and resting on a dining chair, and a cold flannel on his brow. Somewhere, he could smell whisky, possibly brandy, and he became aware of a glass of the former on a small table beside him. Standing in front of him were Henry Bayliss and Eric Hirst, and behind them a woman Carr seemed vaguely to recognise.

"How are you feeling, Mr Carr?" asked Henry.

Carr smiled and nodded his appreciation. "Embarrassed, my boy, if truth be told."

"Nonsense. Are you sure you're all right?"

Carr nodded and pointed at the offending knee with the ferrule of his cane. "This cursed injury gets the better of me sometimes, that is all."

Eric Hirst handed him the glass of whisky. "I don't know a better tonic than this, sir."

It prompted a smile from Carr, who accepted it with pleasure. He looked at Henry. "Did your mother go to church as she wished?"

Henry nodded. "I offered again to go with her, but she refused, of course. So, I planned on walking down to meet her after Matins. That was when I saw you."

"And he came banging on the door here for help," said Hirst. "Lydia's cottage is next door to the church."

Simultaneously, Carr had three thoughts of varying degrees of importance, as it seemed to him. Firstly, that the woman in the room was Lydia Stansfield; secondly, that he was settled so comfortably in her cottage; and thirdly, perhaps most ominously, that her cottage was next door to that of Neville Pym.

"My thanks to you both, gentlemen," said Carr. "And to you, dear lady," he added, nodding to her.

The young woman stepped forward. "Not at all. I hope you're feeling better now."

"Much, dear lady, thank you," said Carr, smiling warmly, and sipping at the whisky. His eyes refused, for the moment, to leave Lydia Stansfield.

It was Henry who broke the spell. "I should get back to the church to meet Mother. Are you well enough to come with us, Mr Carr?"

He felt it, certainly, but Carr gently waved away the question. "I think, if it is permitted, I should rest my leg for just a few moments longer. I have no wish to intrude, dear lady, but…"

Lydia smiled. "By all means, please don't think twice about it."

"You are most kind."

Henry accepted the decision without further debate and gave Carr a reassuring shake of his hand. "If you telephone the house, I'll get Grayson to send a car for you."

"I shall be fine now, my boy, thank you. Go and tend to your mother, who needs you even more than I have done today."

A murmur of laughter brought the matter to a close, and Hirst showed Henry to the door. In the lull, Carr took a moment to consider not only his surroundings but also, more crucially, his temporary hostess.

Like her, the cottage appeared to be both charming and elegant, tastefully and brightly furnished, in a manner that seemed to match her striking blonde hair rather than the funeral black of her dress. There were framed pictures on the walls, sketches of naked ladies, modest rather than provocative, and of faces of unknown people whose features displayed in turn intense fascination with an unseen subject or casual dismissal of it. There was a quality about the sketches, their accuracy of depiction, but their simultaneous absence of finish, that made Carr wonder if they were the work of a gifted amateur rather than a professional artist. In turn, he wondered whether that amateur was Lydia Stansfield herself. The features depicted were not hers, however, of that there could be no doubt. They were those of attractive women, but they lacked Lydia's fine, almost indefinable allure. She had lit a cigarette and had sat down on the settee, crossing one leg over the other, with an almost hypnotically assured elegance. And yet, Carr felt sure, she was not aware of her beauty. If she were, she did not wear it on the sleeve of that finely cut black dress.

Carr was suddenly conscious of the silence in the room. "I am sorry to intrude on you in this way, dear lady."

"Do stop apologising, Mr Carr," she said. Her tone was not irritated, but pleasantly accommodating. "Honestly, it is no trouble, and I'm very glad to help."

"You are most gracious."

Lydia let out an involuntary laugh. His manner of speaking seemed so old-fashioned that it seemed to her almost ridiculous. Her laugh had not gone undetected, but he did not seem offended by it, since he smiled warmly at her, and as he did so, she felt a curiously comforting feeling come over her, as if she might one day find herself freely confessing her darkest secrets to this man. He had that effect on her, this assurance of almost priestly confidence blended with the warm approachability of a favourite uncle. Perhaps, she thought, it was the amiable manner, but it may also have been those dark, compelling eyes.

"I believe we had a mutual friend, Mr Carr," she said.

"It would seem so, dear lady. Although I rather think that you knew Mr Bayliss better than I did."

"The gossips have been talking, have they?"

Even without the tone of voice, it would have been clear how much she despised such people, and Carr had a sudden image of Neville Pym, dead in his chair, only a few yards from where Carr himself now sat.

Politely, but not entirely honestly, Carr gave a shake of his head. "I meant that I have known Mr Bayliss for a short time only."

"I see." Lydia was suitably chastened by the response, but the dark malice in her eyes had not dissipated. "You know about my relationship with him, though."

Carr felt it was diplomatic not to respond, but the involuntary nod of his head worked against him. "Did you telephone Darton House last night,

Miss Stansfield?"

She rose to her feet and walked to the mantel. From a silver case, she took a cigarette and lit it. Even such a mundane task as this, Carr noticed, was done with the same alluring elegance that was so obvious in her.

"Yes, I did," she said. "I suppose it would be foolish to deny it."

"May I ask why?"

Now, she laughed, with more scorn than humour. "If you want the truth, I'm not sure. I don't know what I would have done if he'd been at home. Hung up, I suspect. Not so much a woman scorned as a dirty little coward," she added, but it was a personal reproach, the words meant only for her and not for anyone else.

"Did you leave home after making the call?"

"No." She inhaled deeply on the cigarette, looking at him in a brief, almost insolent sideways glance. "Motive and opportunity, Mr Carr. But no means, unfortunately, since I don't own a gun."

Her knowledge of the method of murder did not surprise him. Eric Hirst would have told her some, if not all, of the details. In Carr's experience, infatuated men were childishly indiscreet if they thought taking a girl into their confidence would make them seem important or exciting.

"I am sorry to hear you talk in such terms, dear lady," said Carr.

"One must be realistic, I think. I'm bound to be a suspect, aren't I?" She inhaled deeply on the cigarette once more. "First, my neighbour is killed, then my lover. And I don't have the ghost of an alibi for either."

"Were you at home on the night Mr Pym died?"

"Yes, alone."

"Did you hear anything unusual?"

"Nothing, as I told the police."

Carr seemed to be on the verge of asking a question when Eric Hirst walked back into the room and closed the door behind him. "Poor Henry. His father's death seems to have hit him harder than anyone might think."

Lydia sat back down on the settee. "Despite their differences, Arthur was still Henry's father."

"There was no love lost between them, though," said Hirst. "We can't deny it."

"That doesn't make Henry a murderer," protested Lydia. "Or does it, Mr Carr?"

Carr shrugged gently. "People kill for many reasons, some of which we cannot understand. It is a matter of individual psychology. What to one person is a meaningless insult, for example, might to another person be a definite reason to kill."

Lydia put a hand to her throat. "What a chilling thought."

Carr took a moment to consider her. Her previous hostility, however minor it had been, had thawed now, it seemed, and her brows had creased in concentration, and her eyes darted around indiscriminately, as if she were considering some new insight into human behaviour that had previously been hidden from her. It was a common revelation, Carr had come to realise, and it remained for him one of the more disturbing consequences of the proximity of murder to individual people. After murder had intruded into their lives, their beliefs, their preconceptions, their opinions, and their assurances about the goodness in people were shaken, betrayed, and changed forever.

"I have been trying to gain a knowledge of the town," he said, as if to provide some form of banal distraction from the horrors of the killings at Darton Vale. "How far is the Bayliss mill from here, for example?"

It was Eric Hirst who replied. "Not far at all. Less than a mile, certainly. You could walk it in five minutes or so, if you cut across the allotments at the back."

Carr was thinking deeply. "It took only a short time also to get to the mill from Darton House."

"By car, yes," said Hirst. "Rather longer on foot, even running as I did last night."

"How long, would you say?"

Hirst shrugged. "Half an hour walking, perhaps, and fifteen minutes or so if one were running."

"Quite so," said Carr, recalling the wait for Hirst to arrive at the mill on the previous evening. "The time of death has been fixed from half past seven to half past eight, when we found the body. If any member of the family were the killer, they would need to leave the house in good time to get to the mill, commit the murder, and be back before we all assembled in the hallway at a quarter to eight."

"That is true," said Hirst.

"You were out of breath and rather exhausted when you met us at the mill last night, my friend."

"One would have to be an athlete to run that distance and not be out of breath."

Carr smiled. "Did any of the Bayliss family display any signs of such exertion when you arrived that night?"

"No, I must confess not."

Carr nodded. "Quite so, and you see the difficulty. If anyone from the house is the killer, they would have to have got to the mill and back before quarter to eight, when we all assembled in the hall, without showing those signs of exertion you displayed, more so since they would have had to run the distance *twice*."

"Unless they used one of the cars," said Hirst.

Carr shook his head. "You will recall that I spoke to the chauffeur before we drove to the mill last night. He confirmed to me that nobody had taken any of the motor cars out of the garage that day, and he was working in the garage all evening."

"Then, we are back to the likelihood that the culprit is someone other than those in the hallway last night." Hirst stared at Carr. "Surely Michael Arden is surely most likely."

Suddenly, Lydia let out a growl of impatience and sprang to her feet. "That's a monstrous suggestion. You mustn't say things like that, Eric. You could get people into serious trouble."

"But it's true, Lydia." Hirst's voice was heavy with implication.

"Whether it is or not, it isn't for us to say." She looked at Carr. "Don't you agree with me, Mr Carr?"

The question was more of a dare to contradict her than a search for support, but Carr smiled amiably and shook his head.

"Perhaps, after all," he said, "we should leave the speculations to the police."

"Yes, we should," said Lydia softly, her voice barely audible.

"For now, I must intrude no longer." Carr struggled to his feet, refusing Hirst's attempts to assist, and brought himself to his full height. He shuffled on his coat and hat, wrapped his scarf around his neck, and bowed demurely to Lydia. "I hope we shall meet again, dear lady. And thank you again for your kindness."

"You're welcome," she replied. "It was no trouble."

Carr was sure it had been no trouble in the sense she meant it, but he was equally certain that her mind was far from peace. He was almost out of the room before she called to him.

"A thought, Mr Carr, which I thought I should share," she said. She was smiling, her expression one of friendly assistance, both of which were at odds with the dangerous intent behind her eyes, which impressed on Carr the discomfort that the scrape of a knife across an empty plate might produce.

"Indeed, dear lady?"

"You say the Bayliss chauffeur said nobody took one of the cars out of the garage that night."

"Indeed."

"Is there not such a thing as buying silence?"

"There is," said Carr gently.

"And being a servant, I suppose one does as one is told. It isn't easy for ordinary people to make their way in the world having been dismissed from previous employment."

"Quite so."

"So, someone in the family, Henry Bayliss, to use your own example, could have bribed or otherwise coerced the chauffeur into complicity in their crime, couldn't they?"

After a moment's silence, Everett Carr smiled and gave a solemn bow. "How very perceptive of you, dear lady. Good day."

It was a thought that had already occurred to him; his manner and the impish smile beneath the ridiculous moustache told Lydia as much. As he limped out of the room, Hirst following him out of a sense of hospitable duty, she wondered whether any of it mattered. Lydia doubted it, but there was no way she could know for sure. Nevertheless, whatever had been in Carr's mind, she felt able to tell herself that she had at least tried to throw some fog into his headlamps. Reasonable doubt, was that not the phrase? As long as Lydia could continue to insinuate that doubt into the minds of the police—and Everett Carr, if need be—all might still be well, and perhaps, after all, she might never have to tell the truth about the murder of Arthur Bayliss.

# Chapter Thirty

They had arranged to meet at Layton Brook. It seemed fitting to Rosamund that any confrontation with George Toole should be at the place where she had first realised that her feelings for him were compromised, and where she had made those first tentative steps to express the fact. If Toole had recalled the significance of the place, he had not said so. Whether Rosamund had expected him either to remember or to comment on it was not certain. Nor was it clear why she had instigated this meeting, beyond her belief that there was something more to be said between them, even if it was easier to believe there was not.

He was on time, but then when was he not, and it was not without some regret that she watched him walk up the incline of the road. How she hated this fluctuation, this indecision, this confusion of her heart that seemed impossible to shake. She had read once that some poet or other, she forgot who, had said all art was useless. Rosamund didn't know about that, but she strongly suspected that all love was hopeless.

"Thank you for coming," she said.

Toole looked out over the brook. "Thank you for asking."

"I wasn't sure you'd come." She looked at him. "After how things have been."

He could think of several responses, some honest, some petulant, and some too easily misinterpreted, and so he said none of them. Instead, he picked a small branch from an overhanging tree and began to pick at it. Rosamund watched the childish action with a curious fascination.

"I'm sorry about your father," Toole said. "Whatever else you think of me,

I hope you can believe that, at least."

"Thank you," was all she said.

Her mind drifted back over the telephone conversation earlier that morning. Rosamund had taken advantage of Marjorie's desire to be at church and Henry's insistence on meeting her after the service, and, partly inspired by Everett Carr's words of advice, she had telephoned Toole.

"Daddy's dead," she had said, surprised at how easily the words had come. "Somebody shot him in his office at the mill."

Toole had betrayed no surprise at the news, and Rosamund had wondered whether town gossip had broken the news earlier than her. He had sighed down the line, and his voice had followed it in a suitably morbid tone. "I'm so sorry, Rosamund."

She had not considered the reaction to be strange. Only later did she wonder why he had not asked how Arthur Bayliss's life had ended. A lack of interest, she wondered, or pre-existing knowledge?

"I think we need to talk, George," she had said.

And now, standing together for the purpose, neither of them seemed to have any words to say. Rosamund looked around her, as if she might find some of those words on the exposed branches or the stray birds that flew above them. And suddenly, without warning, she began to weep. Without hesitation, Toole put his arms around her, and she fell against him. Whatever it meant, neither of them expressed it. To them both, it was simply grief and support. Nothing more.

From somewhere in the distance, a crow or some other bird of the sort cawed. To Rosamund, it seemed dangerously ominous. "Where were you when Daddy was killed, George?"

"At home."

The lie, so easily told, sounded like screeching brakes in her mind. "Henry telephoned you to ask you to come over. It was Mr Carr's suggestion. You didn't answer."

"I must have dozed off."

She laughed, but there were tears in her eyes. "You're still lying to me."

Toole looked into her eyes. "All right, Rosamund, have it your way. I wasn't at home. I was in Manchester. Why I was there doesn't matter. And frankly, given the position between us, I don't see it's any of your business."

She was hurt by the comment, more so than she might have expected, and it must have shown in her expression, because Toole had the grace to look ashamed of himself.

"I suppose I deserved that," she said.

"No, you didn't," he replied, meaning it.

She looked deeply into his eyes. "I don't want there to be any secrets between us now, George. It's time for the truth."

"Very well."

After a pause, she said, "I hated Daddy, George."

The words, brutal but honest, were surprisingly easy to say and, once spoken, she felt an immediate relief. How long, she wondered, had she needed to say them, and why had it been at this particular moment that they had come to her without restriction? She told herself that it was not important to know, but that what mattered above all else was that they had been said. And yet, with them came a terrible but obvious implication, and she pulled away from him in order to address it.

"I hated him," she repeated, "but I didn't kill him."

His eyes betrayed no suspicion otherwise. "I know that, Rosamund. You had no reason to."

"I may have done."

He stared at her, knowing that there was more to come. He did not force her to speak. It would have been neither appropriate nor productive. Instead, he waited for her to say more, but she did not immediately oblige. Then, Rosamund took out a cigarette, and he stepped forward to light it for her.

"I told Daddy that I'd ended our engagement," she said. "He was furious, of course. He said I either made things right with you or I'd be disinherited. And that's a motive, George."

"Only if there was no chance of us putting things right," he said.

Her expression said enough, but she wanted there to be no doubt. "It is a motive, George."

"I see," he said. He was not about to pretend that he hadn't hoped this meeting might be the first step to a reconciliation.

"I'm sorry."

He shook his head. "I could hardly expect otherwise, even if I did hope for it."

"Did you hope for it?"

"Part of me did, yes," he said. "Despite everything, I think I still love you. Then, and now."

She inhaled deeply on the cigarette. "I don't know what love is, or what it means."

"I can't believe that." Toole smoked in silence for a moment. "Did you ask me to meet you just so you could tell me that you hated your father?"

"No," she said, inhaling on her cigarette. "I wanted to ask you what you meant the other day, when you said our engagement was something to do with Daddy."

Toole stared out towards the horizon, as if there might be some answer to his problems beyond it. "I don't know if now is an appropriate time."

"When is there ever going to be an appropriate time, George?"

There was a frankness to the question that startled him. There was truth in it, he knew, but how he could tell her of Bayliss' proposition to him in the Midland hotel all those weeks ago was beyond him. She had asked for the truth, but it seemed to Toole that the truth sometimes was so difficult to tell. He contemplated a lie even now, so much easier to give than honesty, but he suspected that if he lied now, there would never be any end to his dishonesty.

"All right," he said, as if to prepare himself rather than her, "you want to know, Rosamund, and I'll tell you. First, I want to say this. I love you, no matter what comes out of all this. I think I always have. You don't love me, and I shall have to live with that. After this, you certainly won't change your mind, and you will probably despise me, but you should know how I feel."

She had listened, with some impatience, and now she gave a small nod of her head. "Just tell me, George."

He turned to face her. "Our engagement was a plot by your father to disinherit Henry."

Rosamund stared dumbly at him. She had thought that she could anticipate what he would say, but she saw now how wrong she had been and, in the instant, she hated herself. She had thought it had all been about her, that she had been some sort of pawn in a business game, a prize to be won if the merger went ahead, but she understood now that her ideas had been nothing more than self-obsession, as if everything had to be about her. And now, she learned, it was in fact about Henry. A foolish, sickening spite seemed to burn through her like the sting of a whip.

"You thought it was all to do with you?" Toole shook his head. "I don't think any of you realised just how much Bayliss hated Henry. He loathed everything that Henry stood for. Worse, I think he was afraid of what Henry might be."

"I knew that," said Rosamund. "So foolish."

"He thought Henry would squander any money your father left him after his death, so he wanted to leave him nothing. Spiteful, but true."

Rosamund was shaking her head. "But why did he involve you?"

Toole inhaled deeply. "If Henry had been left with nothing, what would you and your mother have done?"

She knew the answer immediately. The ice-cold calculation of it all, on her father's part, perhaps should have sickened her, but she had known him too well.

Instead, she simply said, "I see."

"If he left yours and Henry's legacies to me, and you and I married, he could ensure your happiness and Henry's misery. He knew I wouldn't buckle to Henry's pleas like you. He thought he'd win on both counts."

"Yes," said Rosamund, a tear running down her cheek, "he would."

Toole leaned in closer to her. "I didn't propose to you because he forced me to, Rosamund, I promise you that. I genuinely did, and do, love you."

"But it was a consideration, it was part of the deal." She said the final word with scorn.

"It perhaps hurried things along." Now, he swallowed hard. "Your father said he'd give me yours and Henry's inheritance if I married you, and in return, he wanted my family's mill."

"But you weren't able to run it."

"Which is why it seemed so obvious that your father should take it over. After he was dead, your father said I could sell both mills because I wouldn't be able to run them properly, and I could live off the profits as a wealthy man and with you as my wife."

"It's monstrous," Rosamund hissed. "What about Mummy?"

Toole shook his head. "I don't know what he had planned for her. All I know is that he was disinheriting Henry, leaving everything to me, on condition that I sold him the mill and married you. He said it was the only way to make sure we all got what we wanted."

Rosamund's mind was awash with confusion. "I don't understand."

Toole turned to face her. "Your father wanted to cut Henry out and prevent you and your mother from helping him after Bayliss was dead. I wanted to marry you, but I was a failing prospect because the mill was dying. Your father saw an opportunity for us both. He got what he wanted regarding Henry, and he could get my family's mill to turn into his own. In return, I got you, and I got…" But the words would not come. Instead, Toole spluttered, as if choking on his own regret. "I couldn't say no, and he knew it."

"Of course you could have said no!"

"I *couldn't*," he hissed.

Rosamund glared at him, suddenly aware that they were reaching a crisis. The truth she had wanted, she felt sure, was about to be told, and now that the moment had come, Rosamund realised that she was afraid of it. "Why couldn't you?"

"Because marrying you and selling the mill to your father would mean having money right now, Rosamund," he said. "And I need money. I need it badly."

"Oh, God," Rosamund whispered, understanding now what was unfolding before her eyes.

Toole was shaking his head, as if fighting against himself and the urge to say no more. "You want to know where I've been going. To Hell, Rosamund, that's where, straight to a Hell of my own making."

She seemed to understand at once. "You're in debt."

He laughed, spittle flying from his lips, as if the pressure of concealment had become too much for him to contain any longer. "To some bad people."

"Gambling?" She could barely bring herself to say the word. "That's illegal, George!"

"I know it is!" he roared. "That's the bloody point, my darling!"

"Don't you dare shout at me," she hissed.

"I'm sorry, but…" He breathed deeply, trying to bury his anger. It was not helping the situation. "You wanted to know where I was, and that's my answer. Trying to win back what I owe. It's where I was on the night your father died."

"You have an alibi?"

He shrugged. "If the word of a bunch of criminals can be called an alibi."

A memory returned unbidden to Rosamund's mind. "Daddy knew. That's what he meant when he told you to be careful because some people don't play fair."

Toole sighed heavily. "I think so. He must have. It's why he suggested this whole thing."

"I don't believe any of this."

"I wanted to tell you the truth so many times." He was surprised by how calm his voice now sounded. "That day at Layton Brook, when you asked if I was happy, I wanted to tell you then. And when you came to dinner the other night."

"Why didn't you?"

He shrugged. "Shame."

"You deserve to feel ashamed." It was brutal, she knew, but necessary. "How long has it been going on?"

"Months. It started as a bit of fun. Small stakes at first. I won initially, several times. Each time was better than the last. But then came the losses."

"Why didn't you stop then?"

"Because it doesn't work like that, my darling. One thinks the next hand will win back the money, but it doesn't. So, one looks to the hand after that.

And after that."

"I don't understand it at all."

"Nor do I." His voice was now so composed that the honesty underlying it was impossible to doubt. "I don't understand any of it. But what I know is that I couldn't stop. Something about the possibility of winning next time just consumed me. More and more."

"You sound like an addict."

And there it was, the first use of the word that had increasingly troubled him over the last few months. Even now, with it out in the open, he could not bring himself to respond to it. His silence was deafening, he knew, but he could not break it. The only way he could do so was to accept what he was, and he still could not bring himself to say the word.

Instead, he whispered meekly, "I don't know what I am."

If Rosamund recognised his agony, she found it difficult to sympathise. The stupid, stupid man, she was thinking, the damned idiot. It made idiots of them both, perhaps, this truth of his. It was the reality behind the lies, the precious honesty that she had craved, and what had it achieved? Not the reconciliation she had desired, she was sure of that.

"Have you paid any of it back?" she asked.

"Some, but nowhere near enough. The money from the mill was going to deal with the worst of it, as I said, but your father and I hadn't finalised the sale."

"How bad are these people?"

He laughed, but there was no trace of humour in it. "Bad enough that you don't want to hear about them."

Rosamund believed him. These faceless terrors from Manchester were the sort of demons who became twice as horrifying if their features became identifiable.

"I made myself a promise," Toole said. "I know your father engineered the proposal, but I was going to ask you to marry me of my own accord."

"How noble," she said.

He ignored the sarcasm. "And when we were married, and the mill was sold, the debts paid, I promised myself that I was done with the cards. Once and for all."

"Can you keep that promise to yourself?" she asked.

It was not a question he had dared to ask himself, and now, faced with it, he was not sure how to answer it. Confirmation would seem simplistic, almost naïve; rejection would make him seem weak and rob any attempt at redemption of any veracity at all. At last, he gave the only honest answer he could.

"I hope so," he said. "With your help."

If he had expected her to be enraged by the reply, he was to be disappointed. On the contrary, she nodded slowly at him and gave a small smile.

"At least now we finally have some honesty," she said.

"Of course, you realise what that honesty means for us," said Toole, inhaling deeply on his cigarette. "It gives the three of us, you, me, and Henry, a very strong motive for…"

She interrupted him quickly, as if she could not bear to hear the word. "Don't say it."

"But it's true. We have to face it. You can't pick and choose what honesty you want to hear, Rosamund."

He was right, and she knew it, but admitting it to herself was a far more terrifying prospect. This situation was all so alien, so unprecedented, that she felt as if she had no control over her involvement in it. It seemed to her that murder had intruded into their lives, like an unwanted and insidious guest at a dinner party, and it was now tearing their lives apart, breeding suspicion and fear, and all any of them could do was to sit and stare as it happened. Suddenly, regardless of how much she had despised the man, she wanted Arthur Bayliss to be alive again. No matter how cruel, obnoxious, or manipulative he had been, she wanted him here. She wanted him to come around Devil's Corner now and interrupt their privacy. She wanted him to be there to be malicious to Henry, or to roar his abuse and commands at her and her mother. She wanted it all back because if he were alive again, this horror she was living would not be happening.

She was crying, and Toole held her in his arms. There was no resistance from her, nor was there any attempt to shift the embrace into another, more romantic aspect. There was simply support, warmth, and humanity, but still murder loomed over them.

"The question," Toole whispered into her hair, "is what we do about it."

She looked up at him, but the embrace was not broken. "What do you mean?"

Toole was looking into the distance once more. "Henry was going to be disinherited; that's a motive. You were also going to be cut out of the will unless you married me; that's a motive."

"You have no motive," she argued, "because you needed the mill sale to go through. It would have cleared your debts."

Toole was shaking his head. "But under his new will, if I married you, my darling, *I would have got the lot!*"

Rosamund thought for a moment, her brows furrowed. "What if Daddy hadn't got around to changing his will to reflect this sleazy deal of his to leave Henry in the cold? If he hadn't, then you'd inherit nothing, marriage or no marriage. You'd have the proceeds of the mill sale, of course, but you'd have them anyway. That's no motive."

"My God, that's right."

"As a matter of fact, we don't know what Daddy's original plans had been for Henry. Perhaps none of us has a motive."

Toole was thinking deeply. "We need to see your father's will."

"Isn't it all so horrid?" Rosamund spoke with more frustration than sadness. "What does it say about us, George, that we can allow ourselves to help each other after everything that's happened? How is it right that we can be united like this because of murder, but not because of love?"

It was a question that neither of them could answer, even if they dared to. Slowly, she shook her head, kissed him briefly on the cheek, and walked away. He called after her, but she did not turn back. And somewhere in the distance, there came again the cawing of birds. This time, however, Toole saw the crows flying across the sky above him. It was apt, he thought, that they should appear, like spectres at a feast, especially given the collective noun for such birds.

And that word lingered in George Toole's head, as he made his slow, lonely way back to Darton Vale.

# Chapter Thirty-One

Church had not provided Marjorie Bayliss with any of the comfort or peace that she had hoped for. She had sat and listened to the sermon, she had sung the hymns, and she had prayed for her husband's soul, but none of it had meant anything to her, and she had returned home feeling strangely empty. It was curious, she thought now as she sat in the drawing room, staring out over the lawns at nothing in particular, that she seemed to feel nothing. Was this what unnatural death did to a person, she wondered. She had experienced death many times—of her parents, of a brother in the war, of aunts and uncles—but she had never been faced with death on account of murder. It had been a different sensation altogether. This grief did not heal; it was altogether more destructive. It seemed certainly to have destroyed her emotions, leaving her barren of feeling, empty, and incomplete.

But perhaps she was being disingenuous. Perhaps it was not true to say that she felt nothing, but rather that what she felt terrified her, because what Marjorie Bayliss feared she felt inside was a sense of relief. Her husband was dead, and she was thankful. It was so unpleasant, so charged with guilt that she had not been able to admit it to herself, and so she had converted it to this cold emptiness inside her. Was this why her prayers in church had sounded so hollow to her? Was it why God had not spoken to her or comforted her? To be relieved by violent death was hardly something that could be forgiven, perhaps not even by God Himself. How shameful it all was.

Tears came slowly, and she was dabbing them away with a gentle curse of annoyance when the door opened and Everett Carr stepped into the room. He saw at once, of course, that she was weeping, and he made an effort to step back into the hallway.

"I shall leave you in peace, dear lady," he said.

But Marjorie called him back. She felt a sudden need for company, if only to distract herself from her own thoughts. "I'll ring for some coffee, Mr Carr."

"You are most kind, thank you."

"How is your leg?"

"Much better, thank you," he said. "I was grateful to your son for his assistance."

"Yes, he told me about it. I'm so sorry." She lit a cigarette. "How fortunate that the Stansfield girl was willing to help."

"Indeed," said Carr. He did not quite know what else he could say, or even what she expected him to say.

She saw that she had embarrassed him. "Forgive me, Mr Carr, I don't mean to make you feel awkward. The fact is that Lydia Stansfield has been on my mind a lot today."

The coffee had arrived, and Carr poured it, waiting patiently for his hostess to explain herself.

"Henry told me this morning that he knew about his father and Lydia," she said, taking a cup of coffee from him. "He was in tears about it, the poor boy."

"Because he knew but did not tell you?"

Marjorie nodded. "He feels guilty about it."

"Perhaps he feels that he was weak," said Carr, "and too scared to tell you because of the hurt it would cause."

"Henry is a very sensitive boy," she said. "He always has been. Something his father doesn't...didn't understand."

Carr nodded. "But it is not weakness, and Henry should be told as much."

"What do you call it, Mr Carr?"

There was no thought given to the reply, as none was necessary. "Compassion, dear lady. The very fact that he was afraid he would hurt you is proof enough."

"Don't you think it would have been better to tell me the truth?"

Carr smiled. "Undoubtedly. I do not deny that the compassion was misplaced, but I still do not consider it a weakness. I consider it an entirely human response."

"I suppose it is." She sipped at the coffee. "Is it a human response not to hate Lydia Stansfield?"

Carr shrugged. "Perhaps, for you, dear lady."

Marjorie nodded slowly. "Because she was one of many, you mean? Yes, there is that. You become immune after a while. Henry talks about being weak, but I was far weaker than him. At least he dared to stand up for what he believed in. I stayed with a man who treated me and my children like dirt, and I did nothing about it. I let him walk all over me, Mr Carr." Her voice had become bitter as she spoke, and when she looked into his eyes, it lowered into darkness. "Well, now he'll never walk over anyone ever again."

Carr stared at her intently, his dark eyes unflinching. He may have been mistaken, but he was sure that he could detect gratification in her voice. It was evidence of nothing, but he could not help but begin wondering about the confessed weakness of hers. Had she been so submissive in the relationship as to permit these affairs, or had the mounting number of them slowly eaten away at her soul until she could take no more of it? Either was possible, but where one might mean only tears and regret, the second might easily mean a bullet fired in a quiet office.

"My father never wanted me to marry Arthur," Marjorie was saying. "He was a prominent man, my father. A solicitor, a magistrate, and a Freemason. He had no time for Arthur. He thought the whole Bayliss family was opportunistic. My father was very much in favour of people knowing their place in the world, and the Bayliss family's place was not to be alongside the Ashcrofts."

Carr smiled. "Such a Victorian attitude. And it has not disappeared. One wonders whether it ever will do."

"Looking back, of course, my father was absolutely right." She put down her barely touched cup of coffee. "My marriage was a disaster. How strange it is," she added sadly, "that it takes murder to open one's eyes to such a truth."

Again, Carr did not know how to reply. "Your father allowed the marriage to proceed, however?"

She nodded. "I think my mother talked to him. He never accepted Arthur, but he raised no more objections to the marriage. But we never had his blessing."

"How sad."

"He died soon after the wedding." Marjorie brushed something away from her cheek. It might have been a stray tear. "I don't say that my marriage to Arthur caused it, but…"

"But you feel it?"

"Sometimes. Is that foolish?" She watched Carr shake his head. "I feel it is foolish. And I think now that the marriage was foolish."

Carr leaned forward in his chair. "You have your children, dear lady. They are the goodness out of the darkness."

Marjorie looked into his eyes. "Will you say that if it transpires one of them killed their father?"

Carr frowned. "Do you believe one of them did?"

She shook her head. "I don't know what I think anymore."

Carr pulled himself slowly out of his chair and paced slowly back and forth across the hearth. "Perhaps you should talk to your daughter, dear lady."

"Do you think my daughter murdered my husband, Mr Carr?" she asked, almost choking on the words.

Carr could not lie. "I think it is possible, dear lady."

Marjorie held his gaze for a long moment before turning away from him. Her mind was awash with ill-conceived ideas and half-formed fears already, and Carr's words, softly spoken but heavy with intent, only added to them or, if she were honest, helped to make some of them more concrete in her imagination. Now, it was Rosamund who entered her mind, gun in hand and standing in the doorway of the office. Did Rosamund own a gun? Marjorie had no idea. She couldn't even say for certain whether Rosamund would be able to get hold of a gun, assuming she did not own one.

"I have heard, Mr Carr," she said, "that Harrods sell guns to young girls as fashionable accessories. Is it true?"

"I believe so," said Carr, unsure of the significance of the question.

"It seems wholly repugnant to me," Marjorie said.

So, it was true after all, and it meant that there was every possibility that Rosamund had bought a gun. Marjorie could be certain that Rosamund had not gone to Harrods, of course, but if one luxury department store was willing to engage in the sale of firearms, it was perhaps not unreasonable to assume that another would, too. Rosamund could easily have bought one from one of the several such stores in Manchester. Perhaps even George Toole owned a gun, and Rosamund had used that. Either was possible and, in the wake of the realisation of it, Marjorie felt suddenly sick.

"Do the police suspect her?" she asked.

Carr shook his head. "I am not privy to that information, Mrs Bayliss. Whether she killed her father or not remains to be seen. She certainly is not the only person capable of doing it."

She turned to face him. "You suspect someone else?"

He shrugged gently. "As I said on the night of the murder, nobody in this house has a definite alibi."

"None of us could have got to the mill and been back in time without showing some signs of exertion," she said with assurance.

"One could easily do it if one used a motor car." Carr stepped towards her. "And there are plenty of them in the garage."

The thought may have occurred to Lydia Stansfield, but it apparently had not done so to Marjorie Bayliss. "Is that what you think?"

"It is a valid theory."

"Which means you suspect all of us? Me, Henry, and Rosamund."

Carr bowed his head. "Tell me, dear lady, have you ever been to a restaurant in Manchester called *Sinclair's*?"

The sudden change of subject disturbed her, but it was so bewildering that she seemed unable to question it. "Many times."

"With your husband?"

"Yes."

"Forgive my impertinence," Carr said, with an uncomfortable smile, "but might he have taken other ladies there?"

Marjorie glared at him. "I couldn't possibly know that. Or want to."

Carr nodded. "Naturally not. Let me ask this then: might he have gone there with Michael Arden?"

For a moment, Marjorie seemed not to have understood the question. She blinked curiously at Carr, wondering whether she had misheard him, but the seriousness of his expression told her otherwise. "Why on Earth would he do that?"

Carr shrugged. "I cannot say."

"Whatever made you think it, I can't imagine why he would."

Carr smiled. "No, it seems very unlikely, does it not?"

And yet, there was the napkin with the threatening message on it. A napkin from that very restaurant, with the initials of that very man whose presence in that restaurant with Arthur Bayliss was so unlikely that it seemed almost impossible. And yet, that napkin had to be explained somehow, and as Carr settled back into his chair in a contemplative silence, he looked at the woman who stood now by the window, looking back over the lawns. He began to wonder whether she realised the importance of one particular thing she had said, although, on balance, he doubted it. But Everett Carr had seen the significance at once, and now he sat back in his chair, thoughtfully preening his moustache, and staring at the woman who, by her own admission, had not only been to *Sinclair's* but also had been born Marjorie Ashcroft.

# Chapter Thirty-Two

The inquest took place early on the following morning in the church hall. The verdict in the cases of both Neville Pym and Arthur Bayliss was one of murder by person or persons unknown. Inspector Barber had given evidence surrounding the police investigation to date, and the police surgeon had confirmed that Mr Pym's murder, as Carr himself had suspected, was due to asphyxia, the velvet cushion being named as the most likely weapon. In Bayliss' case, of course, the cause of death was obvious, but now it became a matter of official record. The verdicts held no surprises for any of the assembled witnesses, officials, or those present out of morbid curiosity, but the official declaration of murder did seem portentous, and it had the effect of making what had previously been a source of excitable scandal now seem dangerously and frighteningly real to the residents of Darton Vale.

Everett Carr had sat at the back of the hall, watching and listening. He had given his own evidence in relation to the murders, and his role in the discovery of both, in a typically clear and precise fashion. He had not elaborated on his replies with any theories or speculation, nor had he offered any comment other than to give direct answers to the direct questions he was asked. However, having done so, and sitting quietly at the back of the hall afterwards, he was confronted again by the infuriating question of why the murders appeared to be the wrong way round. Now, the inquest over, Carr stood outside the church hall, his brows furrowed in deep thought, but with no answers forming in his head. At last, he gave a gruff growl of frustration and limped away from the whole business of the inquest.

Had he looked to his right as he walked, he would have seen the graves in the churchyard, and had he taken a moment to consider what he saw, Carr would have seen one man he recognised, standing over a particular grave. If Carr had lingered for a moment longer, too, he would have seen a second man approaching. And seeing the two men together might have prompted Carr to wander towards them, because he would no doubt have found their ensuing conversation of immense interest.

Similarly, if Michael Arden had looked up from the graves, he would have seen Everett Carr passing by. But he did not. In that moment, only the grave before him existed in the world. He did not come to her grave regularly, although he frequently wondered whether he should. Instead, he came when he felt he needed her the most, on those occasions when he would have sat down with her and talked through a concern, discussed with her some anxiety, of his or of hers, or simply wanted to put a day's troubles behind him and sit in peace. After her death, the closest he could get to those moments was to visit her grave, but every time he did so, Arden felt as if he were somehow taking advantage of her, and that he only came when he needed her, not out of any genuine respect for the dead. But today, he felt none of that guilt, because today, he needed her badly.

"I lied, Mum," he said to the grey stone with her name carved across it. "At the inquest just now, I lied." The wind seemed to rise around him, as if she were somehow responding to him. Suddenly, a sickening taste of vengeful bile came into his mouth. "You should've told me, Mum," he spat, wiping at his eyes with the ball of his palm. "You should have bloody told me."

"Michael?"

The voice, unexpected and morose, coming from nowhere, startled him. Turning round, he saw someone standing behind him, hands in the pockets of a long overcoat, a look of serious concern across the features of the face. It was someone Arden had not expected to be there, someone who had no business being near his mother's grave, someone to whom Arden felt he had nothing to say.

"What do you want?" he asked.

Eric Hirst shook his head. "Just to talk."

As Hirst began to approach him, Arden felt his hands tighten into fists. "About what?"

"The inquest was hard for everyone," said Hirst, without any hint of evasion. "I suppose murder by person or persons unknown makes it all seem… more real. It's daunting. I found it so, certainly."

"What are you doing here, Mr Hirst?"

"Same as you. Reflecting, trying to find some perspective, remembering." Hirst inhaled deeply. "I've been to see Emma."

Arden turned away, as if the mention of his former lover's name was impossible for him to hear. Her grave was on the other side of the cemetery to Beatrice Arden, and it was another grave that he felt unable to visit as regularly as he perhaps should.

"These are terrible times for all of us, Michael," said Hirst. "Two murders, fear, suspicion. It's made me think about things. About Emma, about me. About you," he added gently.

Arden turned, his hands still primed for confrontation. "What about me?"

"What's happening in this town at the moment is hard for everyone," said Hirst. "We don't need to create or maintain more problems for ourselves."

"Meaning?"

Hirst raised his eyebrows. He had hoped he wouldn't have to say the words, but Arden seemed determined to prise them out of him, missing the point either deliberately or maliciously.

"I'm trying to say I'm sorry, Michael," he said.

"Why?"

Hirst looked over his shoulder, back towards Emma. "She wouldn't want us to be like this."

Arden glared at him. "I never wanted any of it to be like this."

"I know. And I'm sorry for it." Hirst held out his hand. "I'd like to make peace, Michael. For Emma's sake. For all our sakes," he added with a shrug.

Arden ignored the outstretched hand. "Too much has been said."

"It's not too late," said Hirst.

Arden looked up to the sky, as if the sight of Hirst's face would make him descend into a rage. "You remember what you said to me, Mr Hirst, when you heard about the baby?"

Hirst had hoped the conversation would not go this way, but he realised now how naïve it had been to wish it. Arden was quick to temper, it was true, but he also had a long memory that made him vindictive.

"I remember," he said.

Arden stepped towards him. "Say it to me again."

Hirst looked into the younger man's eyes. "I don't have to say it again. It was wrong, I was wrong."

"Say it," hissed Arden.

But Hirst shook his head. "I won't say it, but I will say how much I regret it."

Arden leaned into Hirst's face now. "I loved your girl, Mr Hirst, and to say I'd ever do that to her, to say I'd force her into it, is fucking filth."

And Hirst now recognised his mistake. "I shouldn't have disturbed you."

"If I had my way, Mr Hirst, it'd be you they found next with a bullet in you."

The threat, so real that Hirst could almost smell it, was made all the more terrible because it was spoken with a grim assurance and a cruel smile. Hirst, however, maintained a demeanour of resilience.

"I thought hand irons were more your weapon of choice, Arden," he said, recalling the incident in the mill.

"That wasn't aimed at you." Arden stabbed Hirst in the chest with his finger. "You and Bayliss, I hate you both. And if I had my way, it'd be you and him whose deaths that inquest was about, not him and old Pym."

"You should be careful what you say, Arden," snarled Hirst. "You might find yourself called a killer as well as a rapist."

And so, the word had been said. Hirst had said it once before, and now it was out of his mouth again. Arden smiled dangerously at it, knowing it meant he had won. With little effort, he pushed Hirst in the chest, causing the older man to wheeze in response. The sudden force and the explosion of air from his lungs propelled him backwards, and gravity did what was left to be done. Hirst fell to the ground, twisting backwards as he did so, so that he fell face forwards in an awkward and undignified heap, fighting for breath. Before he could move, Arden had grabbed him by the lapels and dragged him up to his knees. Hirst croaked in futile retaliation.

"I'm not either of them things, you bastard," Arden growled, "but you can take it from me that if I'd shot him and then shot you, I'd reckon I'd done the best day's work of my life, even if I swung for it."

He spat out some contempt, not into Hirst's face but to the ground beside him, before releasing his grip on the older man's coat with a shove, sending Hirst back to the ground with a further growl of shame. Arden straightened and turned back to look at his mother's grave. And there was the worst of it, that such a scene had been played out in front of this marker to her memory. For all Hirst's injustice towards him, Arden felt like killing Hirst for this maternal transgression above all else. Instead, he stepped over the prostrate man and walked away, leaving Hirst to breathe in the smell of dirt and wet soil.

Slowly, Hirst got to his feet. He felt angry, ashamed, humiliated, and not a little afraid. As he brushed himself down, a pointless effort to wipe away some of the grime of the encounter, he knew that he deserved to feel all those conflicting emotions. They were to be expected. But what Hirst had not anticipated, and what he found more shocking than surprising when he realised it, was that he should be weeping as hopelessly as he was.

# Chapter Thirty-Three

Everett Carr was sitting in a tea shop when he saw Eric Hirst approaching the small town square. Even from a distance, Carr could see that Hirst was in some distress. His gait was uncertain, the flaps of his overcoat billowed out like the straggled wings of an unkempt bird, and he seemed to be wiping his face in an excitable frenzy. Carr had the immediate impulse to imagine that Hirst was wiping blood from his face, but there was no way of knowing for sure from this far away. But his instincts were roused, and Carr dabbed delicately at the corners of his mouth, erasing any trace of the potent tea and rather hard, half-eaten scone from his lips, rose to his feet, pulled on his coat and hat, and left the café, dropping a generous share of shillings onto the counter as he went.

Whether it was design or divine, Carr could not say, but his appearance in the high street coincided with Hirst's approach past the tea shop almost exactly. What was intentional on Carr's part, however, was the amiable collision that occurred between the two men. Offering an apology, perhaps rather too effusively, Carr took the opportunity to look closely at Hirst's face. It was not blood that covered him, but mud, a fact that Carr found curious.

"My dear boy, are you all right?" he asked.

Hirst, if truth be told, would have preferred to have gone home without discovery or interruption, especially from a comparative stranger, but there was nothing he could do now. "I'm fine, thank you, Mr Carr."

Carr smiled. "We have both been in the wars, it seems, but this time it is I who can assist you."

"Honestly, there is no need. I'm embarrassed more than anything," Hirst added.

"As, indeed, was I. Come, let me help you."

Resigning himself to this unwanted assistance, Hirst complied, and together the two men walked towards Hirst's cottage. Once there, Hirst opened the door and stepped inside, Carr following slowly behind him.

Hirst looked at his watch. "I suppose it isn't too early for a small whisky rather than tea. The inquest was a trial for us all, for one thing, and I think my nerves need it." He smiled warmly. "Would you pour us both a glass, Mr Carr, while I go to make myself look a little more respectable?"

Carr bowed as Hirst pointed him in the direction of the living room, before making his way up the stairs that led from the small hallway to the upper floor of the cottage. Carr poured two small measures of whisky and stood silently in front of the fireplace.

The house smelled of loneliness. It was not simply an emotional impression on Carr's part; there was a physical trace of it, too. The room in which he stood was clean, just as it was tidy, but there was a mustiness to it also, the vague smell of forgotten books and old paper, as if the space was seldom allowed to breathe. Casually, Carr walked over to the windows and tried to release one of the catches, but it remained stubbornly closed. The furniture, too, seemed a little tired and in need of either an upholstery repair or complete replacement. The wallpaper was curiously feminine, covered in what once would have been pastel-shaded roses, but whose colours had now faded. The ornaments on the mantelpiece and the small coffee table were free of dust, but they seemed to suggest a feeling of abandonment, just as the ashtrays on the side table beside the overused armchair in the corner spoke of a private isolation. The house was not dirty, nor was it unpleasant, nor was it distasteful, but it possessed a certain degree of neglect. And yet, still, Carr felt something else about the room, something more closely associated with a mausoleum, a sense that time had ceased.

Only the photographs on the walls, and smaller ones on the mantel, betrayed any sense of vitality. The majority were of Hirst himself, flanked by two ladies, clearly a wife and daughter. Gently, Carr picked up one of the frames, and he found himself looking at a woman of immense beauty, whose features were reflected, in suggestion if not in absolute replication, in the younger girl. Both had blonde hair, and both had radiant eyes whose mutual thirst for life seemed to reach out beyond the photographs, so that Carr found himself smiling in appreciation of it. The loss of the obvious radiance of the presence of both ladies must have seemed like the sun burning out, leaving behind only a grey, shadowy negative of the past. Carr felt suddenly intrusive, and he placed the frame back in its place, showing care not to leave evidence of having tampered with it, but also with a curious sense of respect for disturbing the dead.

"My wife and daughter, Mr Carr."

Startled by the voice, Carr turned round swiftly to find Hirst standing in the doorway. He smiled and stammered an apology. "Forgive my inquisitiveness. I had no right."

Hirst shook his head. "If I didn't want people to see them, I wouldn't have them on display. Although," he added after a moment's thought, "I'm not sure that's altogether true."

He took the whisky that Carr handed to him. He sat down in the armchair, but he made no attempt to offer a similar comfort to Carr, whose innate politeness forbade him from sitting of his own accord. Instead, he walked across the room and began to look at the photographs on the walls. These were clearly of the daughter, but in maturity, whereas the ones on the mantelpiece were of her in adolescence. In these later images, however, the spirit of her mother seemed even keener than before. Emma Hirst had grown into a beautiful young woman, and a comparison between the two sets of photographs clearly demonstrated that she was a spiritual reflection of her mother at a similar age.

"Your daughter was a handsome woman," he felt obliged to say.

"Like her mother," said Hirst.

"I am sorry for your loss."

The words, so often little more than a platitude, seemed to be entirely genuine, and Hirst wondered briefly whether Carr himself had suffered a similar tragedy in his life. Certainly, something about the dark eyes and the sombre expression that had fallen across his face suggested it, but they also gave the impression that enquiry into the matter, however polite, would be unwelcome.

"It may sound callous, Mr Carr," he said instead, "but Jean's death was easier to bear than Emma's."

The admission was unexpected and, Carr thought, somewhat difficult to understand. His face must have betrayed him, because Hirst began softly to explain himself.

"It was natural," he said. "Cancer. A horrible way to die, but at least it was a natural death. It was uncontrollable, God's will, if you like. Emma's was circumstance. It was avoidable, it was unnecessary, it was..." He fought for the word, and when he found it, he spoke it with bitterness. "Meaningless."

Thoughts of Miranda's death flooded Carr's brain. "I can understand that well enough."

"Can you?"

Carr nodded, but he did not meet Hirst's gaze. "My wife was killed."

"An accident?"

"No." The tone of voice in which the single, negative syllable was spoken told the story well enough that Carr felt no need to offer further details.

And Hirst, for his part, understood. "I'm sorry. I don't find that the pain ever goes away."

"No," repeated Carr.

"It hasn't even eased," said Hirst. "Not where Emma is concerned, at least. I know that Jean would not have wanted me to be alone, and I think you know I have developed feelings for Miss Stansfield, even if they are not reciprocated. To that extent, having those feelings, perhaps I have in some way come to terms with Jean's own death. But Emma..." He shook his head sadly. "Losing a child is a different kind of grief. It leaves a different, much darker void inside a person."

Carr nodded slowly. "They say time heals, Mr Hirst, and I have known it to do so."

"As far as Emma's death is concerned, time has come to an end," Hirst said. "Come with me, Mr Carr. There's something I'd like to show you."

He led Carr up the narrow staircase leading off from the hallway. There was a bathroom immediately in front of them, and three doors opened out onto the landing. Two bedrooms, Carr assumed, and a spare one, used for whatever purpose. Hirst led him to the first of these three doors and, taking a moment to compose himself, he pushed it open slowly.

"This is Emma's bedroom," he said simply, allowing Carr to enter.

It was a fair-sized room, neither too large nor too cramped, simply furnished but not without some degree of elegance. There was a single bed behind the door, a wardrobe in an alcove beside the window, and a small dressing table to the side, made of varnished wood, the chair neatly placed under it. Various accessories were neatly placed in front of the mirror: hairbrushes, compacts, and a jewellery box with an intricate pattern carved into its lid. There was a musical box on one side of the table, under whose lid, no doubt, stood a small figure of a poised ballerina, ready to pirouette to the chosen tune. Set against the wall opposite, there was a tall bookcase, to which Carr impulsively gravitated. The shelves were filled with novels, and whilst there was an admirable selection of what Carr would consider classic literature, the predominant theme of this personal library was detective fiction. Some of the authors' names Carr recognised, and many he did not, but it was clear that Emma Hirst had been not only an avid reader of the genre, but very possibly a connoisseur of its convoluted plots, elaborate puzzles, and linguistic tricks. On the bed itself, there was a small, stuffed bear, whose frayed ears and single button eye showed that it had seen better days, but that it had been a companion for the girl since her early years of existence. A nightgown made from silk and expensive, if Carr was any judge of such matters, was tossed carelessly across the pillows, as if it had been discarded in a hurry, and now Carr realised why he had been invited into the room.

The nightgown was not the only example of such sartorial dismissal. Carr saw now the skirt that had been tossed over the chair of the dressing table. He saw the pairs of shoes, taken off and abandoned in various places around the room, and he saw the dresses and blouses that had been considered but discarded as choices for the day, and tossed onto a small chair by the window.

He saw crumpled-up humbug wrappers scattered across the bedside table, no doubt eaten whilst reading the detective novel that lay open by the bedside lamp, and whose improbable solution she now would never learn. Suddenly, Carr saw the room as a whole, a place frozen in time, just as Emma Hirst had left it when she had last walked out of it. But for her death, she would have returned here, folded away or hung up the clothes, tidied away the shoes, and cleared away the sweet wrappers. She had expected to return later in the day to do all those things, the mess being only temporary, but fate had prevented her, and tragic misfortune had made the clutter permanent. And now, in the wake of her death, her father had found it impossible to interfere with the room as she had left it, as if doing so would be to disturb her memory or somehow intrude on her privacy. Carr felt a moment of immense sadness wash over him as he looked once again, with sadder eyes, around the room of this dead girl whom he had never known.

Slowly, Carr turned to face Eric Hirst. "Such a tragic accident."

Hirst had been staring at the floor of his daughter's room, but now his eyes lifted and he glared at Everett Carr from over the rims of his spectacles. "I know it was murder."

Carr stared at him. "Murder?"

Nobody who knew the area would have been travelling at sufficient speed to force her car off the road," said Hirst. "The inquest concluded that it must have been a stranger. Someone who didn't stop, didn't try to help, didn't come forward. Is that not murder?"

Carr was not about to enter into the debate. "Did they ever trace this stranger?"

"Tommy Barber tried, of course, but there was never any hope of finding him. No witnesses, no details of the car, nothing to help find him. You see? Totally meaningless."

He said no more, and nor did he need to. Carr's imagination, like Hirst's, could fill in the blanks. It could picture the car hurtling towards the brook, the rocks doing their damage to flesh and metal, and it could hear the screams of agonised realisation from Emma Hirst as her death was set out in front of her with a terrible inevitability.

Suddenly, Carr had no wish to remain in the room. "Perhaps we should go down."

Neither of them spoke until they were back in the sitting room. Hirst replenished his glass of whisky, but Carr refused a second. It was still barely lunchtime, after all, but he understood Hirst's needs. It was a matter of fortification rather than indulgence. For his part, Carr sat on the arm of the settee and stretched out his leg.

"I had come here to try to help you, my boy," he said, "but I seem only to have raked up painful memories."

Hirst shook his head. "The memories never leave me, Mr Carr."

Carr smiled gently. "What happened earlier? You looked as if you had been in a tussle."

Hirst, his cheeks still pale and drawn from the events of the morning, removed his spectacles and ran his hand across his face. "I was. On account of Emma, too."

"Michael Arden," said Carr, almost to himself.

Hirst looked at him in surprise. "How did you know?"

"I understood there was some affection between him and your daughter. It is difficult to see who else you could have fought with about her other than him. And, if I may say so, he is a young man who is more adept with his fists than his brain. So, a physical fight involving your daughter could only have been with him."

Hirst smirked bitterly. "How very Sherlock Holmes of you."

If the cynicism offended Carr, he did not say so. "What happened?"

"I tried to make amends. Arden and I have had a difficult relationship over the years. I never approved of his relationship with Emma. I thought he was no good for her and, quite frankly, I still think it."

Carr took a moment to find the right words. "I understand that your daughter was…"

Hirst understood. "She was pregnant, yes."

"With Mr Arden's child?"

"I always thought so. It was one of the reasons Emma and I argued about him." His eyes brimmed with tears. "Recently, with all this talk of murder and violent death, I thought about Emma and what happened to her and to my grandchild. And I realised that she would hate the fact that there remained this rift between Arden and me. I couldn't make it right while she was alive, so I thought I owed it to her to do so now."

"But Arden refused to take the olive branch?"

"He said it was all too late."

Carr was silent for a moment. "I'm beginning to wonder whether Michael Arden might be more sinned against than sinning. Would he be so caustic if someone tried to talk to him as a friend?"

"I did try," said Hirst. "He wasn't interested."

Carr lowered his gaze. "He thought it was too late. Wasn't it?"

"I don't think it's ever too late to try to make amends."

Carr looked up slowly. "And would you say that to the man who caused Emma's accident?"

It had not meant to be insulting, but it could hardly have avoided being provocative. Carr recognised as much, but the point made was one of importance, and he felt no regret about making it. Hirst, predictably, was less academic about the matter, although Carr suspected that he could not fail to recognise the truth of it, and when he looked at Carr, his eyes burned with a rage that Carr suspected was equally balanced between Hirst and himself.

"I think you'd better leave now, Mr Carr," Hirst said, rising slowly to his feet. "Perhaps you would prefer Michael Arden's company to mine right now."

The slur, as obvious as it was petty, was nevertheless understandable. Carr still offered no apology, but he gave a courteous bow and offered a word of hope that Hirst would feel better in due course. He thanked his host for the drop of whisky and, however hollow it might seem to Hirst, he expressed sorrow once more at the man's loss. It was as Carr was walking down the small garden path towards the gate leading to the main road that Hirst called his name.

"Before you get too cosy with Arden, Mr Carr," Hirst said, "perhaps I should let you know something he said to me earlier."

# CHAPTER THIRTY-THREE

"Indeed?"

"A few days ago, I was standing on the gantry outside the mill offices when Arden threw a hand iron in what I assumed was my direction. It was an act of malice, although he will no doubt call it defiance. Either way, it was violence and could have done some serious harm to a man."

"But it didn't?"

Hirst shook his head. "Arden missed his mark. Now, as I say, I assumed that I was that mark, but he told me this morning that he wasn't aiming the iron at me at all. And only two people were standing on that gantry. If I wasn't Arden's target, Mr Carr..."

Even though he knew the answer, and it sent a shiver down his spine, Carr asked, "Who was standing next to you, Mr Hirst?"

"Arthur Bayliss." There was satisfaction in the voice, but no smile on Hirst's face. "Arden must have had a reason to throw that iron at Bayliss, mustn't he, Mr Carr? And only a few days later, Bayliss is shot to death, and a piece of evidence with Arden's initials on it is found at the scene of the murder. Who's to say that Arden's reason for throwing a piece of mill equipment at Bayliss didn't then escalate into a reason to kill?"

It was a good question, but Everett Carr offered no answer to it. Instead, with a polite smile, he doffed his hat, turned on his heel, and walked away.

# Chapter Thirty-Four

Lydia Stansfield returned home from the inquest tired by the ordeal and relieved that it was over. She had not asked Eric Hirst to come back with her for coffee. She desired no company at all. The inquest had been both intimidating and upsetting. It had stirred memories in Lydia's mind that would have been better left sleeping. Not all unpleasant; she had recalled moments of happiness with Arthur, the dinners at *Sinclair's*, the gifts, the rare moments of tenderness. But mostly, the court proceedings had brought back to her mind the coldness, the snide cruelty of his abandonment of her, and the fact of his death, and everything she knew about it. Only once had she glanced over to Michael Arden during the inquest, and only in that one instant had she considered rising to her feet and telling the truth. She had not, of course, because to do so would have meant exposing her own secrets. And so, she had averted her gaze from Arden and concentrated on the clenched hands and white knuckles in her lap, until the moment when the dreaded words—*murder by person or persons unknown*—were announced with a fatal inevitability by the coroner. As soon as she had heard the words, Lydia had known that she wanted nothing more than to be alone, away from it all, safe inside her cottage, the doors and windows closed to the outside world.

But now that she was sitting on her settee, a cup of tea slowly going cold in front of her, she felt horribly lonely. The sanctuary of the cottage seemed like the confines of a prison cell. The quiet solitude she had craved during the inquest felt like condemned isolation. The time alone that she hoped would clear her mind served only to fill it with questions, suspicions, and fears. Strange, she thought, how some wishes turned into curses once they came true. Like falling in love. If only she had been able to do that with a man who would see her as something more than a passing flirtation, a temporary frolic away from his wife, an easily disposable commodity. In the first few weeks of their relationship, Bayliss had made Lydia feel as if she were the only girl in the world, that she mattered more than any previous lover, including his wife, and she had begun to forge hopes that there would be a life together for them, perhaps even marriage. It would be an honest life, too, she had thought, not one spent snatching moments of time together, always fearful that someone would see them, never able to take their eyes off the clock as their precious moments ebbed away. Now, looking back, Lydia knew that those thoughts had been naïve. In the wake of Bayliss' death, she knew what she had been, and the realisation not only sickened her, but made her feel dirty, and she felt now as if she should have charged him for her time and body. There was little difference between that and how things had been, and at least she would have made something from it. How bitter she felt, how betrayed, and, worst of all, how stupid.

She was crying, for longer than she had realised, no doubt, and she did nothing to wipe away the tears or to clean her nose. "Let it come," her mother would have said, "it'll do you no harm to get it all out." So, she did. Whether it was the shame, the regret, or the pressure of keeping her secrets that was causing the tears, she couldn't say, nor did she care. She simply wept until her eyes were raw, her throat dry, and her body limp.

The knock on the door brought her back to herself. It was unexpected and unwelcome, but she somehow lacked the courage to ignore it. She took out a handkerchief, dabbed her eyes perfunctorily, and blew her nose before getting to her feet and walking to the door. Whoever it was, she thought, she would tell them she was feeling unwell. The aftermath of her weeping would be clearly marked across her face, she had no doubt, and this unwanted caller would surely recognise their intrusion and leave. Allowing these thoughts to console her, Lydia felt assured as she pulled open the door. Then, as soon as her eyes met those of her visitor, she felt her world crumble.

"Hello, Miss Stansfield," said Marjorie Bayliss. "May I come in?"

Lydia's instinct was to refuse, but there was something about Marjorie's expression that suggested amnesty rather than attack. She opened the door wider and stepped aside to allow Marjorie to enter. As she followed Marjorie into the sitting room, Lydia had a curious sense of protectiveness towards her cottage. It was a foolish and sentimental wave of emotion, but she found herself unable to resist it. She wondered whether Marjorie was contemplating her furniture and décor with aloof amusement or, worse, with haughty disdain. Nothing in the cottage would match the fineries of Darton House, Lydia was sure of that, and she found herself growing increasingly convinced that Marjorie was indulging in some sort of patronising pity that this was all the shop girl who had been sleeping with her husband could afford. Respectable, no doubt, but rather tawdry. In return for this imagined disdain, Lydia found herself silently defending her possessions. Perhaps they were small and lowly compared to the lavishness of the big house, but they had been bought with money made honestly by Lydia's own hands, personality, and graft. Nothing in the house had been given to her, but everything in it had been earned. That was their merit.

"Would you like a cup of tea?" Lydia asked, the words almost strangling her.

Marjorie shook her head. "I don't want to trouble you longer than necessary, Lydia. May I call you Lydia?"

"If you like."

"I feel I know you." The words seemed to have been a mistake, and Marjorie felt as much. The girl's eyes said as much. "Of course, I don't know you at all."

The attempt at recompense was not acknowledged. "What do you want, Mrs Bayliss?"

Marjorie peeled off her gloves. Perhaps tea would have been a good idea, after all, but it felt as if it were too late to change her mind. Walking here from the inquest, she had known precisely what she would say to this girl, but now that she was here, the words had either deserted her or seemed, on reflection, too trite to be convincing.

"I wanted to get to know you," Marjorie said.

"Why?"

Suddenly, Marjorie had no idea. "Did you love my husband?"

"Yes."

"And did he love you?"

This time, the answer was not so definitive. "I thought he did."

"You know you weren't the only one?" Marjorie needed to ask the question, but she had not expected it to sound as confrontational as it did in her head.

Lydia nodded. "Yes, I knew that. I didn't expect to be."

"Did you expect to be the last?"

Frustratingly, Lydia felt suddenly ridiculous, foolishly naïve. Her voice, when it uttered the simple reply, sounded like a disappointed, spoiled schoolgirl. "Yes."

Marjorie nodded slowly. "We all think it, my dear. It's the hardest part of loving him."

Lydia raised her gaze from the floor to Marjorie's face. Was this a statement of solidarity? Marjorie's expression showed no anger, no contempt, no jealousy, nor any other emotion that a betrayed wife might be expected to convey. Conversely, almost disturbingly, there was empathy in those sad eyes, and when Marjorie gave a gentle nod of her head, Lydia began to understand something of Marjorie's motives for the visit.

"Why did you stay with him?" she asked.

"I loved him," Marjorie said.

"He betrayed you."

"Perhaps you won't be able to understand this, Lydia. You seem a much more confident woman than I ever was, and far less compliant than I fear I have been throughout my life."

Lydia smiled thinly. "You don't seem so weak now."

"Things have changed, haven't they? Arthur has gone. I have nothing left to fear."

"Were you afraid of him?"

Marjorie held the girl's stare for a long moment. "Oh, yes."

"Why didn't you leave him?"

"One didn't leave Arthur, you know that. He was in control, in command. He would leave you, but you could never leave him."

Lydia felt a surge of emotion. Had this very thing not happened to her?

"I loved my husband," Marjorie was saying. "Despite it all, despite his overbearing control over me, I loved him. So much that it was easier to have a life with him in it than not."

"I hated it when he would go home to you," said Lydia. "I was jealous."

Marjorie smiled gently. "But you never ended the relationship, did you?"

"No."

Marjorie took a step towards her. "And that is my point. I have every right to despise you, Lydia, and in my darker moments, I can convince myself that I do. But, you see, we have more in common than we would like to pretend. Not least, the man who harmed us both."

"Harmed us?"

Marjorie nodded. "We're not enemies, Lydia. We should be, no doubt, but I can't see it that way. The deceit, the betrayal, the manipulation, it was all Arthur. He broke our marriage vows, not me, and not you."

"I should have refused him," argued Lydia. "I knew he was married, after all, so I should never have…"

Marjorie shook her head. "Nor should he. That is my point. Besides," she added, "you say you *should* have refused him. Be honest with yourself, Lydia. *Could* you have refused him?"

The girl needed no time to respond, but she did so with a shake of her head and the first glistening of tears in her eyes. Marjorie made no effort to comfort her. It would have been neither appropriate nor welcome, she thought, but she did suggest that tea, after all, might be in order. They walked through to the kitchen together, and it seemed somehow natural that they did so. Marjorie had said that they were not enemies, and as she filled the kettle and reached for tea cups, Lydia began to wonder whether it could be true. Certainly, she felt no animosity and nor did she feel any resentment. Marjorie's view of their situation was hardly one Lydia could have expected, or even had a right to, but it was one that seemed to her to possess a degree of merit.

The tea made, they walked back into the sitting room and sat beside each other on the settee. Marjorie was not so presumptuous as to take it on herself to pour, and she waited whilst Lydia performed the task. She did so with a certain graceful confidence, the slim hands manipulating the china cups and pot, pretty rather than elegant, with dextrous ease. The tea itself was sweet, fragrant, and strong, not perhaps, thought Marjorie, like the girl who had brewed it.

"Do you make peace with all Arthur's lovers?" Lydia asked.

"Not personally," said Marjorie. "I fear that if I did so, I would have to spend my life travelling around Lancashire."

Lydia smiled, but it was barely with any humour. "Even further, perhaps."

Marjorie could have considered the remark to be in poor taste, even insulting, and perhaps she did to a degree, but she did not say so. "If I chose to do it, though, I would say the same thing. All of us, all the women who fell for him, we were all his victims."

"Victims?"

Marjorie nodded. "We were all used by him, betrayed by him, manipulated by him, hurt by him. Wouldn't you say we were victims?"

"I've never thought of it like that."

Marjorie sipped the tea. "I have, many times. It's part of the reason I don't blame the girls concerned. I only blame him."

Lydia allowed a moment to pass before she dared ask her question. "Why did you come to see me? What makes me so different from the others that I deserve a visit from you?"

Marjorie replaced the cup and saucer on the tray carefully, so as not to spill any of the tea that remained inside. "Because none of the others were involved in murder, Lydia, but we are. And I think that changes everything."

Lydia seemed to develop the look of a wild creature cornered. Her eyes widened, and her lips parted in a silent scream, and slowly her head began to oscillate, as if she were silently trying to shake her mind free from any association with murder. It seemed to Marjorie as if this was the moment that the truth of what had been happening in Darton Vale became clear to the girl, as if before now, it had only been some sort of dark fantasy that could have no real consequences.

"What are you saying?" Lydia stammered.

"I'm saying that you and I need to be honest with ourselves and each other. We both had reasons to kill Arthur, after all."

"I hadn't."

"Don't be naïve, Lydia. Stubborn denials like that will get us nowhere. You had possibly the oldest motive of all. Love," Marjorie added, sadly and unnecessarily.

But Lydia's unwillingness to face the truth persisted. "You didn't have any reason to kill him, if what you said just now is true."

"But I *did* have reason. Do you think for a moment that the police will believe what I've said to you?"

"It wasn't true?"

"Yes, it was true, but whether Tommy Barber can bring himself to believe it is an entirely different matter. On the face of it, I was a betrayed wife, and my husband had multiple affairs. To the police, perhaps you were one infidelity too many. And then there are my children."

"Your children?"

"Arthur made Henry's life unbearable, and although he preferred Rosamund, I think, he treated her no better. You're not a mother, Lydia, so you may not understand this, but a mother will do anything to protect her children. And anything to save them. Oh yes, I had good reason to kill Arthur," she added. "More than one, in fact."

Lydia took a moment to digest the words. They were so frightening, so momentous, that she could barely interpret them, beyond this innate assurance within herself that what Marjorie was saying was horrifyingly true.

She looked into Marjorie's eyes. "Did you kill him?"

The older woman took a moment to reply. "As a matter of fact, I didn't. Did you?"

"No." This time, the reply to the question seemed to come too quickly.

Marjorie fixed Lydia with a disbelieving glare. "Did you?"

Lydia shook her head, and this time, the denial was more forceful. "No, Marjorie, I didn't."

"I saw you at the inquest. You looked terrified, Lydia. What was it that frightened you?"

The question seemed foolish, and Lydia took advantage. "Weren't you scared, too?  I'd have thought an inquest into a murder would terrify anybody.  Having to give evidence, stand up there, and tell your private matters to a room filled with people.  Perhaps you can take that in your stride, but I can't."

Marjorie shook her head. "The fear I saw in your eyes this morning, Lydia, was the fear of someone who was hiding something."

Lydia rose to her feet. "I'd like you to go now, please."

Marjorie stared at her.  "I'm sorry, Lydia, I didn't come here with the intention of antagonising you. I came to offer solidarity, and I seem to have achieved the opposite."

"No, you haven't. I appreciate what you've said, and I am grateful for it." Lydia smiled, but with difficulty. "But I didn't kill Arthur or Mr Pym, and I'm hiding nothing."

Marjorie stood up now. "Yes, poor Mr Pym. Nobody seems to be able to explain why he had to die."

"I hardly knew him."

Marjorie looked at the girl. "Well, perhaps that's just as well."

"Why?"

"Because it's hardly likely that there are two killers in the town, so if you didn't know one of the two victims, you couldn't have any reason to kill him. And if you didn't kill one…"

Lydia, despite her fears, smiled. "Yes, I see."

Marjorie was smiling too, but her eyes were heavy with suspicion. The girl was being amiable, she thought, but there was still a conviction in Marjorie's soul that Lydia Stansfield was hiding something. A further verbal warning about the matter, however, would do no good.

"I want us to be friends, Lydia," she said.

"Me too," said Lydia, although her voice was less assured.

Only a few moments after Marjorie had left, Lydia began to brood. The more she thought about Marjorie's visit, the more it disturbed her, until eventually Lydia began to feel very frightened indeed. Marjorie had been correct to say that the inquest had terrified Lydia, and it was possible that Marjorie had come to the cottage simply to find out why Lydia was so frightened by the proceedings. It was equally possible that the purpose of the visit had been to make peace with her late husband's former mistress.

And yet...

Lydia's paranoia was forcing her to ask a different question. Was it not far more reasonable to assume that, far from being a matter of instinct, Marjorie *knew* why Lydia was so frightened?  If so, there was only one conclusion to draw—that *Marjorie Bayliss had been at the mill that night.*

And if that was true, this unwanted visit from her former lover's widow had not been a matter of reconciliation between the two women, but rather more a question of self-preservation, and one prompted not by kindness but by guilt. Unbidden, a cold fear took hold of her, and tears began to form in her eyes. Suddenly, it was Marjorie Bayliss that Lydia could see with a gun in her hand and hatred in her heart. And it was Marjorie Bayliss that she watched now as she walked away from the cottage, stopping only once to turn back to look towards Lydia, and to slowly raise her hand to wave.

# Chapter Thirty-Five

Henry Bayliss sat in the library of Darton House, with a book open on his lap and a glass of whisky in his hand. The plot of the novel, derivative and unconvincing, had been unable either to engage him or to distract him from reality. The inquest had been as difficult as he had feared, and he recalled now the nervous frenzy with which he had given his evidence, his voice faltering and hesitant. He had feared, both during and after the ordeal, that his nervousness had suggested guilt, and the more he looked back over the morning and his participation in it, the more assured he was of it. Perhaps he did feel guilty, he thought. And yet, he could not bring himself to say that he was glad his father was dead. To do so seemed somehow monstrous, no matter how monstrous the dead man had been himself. These thoughts, as contradictory as they were unpleasant, danced around Henry's mind with a dark persistence, and they left him with the distinct impression that he simply did not know how he felt, other than acutely despondent and helpless.

He finished the drink and rose to his feet to get another. Henry was not a serious drinker, but that evening he felt inclined to succumb to the worst time of drunkenness. He had returned home after the inquest with Rosamund, who had promptly gone to her room. His mother had not come home with them, and Henry had wondered for a long time afterwards where she could have gone and why she had felt it necessary to keep her plans secret. His kinder instincts had told him that it was arrogance that assumed his mother was obliged to divulge her intentions to him, but the whisky now told him that this display of arrogance was something he might have expected from his father. The thought both alarmed and disgusted him. He threw some whisky down his throat, as if to burn away the taste of indignation from his mouth. Then, he poured another measure and this time added ice to it, to temper both the harshness and possibly the effects of the drink. Perhaps, after all, he should try to distract himself from these thoughts once more, and so he turned back to the chair, sat down, and picked up the novel once more, with a renewed determination to concentrate his mind away from real events and back towards a fictional narrative.

His mind was beginning once more to wander, however, when he heard the noise. It was a curiously delicate sound for something so obviously sinister. The house was still, otherwise Henry doubted he would have heard it, but in the heavy quiet of the late evening, the sound of breaking glass was unmistakable. Almost instinctively, Henry seemed to know that the sounds had not been the breaking of a tumbler or wine glass, or indeed anything of the sort. Nor, he thought, had it been the shattering of the glass of a dropped photograph frame. It had been, without doubt, the pane of a window. Henry set down his glass on a small side table, closed his book, and placed it beside the glass, then rose gently and uneasily to his feet.

He stood for a moment in the hallway, his ears searching for any further noise that would betray the source of the intrusion. An unquantifiable length of time seemed to pass, and Henry was beginning to wonder whether he had imagined the sound, although his intuition was adamant that he had not. And then, as if to corroborate his instinct, Henry heard the sounds of activity coming from his father's study. Drawers pulled open, he thought, and, as he moved closer to the study door, papers being shuffled.

Sweat beading coldly on his brow and temples, Henry reached for the handle of the door, gritting his teeth against the possibility of making any noise. Slowly, he turned the handle of the door, closing his eyes tightly as the faint creak of the turning handle seemed to scream like a banshee in the stillness. Then, with his breath held anxiously in his lungs, Henry threw his shoulder against the door and burst suddenly into the room.

The figure was illuminated only marginally by the sudden shaft of light that Henry's arrival shone into the room, but it was enough for Henry to discern a tall, athletic man, dressed in black, with a scarf wrapped around the lower part of his face, and what seemed to be a chimney sweep's black peaked cap pulled low over his eyes. Henry had a sudden recollection of the description his father had given of the man who had poured acid over the Bentley. Was this the same person, now an intruder as well as a vandal? With a surge of excitement, Henry wondered whether he was now confronting the mill's poltergeist and, if so, he was determined not to let him get away.

The intruder was standing by the study safe, set in the wall behind a reproduction of Lowry's *Coming Home from the Mill*. Henry, his eyes growing accustomed to the gloom, could see that the safe door was open, just as he could see the signs of destructive searching across the top of the desk. He looked from one to the other, and then to the intruder caught in between. For what seemed like minutes, but what could only have been mere seconds, the two men stared at each other, neither knowing what to do next.

Then, it happened.

The two men moved simultaneously. The intruder picked up a paper-weight from the desk beside him and threw it in Henry's direction, forcing him back into the hallway to take shelter behind the open door. The paperweight hit the wall, causing the wallpaper to tear and the plaster beneath to crack, forming a small but curiously artistic spider's web pattern. Letting out his breath and grunting with effort, Henry charged back into the room.

The intruder had wasted none of the time that the paper weight distraction had provided him. He had turned back to the French windows, one of whose panes he had broken in order to gain entry, and had raced through them. Henry was swift on his feet, however, and he was back in the room in time to see the burglar disappear through the doors and out into the darkness of the night.

Henry gave chase.

The unknown man was quick, but Henry had not been a disgrace on the athletic tracks of his schooldays.  His lungs burned with the effort, and he could feel the tension in his legs as he ran, but his mind remained concentrated on the back of the man who fled over the lawns of the house. Henry called out once, but it did no good. Ahead, Henry could see the trees that surrounded the grounds of the house, and he knew that if the burglar reached those, Henry would lose him in an instant. The woods were dense, and under their cover, a man might disappear as easily as a beautiful girl in a magician's trick. But first, the man would have to get over the garden wall.

Spurred on by his determination, Henry quickened his pace, ignoring now the rising pain in both his legs and lungs. He let out a feral grunt of exertion as he ran, and he called again for the man to stop. The command was disobeyed, and Henry watched in alarm as the man seemed to crouch low without slowing his speed, and then sprang like an acrobat into the air. In an elegant windmill of limbs, the man was almost over the wall. Henry made a leap of his own, less powerful and less gracious than his opponent's, but still effective, as far as it went. Henry felt his fingers close around the ankle of the burglar, and he felt the air be expelled from his protesting lungs as he collided with the wall. For a painful moment, the two men hung there loosely, the intruder half over the wall, one leg dangling on the other side, and the other stretched to its limit and trapped in Henry's grasp, and Henry himself hanging onto the limb and huddled in agony against the wall.

At last, Henry's grip began to fail him and, as if sensing the weakness, the intruder kicked hard with his trapped leg. The action was too much for Henry. His fingers gave way, and he slumped against the wall, breathing like a drowning man gasping for air.  He looked up to see the intruder towering over him, straddling the wall as if it were a horse, and breathing hard with his exertions. To Henry, who now had collapsed in a heap under the pressure of the exploit, the silhouetted figure of the burglar seemed so high above him that he was beyond reach, even if Henry could have trusted his knees to allow him to stand. For a moment, both men glared at each other before the one on the wall kicked his leg high and dropped over the other side of the wall and into the trees.

Henry heard an owl somewhere in those trees, but the sound made no impression on him. All he could hear, reverberating around his skull, was the sound of his own blood pumping and the mocking laugh the intruder had given as he disappeared into the darkness.

# Chapter Thirty-Six

When Henry got back to the French windows, he found Everett Carr standing in front of the safe. He was dressed in an elaborate brocade dressing gown, decorated with crescent moons, tied with a length of tasselled cord, and a pair of patent leather slippers protruding from the bottom of it. As Henry approached, he turned away from the safe and limped over to the windows to assist the younger man into the room and close the doors behind him.

"He was too quick for me," gasped Henry.

"You gave a good account of yourself, my boy," said Carr. Then, in answer to Henry's puzzled expression, he added, "I saw your little adventure from my bedroom window. I thought I might be of some assistance in its aftermath."

"Thank you," said Henry, his breath returning to him. "If he hadn't been so fast, I might have been able to tackle him."

"You did not see who it was?" Carr asked.

"His face was hidden," replied Henry, helping himself to a brandy from a small drinks table in the corner of the room. "I assume it was the poltergeist from the mill."

Carr shook his head slowly. "I think not, my boy."

"He was dressed very much how Father described the man he chased away from the garage the other day."

Carr shook his head. "That in itself does not prove it was the same man."

A realisation seemed to hit Henry. "Mr Carr, do you know who the poltergeist is?"

Carr nodded, but it was clear that his attention was focused elsewhere. "I know who both of them are."

Henry glared at him. "Both of them?"

The question seemed to bring Carr out of himself. He looked at Henry as if seeing him for the first time, and he seemed momentarily confused by his presence in the study. At last, however, he gave a short laugh and shook his head.

"Forgive me, my boy, I was lost in my thoughts," he said. "Tell me, did you see the intruder take anything from the safe?"

"No."

"Or put something in his pocket?"

"No."

He turned back to the safe and craned his neck to look inside once more. It was filled with papers, some loose, others folded, a fair number still in opened envelopes, some tied together with ribbons. There were folders and files, too, and what seemed to Carr to be account ledgers, leather-backed and sombre, along with various certificates for numerous stocks and deeds. Carr flicked through them, but none of them seemed to be of particular relevance. As soon as he had looked in the safe, he had felt the familiar chill of trepidation freeze his spine, and now, as he looked more carefully through the papers and files, it grew even colder. Something was missing from the safe, Carr was certain of it.

"Who knows the combination to this safe?" he asked.

"Mother, probably" was Henry's instinctive response. "But it most certainly wasn't her I chased just now. I wouldn't put it past Rosamund to have spied on Father so that she could learn the combination."

"Did you know it?"

"No." Henry was careful to make the word emphatic. "And you could hardly have seen me chasing myself, could you?"

Carr's smile broadened. "Indeed not."

He turned to Henry. "Do you know what these papers are?"

"No. Father would never have confided in me about them."

"What might you have expected him to keep in this safe?"

Henry gave the matter brief consideration and joined Carr at the open safe. "Private papers, I suppose, business and personal. Financial matters, too, I suppose."

Carr was nodding, and he turned back to look inside the safe once more. "I expected to find something in this safe, and it isn't here."

"What?"

But Carr seemed not to have heard. His dark eyes had narrowed, and his lips were pursed under the heavy moustache. Absently, he stroked the Imperial beard on his chin and began to pace the room. He looked from the safe to the French windows, from the mess on the desk to the newly formed spider's web of cracks in the plaster of the wall, and finally at Henry. Slowly, a smile formed on his lips, and the dark eyes shone with a triumphant gleam.

"Now, my boy," he said, "I think it is as well for us to secure those French windows, leave this room as it is, and lock the door. I shall keep the key. We must allow the good Inspector Barber to draw his own conclusions from the events of tonight."

"But, Mr Carr—"

"We must sleep, my boy. Be patient, and all shall be made clear."

And he would say no more. Once the room was secured, Carr took the key to the door and dropped it into the pocket of his dressing gown. Then, with a polite bow, he bid Henry good night and slowly ascended the stairs.

# Chapter Thirty-Seven

On the following morning, the news of the attempted burglary was greeted with a mixture of emotions, ranging from shock to outrage, with a certain degree of admiration for Henry's courage. Marjorie insisted on looking in the safe, despite the protestations of Everett Carr and his desire to preserve the room as carefully as possible for police inspection. But Marjorie was adamant, and Carr, albeit reluctantly, assented on the condition that he accompany her. As it transpired, he need not have worried, for she did little more than glare with anger at the cracked plaster, take a cursory look in the safe, and bemoan the broken pane in the French windows. Only after they had stepped back into the hallway and Carr had locked the door once more, did Marjorie seem to display any deeper emotion than an apparent but mild inconvenience.

"Will this nightmare never end?" she asked. "What have we done to deserve all this?"

It was a simple but agonising question to hear, and Rosamund seemed to feel it most keenly, since she went to her mother and threw her arms around her neck.

"Oh, Mummy, I'm so very sorry," she said. Marjorie held onto the girl, as if feeling her child against her body was a comfort in itself, an anchor of something approaching normality amid the crashing waves of despair. At last, Rosamund ended the embrace and looked into her mother's eyes. "Has anything been taken?"

Marjorie shook her head. "Not by the look of it."

"That's a relief, at least." Rosamund looked at Henry. "A good job you disturbed him, otherwise who knows what he might have taken?"

"If the police are coming," Marjorie said, "we should all at least be dressed to greet them. And we can certainly do no good standing around in the hallway."

There was a murmur of consent, and the party dispersed. As Rosamund passed him, Carr made a gentle movement and subtly placed his hand on her arm.

"I wonder, my child," he said, "whether I might have a little word with you."

"Of course, Mr Carr. Now?"

"No, no," he said, as if the idea was a monstrous one. "Once you have had your breakfast and Inspector Barber has spoken with you. There is no hurry."

"Very well," Rosmund said with a smile. But as she walked away from him and up the stairs, she wondered whether he had detected the fear in her eyes that she had tried so hard to conceal. And whilst she tried to convince herself otherwise, she somehow felt certain that he had.

Breakfast was a muted affair. It was difficult to think of a topic of conversation that would not in some way come round to the burglary or, more frighteningly for them all, to the murders. Later, when Inspector Barber arrived, the atmosphere of gloom that had gently pervaded the meal somehow seemed to intensify. To the family, it seemed strange that a man they had known so well and for so long could now instil in them a very definite sense of fear. Once, he had simply been Tommy Barber, the local copper. Now, circumstances had turned him into a fearful entity of official suspicion.

For his part, Everett Carr made no reference to his deductions about the contents of the safe, but gave a clear and elegantly balanced account of the previous evening's events. Barber listened, making the occasional note, but if he was suspicious of any reticence on Carr's part, he did not show it.

"I'm grateful to you, Mr Carr, for locking the door," said the inspector. "Very helpful indeed. Although I wish you'd been able to stop Mrs Bayliss from going in there."

Carr gave a shrug of defeat. "She is a strong-willed woman, Inspector."

"She is that," said Barber, in a tone of voice that suggested that once upon a time he had experienced the phenomenon first-hand. "One thing has occurred to me, Mr Carr, that I would welcome your views on."

Carr was flattered rather than surprised at this sudden desire on the inspector's part to confide in him, and the cause of it was not difficult to see. Barber's pale blue eyes were heavy with stress, his cheeks blanched with the signs of anxious insomnia, and his broad shoulders were slumped with professional fatigue. Carr had seen the symptoms many times, even in Scotland Yard detectives, but in this gruff provincial policeman, they seemed even more prominent. Murder did not feature prominently in this simple community, Carr reflected, and its presence twice over would be monumental, and its pressures affected nobody as acutely as they did Barber.

"Whatever I may do to assist," said Carr gently, touching the inspector's forearm briefly but comfortingly. "I am here to help."

Barber, seldom sentimental, nevertheless gave a grateful bow of his head. "It's the matter of these acts of sabotage, you see. Are you convinced that they're the work of one man?"

It was a question that Carr understood to require no formal response, and so he said nothing and allowed Barber to continue.

"You see," the inspector went on, "I can't help thinking there's something not quite right about them. For example, why does this poltergeist attack the mill one moment and Bayliss' car the next?"

Carr frowned. "I do not follow, my boy."

"It's professional and domestic, isn't it?" Barber said. "Why does the poltergeist suddenly shift his focus from the mill to Bayliss' private property?"

"The culprit would not recognise any such distinction if his target was Bayliss. The man was master of both the mill and the house."

But Barber was not convinced. "Perhaps, but I can't shake the idea that whoever poured acid on Bayliss' car wasn't the same person who carried out the other attacks. After all, Mr Carr, if you're right, and Bayliss was the target, why does the poltergeist strike at the factory all those times and only once at Darton House? Surely, he'd attack wherever he could."

"You're saying that there is a change of emphasis from the factory to the car, from the professional to the private, that does not seem in character for this poltergeist?" Carr's tone of voice showed that he was becoming increasingly fascinated by the idea.

And Barber was nodding. "And perhaps it only makes sense to me if there are two poltergeists."

But Carr held up a warning finger. "We must not run before we can walk, Inspector. But it is an intriguing notion, to be sure. Bayliss himself, of course, thought it was the same person."

Barber seemed not to have heard, and, indeed, Carr's voice had lowered as he spoke those final words, as if they had been for him alone, private thoughts unintentionally given voice.

"But I still think there is only one killer," Barber was saying. "Do you?"

Carr nodded. "May I ask, Inspector, whether you have made any progress in the matter of the deaths of Mr Pym and Mr Bayliss?"

Barber shook his head. "We've found nothing, Mr Carr, at least not insofar as Mr Pym's death is concerned. I can't find any motive for that at all, I must say. Bayliss, of course," he added, lowering his voice, "was a man not short of enemies. Michael Arden remains the prime suspect, but I can't see any reason for him to murder Pym. There seems to be no reason for it."

"Be sure, Inspector, that there was a reason."

There was something in the tone of voice that caught the inspector's attention. "If you know something, Mr Carr, it is your duty to tell me."

Carr smiled and waved away the official warning. "I *know* nothing, Inspector, but I *think* many things."

Despite the inspector's protestations, which Carr cut off with polite deflections and an amiable wave of his hand, no more was said. Carr took his leave of the inspector with a gentle handshake and a bow of his head.

He found Rosamund in the garden, having searched the house for her. She looked tired. Her cheeks were paler than normal, and her dark eyes were heavy with the mixed emotions that violent crime so often caused.

He could sympathise, and he did so, and he walked towards her slowly, a gentle smile of friendship rather than confrontation on his lips, and one hand outstretched towards her, as much in support as it was in greeting.

When she saw him, Rosamund felt a shiver of anxiety pass through her, and she wondered what it was about him that suddenly caused such fear within her. Surely, he was the same harmless and polite man who had arrived at the house a few days ago. Nothing had changed, other than he now seemed somehow dangerous. His dark eyes now seemed predatory where once they had been engaging. Then, almost inevitably, it occurred to her that perhaps it was not Everett Carr who had changed at all, but her. Her perceptions had shifted, she thought, not because of him but because of her guilt, of her suspicions, and of the impact of the situation in which she found herself. How she wished, not for the first time, that things were how they used to be.

"I couldn't stand it in the house anymore," she said. "The whole place seemed tainted by everything that has happened."

"Quite so," said Carr. "I suspect it will do no good to tell you that what you're experiencing is a perfectly normal reaction to these extraordinary circumstances in which you find yourself."

Rosamund shook her head. "I'm afraid that doesn't help a bit, Mr Carr."

"I hope, my child," he said, his voice suddenly so serious that the innate politeness and formality of speech seemed to her almost ludicrous, "that you will treat me not as an enemy, but as a friend. I assure you that I wish only to help you."

"Very well," she said, uncertain of how she was expected to respond.

"Then perhaps, my child, we might speak to young Mr Toole together."

Rosamund stared at him with an uncertain expression. "What for?"

But Carr did not offer any reply other than a deeply ingratiating smile, one that she found so persuasive that it was almost hypnotic. She checked her watch.

"He might still be at home," she said. "He may not have left for his office at his mill as yet."

Carr nodded, as if sealing a deal. "Good, then let us waste no time."

"I still don't understand what this is all about."

With a strangely conspiratorial glimmer in his eyes, Carr leaned towards her. "All shall become clear, my child."

Rosamund insisted on driving to George Toole's cottage, although Carr was certain that it was not so great a distance that a morning walk could not have achieved it. As she climbed into the driver's seat, however, Rosamund gave no indication that she was willing to relent on the matter. If they must see George Toole, her expression seemed to say, it would be on her terms. She waited in silence for Carr to acquiesce, which he did with reluctance.

"Daddy never let me drive these things while he was alive," she said, with perhaps a trace of sadness in her voice. "Perhaps now I can."

"I did not realise that you enjoyed motor vehicles so much, my child."

"I don't, not really. It's just a whim." She looked at Carr. "And I presume you want to see George urgently."

"Indeed," said Carr uncomfortably. A premonition had set in his mind that Rosamund would drive this mechanical beast not with care but with abandon. He was proven correct almost at once, but his mind lingered not on that rather obvious prediction but on the fact that, had she desired to do so, Rosamund Bayliss could have driven to the mill and back to the house in more than sufficient time to kill her father.

Toole had finished his breakfast and was sitting by the fire, smoking a cigarette and reading the newspaper, when he saw the car pull up outside his house. He watched through the window as Rosamund got out of the car. He was as surprised to see her as he was elated. Was this a step closer to reconciliation, he wondered. She had come here of her own volition, without either invitation or insistence from him. He could guess her primary motive, no doubt, but surely a telephone call would have sufficed to satisfy any curiosity about recent events. And yet, he thought, smiling to himself, she had chosen to come here in person. How strange that crime would be the thing that brought them together again.

No sooner had Toole indulged himself in this false optimism than he saw Everett Carr emerge, too, from the motor car. At once, the sense of excitement Toole had brought upon himself shifted its focus and altered its form into a malevolent sensation of dread. The knocking at the door sounded grotesquely ominous, and the simultaneous chiming of the clock in the hallway seemed somehow to mark the dawning of a day of reckoning.

Rosamund was standing on the doorstep, her eyes flashing a silent warning to him. Behind her, he could see the smiling and amiable face of Everett Carr, muffled both by his scarf and moustache. There was a benevolence about his expression and his attitude that almost made Toole feel foolish for this overwhelming premonition of disaster that had taken hold of him.

"Let us in, George," said Rosamund. "It's a nice day, but the wind is bitter."

He showed them through to the parlour. It was a charming room, thought Carr as he entered it, which made the unpleasantness of the visit all the more regrettable. The furnishings were simple but expensive, although they were now showing signs of their age. The leather of the obviously comfortable armchair and settee was cracking, and the edges of the rug placed over the wooden flooring were beginning to fray. The lace trim of the cloth placed over the small table beside one of the armchairs was likewise showing signs of decay, as was its counterpart draped over the mantel. It seemed strange to Carr that a man of Toole's position should have allowed such signs of neglect, however small, to show, and he wondered what the origins of this apparent disregard for external decency were. Disregarding them for the moment, Carr looked at the items that decorated the mantel itself: the small but elegant carriage clock, the gilt candlesticks, and, most interestingly of all to Carr's mind, the various trophies and cups, both silver and gold, that spoke of Toole's athletic prowess.

"You are a sportsman, Mr Toole," said Carr. "An athlete, in particular."

"I'm a pretty effective leg-spinner, yes," said Toole, not realising the significance of the statement, and being only vaguely aware of it from the beaming smile on Everett Carr's face. "Forgive me, I have no wish to be rude, but what is this about?"

It was Rosamund who replied. "Mr Carr wanted to speak to you."

Toole registered the anxiety in her eyes, but strove to hide his own. He looked over to Carr with a placid innocence. "Oh yes?"

Carr bowed. "I wished to speak to you both together."

"About what?"

Carr indicated the leather armchair and, with a nod of approval from his host, lowered himself into it. Rosamund, without invitation, sat on the settee, leaving Toole standing on the hearth rug between them. He felt suddenly awkward and strangely exposed as he towered above the two of them.

"Would you like coffee, tea?" he asked.

Rosamund shook her head. Carr, too, waved aside the offer with a subtle shake of his head. Toole lit a cigarette and shifted his weight from one foot to the other.

"Well, I'm all ears, Mr Carr," he said. The voice was jaunty enough to suggest a lack of concern, but the constant flicking of ash from his cigarette into the grate and the suppressed nervous shaking of his leg spoke otherwise.

Carr looked at him for a long moment. "I would simply like to know whether Arthur Bayliss' will said what you expected."

Rosamund began to tremble. She could feel her innards quivering with emotion, so violently that she felt sure it would have been visible to Carr, had his attention not been reserved for George Toole. She glared at Carr, sitting motionless, looking up into Toole's eyes, and Rosamund could see that whilst there was a smile beneath the imposing moustache, the dark eyes above it were serious and persuasive in their intensity.

"I don't know what you're talking about," Toole said at last, forcing a smile to his lips.

Carr looked over to Rosamund. "Can you answer my question, my child?"

Rosamund shook her head. "I don't know anything about it."

"It is better to trust me." Carr waited for her to respond, but she had no words to give him.

Toole tossed his cigarette into the grate. It might have seemed casual had he not instantly lit another. "You've made a mistake. I didn't even know Bayliss had made a will."

Carr looked from one to the other of them. "He most certainly did, I can assure you."

"Did he tell you as much?" asked Toole.

"No," conceded Carr. "But I know he did, all the same."

"I don't follow you, Mr Carr," said Toole.

Rosamund looked at Carr. "How *do* you know there's a will?"

Carr began to twirl his cane between his fingers, the silver handle sparkling in the morning light. He looked at Rosamund.

"Your father threatened to cut you out of his will if you did not reinstate your engagement to Mr Toole," he said. "You will recall the very unpleasant scene at dinner a few nights ago, when you asked your father about his argument with Mr Arden in the public house."

"Yes." Her voice showed that the memory was still a painful one.

"Quite so," Carr said, nodding his head. "It seemed to me that a businessman such as Mr Bayliss would keep a copy of his will at home, as well as at his solicitors' offices. The safe seemed an obvious place for him to do that, and yet there was no will inside."

"You're a very clever man, Mr Carr."

The compliment was spoken in a tone of voice that suggested defeat rather than admiration, and the smile that flickered across Rosamund's lips as she said it was one of resignation rather than affection. Carr did not acknowledge either the words or the smile, however, and his eyes remained fixed on George Toole.

Toole, for his part, was smoking incessantly, but his expression showed a forced lack of interest. "Forgive me, Mr Carr, but I don't see what any of this has to do with me."

Carr's smile was faintly condescending, like the smile of a parent indulging a recalcitrant child. "I think, perhaps, that you do, Mr Toole."

"I think, perhaps, that I do not."

Carr rose slowly to his feet. Although the smile retained its derision, his dark eyes had hardened with a determined authority, as if he were daring Toole to say one more word of untruth.

"You will forgive me, Mr Toole," he said, the voice so gentle and calm that it was almost terrifying, "if I ask you what will be a very personal question." Carr allowed no time for any riposte or evasion from the man. "How much do you owe?"

The question had a startling effect. Rosamund gave a short gasp of frightened shock, and Toole's eyes widened with fearful surprise. Carr could almost see the half-formed lies and instinctive denials form in Toole's mind, and the lips attempted to form them, but the words refused to be said.

"I don't know what you mean," he stammered.

"Miss Bayliss has made no secret of the fact that your relationship with her was over," said Carr. "There has to be a reason for that, even if she is unwilling to give it. Similarly, there must be a reason for your attempts to deceive both Miss Bayliss and the police about your whereabouts on the night Arthur Bayliss was murdered. The fact that you have lied about where you were on other evenings suggested to me that you were not Bayliss' killer. If you were, you would only need to lie about your movements on the night he died. And yet you were lying about them in any event."

Toole looked at Rosamund, who simply lowered her head, as if by doing so, she could distance herself from the events unfolding in front of her.

"I may have suspected another woman," Carr was saying, "but I rather fancied that money lay behind your deceptions."

"Why?"

Carr gave a small shrug. "I was certain in my mind that the object of the burglary was to steal a will that simply had to exist. Wills are far more closely connected with money matters than romantic ones."

"I said you were a clever man," said Rosamund sullenly.

Carr did not reply. "And then, Mr Toole, whoever broke into Darton House last night knew the combination of the safe. Henry Bayliss suspected that Miss Rosamund here might have spied on her father in order to learn the combination. I could hardly imagine it myself," he added, looking at her, "since it was not her that I envisaged as being in need of money. But you, Mr Toole, would have been in the study many times with Arthur Bayliss as part of your mutual business concerns, and I could very easily imagine you idly taking note of the combination of his safe on those occasions when he opened it, not knowing how you would later come to use the information."

# CHAPTER THIRTY-SEVEN

"You have no proof of that," cautioned Toole.

"No," conceded Carr without concern, "but I have the balance of probability on my side. And I have the frayed edges of this rug," he added, tapping his cane along them, "and in the tablecloth, and I have the cracked leather of the chairs and settee, well past their best. All of it speaks of financial difficulty."

Toole finished his latest cigarette and tossed the end into the grate. Slowly, he put his hands in his pockets and looked into Carr's eyes. "It doesn't prove a thing."

Carr was undeterred. "I watched Henry Bayliss chasing the burglar across the lawns. Henry himself said how quickly the man had run. And here," he indicated the trophies on the mantel, "I see evidence of your sporting prowess. You talk about proof, Mr Toole, as if I require it. I do not. I am not a policeman. I have no power over you, but neither do I have the burden of evidential proof. What harm is there in telling me the truth that is already so obvious to me?"

"If it's obvious to you, I needn't say anything," replied Toole.

But Rosamund had heard enough. "If you don't tell him, George, I will. I can't live with any more lies. I just want everything to be back to normal. I want us to be able to speak to each other without deceit or mistrust. No more scheming, no more lies. Please," she added, as the tears flowed down her cheeks.

Toole stared down at her. "Very well. I suppose it is time for the truth to have its day. You're quite right, Mr Carr. I am in serious debt."

"In business or personally?"

"Personally," said Toole. "Gambling."

Carr looked sadly into the younger man's eyes. "Was Arthur Bayliss blackmailing you?"

Toole stared. "What makes you say that?"

"Something he said to me one evening at the Icarus Club in London," said Carr. "He said that taking over your father's mill was a good business opportunity and that you had no choice about it."

"I didn't."

"He was blackmailing you about your gambling habit."

"Not quite." Toole looked over to the woman he loved. "He was blackmailing me into a marriage I already wanted."

Carr looked from one to the other. "I fear I don't understand."

"Arthur wanted to disinherit Henry, and he wanted to use my relationship with Rosamund to do it," Toole said. "My debts were a way of making sure I went along with his plan."

Carr looked at Rosamund. "Did you know of this, my child?"

The girl nodded. "George told me a couple of days ago."

"And what precisely was this plan of your father's?" asked Everett Carr.

He listened to the story, told in a few but tearful words by Rosamund. He felt sickened by what he heard, certainly, but Carr felt a simultaneous sadness shudder through him at the realisation that none of what the girl said came as a surprise to him. On the contrary, it merely confirmed his opinion of Arthur Bayliss as a repulsive, manipulative, and almost monstrous individual. Was murder, Carr thought, not for the first time, ever justified?

"You knew about the plan to burgle the house?" asked Carr, looking at Rosamund.

"Yes."

Carr turned his attention to Toole. "You needed to know what that will said, and whether Bayliss had indeed disinherited his daughter."

Toole nodded. "It was vital if we were to know whether Rosamund had a motive or not."

"Or, indeed, whether you had one?" Carr nodded.

"Yes." Toole's cheeks flushed with shame.

Everett Carr allowed a long pause to pass before he asked the most important question of all. "And had you a motive?"

In response, Toole walked over to a sideboard that stood in the corner of the room. He pulled open a drawer and took out a long, slim document, folded lengthways and tied with scarlet ribbon. He handed it to Carr, who took it warily, as if holding it alone might contaminate his personal morality.

"See for yourself, Mr Carr." Toole lit a cigarette. "Or perhaps I can save you the trouble. The will leaves nothing to Henry Bayliss, but it does leave everything to Marjorie and Rosamund, to be split equally."

"Oh, God…" whispered Rosamund.

Carr was reading the will intently. "So, he never got around to changing it to reflect his deal with you?"

Toole shook his head. "Apparently not. I am sure you can see where it leaves us."

"Mrs and Miss Bayliss have significant motives to kill," said Carr, looking sadly at Rosamund.

Rosamund's attempt to deny the fact was interrupted by Toole's voice. "But Henry Bayliss and I have none."

Carr shook his head, folding the will neatly together once more. "I shouldn't say so. Henry may have no financial motive, but his father's treatment of him must be taken into account. Indeed, Bayliss' treatment of his wife and daughter might also constitute motives for Henry."

"And for me?"

Carr smiled gently. "You had no way of knowing that Bayliss had not as yet changed his will. The deal you agreed with him was entirely favourable and beneficial to you. And, of course," he added, "you still love Miss Rosamund. Her father's treatment of her is a motive you share with Henry Bayliss. And whilst your engagement is currently broken, nobody can know what the future might hold. Her inheritance might still be of some benefit to you."

"That's an appalling thing to say," seethed Toole.

Carr nodded. "Perhaps, but it is no less true for that."

Rosamund had risen to her feet and was staring out of the window. So, she thought, they all had a motive. Any single one of them could have done it. And it all came down to money. Which of them was a killer? Which of them valued money over human life? Which of them would she never be able to trust, believe, or love again? She felt tears sting her eyes once more, as the weight of her thoughts crushed the sound of the voices behind her, leaving her only with her own fears and suspicions.

# Chapter Thirty-Eight

Lydia Stansfield had slept badly. It was rare for her to lie awake in the darkness, distracted from sleep either by bad dreams or personal concerns, but the previous night had been one of those rare occasions when slumber, deep or transient, had abandoned her. The reason, of course, was obvious, and whilst Lydia could convince herself that it was Marjorie Bayliss' visit to her and the words that they had exchanged that troubled her mind, she knew that this was not the primary cause of her nocturnal disorders. No, Lydia thought, as she finally abandoned hope of any sleep at all, what kept her awake was her increasing need to confess. It had been gnawing at her, like a parasite on a host, for some days now, and finally, it was threatening to consume her peace of mind entirely. Confession, she thought, like some religious zealot, was the only remedy for this illness of deceit.

She had given up the attempt at last and had gone downstairs. She had sat at the kitchen table, a cup of coffee in front of her. The room had been eerily silent, the darkness almost absolute, and she had become slowly aware of the feeling of a strange but contradictory sense of peace. The quiet had been so extreme that she felt as if she could taste it, and she had known that the slightest sound would seem like a terrible explosion in her head. No such sound had come, however, although sleep must have overpowered her at last, because she had woken up slumped over the kitchen table, with a terrible throb of discomfort along her spine, and the untasted coffee still before her, now cold and unappealing.

But Lydia had woken with a clearer mind. Her sleep may have been erratic, even sporadic, during the early hours of the morning, but somehow, she felt refreshed, and she could detect within herself a calm determination not only to face the day but to tell the truth. The lingering question in her mind was in whom she should confide. The natural choice was Eric Hirst, of course, but what Lydia had to confess would perhaps cause Eric more pain than it would give her comfort. Eric was a dear man, even if Lydia could not bring herself to feel as strongly for him as he did for her, and she would not want to harm him unnecessarily. But whom she could trust apart from him, she could not think. The problem plagued her as she made her way back upstairs to wash and dress, and it continued to do so as she walked downstairs. Names passed through her mind continuously, but they were dismissed as soon as they had occurred to her. The reality was, she knew, that she should go to the police, but the idea terrified her. It seemed so final, not to say fatal, as if once she had said the words to Inspector Barber, there would be no going back, no escape.

The answer came to her in the sound of a small, delicate tapping on her front door. She was expecting nobody, so the noise surprised her, and the idea of ignoring it existed in her mind for only a passing moment. She walked to the door and pulled it open. Whether she understood in that moment that the solution to her dilemma was standing in front of her, she could not say for certain, but she did know that it was somehow important and strangely comforting to see Everett Carr standing on her front step, smiling benevolently at her, and his dark eyes filled with a majestic allure.

"I had hoped I might catch you before you left for your employment, dear lady," he said.

"I'm not going into the shop today," said Lydia. "I've telephoned to say I'm not feeling too well."

A look of concern darkened Carr's features. "I am sorry to hear it."

Lydia shook her head. "I'm afraid it's not true. I just couldn't face it."

Carr tapped the side of his nose with a gloved finger. "Our little secret."

Despite herself, Lydia laughed. There was something so childishly innocent about this little man that she knew she should find irritating, but which she in fact considered foolishly charming.

"To tell the truth," she said, "I do feel rather under the weather, but it's nothing physical."

Carr placed a hand on his heart as if he were some sort of exaggerated cleric. "Perhaps what I have to say to you will ease all your troubles."

"I don't see how."

"Because, dear lady, I know about the night Mr Bayliss was killed, and I know what part you played in it."

Lydia glared in horror. "You can't know."

Carr nodded slowly. "But I do. And I come here as a friend, not as an accuser."

She stepped aside slowly to allow him to enter and, as with her consideration of confessing to the police, she felt somehow burdened with a sense of finality, but, unlike before, she found it neither overwhelming nor terrifying.

They sat at the kitchen table, and Lydia prepared tea. Carr would have preferred coffee, but he was not given the choice, and such a petty consideration could hardly matter in the circumstances. Sitting opposite him, Lydia saw a quiet confidence in those dark eyes, but there was nothing about his expression that spoke to her of danger or confrontation. He seemed harmless, politely benign, although the stark contrast between the scarlet tie and handkerchief with the funereal black of the suit, and the elaborate but careful styling of the large moustache and trim Imperial beard spoke of a certain eccentricity.

"Tell me," he said now, his voice quiet but authoritative. "Do you know who killed Arthur Bayliss?"

"No."

He looked at her keenly. "But you suspect someone?"

"Yes." It seemed futile to deny it.

"The person you saw at the mill that night?" The question was asked with such quiet assurance that, although Lydia tried not to react, the slight quiver of an eyebrow betrayed her surprise. Carr smiled in satisfaction. "Was it Michael Arden?"

Lydia said nothing. She looked down at the cup of tea in front of her, as if she might find some way out of the situation that she had allowed herself to fall into in the cooling, stewing brew.

Carr leaned forward in his chair. "The police suspect Mr Arden. There is evidence that he was at the mill."

Now, she did look up at him. "Evidence?"

Carr nodded. "A note, signed with his initials. A threat against Mr Bayliss' life," he added slowly.

Lydia's cheeks had blanched, and her eyes glistened with anxiety. "A threat?"

Incongruously, it seemed to her, Everett Carr smiled soothingly. "The police say so."

"And you?"

"I rather think it was something else entirely."

A gurgle of tearful relief rose in Lydia's throat, and it expelled from her mouth like a drowning man sucking for air. Carr stretched out a hand and held her forearm gently for a moment of reassurance.

"*I won't let you get away with it again,*" he quoted. "You can see how it might be construed as a threat. But it was written on a napkin from a restaurant. A very exclusive restaurant in Manchester, if I understand correctly. *Sinclair's.* Have you ever been there?"

"Yes," she said with a choking sob.

Carr nodded. "Does a napkin seem a likely place to write a threat? The anonymous letter delivered to Mr Bayliss' office was not on a napkin. It seems to me, dear lady, that the use of a napkin suggests a message written on the spur of the moment, using the first thing that comes to hand. Very naturally, in a restaurant, a napkin is clearly to hand. So, you see, the meaning of this message suddenly takes on a different form. In my eyes, that is," he added with a smile.

"Yes," she repeated, the tears now heavy in her eyes. Did he enjoy this sort of slow breakdown of a person's defences, she wondered? She had woken up determined to confess what she knew about the night Bayliss was killed, but this deliberate dissection of the matter terrified her, and she wished now that she had never let this man into her house and that she had remained closeted by her own deceit.

"This was not a threat," Carr said. There was now a sliver of ice in his voice. "It was a promise. What sort of promise could be made like this, on impulse, on a restaurant napkin, *other than a promise that next time the person concerned would pay the bill?* Bayliss had paid too many times before, and next time, the guest would pay. Does that not make more sense than a threat?"

Lydia rose to her feet and strode towards the sink. It was an almost meaningless gesture. She had no reason to wash her hands, nor to fetch clean cups, nor to grab a cloth to mop up any spillage. There was no reason to go to the sink, only the instinctive urge to be away from him. She had wanted the truth, yes, but on her own terms, not delivered to her on a plate of courtesy and amiability. She gripped the sink with her hands and sobbed silently.

Carr rose and approached her. "You found the napkin, my child, and you knew what it meant. Mr Bayliss only went to *Sinclair's* with those ladies he convinced to love him. Including you, I think."

"He told me it was our special place. That he would never bring anyone else there because it was reserved for us."

"A cruel lie," said Carr.

"He fooled us all." She looked into his eyes now, the pain seeming to ease as she stared into them. "Marjorie was right in what she said to me. We were Arthur's victims, not his lovers. He used us all for his own pleasure."

"Mrs Bayliss came to see you?" He listened intently to Lydia's explanation. Then, he nodded with quiet admiration. "A brave lady, as indeed, are you, my child."

"I don't feel very brave." She wiped a tear away from her flaming cheek. "I feel completely stupid."

"But there is your bravery, in your ability to recognise and admit it. There are times when it takes courage to be honest, Miss Stansfield, particularly with oneself."

He took a glass from the sideboard and leaned over to turn on the tap. He let it run cold and then half-filled the glass, handing it to her with the unnecessary command to drink. She did so, hesitantly at first, but then almost greedily, as if she hadn't realised how badly she needed to quench her thirst.

"I found the napkin in his wallet," she said. "Not long before he ended the relationship, he told me to take some money to buy myself something pretty for the next time we met. You have no idea how I feel about that now, Mr Carr. At the time, I was stupidly happy that he was lavishing me with gifts, treating me, and spoiling me."

"Something he did with all his lovers," Carr said, almost to himself.

"Now, it makes me feel like a whore. They weren't gifts, they were *payment*." The words seemed to hurt him as much as her. There was a moment of silence before she spoke again. "He must have forgotten the napkin was in there, but I found it. I didn't say anything. Shock, I suppose."

"You believed you were his only lover, that only you were treated to meals at *Sinclair's* and received expensive gifts."

"Yes. And then, here was proof that I wasn't." She sipped at the water. "Days later, he ended things altogether. I could only assume it was because of the woman who had written that message."

"It could have been in his wallet for months," Carr argued.

Lydia shrugged. "Perhaps, but that didn't alter how it made me feel."

"And you kept it. You took it that night to confront him with it."

She nodded. "That was why I telephoned the house."

"You wanted to know where Mr Bayliss was."

"Eric had told me he was dining that night at Darton House. I knew that if Arthur was there, I could do nothing. If he wasn't, I knew he'd be in his office. It was his second home, after all."

"And so, you went to the mill. At what time?"

"I was running a bath, and Eric called. That was twenty to eight, perhaps. I thought about everything for a moment or two, then telephoned Dartford House."

"That was a quarter to eight," said Carr.

"And I left home as soon as I'd hung up."

Carr did a mental calculation. "Mr Hirst says that it would take no more than five minutes from here to walk to the mill if you went over the allotments." He pointed to them through the window above the sink. "That would mean you arrived at the mill for ten to eight, five to at the outside."

"That would be about right."

"What happened?"

Lydia took a moment to compose herself. Here, she thought, was the truth she had so desperately wanted to tell. Now that it had come to it, the words were difficult to find.

"I got to the mill at the time you say," she said, "give or take a minute or so. I was just turning through the gates when I heard footsteps. Running, they were. I had the feeling they were coming towards me rather than going away from me. Obviously, I didn't want to be seen, so I stood close to the wall and hid in the shadows. I could hardly breathe; I was so frightened. My heart seemed to be in my mouth all the time." She took a gulp of what remained of the water. "In a matter of seconds, Michael Arden came running through the gates."

"Did he see you?"

"No."

"You are sure?"

"Yes, he never once looked in my direction. He ran through the mill gates and away from me."

"You are certain it was Mr Arden?"

"Oh, yes," she said. "His face was lit by the streetlamps."

Carr nodded slowly. "What did you do then?"

"I ran down the pathway to the mill. It looked so large, so imposing in the darkness."

"Was the main door open?"

"Yes, so I knew Arthur was inside."

Carr recalled the evening of the murder. A similar thought had occurred to him, as he had expressed to Eric Hirst. "You went up the iron staircase?"

"To Arthur's office…" The memory was dawning once more on her, and her widening eyes betrayed the fact. "I saw…"

Carr spared her the pain. "I know all that you saw. And the horror of it…"

"I dropped my handbag. Everything fell out on the floor."

"Including the napkin?"

She nodded, the tears returning. "It was all such a mess. Suddenly, I wanted to be out of there, away from it all, at home, just anywhere that wasn't that place."

"In your haste," Carr murmured, "you left the napkin behind."

"I didn't realise until the next morning."

Carr swung his cane loosely between his fingers, leaning against the sink for support. "When you recalled the fact, the initials on the napkin reminded you about Michael Arden?"

"Yes."

Carr nodded. "I wondered why you were so quick to defend Mr Arden when Mr Hirst suggested that the initials were his. You recall when I was brought here after my fall?"

"I remember."

"Mr Hirst did no more than voice your own fears, and they shocked you."

Lydia sat down at the table once more, her movements slow and exhausted. "It's strange how frightening it is to hear your private thoughts said to you. They seem so much more terrifying than when they're silently in your head."

Carr smiled softly at her but did not say how often his own mind had drifted into similar territory. Lydia did not look at him. Instead, she stared at the knots in the table and ran her fingers over one of them. The truth had been told now, she thought, and contrary to her expectations, she felt no better for it. Slowly, she became aware that Carr was talking once more.

"Do you know whose initials were on the napkin?" he asked.

"No. I don't know anybody with those initials." Then, a thought hit her. "Marjorie Bayliss' surname was Ashcroft."

Carr nodded. He had contemplated the same thing already. "One thing, I think, dear lady, that we can be certain of is that they are not the initials of Michael Arden."

"No," Lydia conceded. "But he was at the mill that night, Mr Carr. I saw him."

"Do you believe him capable of murder?"

Lydia was unsure how to respond. Whatever she thought to say sounded either incriminating or deceitful. At last, she just shrugged and settled for evasion.

"I don't know him well enough to say," was her reply. "But he was there, Mr Carr, and he seemed badly frightened when he came running out of the gates."

Carr was frowning. "Frightened? You said only that he was crying."

Lydia nodded. "He was, but it wasn't sadness, Mr Carr. It was *fear*."

"Fear of what?"

Lydia shrugged again. "I don't know, Mr Carr. God knows what it was."

Everett Carr had leaned back in his chair. When he spoke, there was a strange, almost ominous timbre to his voice, and the dark eyes had narrowed in disturbing concentration.

"God may indeed know, dear lady," he said, "but I know, too. I think I know, too," he repeated, as if he needed to assure himself of the fact.

# Chapter Thirty-Nine

Everett Carr had walked in sombre silence since leaving Lydia Stansfield's cottage. He had no destination in mind, but it was no surprise to him that, once he had broken his reverie and taken stock of his surroundings, he found himself once more overlooking Layton Brook. From here, the scene of such beauty and tragedy, he could see the small mill town of Darton Vale spread out beneath him, as if he were some sort of God overlooking the feats of its divine labour. A heavy raincloud hovered over the town, but it had not yet released its downpour, and in a moment of romanticism, Carr could not help but feel that the cloud somehow represented the shadow of murder that had blanketed over the town, as if this nebulous mass of atmosphere and unbidden rain was the personification of the dark secrets and hidden lies that had led to violent death. The cloud may soon break, and the rain fall, and in a similar fashion, those secrets and lies would soon be unveiled, and the truth would pour out from them. Carr was certain that he knew that truth, but proving it was a different matter, and, perhaps for the first time, he was not sure he wanted to. He may know the truth, but Carr had a dark concern around his heart that he did not know what to do with it.

He felt powerless. Michael Arden would be at home, but Carr knew that he would not welcome any attempt by Carr to force his way inside and demand an audience. Besides, Carr told himself, there was still so much that he didn't understand. He needed time to gather his own thoughts before he could feel able to confront Arden. He had the unswerving impression of disaster if he were to play his hand too early. Michael Arden was the key to the business; Carr was certain of that, and it was to him that Carr felt he should speak first.

But if Arden was the key, the mystery of Neville Pym still refused to be unlocked by him. Carr could explain everything about the murders of Darton Vale if he placed Arden at the centre of them, but Pym's murder remained as far from explanation of a plausible motive as ever. A growl of frustration rumbled from deep within his throat, and he slapped his gloved hand against the trunk of one of the trees that overlooked the deep crevice of Layton Brook. Bayliss' murder was so simple, both in terms of its mechanics and its motives, but the death of Mr Pym was frustratingly obscure. Carr began to wish that some piece of information would fall into the palm of his hand, something that would give him a clue, some innocent remark from somebody who had no indication of how vital their words were, a piece of gossip spoken in innocence, yet those words would spark in Carr's mind the light of the revelation of guilt. It happened in detective stories, all too often, he thought with a sneer of condescension. Eric Hirst's daughter, being the devotee that she was, would no doubt expect such things to be a matter of course. But Carr knew the reality. No such tricks of the imagination could work in the dark, unhelpful world as they did in the brighter, more convenient fictionalised version. Perhaps the only way to understand the truth about Mr Pym's murder was to ask the culprit to explain the truth, and there would be time enough for that.

He began to walk back to the town when the whole depraved truth dawned on him. There had been, after all, that spark of imagination, an innocent remark that had revealed the truth, but Carr had been too blind to recognise it. Now, however, it was only too clear to him, and he saw how tragically simple it had all been. Carr had once heard a senior detective say that the detection of murder was all about the study of human behaviour and nature. Carr could not agree more, and if he had paid sufficient attention to the personality of Neville Pym, the truth would have been evident from the beginning. Carr did not reproach himself for his previous failure to recognise Mr Pym's importance, nor to identify what his death had meant, since he firmly believed that it was better to learn wisdom late than never at all, but it was with a solemn heart that he made his cautious and painful way back to Darton Vale.

He consulted his watch as he walked. The public house would be opening in a very short while, and Michael Arden would arrive not long afterwards. Within the hour, Carr calculated, he would know everything. And by nightfall, a brutal killer would have been exposed.

# Chapter Forty

As Carr had anticipated, Michael Arden was a man of routine. If anybody had said as much to him, or suggested that he was in any way predictable, he would have been angered by it, but the fact remained that Carr had expected him to arrive at *The Black Bull* soon after noon, and he had done so. For his part, Carr had been sitting quietly on a small bench under a tree in the town square, watching the public house for Arden's arrival, and nursing the shattered knee, which had been groaning in agony from the exertions caused by the descent from Layton Brook. Now, on seeing Arden approach, however, he struggled once more to his feet and called out to the young man.

On hearing his name, Arden fought with the urge to confront or to ignore. He watched Carr limping over the town square and, sensing no fear, he remained where he stood. Whatever the little man had to say wouldn't take long, Arden would make sure of it, and the lunchtime beer he badly craved wouldn't be delayed any longer than necessary. As Carr came up to him, Arden folded his arms.

"I don't have anything to say to you," he said.

Carr, almost breathless, shook his head. "But I have much to say to you."

The seriousness of the tone of voice alerted Arden to danger. "What about?"

"Your mother," said Carr gently. "And, very possibly, your father."

A quiver of emotion, anger or distress, Carr couldn't be sure, flashed behind Arden's eyes, but he was quick to suppress it. "I didn't know my father, so you couldn't know anything about him. Or my mother," he added, making a move to push his way to the public house.

But Carr was too quick for him, and he placed a restraining hand on the young man's chest. "Neither of those statements is true, my boy. And I can prove it with a single word."

"Which word?"

Carr whispered it. "*Sinclair's.*"

Arden now could not disguise his emotions, but instead of fury, Carr read in the man's expression something closer to sadness and regret.

"How do you know about it?" he asked.

Carr took the man's arm. "This is not the place. Let us go to your cottage."

They walked slowly, Carr's arm still linked through Arden's, so that for all the world they looked like a young man out walking with his father, perhaps even his grandfather, given the white hair and the infirm gait and cane. Neither of them spoke on that short walk. Once or twice, Arden made the attempt, but Carr silenced him. There was a time and a place for the words required, and a public street, Carr's eyes told Arden, was not it.

At the cottage, Arden opened a bottle of beer, and Carr watched as he gulped savagely at it. Arden stood in front of the iron grate. Carr, on invitation, sat at the kitchen table.

"Shall I speak, or will you?" he asked.

"You're the one with something to say." The swagger in Arden's attitude and voice had returned, but only as diluted forms of themselves.

"Very well." Carr nodded gently. "What were you doing at the Bayliss mill on the night he was murdered?"

Arden glared at him. "Who says I was there?"

"You were seen." Carr let the fact settle into the atmosphere between them. Arden was glaring at him, willing him to give a name, but Carr's dark eyes were hardened by a stern refusal to do so. "Will you tell me why you were there?"

"I didn't kill him." It was the only reply Arden seemed able to give.

"You hated the family, did you not?"

"Yes."

"Why?"

"Their arrogance, their privilege."

"Their wealth?"

"More the fact they've never had to work for it."

"Bayliss was a self-made man," argued Carr.

"His children aren't. Born to it all, they were, while the rest of us have to work, and work hard, mind you, for no more than a handful of shillings."

Carr leaned back in his chair. "And you think that things could have been so different for you?"

Arden looked down at the rug beneath his feet. "I don't know what you're talking about, sir."

Carr ignored the obvious irony of that salutation. "You will recall that I told you a napkin with your initials on it had been found at the scene of the murder, and now I learn that you were on that very scene. There is a witness to the fact."

"I didn't kill him!" seethed Arden.

"Then why were you at the mill on that night?"

"It's nobody's business but mine," said Arden, his voice quivering with emotion. He could feel the sting of tears behind his eyes.

"It will soon become police business, Mr Arden," cautioned Carr, "if it is not already."

"I didn't write any notes on napkins."

Carr was quick to interrupt. "But you *did* go into the mill?"

"No, I only—"

Arden glared, angry and confused. His voice sank, and he seemed to Carr to change shape and aspect to that of a sullen schoolboy caught stealing apples from an orchard. "No point lying now, is there? Whoever saw me is right. I was there."

"Why?" Carr's voice was gentle.

"I had something to say to him."

"But you couldn't bring yourself to say the words?"

Arden shook his head. "So, I ran away. Like a coward, I ran away."

"Why did you run?" Carr now rose slowly to his feet and walked towards him. "What was it you were afraid of, Michael?"

Arden looked into Carr's eyes. "I went there to kill him, sir. I'll admit that. I wanted him dead. But when I got there…"

Carr now understood. "You realised that you couldn't go through with it, and the shock of believing that you ever could have terrified you."

Arden nodded, gulping once more at the beer. "I've always been angry, sir. Not knowing who my Dad was, the teasing at school about my Mum, the shame, never having any money, working like a dog for other people. The unfairness, sir, just because of how you're born. You're rich," he added with a sneer, "I don't suppose you understand it."

"Perhaps I am beginning to, my boy." Carr made no further admission. "But you have felt this way since childhood. Something must have been the catalyst to turn that anger and frustration towards thoughts of murder."

Arden shrugged. "It all got too much."

Carr shook his head. "That is a lie, Michael. There was a very definite event that turned your mind towards violence. Something that made all your thoughts about injustice and social privilege boil over."

Arden drained his glass and opened another bottle of beer. "It's my business, nobody else's."

Carr rolled his eyes to the ceiling. He had hoped this would not be necessary, but the lad was leaving him with no choice. Carr leaned on his stick and spoke in a solemn voice.

"*On all the line a sudden vengeance waits, and frequent hearses shall besiege your gates,*" he said.

"What's that?"

"It is from a poem," Carr said. "Alexander Pope's *Elegy to the Memory of an Unfortunate Lady*. Rather apt, don't you think?"

Arden sneered. "Funnily enough, I'm not an expert in poems."

"But you have had to say the final goodbye to your mother, Michael. And she was an unfortunate lady, was she not? And when you discovered the truth about her, did the desire for a sudden vengeance not come over you?"

"Vengeance for what?"

"Rather, vengeance against whom, I should say." Carr was nodding slowly. "And the answer is Arthur Bayliss, of course."

"He'd done nothing to me."

Carr smiled coldly. "Perhaps you mean he'd done nothing *for* you. And he hadn't. He hadn't provided for you, he hadn't cared for you, he hadn't supported you, he hadn't pampered you, and he hadn't even acknowledged you."

"As what?" It was a stubborn refusal to admit the truth, and Arden clung to it, but he knew that the attempt at secrecy now was futile.

Carr's voice was almost without emotion. "As his son, Michael."

The words, now spoken, seemed almost calamitous. Arden slumped against the fireplace and almost lost his footing. Carr made a move to assist him, but he was too quickly back in control of himself. He pulled one of the wooden chairs out from under the table, its legs scraping across the stone floor like the cry of a soul in torment, and he slumped down onto it. Carr, with more delicacy and discretion, did likewise.

"How did you know?" asked Arden.

"The napkin," replied Carr. "When I learned that *Sinclair's* was a place Bayliss took those ladies whom he wished to woo, including his wife, I should say, it hardly seemed likely that you would have been there with him, regardless of those initials."

"They're not mine, I swear,"

"Of course not. It makes no sense to say they are yours. They are the initials of a woman; that much is clear. Bayliss would not have gone to this particular restaurant with anyone *other than a woman*. Including, I suggest, your mother." He watched Arden shuffle in his chair, but any anticipated reply did not come. Carr continued to speak. "Then there was something that Mr Pym had said to Mr Hirst. He had said that Bayliss could not have these affairs with women and not expect some consequences from them."

"Consequences?"

"Children." Carr paused to allow the significance to settle in Arden's mind. "And then I began to think about your hatred of the Bayliss family. About your physical scuffles with Bayliss and his son. In particular, I remembered your fury when Bayliss talked to you about Henry, about how he wished he were more like you. He called Henry his son, and he called you his boy.

*'Don't call me your boy,'* you said. At the time, your reaction to his words and the physical assault that followed seemed to me to be a gross overreaction. Why should you react so violently to words that really should have caused you no pain at all? But," he added, pausing for a brief moment, "if there were a closer bond between you and Bayliss than there appeared to be, it would perhaps explain it. The whole thing began to make more sense. His hatred of Henry, his wish that Henry was cut from similar cloth to you, calling you his boy: your violent response to all of those things made sense to me *if you were his son.*

"And then, there was the sudden animosity towards Henry Bayliss himself. I could not fathom what had caused it. Hating Henry Bayliss for being born into wealth was too vague an explanation to my mind. There had to be more than that for you to attack him as you did. Marjorie Bayliss told me that there had been no such hostility between you before, and I was struck again by the idea that there had been an event, a happening, a change to the normal course of events that had prompted this sudden tendency towards hatred and violence against Henry.

"Once I had asked myself whether Bayliss could be your father, it began to make sense to me, and if you had only just discovered for yourself who your father was, it would explain the suddenness of your hatred towards Henry. It was not simply a division of class or envy of wealth, but it was something much more profound. If you were also Bayliss' son, and if you believed that this same wealth and privilege you professed to despise could have been yours, then I could begin to discern a much more psychologically plausible cause for your venom towards Henry. You should have been his equal. He had what should and could have been yours, were it not for circumstance. He was a legitimate son. You, however, were..."

"A bastard," said Michael Arden. "You can say the word, Mr Carr. I've lived with it all my life."

"Your mother never told you the truth about your father?"

"No. She used to tell me that he was a salesman from London. Up here on business, a bit of a charmer." A memory stirred in Arden's mind. "She once said he was full of promises, but all they were was a way of charming girls into bed, and that there was always a new promise of love or a new flattering compliment."

Carr thought about Arthur Bayliss. "Perhaps that part of what she told you was true."

Arden allowed himself a grim smile. "Sometimes, I wonder what sort of dad I'd have been. If Emma had lived, I mean. I had no role model. How would I have managed, known what to do?"

"You would have known," said Carr softly.

"I didn't take advantage of Emma, sir, no matter what her dad says." Arden's eyes were earnest, his tone movingly candid, as if it somehow mattered very much that Carr believed the words he heard, and that it was equally important that Carr should acknowledge the truth of them.

"I'm sure you did not, Michael," he said, his own eyes deep with assurance. Tell me," he added, after a moment's silence, "how did you find out the truth about Bayliss and your mother?"

"About a week ago." He finished his second whisky. "I went upstairs to look through some of Mum's things. I don't know why. Maybe I felt..."

He could not say the word, but Carr knew it only too well. Arden had felt the loneliness of the survivors of death, that special emptiness that only mourners can truly understand, the void of a lost life that can never truly be filled with anything other than memories and remembered voices and faces. In that emptiness, certain objects could momentarily assume the physical presence of the dead: papers, diaries, kept birthday or Christmas cards, perhaps even napkins from illicit meals in certain restaurants.

"You found the truth in those papers?" Carr said.

"I found a napkin from that restaurant," said Arden. "And she'd written me a letter. It told me everything."

"Did Bayliss know about you?"

Arden shook his head. "She never told him, not according to the letter. I was furious."

Carr could understand as much. It was another burden for the young man to carry. Beatrice Arden had spared Arthur Bayliss the knowledge of an illegitimate child, but she had cursed that child with the full extent of the truth. To Arden, it would seem like an unfair division, even a cruel one, and Carr could empathise. What was Arden to do? Tell the Bayliss family the truth and suffer the consequences? Or keep his mother's secret and watch as his half-siblings lived their lives of wealth and security under his nose? It was little wonder, Carr thought, that Michael Arden was so angry at his position in life. For once, perhaps, Carr could convince himself that if Michael Arden had killed Arthur Bayliss, he, Carr, could well have understood the reason for the crime.

"What will you do?" he asked.

Arden shrugged. "What can I do? I won't be welcome into my father's family, will I? They would never accept me as a son, brother, or heir. People aren't like that, Mr Carr."

Carr lowered his gaze. "Perhaps people should be given a chance to surprise us."

"You think so? I don't."

Carr was thinking of Marjorie Bayliss words to Lydia Stansfield. They had both been victims of Arthur Bayliss, she had said. It had been a courageous point of view, Carr had thought, and he wondered now whether it could be taken once more in relation to Michael Arden. He hoped so. His belief in the goodness of people demanded it. His hope that the world could be a better place desired it. Only his darker impulses strove to deny it.

"Michael," Carr said now, his voice calm but imposing, "do you know who killed Arthur Bayliss?"

"No."

"You didn't go into the mill on that night? You swear that to me?"

"Yes."

"Do you have any idea why anyone would want to murder Neville Pym?"

"No."

"Are you the mill poltergeist?"

"No."

"But you did pour acid on Bayliss' motor car?"

And in that final question, the purpose of the catechism became clear. The questions had been delivered rapidly, like bullets from a gun, and the answers had come with similar speed, but it had been designed to throw Arden off his guard, and he saw as much now. Carr had manipulated him with questions to which Arden could only give honest replies. Now, however, with no change in the timbre or speed of his voice, he had exposed Arden by offering a question that Arden could not answer with anything other than a lie. And yet, his brain had been eased into this false security of truth, so that now, when it mattered, he faltered between the instinctive habit of honesty and the necessary disguise of deceit, and that moment of hesitation had been all the confirmation Carr had needed.

"Rosamund Bayliss told me that he cared more about his cars than his children," said Carr. "Did you feel likewise?"

"I'd heard her say it," said Arden. "I thought it was the spite of a spoilt bitch, quite honestly, until I read Mum's letter. Then, I knew exactly what she meant. And how she felt."

"Did you intend to disguise the vandalism to the car as another act of the poltergeist?"

"I'm not sure I was thinking that clearly." Arden looked into Carr's eyes. "I didn't do those other things."

Carr nodded slowly. "I know, my boy."

"How do you know?"

"It was something Inspector Barber had deduced, in fact. He said that there was a change in the poltergeist's character, reflected in the fact that whoever it was had continually targeted the mill, but then suddenly shifted his focus to Bayliss' private property. I must give credit to the inspector for solving this particular mystery."

"I don't follow," said Arden.

Carr spoke gently, as if explaining to a child. "The poltergeist outrages were all directed towards the mill. The vandalism of the motor car was altogether more personal. That was done in a domestic setting, and to private property. Inspector Barber took that change in focus as evidence of two vandals operating independently. I must say, I could not help but agree. But it did pose a further question of its own."

"What?"

"The smashed headlamps," said Carr. "Did you smash them? You have said that you poured the acid on the car, so it is reasonable to presume, is it not, that you also smashed the headlamps."

"I didn't. I swear I didn't."

Carr was smiling. "I am glad to hear you say so."

"Why?"

"Because it confirms what I thought was the truth. Now, I *know* it is the truth."

Arden did not understand, but he made no attempt to do so. "I don't regret the acid on the car. I'm damned if I do."

Carr laughed softly. "My boy, I would not have thought otherwise. I doubt the poltergeist regrets its actions, either."

"Do you know who it is?"

Carr smiled and rose to his feet. "Perhaps I do."

Arden watched him carefully. "And the murderer? Do you know who that is, too?"

Everett Carr looked into Michael Arden's scowling eyes for a long moment before answering. When he spoke, his voice was that of an absolving priest addressing an errant member of his flock.

"I do, Michael," he said. "And if you consider everything that we have said together this afternoon, so do you."

The words lingered in the room long after Carr's departure, but no matter how loudly they resonated in Arden's head, their meaning remained resolutely and frustratingly beyond his reach or understanding.

# Chapter Forty-One

Eric Hirst poured himself a generous measure of whisky, gently placed the needle on the vinyl to allow Mahler's Second Symphony to begin, and settled down to examine the chess problem that he had set himself. It was a moment of solitary relaxation that he had coveted that day in particular, for a reason he could not define. The day's work at the mill had been no less fraught than normal. A meeting with George Toole about the future of the mill, the merger with Toole's own mill, and financial matters concerning the business generally had been promising but far from conclusive, which had irritated rather than concerned Hirst. None of these issues was sufficient to force Hirst into a desire for solitude, and yet he desperately wished for it. Perhaps it was the trauma of other matters, beyond the mill, that had unfolded over the past week, finally overtaking him. Whatever the cause, Hirst was glad for this nocturnal isolation, even if it was outside the normal course of events for him. Ordinarily, he would have wanted to telephone Lydia Stansfield to invite her over for a drink or a meal, but on that one night, he preferred his own company. Perhaps, he thought later, it had been something of a premonition, but in the moment, he wanted only to be with himself and his pleasures.

It was with something more than irritation but rather less than outrage, therefore, that he heard the clatter of the door knocker. He had barely begun to ponder the chess pieces and their positions, and the whisky had certainly not come close to having its soothing, warming effect, and Mahler's funereal *Allegro maestoso* had not yet begun to swell. The repetitive dull rhythm of the knocker was a rude intrusion into Hirst's evening of quiet bliss.

He wondered whether it would be Lydia herself, calling on him of her own accord. That would be, at least, a reward of sorts for the interruption, but when Hirst opened the door, his minor optimism was instantly swept away by a wave of disappointment. Standing on the front step, one hand clasped around the handle of his cane and the other behind his back, the lower part of his face muffled by the scarf and coat, so that only the tips of the waxed moustache peered over the edge, was Everett Carr.

"What are you doing here?" asked Hirst. If it was rude, he made no apology for it.

"I have been trying to silence my doubts, my friend, and I thought you might help me," said Carr. "I am interrupting something?"

Hirst resisted the temptation to agree. Manners, he thought, maketh man. "Not at all. Come in." Then, as Carr stepped over the threshold, he asked, "Will you have a whisky?"

"I should be most obliged," Carr replied. "I see that I am interrupting you, after all," he added, looking at the chessboard and hearing the music. "Mahler's Second is not for the faint of heart, I always think."

Hirst smiled. "I would find it difficult to argue. Please sit down."

Carr, accepting the glass of whisky, did so. He did not settle into the comfort of the armchair, however, but remained perched on the edge of the seat, with the lame leg stretched out in front of him. He savoured the whisky, its smell and then its taste, and sipped at it with a delicate and appreciative precision.

"You said something about silencing doubts," prompted Hirst.

Carr seemed to have forgotten his own words, but now he nodded slowly. "Quite so."

"Doubts about what?"

"Perhaps we could turn off the music, beautiful though it is," said Carr.

Hirst obliged, and the resulting silence bordered on the oppressive. "Doubts about what?"

"My conclusions," said Carr, "about who killed Neville Pym and Arthur Bayliss."

Hirst sat on the arm of his chair. "You think you know who it was?"

"I am sure of it."

"Who?"

Carr smiled briefly and then looked into the pale amber of the drink, watching the reflection of the flames of the fire dance across its surface and glitter in the crystal of the glass.

"You killed them both, my friend," he said gently.

Hirst stared blankly at him before smiling slowly and finally letting out a burst of disbelieving laughter. "You're not serious."

"I am deadly serious," replied Carr. "You murdered Neville Pym for a reason that has eluded everybody, including me, until now, and you shot Arthur Bayliss to death because of what he was and what he did to you."

Hirst was shaking his head, his eyebrows raised in denial. "I don't know what you're talking about, Mr Carr, but I'm afraid I shall have to ask you to leave."

Carr bowed his head. "I shall do so, my friend, once I have said what I have to say. You will allow me that courtesy? If I am wrong, then you have lost nothing but an hour of your time with a madman."

"Very well." Hirst settled into the armchair. "Say what you must."

Carr sipped the whisky, taking the opportunity to gather his thoughts. "Perhaps it is best to begin by setting out how the two murders with which we are concerned came to be committed. In turn, that might explain how it is that only you, of all the people in this little town, were capable of committing them."

Hirst shrugged. "As you wish."

Carr took another sip of the whisky. "The central player in this tragedy is, of course, Arthur Bayliss. In particular, we must concentrate on his numerous infidelities. They were, I think, well-known. Certainly, his wife knew about them, although she turned a blind eye to them, for reasons of her own. Bayliss was a man who cared little for the feelings of others. Marjorie Bayliss herself put it best when she told Lydia Stansfield that they were both victims of her husband. That, I think, is a crucial point. Miss Stansfield herself told me that when Bayliss showered her with gifts, something he did as a matter of routine with his new conquests, she could only look at those gifts now as payments. They made her feel, she said, like a common prostitute. Bayliss was a man who toyed with women, discarding them once he had exhausted his pleasures on them and moving on to the next. One such woman, or victim if you will, was Beatrice Arden."

Hirst frowned. "Michael's mother?"

"You did not know? Yes, she was seduced by Bayliss, along with many others. One thing these affairs had in common, as both Miss Stansfield and Mrs Arden told me, and now as Michael Arden confirms, was Bayliss' choice of *Sinclair's* as a restaurant."

"I told you as much, too," said Hirst.

"Indeed, you did. You remember that?"

"Of course."

"It was when we had discovered Bayliss' body, was it not?"

"Yes. There was a napkin from the place on the floor. With a message from Michael Arden on it."

Carr shook his head. "No, my friend, it was not from Mr Arden."

"They were his initials."

Carr smiled now. "Ask yourself under what circumstances Arthur Bayliss would take Michael Arden to that restaurant. He took only those women he wished to seduce. Again, ask yourself when Arden himself might have gone there in order to pick up one of these napkins."

"Perhaps his mother kept one of them," said Hirst, not without a sneer, "and Michael took it to show Bayliss before he killed him."

Carr held up a finger. "Beatrice Arden did, indeed, keep a napkin, and Arden still has possession of it. No, the napkin found at the scene of Bayliss' murder was one from an assignation with one of his many lady friends, but not Michael Arden's mother."

Hirst leaned forward. "A lady with the initials MA? Do you know who it is?"

Carr nodded slowly. "It is true that Mrs Bayliss' maiden name would give her these initials—Marjorie Ashcroft. But for them to be her initials, this napkin would have to be almost thirty years old. I think it is rather more recent than that."

"Why?"

"Because Miss Stansfield found it in Bayliss' wallet only a few days before he ended their relationship."

"There must be hundreds of women in Lancashire with the initials MA."

"No doubt."

"How do you hope to trace her?"

Carr laid his cane across his knee. "I have done so."

Hirst frowned. "How?"

"We shall come to it," said Carr. "For now, let us consider something Neville Pym said to you, and that you told me. He said, did he not, that Bayliss could not hope to have these affairs with various women and not expect consequences?"

"He did say that, yes." Hirst waved his finger from Carr to himself and back again. "I think we both knew what he meant."

"Children," conceded Carr. "On at least one occasion, Mr Pym has been proved correct. Michael Arden," he said in a lowered voice, "is Arthur Bayliss' son."

Hirst stared blankly, his eyes widened with shock and bewilderment. "It isn't true."

"It is. Mr Arden has confessed it to me."

"My God..."

Carr raised a finger. "Now, if Mr Pym was correct on one occasion, it occurred to me that he might have been correct on another. Could there be, I wondered, another illegitimate child of Arthur Bayliss' in Darton Vale? The child, perhaps, of this mysterious woman with the initials MA?"

Hirst scoffed. "Someone with a secret identity living in the town?"

"It sounds melodramatic, does it not?" smiled Carr, with a gentle laugh. "Like something out of a detective story."

"It does, indeed!" laughed Hirst.

And then, Carr clicked his fingers loudly, like a small pistol shot, and he hissed, "Exactly!" with a dramatic flourish. His dark eyes blazed with accusation.

"A detective story," he said, his voice suddenly dangerous. "Once I realised the possibility, all became clear."

"You'll have to forgive me, Mr Carr, but I don't understand the significance," said Hirst. His manner was casual, but there was a darkness behind the eyes that suggested a creeping terror.

"Your daughter was a devotee of such literature. I saw her collection myself upstairs in this very house. Such tales typically involve obscure clues, tricks, deception, and often coded messages in order to achieve their effect. An avid reader of such stories could not help but be influenced by them, of drawing from their example, particularly if they were seeking to keep some sort of secret."

"What sort of secret?"

"A love affair with a thoroughly unsuitable man."

Hirst's eyes had hardened, and his expression darkened. "What exactly are you saying, Mr Carr?"

Carr held his gaze. "Those were not initials. The message on the napkin was not, as Inspector Barber thought, a threat. As I said to Lydia Stansfield, given that it was written on a napkin from a restaurant Bayliss went to exclusively with women, it seemed far more probable to me that it was a message written on the spur of the moment, instinctively, on the nearest thing to hand. Bayliss was known for showering his ladies with gifts, such as meals at *Sinclair's*, perhaps jewellery, or similar tokens of affection. It occurred to me that this message was not a threat, but a promise that on the next occasion, he would not be permitted to pay."

"Written by someone with the initials MA," said Hirst.

"No," said Carr with defiance. "Written by someone who wished to keep those meals and assignations a secret, and *who used her love of detective stories to do so*. They are not initials, Mr Hirst," he added after a brief silence. "They are a phonetic mnemonic. *They represent the name Emma!*"

Hirst rose to his feet, slamming down his glass. With a violent gesture, he waved towards the door. "Get out! Go on, go!"

"When you showed me Emma's bedroom, I saw an expensive silk nightgown. It was just the sort of gift I could imagine Bayliss buying for one of his secret lovers."

"I said, get out!" Hirst shouted.

But Everett Carr remained seated. "Why were you so eager to make amends with Michael Arden?"

"I told you why. I didn't think Emma would want us as enemies."

"A lie!" hissed Carr. "It was because you had learned that the baby she carried was not his but Arthur Bayliss'! You had maligned Arden without justification, and you felt ashamed of it."

"No," said Hirst, but the word had no meaning.

Carr now stood up slowly. "You lied about not recognising the handwriting on the napkin because you knew only too well that it was your daughter's."

"No."

Carr ignored the denial. "When I asked you if your daughter's baby was Michael Arden's, you replied not with a definitive answer, but with the words, *I always thought so.* I thought nothing of it at the time, and only later did I realise the significance. You had always thought the baby was Michael's, since whose else could it have been? But then, Neville Pym talked about the consequences of Bayliss' affairs. It set a train of thought in motion in your mind. Emma had ended her relationship with Arden. Had she met someone else? And was he the father of her baby?

"When you talked to me about the circumstances of your daughter's death, you said you knew it was murder. The coroner had ruled it an accident. I wondered why you would be so sure it was murder. If you had come to believe that Arden was not the father of Emma's baby but someone else was, the idea of murder would be impossible to resist. Arden would not kill the girl he loved because she was carrying his child. Why should he? They were in a public relationship. All he would need to do would be to marry her. He certainly would not need to kill her.

"But a man who did not wish his relationship with Emma to become known, and for whom an illegitimate pregnancy would be a devastating scandal in view of his potential place in the Honours list, might certainly wish to silence her. Remember, he broke off the affair with Lydia Stansfield for that very reason. Emma's pregnancy would be even more devastating to his ambitions."

Hirst stood in the centre of the room, his shoulders slumped and his arms hanging loosely by his side. He looked like a man condemned to death who had given up trying to proclaim his innocence.

"Neville told me that he'd seen Bayliss at Layton Brook with some of his lovers," he said. "He'd said some were half Bayliss' age, then he started talking about consequences, as you said. It set me thinking."

"About Bayliss and Emma?"

Hirst nodded. "I thought it would be nothing, foolish paranoia on my part."

"But you found proof of their relationship?"

"Letters, diary entries, photographs." Hirst wiped the silent tears from his cheeks. "It was all there. God knows, I would have taken Michael Arden as a son-in-law over Arthur Bayliss any day of the week."

"You knew what Bayliss was?"

Hirst nodded. "I knew. Everybody knew. How he treated women, how he had his way with them, and then cast them aside. He was going to do it with Lydia, I could see that, but I found out that he'd already done it with my daughter."

Carr's voice was gentle, but the words he spoke were horrific. "The broken headlamps on his car were taken to be the work of the poltergeist, but they weren't. The coroner assumed that whoever crashed into your daughter's car at Layton Brook was a stranger to the area, as did everybody else, since only a stranger wouldn't know to take care on that treacherous bend in the road. What nobody considered was the possibility of *deliberate murder*."

"I couldn't prove anything," Hirst said, "but I was in no doubt about it."

"All because of what Neville Pym had said and the train of thought it set in motion in your mind."

Hirst shook his head. "The letters and the diaries were proof of the affair. Neville was trying to warn me without saying it outright."

"Bayliss told me that he thought Mr Pym was spying on him. I put it down to coincidence, and perhaps it was. But the fact remains that Mr Pym and Arthur Bayliss were frequently in the same place. Mr Pym no doubt saw your daughter and Bayliss together."

"Is that so?"

"Beatrice Arden had never told Bayliss about her pregnancy," continued Carr, "but your daughter was not so hesitant. She told him at once."

"And he killed her because of it." Hirst experienced an explosion of grief. "And he killed my grandchild in the process."

Carr's voice was as low as it could be without passing unheard. "And so, you killed him."

Hirst's blood-red eyes seemed to drill into Carr's soul. "I couldn't have. I told you it's about half a mile away from here to the mill. It would take at least half an hour to get there on foot. I was on the telephone with Lydia at twenty to eight that night, and she confirmed it. I couldn't possibly have got to the mill and back in time to be at Darton House at a quarter to eight."

"We discussed the possibility that one of the family could have made that journey in a motor car."

"You said yourself that the chauffeur disproved that theory. And besides," he added, "I don't own a car. I haven't been able to drive since Emma's death."

"So Mr Pym told me."

"Then I couldn't have done it."

Carr was nodding. "You have your bicycle, Mr Hirst."

Hirst shook his head. "The tyres were slashed by the poltergeist."

"Mrs Bayliss told me that her husband had said you had repaired your tyres. I presume that we will find them in working order if we go to look at the bicycle now. No doubt it will also have mud on those same tyres from the journey you made from this house to the mill on that night." Carr began to pace the room. "On a bicycle, you could have made the journey in half the time it would take to walk the same distance. You were careful not to ride with Henry Bayliss and me in the motor car on the night of the murder. You opted to run to the mill instead, blaming your aversion to motor cars."

"I do have that aversion."

"No doubt, but you could have used your bicycle, your normal mode of transport, to make the trip. It would have made far more sense than running, and I began to wonder why you insisted on doing so. I realised, of course, that you had to distance yourself from your bicycle. There could be no mention of it, in case it prompted me to consider it as an alternative means of transport. You had been careful to emphasise the use of a motor car to make the trip from Darton House to the mill, but there could be no suggestion that a bicycle could be used for the same purpose."

"But the telephone to Lydia," protested Hirst.

Carr nodded. "A clever trick, but not quite clever enough."

"You don't think Lydia lied?"

"Not at all. The call was genuine, of course, and Miss Stansfield will testify to it."

"Then what are you saying?"

Carr stopped his pacing and looked into Hirst's eyes. "When we drove back to Darton House after discovering Bayliss' body, I was troubled. I felt that a crucial fact had come to light and I had failed to recognise it. That, my friend, is no longer the case."

"What fact?" Hirst was getting lost in Carr's rhetoric.

"Miss Stansfield's gloves," said Carr. "She had left them behind in this house on that night, and you had telephoned her to tell her so."

"Yes."

"*But why?*" hissed Carr. "Why was it so important that she should know about the gloves at that moment? You would surely see her the next day. She would no doubt realise that she had forgotten them and rectify her mistake on the following day of her own accord. Why was it so vital to tell her *immediately* that she had left them behind?"

"I don't know what you're driving at," said Hirst.

"An alibi, Mr Hirst. A crude one, but it transpires, an effective one, since the police do not, I think, suspect you. It was impossible for you to have spoken to Miss Stansfield at twenty to eight, got to the mill, shot Bayliss, and been back at Darton House by a quarter to."

"Even on a bicycle," said Hirst.

"Just so, a perfect alibi. Except for the very real possibility," Carr added, "that Bayliss was murdered *before* that telephone call. The police surgeon, if you recall, said that the time of death was between seven o'clock and when we found the body at around half past eight. What time did Lydia Stansfield leave here?"

"Seven o'clock," said Hirst sadly.

Carr nodded. "As soon as she was gone, you went to your garage to get your bicycle. You rode down to the mill, shot Bayliss, and cycled back. The whole operation would have taken you perhaps half an hour, thirty-five minutes at the outside. You regained your breath, telephoned Miss Stansfield, then set out for Darton House, as calm as an innocent."

"You can't prove any of this."

"But it is undoubtedly what happened," said Carr. "And it will not take Inspector Barber long to look into your daughter's death at a different angle. There will be proof, Mr Hirst. It will simply need to be found. I wonder how easily you will sleep whilst the police go searching for it? How clear is your conscience, Mr Hirst?" This final question was asked with an element of judicious malice.

Hirst, however, remained defiant. "Even if what you say is true, why would I kill Neville Pym? He was harmless, and he was my friend."

Carr shook his head. "He was dangerous to you. You killed him to prevent him from talking."

Hirst laughed. "From talking about what? A murder I hadn't yet committed? A fine theory, Mr Carr, but wouldn't it make more sense if Neville was killed *after* Arthur Bayliss?"

Carr smiled. "The motive for Mr Pym's murder had been a factor in this matter that has eluded everyone. I, myself, could not fathom it for a long time. Everybody was at pains to tell me what a gossip Mr Pym was, and I had a taste of his capacity for it personally. And it was this taste for gossip that got him killed. The motive for his murder is really very simple."

"What could he have possibly said, though? The murder of Arthur Bayliss hadn't happened."

Carr was nodding his agreement. "But what *had* happened was that Mr Pym had told you about Bayliss and Emma. At least, he had told you enough to set your mind working. If Bayliss was subsequently killed, Mr Pym would certainly have suspected you, and his nature would no doubt have meant that he would not have been able to keep those suspicions to himself.

"Ordinarily, in such circumstances, a murder is committed, and a third person discovers something about the crime that makes them a danger to the killer. In Mr Pym's case, it was this situation *in reverse*. His killing was pre-emptive rather than reactive. Such a simple reversal," he added, "so simple that everybody has overlooked it."

Hirst nodded slowly. He walked to the whisky bottle and poured out another large measure. He had no appetite for it, but he was in very great need of it.

"You still can't prove any of this," he said. "But I take your point about the suspicion and my conscience. You will put everything you've said to Inspector Barber, I have no doubt."

Carr nodded. "Tomorrow morning."

"Why not tonight?"

"I wanted to set it out before you first." Carr accepted the offer of another glass of whisky. "I accuse you of murder, Mr Hirst, but it does not mean I have no sympathy or compassion for you."

"I don't want either."

"Nevertheless," said Carr softly, and not a little sadly.

"I feel no pity. Not for Bayliss, not for myself." Hirst sipped the whisky. "But I do for Neville. It is his face I see when I can't sleep at night."

Carr nodded slowly. "When we were in Mr Pym's sitting room, with Inspector Barber, you wept. I thought at the time it was because of the death of your friend. Now, I understand that it was…"

"Guilt," said Hirst.

"Outside Mr Pym's cottage, you betrayed similar emotions, your head buried in your hands. When I spoke to you then about a reason for Mr Pym's murder, you were very quick to change the subject. You deflected my attention by suggesting that Mr Pym was the wrong victim and hinting that Arthur Bayliss was a more likely victim of murder. It was a mistake. Mr Pym must have died for a reason, and I began to wonder why you would wish to distract me from finding out that reason."

"You suspected me that early on?"

Carr shook his head. "No. But later in the same conversation, you distracted me again. I was talking about Neville Pym's suggestion that Bayliss might have fathered children he did not know about. You were quick to dismiss it as a figment of Mr Pym's imagination. You made it clear that there was no proof he was correct."

"I remember." Hirst held Carr's gaze steadily. "Neville wasn't spying on Bayliss, but he did see him with Emma. It was pure chance, but it has led to so much."

"And Mr Pym told you what he had seen."

Hirst nodded. "And it set me thinking, as you said. I didn't plan any of it. I was learning to live with the idea that I would never know who killed Emma, but when Neville told me what he had seen, everything changed. It was all so sudden."

Carr stared into the space between them. *"On all the line a sudden vengeance waits, and frequent hearses shall besiege your gates."*

Hirst seemed not to have heard. The tears in his eyes began to fall, as silent as the grave. For a moment, there was no sound between the two men, between accuser and accused, save for the quiet ticking of the clock on the mantel, set between the images of a dead girl and her dead mother. To Carr, the cottage seemed to be nothing more now than the house of the dead.

At last, he spoke. "Where did you get the gun, Mr Hirst?"

Hirst took a moment to reply. "I found it in Emma's belongings."

"Where is it now?"

"Back in her bedroom, where I found it. I didn't know she had it. Such a dainty thing, almost pretty. I have no idea where she got it or why."

Carr was remembering Marjorie Bayliss. "They sell such items to young girls as fashion accessories. In Harrods, certainly, possibly elsewhere."

"I see," said Hirst. "I suppose there is some poetic justice in that."

"Perhaps," said Carr.

"In case you're wondering, Mr Carr," said Hirst, turning to look at him, "I realise that what I have said is essentially a confession."

"Yes," said Carr, "it was."

Hirst smiled, but there was no humour in it. He drank more of the whisky. It tasted now of deceit and death. "So, what happens now?"

Carr got to his feet. "As I said, the truth will be with Inspector Barber in the morning."

"Of course."

Carr finished his drink and replaced the glass on the silver salver on the small table by the fireplace. "I suggest you get some rest, Mr Hirst. Go upstairs, lie down, and sleep."

Hirst nodded. "Do you know, Mr Carr, I think I might just do that."

Moments later, Carr was walking along the lane back towards the town. The night was still, the breeze only a delicate wisp across his face, and no sound reverberated along the lonely stretch of road. Carr strained his ears, listening for the sound he expected to hear, but nothing came to his ears. He closed his eyes and wondered, sadly, what the following day would bring. He dared not hope for one outcome or the other. What would be would be, he told himself, and there was nothing he could do to influence a man's destiny one way or the other. He was walking through the gate of Darton House when, if he had only been able to hear it, the sound of a gunshot sang through the air, and the life of Eric Hirst came to its own violent end.

# Chapter Forty-Two

The news of Eric Hirst's guilt and his suicide spread across Darton Vale like a plague. Some expressed astonishment, some suggested that they had always had doubts about the man; some called the suicide a killing of honour, some said it was cowardice. Nobody, however, expressed any disagreement with his motives. As a killer, Eric Hirst inspired sympathy, whereas Arthur Bayliss was almost universally painted as a villain, rather than a victim. For Everett Carr, such distinctions were pointless as well as dangerous. Life and murder, he thought, were not to be so easily dismissed or categorised.

Hirst had left a full confession in his own handwriting, addressed to Inspector Barber. It had set out the history of the murders and his reasons for committing them, plainly and without any attempt to justify his actions. It was a statement of facts, not an excuse for those facts. Carr had been correct in his conclusions, but it had given him no pleasure to learn it.

"You'll go back to London now, I suppose, Mr Carr," Rosamund said, as they sat together in the drawing room of Darton House.

"Indeed, my child."

"I don't suppose you'll ever return here."

He did not reply. He doubted it, and so did she, so he felt no reason to voice the obvious.

"Tell me, my child," he said, "has Michael Arden spoken to you?"

"Michael? No, why?"

Carr shrugged. "It is of no matter."

Curiously, he felt saddened that Arden had not confessed his secrets to the Bayliss family. Perhaps he could not bring himself to do so or had no desire to do so. Whichever was the case, Carr could not shake the feeling that at some point in the future, if nothing was said, Michael Arden would come to regret his decision to remain silent. But it was not for Carr to interfere, however much he may wish to.

He looked now at Rosamund. "How are you and Mr Toole?"

She smiled. "Better than we were. You were right in what you said, Mr Carr."

"What was that?"

"That my inheritance was of use to George. He isn't happy about it, but I'm using some of it to clear his debts, on the condition that he abandons gambling altogether."

"With your help, my child, he will." Carr patted her forearm and smiled. "And your brother?"

"He's going to try his luck in America. Go find out if he really has talent, he says." She scoffed. "The stupid boy should know that he has without going all that way to prove it."

Carr did not return the smile. "And the mill?"

Rosamund shrugged. "That's for Mummy to decide. She will sell it, no doubt. Henry has no interest in it, George can't run it, and the accountant has shot himself. Altogether too much bad luck surrounding the damned place."

"You have no interest in it yourself?"

Another scoff. "Damned right, I haven't. I hate the place."

Carr nodded. "Which is why you broke the windows, slashed Eric Hirst's tyres, cancelled the orders, and so on."

She glared at him. "What on earth do you mean?"

Carr closed his eyes for a moment. "It is useless to deny it, my child."

"Nevertheless, I do!" She laughed incredulously. "What makes you think I'm the poltergeist?"

Carr smiled gently. "Those initial acts of vandalism at the mill I have just mentioned were hardly likely to cause anything more than minor irritation. In many ways, your father was right to dismiss them. The more I thought about them, the more they suggested spite rather than deliberate malice. Like a child having a tantrum," he added softly.

Rosamund looked away from him, and a moment of unease passed between the two of them.

"But in dismissing them," Carr continued, "Mr Bayliss angered the poltergeist. His reaction to the matter trivialised it, almost mocked it, and the poltergeist could not allow that to pass. Hence, the escalation to the dead rat and, ultimately, the death threat."

"And the acid on the car?" Rosamund said, striving for innocent outrage. "Was that me, too?"

"As to that point," said Carr, "I must give credit to Inspector Barber. It was he who suggested the truth of the matter to me."

"What truth?" Rosamund was fighting to remain dismissive.

"That there was a change in the poltergeist's manner," said Carr. "It reminded me that when your father said that whoever poured acid on his car was the same person who left the dead rat in his drawer, you were quick to disagree."

She was growing impatient. "Mr Carr, do you have any actual evidence to back up this accusation?"

He held up a finger, and his dark eyes glowed with triumph. "A small but significant detail."

"Which is?"

"*It was a woman who had cancelled the Carnaby order.*" Carr allowed the revelation to settle. "Your mother told me so. Therefore, the poltergeist could only be your mother, you, or Lydia Stansfield. I doubted Mrs Bayliss would incriminate herself."

"Then it must be Lydia," said Rosamund.

Carr shook his head. "On my first day here, you said that you had gone to the mill to speak to your father, but he wasn't there."

"He wasn't," said Rosamund, missing the point.

"*But you were,*" said Carr. "And it meant you had the opportunity to leave the anonymous letter on the outer door. In fact, I think that was *the only reason you went to the mill at all.* The poltergeist had to be you, my child. You broke the windows, you slashed Mr Hrist's tyres, you cancelled the order.

She stared at him, wondering initially if he was joking. His eyes showed her very clearly that he was not. "And the rat. Don't forget the rat. I found it down by Layton Brook."

"It was spiteful and wicked."

"I felt spiteful and wicked." She got to her feet and walked to the window. "Daddy loved the mill more than his family. He hated us, and we hated him. He felt nothing for us. I wanted him to *feel* something."

"Afraid?"

"Yes, afraid, outraged, paranoid, anything. I wanted him to feel something because of me."

"Why?"

"Because of what he did to me." Rosamund looked into Carr's dark eyes. "Do you remember asking me if I thought Daddy was wicked, sadistic, or perverted?"

"I do."

"I lied to you."

If Carr had known it at the time, he did not betray the fact now. He simply waited for her to explain.

"He used to lock me in the cellar without any light," she said. Her voice was distant, travelling back into the past. "Sometimes, he would shut me in the cupboard under the stairs. I'd be in the dark for hours, cold, hungry, and scared. Above all else, scared."

"I can well imagine, my child." He placed a hand on hers.

"I don't know why I lied to you." She laughed without humour. "Except I do, of course. Altogether too difficult to talk about."

"Especially to a stranger," said Carr.

Rosamund looked out of the window, wondering whether she would ever be able to accept that truth. She hoped so. Now, she thought, in the aftermath of this wickedness and violence, there was a time to heal.

"I did what I did partly because of that fear," she said. "Because of all the years I spent being frightened of my father, being locked in the dark by him. I wanted to hurt him, to make him feel as frightened as he made me feel."

"But he dismissed your actions as trivial," said Carr.

Her eyes came back to the present, and her voice hardened. "He felt *nothing*. None of it mattered. He didn't care about any of it."

"And so, you increased the severity of the pranks with a threat against his life."

She turned to face him, pale with anguish and regret. "I didn't mean what it said. Father was right about that. I would never have had the guts to actually do it."

"I know that, my child," said Carr.

"It was stupid. But I just wanted him to have a reaction. I wanted to affect his life somehow, even in a terrible way." Rosamund wiped a stray tear away from her cheek. "I suppose you think I'm a bitch."

Carr shook his head. "No, I do not, my child. Your father was cruel, and cruelty often drives one to despair. What you are, what acting as you did makes you, is a matter for you and your conscience."

She looked at him for a long moment. "You're so very understanding, Mr Carr."

"We all have that quality of mercy, my child," he said. "I am not unique."

She laughed. "I rather think you are, Mr Carr."

He bowed his head in acknowledgement of the compliment, but he said no more. There was, he thought, nothing more to say.

# Chapter Forty-Three

It was as he was being driven to the railway station that Carr saw Michael Arden walking down Church Lane. Carr demanded that the driver stop the motor car, and he climbed out unsteadily onto the road. Arden faltered when he saw him, but he did not retreat. Instead, he walked slowly towards Carr, with his head on his breast and his hands in his pockets.

"You're leaving?"

"Indeed," said Carr, smiling.

"I heard about Eric Hirst. And I heard about Emma."

Carr placed a hand on his shoulder. "I am sorry, Michael. You have lost so much in life. Please, do not lose any more."

"What else is there to lose?" Arden shook his head. "Mum, Emma, and now the baby I thought was mine turned out not to be. I can't bear to think what it was."

A sibling, thought Carr. A perverse, tragic sibling. The thought was nauseating. "What will you do?"

"I can't stay here," Arden said. "Too many memories, and they're all too close."

"You still have family here, Michael, however painful it is to admit it."

Arden shook his head. "I can't do that to them. They're better off not knowing."

Carr fought to find some words, but none came. Those that he found sounded like little more than trite platitudes, with no more meaning than chance in a chaotic world. Instead, he shook Arden's hand and wished him good luck. Whatever decision Arden took, Carr told him, would be the right one for Arden himself. Of that at least, he could be sure.

Carr walked slowly now from the car to the railway station. He purchased his ticket after waiting a few moments in the small queue that had formed, and then made his way to the platform. To his surprise, the people gathered there were not all strangers. He walked up to the woman he recognised and tipped his hat in greeting.

"You are going somewhere, Miss Stansfield?" he asked.

If Lydia was surprised to see him, she did not say so. Nor did she display any inconvenience at his presence.

"As far away from Darton Vale as I can manage," she said.

Carr thought back to Arden. "You are not alone in wishing as much."

Lydia did not pursue the point. "Why didn't Eric talk to me about what Neville Pym had said? I thought we were friends. I thought he trusted me."

"Perhaps he did not wish to involve you. He cared for you very much."

Lydia had promised herself she would cry no more over the events of the last week or so, but her eyes refused to stay dry.

"What he did was terrible," she said, her voice breaking. "Whenever I think of it, I could be sick."

"Then you must try not to think about it," said Carr, gently. "What he did was terrible, yes, but he did it out of the poison of deep grief, dear lady. And none of us can know how we will react when such grief is visited on us."

"You're saying I shouldn't blame Eric for what he did?"

"No, I am not saying that," said Carr. "I am saying only that perhaps you might try to understand why he did it."

She looked into his eyes. "Can you understand it?"

"I believe so."

She smiled now, but the tears had begun to fall. "Then you're a better person than me, Mr Carr."

Her words were almost lost under the screech of the incoming train's whistle, just as her features, tragic and abandoned, were blurred by the smoke from its funnel. She leaned forward towards him and kissed his cheek softly. She smelled of rose water and sadness.

"Goodbye, Mr Carr," she said, and in the next moment, she was gone.

"Goodbye, dear lady," he replied.

But she did not hear him and, a minute later, the train and Lydia Stansfield had vanished.

He remained on the platform, now alone, and waited for his own train to arrive. Within moments, he would be journeying back to London, back to his own realm, and far away from the Lancashire landscapes. But the memories of his time in Darton Vale, he feared, would not leave him as swiftly as the train would carry him home. Those ghosts could not be so easily banished from his mind, any more than those spectres that already haunted him could. He would have to learn to live with these new ghosts, just as he had learned to live with the old ones. To a lonely man, Everett Carr thought, even the company of these ghosts of the past was preferable to no company at all.

# About the Author

Matthew Booth is the author of the Everett Carr mysteries, novels inspired by the famous Golden Age of detective fiction, featuring a retired judge and amateur sleuth, who not only survived an assassination attempt on his life but is also plagued by survivor's guilt as a result.

As an expert in crime and supernatural fiction, Matthew has provided a number of academic talks on such subjects as Sherlock Holmes, the works of Agatha Christie, crime fiction, Count Dracula, horror fiction, film noir, and the facts and theories concerning the crimes of Jack the Ripper.

He is a member of the Crime Writers' Association and is the editor of its monthly magazine, *Red Herrings*. He is the co-host of the film noir podcast, *Mean Streets*. He lives with his wife in Manchester, England.

SOCIAL MEDIA HANDLES:
Twitter: @HolmesBooth
Facebook: Matthew Booth
Instagram: matthewboothauthor
Threads: matthewboothauthor

# Also by Matthew Booth

The Everett Carr Mysteries
*A Talent for Murder* (Level Best Books)
*The Dangers of this Night* (Level Best Books)
*A Killing Amongst the Dead* (Level Best Books)
*The Serpent's Fang* (Level Best Books)
*A Sudden Vengeance* (Level Best Books)

Other Crime Fiction
*The House of Skulls* (Pegasus Mackenzie Publishing)
*When Anthony Rathe Investigates* (Sparkling Books)
*The Further Exploits of Sherlock Holmes* (Sparkling Books)
*Sherlock Holmes & the Giant's Hand* (Breese Books)

Anthologies – Editor / Introduction
*Secrets in the Snow and Other Christmas Crime Stories* (Macmillan Collector's Library)